The Feminist Alcott

THE
Feminist
Alcott

Stories of a Woman's Power

EDITED WITH AN INTRODUCTION BY

Madeleine B. Stern

Northeastern University Press

BOSTON

Northeastern University Press

Copyright 1996 by Madeleine B. Stern

Library of Congress Cataloging-in-Publication Data

Alcott, Louisa May, 1832–1888.
The feminist Alcott : stories of a woman's power / edited with an
introduction by Madeleine B. Stern.
p. cm.
Includes bibliographical references (p.).
ISBN 1-55553-265-9 (hard : alk. paper). —
ISBN 1-55553-266-7 (pbk. : alk. paper)
1. Women—Social life and customs—Fiction.
2. Feminism—Fiction. 3. Sex role—Fiction.
I. Stern, Madeleine B., 1912– . II. Title.
PS1016.S73 1996
813'.4—dc20 95-52241

Designed by Ann Twombly

Composed in Bembo by Coghill Composition Company,
Richmond, Virginia. Printed and bound by Hamilton Printing
Company, Rensselaer, New York. The paper is Renew Antique, an
acid-free stock.

MANUFACTURED IN THE UNITED STATES OF AMERICA
00 99 98 97 96 5 4 3 2 1

Contents

⁀⋅⋅⁀

Introduction

✝••✝

    *F*eminism was in Louisa May Alcott's genes. Both her
    parents participated in most of the reforms of their day,
    but according to her philosopher father, Bronson Al-
    cott, the "reform of reforms" was woman suffrage.
Her mother, Abby May Alcott, agreed with Margaret Fuller, author
of *Woman in the Nineteenth Century*, that the rights of woman as "wife,
mother, daughter, and owner of property" must be protected, that
the opening to women of "a great variety of employments" could
have only salutary effects, and that "extension to woman of all civil
rights" would contribute to the "welfare and progress of the State."
Bronson and Abby May Alcott did more than support feminist lead-
ers; they petitioned, appealed, and spoke to advance this "reform of
reforms." As Bronson Alcott put it, "Does any reasonable man question if there be not as many women having public gifts as there are
men? . . . Where women—the best women, lead is it unsafe for any
to follow?"[1]

    In the American mid-nineteenth century the motivations for
such queries were rampant. At a time when women's inequality un-
derlay the laws of the land, when women were taxed but not represented, when their status as individuals and as citizens yielded few
legal advantages, women in general and the Alcotts in particular had
good reason to endorse feminist causes.

    Louisa May Alcott at age nineteen had additional cause for anger
against the inequities sponsored by "male lords of creation." In 1851,

when the family poverty was extreme, her mother worked as a city missionary in Boston and opened an intelligence or employment office. One customer was the Honorable James Richardson, a lawyer of Dedham, Massachusetts, who wished to hire a companion for his sister. Learning of his need, Louisa, who had worked from time to time not only as teacher but as seamstress, laundress, and second girl or chambermaid, decided to fill the position herself. As it turned out, James Richardson was less honorable than his title. The young hired help, who had been assured that only light housekeeping would be required, was expected to kindle fires, destroy cobwebs, and become the recipient of her employer's maudlin attentions. When his pursuit proved unsuccessful, he assigned all the household work to her, including fetching water from the well, splitting the kindling, sifting the ashes, and digging paths through the snow. He especially enjoyed having her blacken his boots. After seven weeks of humiliating drudgery, young Louisa received four dollars in payment. Actually, she had garnered much more from her experience. Decades later she would write an amusing story about it entitled "How I Went Out to Service." But long before that her humiliation in Dedham would filter into her more sensational feminist fiction. There, either anonymously or over her pseudonym of A. M. Barnard, she could vent her fury in sexual power struggles that reversed the roles of male masters and female slaves.[2]

Other episodes contributed both to her attitude and to its tangible results. In the climate of her own life as well as in the climate of her times there was cause for resentment. If the Reverend Theodore Parker's sermon "The Public Function of Woman" fortified her faith in the power of her sex, editor James T. Fields's chilling estimate of her ability fortified her resentment and her determination to prove him wrong. "Stick to your teaching, Miss Alcott," he had pontificated. "You can't write."[3]

And so, Louisa May Alcott became a writer. In the course of her prolific career she would advance the feminist cause in much that she would write. From *Little Women*, where the independent heroine, Jo March, has become a role model for the twentieth century, to her letters in the *Woman's Journal* supporting women in all their endeavors, Alcott would prove herself a staunch feminist. Nowhere, however, does her belief in the power of women appear as graphic or as dramatic as in the thrillers she never acknowledged but sent forth anonymously or pseudonymously—pageturners for an all-but-insatiable readership.

In almost the entire corpus of sensation narratives that Alcott produced during the 1860s, a feminist theme can be traced as men's dominance is challenged and women's power asserted. Alcott's concept of feminism reflects a conviction that transcends egalitarianism. She seems to have held that women could be not merely the equals of men but their superiors. What men could accomplish, women might, given certain motivations and circumstances, accomplish better. And, as her shockers indicate, those accomplishments might on occasion be constructive and good, and on other occasions destructive and evil. Sometimes Alcott's feminist theme is presented obliquely; sometimes it is more boldly enunciated. The theme winds in and out of such stories as "A Marble Woman," "A Pair of Eyes," "The Fate of the Forrests," and other tales in which female slave tilts with male master.

The four serials included in *The Feminist Alcott* have been selected because in them the sexual power struggle is not simply one of many threads running through a complex plot, but the fiber that knits the narrative together. What is significant too is the fact that in each of the four titles the canny author has offered fascinating variations on the theme. In each the success of the heroine—the woman's power—is achieved to a different degree; and in each the protagonist's character ranges from the depths of evil to the heights of ideality. The women are not homogeneous. Their goals may or may not be fully attained, but the theme of woman's power resonates with intriguing variations throughout this quartet of nineteenth-century sensation stories.

In three of the four stories in this collection the leading lady is both feminist and femme fatale, with varying degrees of "fatality." Pauline Valary of "Pauline's Passion and Punishment"[4] plays this double role seductively but fails in the end to accomplish her purpose.

The opening description of Pauline captures immediate attention, suggests the aura of "sumptuous life" that pervades the heroine, and arouses the reader's curiosity:

> To and fro, like a wild creature in its cage, paced that handsome woman, with bent head, locked hands, and restless steps. Some mental storm, swift and sudden as a tempest of the tropics, had swept over her and left its marks behind. As if in anger at the beauty now proved powerless, all ornaments had been flung away, yet still it shone undimmed, and filled her with a passionate regret. . . . and over the face, once so affluent in youthful bloom, a stern pallor had fallen like a blight, for pride was slowly conquering passion, and despair had murdered hope.

As the explanation for Pauline's metamorphosis unfolds, her character is fleshed out. "Pride sat on the forehead" of this ardent, dominant woman who dared "to act where feebler souls would only dare desire." In this two-part serial, such a woman must have a powerful motivation for revenge. Pauline has been deserted by her perfidious lover, Gilbert, who has married a woman of reputed wealth. And so, seeking a "subtler vengeance than men can conceive," she marries the devoted and wealthy nineteen-year-old Manuel and resorts to the manipulations of a woman scorned but still magnificent. The quartet meet against a tropical background, "the green wilderness of a Cuban *cafetal*," and play out the fates to which the inventive Alcott dooms them. A surprisingly modern touch is given to the fabric of the story when it is learned that Gilbert, who comes from a broken home, now abuses his young wife. Moreover, he still loves Pauline, whose sexuality, though implicit rather than explicit, is a dangerous power. "The evil spirit to whose guidance she had yielded herself exulted to see his self-love bleed." The sexual power struggle that follows is defined by the author as "the tournament so often held between man and woman—a tournament where the keen tongue is the lance, pride the shield, passion the fiery steed, and the hardest heart the winner of the prize, which seldom fails to prove a barren honor, ending in remorse." Imbued with theatricality, as most Alcott heroines are, Pauline, bent upon Gilbert's destruction, becomes his nemesis. "Passions, not principles, were the allies" of a heroine daring, defiant, and indomitable. In the end remorse is indeed in the ascendancy, for in an ironic and unexpected finale, Gilbert throws his wife and Pauline's husband over a precipice, and the two leading characters are left in mutually loathing confrontation. After all Pauline's passionate machinations, her long punishment begins.

"Pauline's Passion and Punishment" was Alcott's first success in the sensation genre. *Frank Leslie's Illustrated Newspaper,* a New York weekly filled with graphic accounts of murders, prizefights, and gaudy gossip, also ran serial narratives in keeping with its lurid style. When publisher Frank Leslie offered a hundred-dollar prize for a story, Louisa May Alcott, author of *Flower Fables* and the soon to be published *Hospital Sketches,* based upon her experience as a Civil War nurse, contributed the anomalous tale of the passionate Pauline Valary and her punishment. The author had begun to indulge in the literary deviations that would delight her. She was developing a professionalism as she attempted various literary techniques. She was also earning money. Where *Flower Fables* had netted her only thirty-odd dollars, Leslie paid one hundred for the prize story.

Alcott learned the results of the competition during her brief period as nurse in the Union Hotel Hospital in Georgetown, where she received a letter from editor E. G. Squier informing her that "Pauline" had won the prize and recommending that the author submit whatever she might write of the same sort for Mr. Leslie's acceptance.[5] The newspaper itself announced that, after deliberating over the moral tendency and artistic merit of more than two hundred manuscripts, the editor had decided to award first prize to "a lady of Massachusetts" for "Pauline's Passion and Punishment." In the next number—that of 3 January 1863—the first half of the serial appeared, presented as a narrative of "exceeding power, brilliant description, thrilling incident and unexceptionable moral." The conclusion was issued the following week, and the story was emblazoned with illustrations of Pauline in despair, Pauline with Manuel, and Pauline with Gilbert. In April 1863 the author mentioned in her journal: "Received $100 from Frank Leslie for a tale which won the prize last Jan. Paid debts & was glad that my winter bore visible fruit."[6]

The fruit the winter had borne was indeed visible. Alcott had not merely earned a hundred dollars but produced her first full-scale portrait of a richly sexual femme fatale who indulged in a power struggle with a male antagonist. The struggle was certainly not entirely successful, but the heroine had defied and challenged her treacherous lover and used "with feminine skill" daring feminist methods and machinations. In later sensational serials the "lady of Massachusetts" would sketch other portraits in her gallery of heroines and devise for them a succession of different denouements. The theme of woman's power would continue to intrigue her, but she would pursue it with variations.

In September 1864 Alcott recorded in her journal: "Wrote a blood & thunder story or novelette of several hundred pages to relieve my feelings & called it 'V.V.' "[7] She did not add that she had relieved her feelings by portraying her most evil and unregenerate heroine, Virginie Varens. The protagonist of "V.V.: or, Plots and Counterplots"[8] would succeed in her goal no better than Pauline Valary, but the plots and counterplots she devised would reflect a feminist fury almost out of control.

Like her predecessor Pauline, Virginie is a femme fatale. Unlike Pauline, who had been bent on revenge, Virginie is motivated principally by social and mercenary ambition. A captivating dancer, she is introduced as she appears in the greenroom of a Paris theater: "A sylph she seemed, costumed in fleecy white and gold; the star that glittered on her forehead was less brilliant than her eyes; the flowers that filled her graceful arms were outrivaled by the blooming face that smiled above them; the ornaments she wore were forgotten in admiration of the long blond tresses that crowned her spirited little head; and . . . she crossed the room as if borne by the shining wings upon her shoulders."

Those wings are mere theatrical props—there is nothing angelic about Virginie. Her cousin and dancing partner, Victor, has set his mark upon her: two dark letters "tattooed on the white flesh" of her wrist, the monogram "V.V.," which she conceals by means of a bracelet with a golden padlock. She has, of course, many suitors, but, being "mercenary, vain, and hollow-hearted," she accepts without loving the Scotsman Allan Douglas who offers her an honorable name and a home. Within the first few pages, the "fiery and fierce" Victor, enraged with jealousy and "reckless of life or limb," takes "the short road to . . . revenge" by stabbing Virginie's bridegroom. After one "night of love, and sin, and death," the bride is transformed into a widow and the manipulator of the plots and counterplots that follow.

Virginie now sets out in hot pursuit of the dead Allan's cousin, a noble Scot also named Douglas who looks like her slain husband's twin. The action shifts to the Scottish estate of Lady Lennox, where the remainder of the narrative is set and the complicated plot unravels. There, too, Virginie's character is elaborated as she perpetrates sins both venial and venal and proceeds to captivate every Scot on the estate except her target, Cousin Douglas. He is pledged to another, the lovely Diana Stuart, whom Virginie determines to eliminate. He detects, beneath Virginie's handsome surface, the character of "a little green viper." Feigning, conniving, and manipulating, she weaves her deceitful web, leads her rival to her death, and dominates not only the story but, except for Douglas, all its male characters. Endowed with "the nerves of a man" and "the quick wit of a woman," Virginie Varens shapes her feminist powers to her baleful purpose. She is an exciting femme fatale with the malignancy of Satan and the skills of Machiavelli. In the end, however, like Pauline, she falls short of success. Her disguises and artifices are penetrated; the plots and counterplots, involving drugged coffee, a feigned pistol duel, and the footprints left by a murderess, are untangled. Virginie is threatened with a punishment intolerable to contemplate and from which "escape is impossible." In what might be viewed as an ultimate if questionable triumph, however, Alcott's most Mephistophelian heroine does indeed escape—by suicide. The suicide is accomplished by means of a deadly poison concealed in an opal ring; to the announcement "Escape is impossible," Virginie is able to reply, "I have escaped!"

Virginie Varens must take a lead position among Alcott femmes fatales, for even as she appalls, she enchants. Certainly her publishers believed this. The Boston market for Alcott's sensation fiction was a periodical, *The Flag of Our Union,* issued by the firm of Elliott, Thomes & Talbot. In 1865 and 1866 James R. Elliott had written to

Alcott the series of five letters discovered by Leona Rostenberg in which the author's pseudonym of A. M. Barnard, her association with *The Flag of Our Union*, and the titles of several of her serials were first revealed.[9] When she came to write *Little Women,* Alcott would immortalize the trio of Boston publishers as "three gentlemen, sitting with their heels rather higher than their hats" in a disorderly room filled with cigar smoke located above "two pairs of dark and dirty stairs." One of the three is Mr. Dashwood of the *Weekly Volcano,* and it was for Mr. Dashwood that Jo March "rashly took a plunge into the frothy sea of sensational literature."

It was for James R. Elliott of Elliott, Thomes & Talbot that Louisa May Alcott "wrote a blood & thunder story . . . to relieve my feelings & called it 'V.V.' " "V.V.: or, Plots and Counterplots" ran in *The Flag of Our Union* as a four-part serial in February 1865. Alcott mentioned in her journal the preceding December: "Sold my Novelle to Elliot for $50. He offered 25 more if I'd let him put my *name to it,* but I wouldn't."[10] Alcott may have relieved her feelings in her sensational narrative, but she apparently respected, if she did not entirely share, Ralph Waldo Emerson's aversion to sub-literature. When it appeared in *The Flag of Our Union,* "V.V." bore the byline "A Well Known Author." It was not until several years later, about 1870, by which time the "Well Known Author" had become the universally known author of *Little Women,* that Thomes & Talbot issued *V.V.: or, Plots and Counterplots* by A. M. Barnard in their series of Ten Cent Novelettes. They did so without informing Alcott, who was then enjoying a grand tour abroad. There, in blue paper wrappers, the temptress Virginie Varens wove her malignant web once more, tested her woman's power, and escaped her intolerable punishment.

If Pauline Valary and Virginie Varens seem more femme fatale than feminist, a third Alcott heroine is an extraordinary combination of both. Jean Muir of "Behind a Mask" is not only feminist and femme fatale in one—she is completely successful in the exercise of her woman's power. Moreover, while Pauline and Virginie seem at times ambivalent and covert in carrying out their feminist intentions, Jean Muir is a bold practitioner. The reader is almost immediately aware of her purpose, is immersed in her power struggle against male chauvinism throughout, and is exultant at her ultimate triumph. With its very title the author pointed the way she was headed, and "Behind a Mask: *or,* A Woman's Power"[11] may well be judged the most successful of Alcott's sensation fiction.

The first chapter sets the stage for what will follow and reveals the true identity of Jean Muir behind her mask. She appears in scene one a thin, colorless, nineteen-year-old applicant for the position of governess in the Coventry family. Something in the lines of her mouth, however, betrays strength, and after she has enacted an improvised faint—she is of course a consummate actress—young Gerald Coventry remarks: "Scene first, very well done." To this Jean Muir replies: "The last scene shall be still better." And it is.

Alone in her room, the new governess mutters to herself: "I'll not fail again if there is power in a woman's wit and will!" She proceeds to drink an "ardent cordial" from a flask, removes several "pearly teeth," wipes the pink from her face, and emerges "a haggard, worn, and moody woman of thirty." The reader now knows Jean Muir as a woman of inordinate power directed against the male sex. "Some wrong, or loss, or disappointment . . . had darkened all her life," and, like Pauline Valary, she is bent upon revenge.

In the chapters that follow, the governess—more successful than V.V.—enchants *all* the male Coventrys, even subduing Gerald's wild horse, Hector. It appears that she is multicultural, having lived in Paris, traveled in Russia, and mastered Italian airs. She uses a variety of methods: deceitful lies and forgery, coquetry and subterfuge, a "passion of tears" and a feigned suicide attempt. She wears many disguises. Jean Muir can range from meek governess to lady of the world, from injured female to defiant and proud woman. When Gerald says to her, "You make a slave of me already. How do you do it? I never obeyed a woman before. Jean, I think you are a witch," she replies, "I *am* a witch, and one day my disguise will drop away and you will see me as I am, old, ugly, bad and lost. . . . love me at your peril."

The younger Coventry brother, Ned, besotted though he is, finally penetrates her disguise and reveals that Jean "has the art of a devil," offering as proof the letters she has written to her accomplice,

Hortense. "There was a compact between the two women," he announces. In the course of that sisterly compact Jean has informed her associate that the Coventrys "are an intensely proud family, but I can humble them all . . . by captivating the sons, . . . and marry the old uncle, whose title takes my fancy. . . . What fools men are!" Jean Muir succeeds in her purpose and, having humbled all the men, marries the elderly head of the family, Sir John, and becomes Lady Coventry. "Is not the last scene better than the first?" she asks Gerald in the stunning finale of "Behind a Mask."

On 11 August 1866 James R. Elliott wrote to Alcott: "The story entitled 'Behind A Mask' is accepted. I think it a story of peculiar power, and have no doubt but my readers will be quite as much fascinated with it as I was myself while reading the Ms. I will give you $65. for it."[12] The story was announced in the 6 October 1866 issue of *The Flag of Our Union* as "Another Splendid Romance" and ran serially in four issues. Its byline was A. M. Barnard. When she entered her receipts in her ledger, Alcott noted that "Behind a Mask" had earned her not the promised sixty-five dollars but eighty dollars.[13] Apparently, she had demanded and received a higher price, but certainly not a price commensurate, even at the time, with the value of the narrative. Here Alcott presented one of her most intriguing heroines, a woman proud, passionate, and intensely feminist, who devises a series of suspenseful maneuvers leveled against male dominance.

The twentieth-century readership of "Behind a Mask" has been not only more receptive to the story than its nineteenth-century readership, but far more extensive. The serial was adapted for stage presentation before delighted audiences in 1983,[14] and a recent reviewer has wryly commented: "If they ever make a movie of 'Behind a Mask,' forget Winona Ryder; this Alcott heroine calls for the likes of Leona Helmsley."[15]

There is nothing of Leona Helmsley in the protagonist of the final narrative in this collection. Nor is Sybil Varna a femme fatale. She is, rather, all woman, as independent and straightforward as Jo March and as intensely feminist as Jean Muir. Without manipulation or deceit she triumphs completely in "Taming a Tartar."[16] Alcott's final variation on the theme is neither ambivalent nor oblique but a pellucid and satisfying portrayal of woman's power.

In her journal in December 1866 Alcott wrote: "Paid bills, but never expect to see the end of em. Wrote . . . a wild Russian story 'Taming a Tartar.' "[17] In that "wild Russian story" Sybil Varna is a self-reliant, self-possessed young woman without guile who is exactly what she seems—an English teacher in a girls' "pensionnat"—who becomes companion to a Russian princess settled in Paris. Sybil's foil is the Tartar of the title, the princess's brother, Prince Alexis Demidoff, suggested perhaps by a Russian baron Alcott had met during her journey abroad as companion to a young invalid. At the Pension Victoria in Vevey, Switzerland, the contributor to *Leslie's Illustrated Newspaper* and *The Flag of Our Union* had encountered a stout, turbulent barbarian who served as page to the czar and spent his time smoking, playing billiards, and indulging in an unrequited passion.[18]

The Tartar of "Taming a Tartar" is savage, swarthy, and tyrannical. His features "all betrayed a trace of the savage strength and spirit of one in whose veins flowed the blood of men reared in tents, and born to lead wild lives in a wild land." He is "mad to go back to his wolves, his ice and his barbarous delights. . . . His will is iron. . . . He has always claimed entire liberty for himself, entire obedience from every one about him." "Supremely masterful," accustomed to command, Alexis is male chauvinism personified; Sybil Varna engages him in a mighty sexual power struggle that ends when she has indeed tamed him. Her own power derives not only from her feminist instincts but also from her fearlessness. "You do not fear him," the princess observes, "and it gives you power." Besides possessing the power of fearlessness, Sybil enjoys the struggle. As she puts it, "It was interesting to match him, and . . . exciting to try my will against his in covert ways. . . . over me he had no control."

And so, the rounds of the struggle for mastery are fought out. Round One concerns the postponement of a return journey to Russia; the crux of Round Two is the prince's whipping of his dog, Mouche. Sybil wins those rounds. She confesses, "I was bent on having my own way, and making him submit as a penance for his unwomanly menace. Once conquer his will, . . . and I had gained a power possessed by no other person. I liked the trial." In the course of their contests the prince is, of course, drawn to his opponent, and the sexual struggle is interlaced with sexual attraction. After a little accident in which Sybil hurts her foot and faints, the prince ministers to her. When she wakes she finds that "My bonnet and gloves were off. . . . Who had removed them? My hair was damp with eau-de-cologne; who had bathed my head? My injured foot lay on a cushion; who placed it there? Did I dream that a tender voice exclaimed, 'My little Sybil, my heart, speak to me'? or did the prince really utter such words?" The duel, now tinged with romantic overtones, continues. While the prince's spirit is still defiant, Sybil likes "courage in love as in war, and respect[s] a man who conquers all obstacles."

The final round of the power struggle is fought during the prince's abduction of Sybil to his estate in Volnoi. He admonishes her: "Submit, and no harm will befall you. Accept the society of one who adores you, and permit yourself to be conquered by one who never yields—except to you." Alexis now begs his beloved to tame his wild temper, his headstrong will; indeed, her "feminine wish" is "to see my haughty lover thoroughly subdued before I put my happiness into his keeping." A melodramatic uprising of the serfs at Volnoi brings matters to a head, and in the end Sybil persuades the prince to liberate his serfs and "Come with me to England, that I may show my countrymen the brave barbarian I have tamed." To this Alexis replies in this most satisfactory of endings: " 'I might boast that I also had tamed a fiery spirit, but I am humble, and content myself with the knowledge that the proudest woman ever born has promised to love, honor, and—' '*Not* obey you,' " Sybil breaks in with a kiss.

The four-part serial in which a tyrannical Tartar is tamed by a forthright young English feminist appeared anonymously in *Frank Leslie's Illustrated Newspaper* between 30 November and 21 December 1867. In return for this most explicit of her feminist shockers, Alcott received a hundred dollars.[19] Shortly before the publication of "Taming a Tartar," in September, the author had been invited to edit the juvenile periodical *Merry's Museum* and to "write a girls book" for Thomas Niles of Roberts Brothers.[20] She would shortly comply with both requests. Once that "girls book" began its perennial career in print as *Litte Women,* Alcott noticeably diminished her output of sensational pageturners. Instead, with a succession of domestic novels and stories for young readers, she began to assume the role of "The Children's Friend."

Although Louisa Alcott never abandoned her feminism, she articulated it in different ways. On 1 October 1873, in response to an appeal from the suffragist Lucy Stone, Alcott wrote, "I am so busy just now proving 'woman's right to labor,' that I have no time to help prove 'woman's right to vote.' "[21] It was not long, however, before she found time to help prove both. Between 1874 and 1887 evidence of her support for woman suffrage is reflected in her letters to the *Woman's Journal,* a Boston weekly edited by Lucy Stone and her husband, Henry B. Blackwell, the only woman suffrage paper published in Massachusetts. In its pages appeared repeated evidence of Alcott's affirmative feminism. Her letters to the *Journal* were variously signed: "With a firm belief in the good time coming," "three cheers for the girls of 1876," "Yours for reforms of all kinds."[22]

In October 1875 Alcott attended the Woman's Congress in Syracuse, New York, and the *Woman's Journal* reported the event:

> The author of "Little Women," who is a member of the Congress, was in attendance throughout the sessions. As soon as the papers announced her presence, a great commotion began among the young people. They must see her. A note was sent by them to the President, begging her to invite Miss Alcott to sit on the platform. . . . But their idol could not be coaxed to put herself on exhibition, and so their desire had to be compassed in another way. . . . At first it was the inevitable autograph album that brought the . . . damsels to the rear of the stage, crowding its wings—they wanted autographs. While these were being written, they used the Yankee privilege of asking questions, and their eyes, sometimes assisted by lorgnettes, gave in keeping to their memory, the lineaments of one who has long held them in thrall with her pen.

Indeed, one ardent devotee from the West pushed her way through the crowd to assure Louisa May Alcott, "If you ever come to Oshkosh, your feet will not be allowed to touch the ground: you will be borne in the arms of the people!"[23]

Alcott's reception, as well as the reception of all the women present, was far less effusive when Concord, Massachusetts, celebrated the centennial of American independence. Then, on April 19, 1876, the hospitality of the town seemed to be confined to the male participants. Women, who had no place in the procession, were ordered to wait for escorts who never arrived; the platform of the great tent was reserved for gentlemen, and Concord, that mecca of the mind, gave but cold comfort to the distaff side. Alcott was moved to write a lengthy account of "Woman's Part in the Concord Celebration" for the *Woman's Journal,* ending on a prophetic note:

> By and by there will come a day of reckoning, and then the tax-paying women of Concord will not be forgotten I think, will not be left to wait uncalled upon, or be considered in the way; and *then,* I devoutly wish that those who so bravely bore their share of that day's burden without its honor, will rally round their own flag again, and, following in the footsteps of their forefathers, will utter another protest that shall be "heard round the world."[24]

By the end of the decade, when women were granted the right to vote for school committees, Alcott, as she recorded in her journal, "was *the first woman to register my name* as a voter." Trying to stir up the women about suffrage—"so timid & slow"—she welcomed them to the Alcott house and exercised the very limited privilege accorded her as a woman. In September 1880 she noted in her journal: "Paid my first poll tax. As my head is my most valuable peice [*sic*] of property I thought $2,00 a cheap tax on it. Saw my townswomen about voting &c. Hard work to stir them up."[25]

It was harder still to stir up the men, but Alcott had not forgotten the feminist devices employed in sexual power struggles. When a former Lowell mill girl, Harriet Robinson, compiled a history of Massachusetts in the woman suffrage movement, Alcott appealed to Thomas Niles of Roberts Brothers to publish it: "Cannot you do a small edition for her? All the believers will buy the book. . . . Will you look at the manuscripts by and by, or do you scorn the whole thing? Better not, for we are going to win in time, and the friend of literary ladies ought to be also the friend of women generally." She followed the letter with another even more telling:

> Thank you very much for so kindly offering to look at Mrs. R.'s book. It is always pleasant to find a person who can conquer his prejudices to oblige a friend, if no more.
>
> I think we shall be glad by and by of every little help we may have been able to give to this reform in its hard times, for those who take the tug now will deserve the praise when the work is done.
>
> I can remember when Anti slavery was in just the same state that Suffrage is now, and take more pride in the very small help we Alcotts could give than in all the books I ever wrote or ever shall write.[26]

In many of her books she had and would continue to insinuate her support of feminism. Despite the fact that the heroine of *Little Women* yields to the authoritarian Professor Bhaer in literary or sub-literary matters, Jo March remains the image par excellence of the bold and independent young woman. In 1876, when the town of Concord was celebrating a nonfeminist centennial, Alcott was publishing *Rose in Bloom,* in which the theme of woman's rights is woven into the lives of Phebe and Rose. A decade later, in *Jo's Boys,* the author sounded the trumpet for the women whose hour had struck and among her "Owlsdark Marbles" she placed the figure of Minerva bearing a shield inscribed, "Woman's Rights."

Surely in a gallery of feminist heroines that includes Jo March and "Rose in Bloom," there is room for those unacknowledged heroines who assumed woman's rights, practiced egalitarianism, and engaged with varying degrees of success in the sexual power struggle. In the four stories in this collection, Alcott's feminism is far more boldly stated than in the succession of domestic novels she produced for Thomas Niles of Roberts Brothers. Pauline Valary, Virginie Varens, Jean Muir, and Sybil Varna may never have concerned themselves with voting privileges, but they ruled or sought to rule in men's domain. They grasped privileges denied them by half the human race, and whatever the degree of their success, they courageously challenged the status quo. They dominate Alcott's clandestine narratives, these wielders of woman's power in a quartet of feminist fiction.

NOTES

1. For Alcott's parents' attitude toward woman suffrage and other reforms, see *The Letters of A. Bronson Alcott*, ed. Richard L. Herrnstadt (Ames: Iowa State University Press, 1969), pp. 629–30; "Petition of Abby May Alcott and others," *Una* (November 1853); Madeleine B. Stern, "Louisa Alcott's Feminist Letters," *Studies in the American Renaissance* (1978), pp. 429–31, 436–37.

2. Louisa May Alcott, *Behind a Mask: The Unknown Thrillers of Louisa May Alcott*, ed. Madeleine Stern (New York: William Morrow, 1975, 1995), pp. ix–x; Louisa May Alcott, "How I Went Out to Service. A Story," *The Independent* (4 June 1874); Madeleine B. Stern, *Louisa May Alcott* (New York: Random House, 1996), pp. 63–65.

3. Stern, *Louisa May Alcott*, pp. 67–69.

4. "Pauline's Passion and Punishment" was first published in *Frank Leslie's Illustrated Newspaper* (3 and 10 January 1863).

5. E. G. Squier to Louisa May Alcott, ca. 18 December 1862 (Houghton Library, Harvard University). Quoted in Leona Rostenberg, "Some Anonymous and Pseudonymous Thrillers of Louisa M. Alcott," *Papers of the Bibliographical Society of America* 37:2 (1943).

6. *The Journals of Louisa May Alcott*, ed. Joel Myerson, Daniel Shealy, and Madeleine B. Stern (Boston: Little, Brown, 1989) p. 118 (hereinafter cited as *Journals*).

7. *Journals*, p. 132.

8. "V.V.: *or,* Plots and Counterplots" was first published in *The Flag of Our Union* (4, 11, 18, and 25 February 1865). It was reprinted as Ten Cent Novelette, No. 80, By A. M. Barnard (Boston: Thomes & Talbot, ca. 1870).

9. Rostenberg, "Some Anonymous and Pseudonymous Thrillers of Louisa M. Alcott."

10. *Journals*, p. 134.

11. "Behind a Mask" by A. M. Barnard was first published in *The Flag of Our Union* (13, 20, and 27 October and 3 November 1866).

12. J. R. Elliott to Louisa May Alcott, 11 August 1866 (Houghton Library, Harvard University).

13. *Journals*, p. 154.

14. Dramatization by Karen L. Lewis performed at Theater of the Open Eye, New York City.

15. Maureen Corrigan in *The Washington Post Book World* (3 September 1995), p. 5.

16. "Taming a Tartar" was first published in *Frank Leslie's Illustrated Newspaper* (30 November and 7, 14, and 21 December 1867).

17. *Journals*, p. 154.

18. See Louisa May Alcott, "Life in a Pension," *The Independent* (7 November 1867), p. 2.

19. *Journals*, p. 155.

20. *Journals*, p. 158.

21. *History of Woman Suffrage*, ed. Elizabeth Cady Stanton et al., vol. 2 (New York: Fowler & Wells, 1882; rpt: New York: Arno and the New York Times, 1969), 831–32.

22. *Woman's Journal* (14 November 1874, 15 July 1876, 11 October 1879).

23. Stern, *Louisa May Alcott*, p. 238; *Woman's Journal* (23 October 1875), p. 341.

24. *Woman's Journal* (1 May 1875).

25. *Journals*, pp. 216, 226.

26. Louisa May Alcott to Thomas Niles (12 February and 19 February 1881) in *The Selected Letters of Louisa May Alcott*, ed. Joel Myerson, Daniel Shealy, and Madeleine B. Stern (Athens: University of Georgia Press, 1995), pp. 252–53.

Pauline's Passion and Punishment

⊹⊹⊹

CHAPTER I

*T*o and fro, like a wild creature in its cage, paced that handsome woman, with bent head, locked hands, and restless steps. Some mental storm, swift and sudden as a tempest of the tropics, had swept over her and left its marks behind. As if in anger at the beauty now proved powerless, all ornaments had been flung away, yet still it shone undimmed, and filled her with a passionate regret. A jewel glittered at her feet, leaving the lace rent to shreds on the indignant bosom that had worn it; the wreaths of hair that had crowned her with a woman's most womanly adornment fell disordered upon shoulders that gleamed the fairer for the scarlet of the pomegranate flowers clinging to the bright meshes that had imprisoned them an hour ago; and over the face, once so affluent in youthful bloom, a stern pallor had fallen like a blight, for pride was slowly conquering passion, and despair had murdered hope.

Pausing in her troubled march, she swept away the curtain swaying in the wind and looked out, as if imploring help from Nature, the great mother of us all. A summer moon rode high in a cloudless heaven, and far as eye could reach stretched the green wilderness of a Cuban *cafetal*. No forest, but a tropical orchard, rich in lime, banana, plantain, palm, and orange trees, under whose protective shade grew the evergreen coffee plant, whose dark-red berries are the fortune of their possessor, and the luxury of one-half the world. Wide avenues diverging from the mansion, with its belt of brilliant shrubs and flowers, formed shadowy vistas, along which, on the wings of the wind, came a breath of far-off music, like a wooing voice; for the magic of night and distance lulled the cadence of a Spanish *contradanza* to a trance of sound, soft, subdued, and infinitely sweet. It was a southern scene, but not a southern face that looked out upon it with such unerring glance; there was no southern languor in the figure, stately and erect; no southern swarthiness on fairest cheek and arm; no southern darkness in the shadowy gold of the neglected hair; the light frost of northern snows lurked in the features, delicately cut, yet vividly alive, betraying a temperament ardent, dominant, and subtle. For passion burned in the deep eyes, changing their violet to black. Pride sat on the forehead, with its dark brows; all a woman's sweetest spells touched the lips, whose shape was a smile; and in the spirited carriage of the head appeared the freedom of an intellect ripened under colder skies, the energy of a nature that could wring strength from suffering, and dare to act where feebler souls would only dare desire.

Standing thus, conscious only of the wound that bled in that high heart of hers, and the longing that gradually took shape and deepened to a purpose, an alien presence changed the tragic atmosphere of that still room and woke her from her dangerous mood. A wonderfully winning guise this apparition wore, for youth, hope, and love endowed it with the charm that gives beauty to the plainest, while their reign endures. A boy in any other climate, in this his nineteen years had given him the stature of a man; and Spain, the land of romance, seemed embodied in this figure, full of the lithe slenderness of the whispering palms overhead, the warm coloring of the deep-toned flowers sleeping in the room, the native grace of the tame antelope lifting its human eyes to his as he lingered on the threshold in an attitude eager yet timid, watching that other figure as it looked into the night and found no solace there.

"Pauline!"

She turned as if her thought had taken voice and answered her, regarded him a moment, as if hesitating to receive the granted wish, then beckoned with the one word.

"Come!"

Instantly the fear vanished, the ardor deepened, and with an imperious "Lie down!" to his docile attendant, the young man obeyed with equal docility, looking as wistfully toward his mistress as the brute toward her master, while he waited proudly humble for her commands.

"Manuel, why are you here?"

"Forgive me! I saw Dolores bring a letter; you vanished, an hour passed, I could wait no longer, and I came."

"I am glad, I needed my one friend. Read that."

She offered a letter, and with her steady eyes upon him, her purpose strengthening as she looked, stood watching the changes of that expressive countenance. This was the letter:

Pauline—

Six months ago I left you, promising to return and take you home my wife; I loved you, but I deceived you; for though my heart was wholly yours, my hand was not mine to give. This it was that haunted me through all that blissful summer, this that marred my happiness when you owned you loved me, and this drove me from you, hoping I could break the tie with which I had rashly bound myself. I could not, I am married, and there all ends. Hate me, forget me, solace your pride with the memory that none knew your wrong, assure your peace with the knowledge that mine is destroyed forever, and leave my punishment to remorse and time.

Gilbert

With a gesture of wrathful contempt, Manuel flung the paper from him as he flashed a look at his companion, muttering through his teeth, "Traitor! Shall I kill him?"

Pauline laughed low to herself, a dreary sound, but answered with a slow darkening of the face that gave her words an ominous significance. "Why should you? Such revenge is brief and paltry, fit only for mock tragedies or poor souls who have neither the will to devise nor the will to execute a better. There are fates more terrible than death; weapons more keen than poniards, more noiseless than pistols. Women use such, and work out a subtler vengeance than men can conceive. Leave Gilbert to remorse—and me."

She paused an instant, and by some strong effort banished the black frown from her brow, quenched the baleful fire of her eyes, and left nothing visible but the pale determination that made her beautiful face more eloquent than her words.

"Manuel, in a week I leave the island."

"Alone, Pauline?"

"No, not alone."

A moment they looked into each other's eyes, each endeavoring to read the other. Manuel saw some indomitable purpose, bent on conquering all obstacles. Pauline saw doubt, desire, and hope; knew that a word would bring the ally she needed; and, with a courage as native to her as her pride, resolved to utter it.

Seating herself, she beckoned her companion to assume the place beside her, but for the first time he hesitated. Something in the unnatural calmness of her manner troubled him, for his southern temperament was alive to influences whose presence would have been unfelt by one less sensitive. He took the cushion at her feet, saying, half tenderly, half reproachfully, "Let me keep my old place till I know in what character I am to fill the new. The man you trusted has deserted you; the boy you pitied will prove loyal. Try him, Pauline."

"I will."

And with the bitter smile unchanged upon her lips, the low voice unshaken in its tones, the deep eyes unwavering in their gaze, Pauline went on:

"You know my past, happy as a dream till eighteen. Then all was swept away, home, fortune, friends, and I was left, like an unfledged bird, without even the shelter of a cage. For five years I have made my life what I could, humble, honest, but never happy, till I came here, for here I saw Gilbert. In the poor companion of your guardian's daughter he seemed to see the heiress I had been, and treated me as such. This flattered my pride and touched my heart. He was kind, I grateful; then he loved me, and God knows how utterly I loved him! A few months of happiness the purest, then he went to make home ready for me, and I believed him; for where I wholly love I wholly trust. While my own peace was undisturbed, I learned to read the language of your eyes, Manuel, to find the boy grown into the man, the friend warmed into a lover. Your youth had kept me blind too long. Your society had grown dear to me, and I loved you like a sister for your unvarying kindness to the solitary woman who earned her bread and found it bitter. I told you my secret to prevent the utterance of your own. You remember the promise you made me then, keep it still, and bury the knowledge of my lost happiness deep in your pitying heart, as I shall in my proud one. Now the storm is over, and I am ready for my work again, but it must be a new task in a new scene. I hate this house, this room, the faces I must meet, the duties I must perform, for the memory of that traitor haunts them all. I see a future full of interest, a stage whereon I could play a stirring part. I long for it intensely, yet cannot make it mine alone. Manuel, do you love me still?"

Bending suddenly, she brushed back the dark hair that streaked his forehead and searched the face that in an instant answered her. Like a swift rising light, the eloquent blood rushed over swarthy cheek and brow, the slumberous softness of the eyes kindled with a flash, and the lips, sensitive as any woman's, trembled yet broke into a rapturous smile as he cried, with fervent brevity, "I would die for you!"

A look of triumph swept across her face, for with this boy, as chivalrous as ardent, she knew that words were not mere breath. Still, with her stern purpose uppermost, she changed the bitter smile into one half-timid, half-tender, as she bent still nearer, "Manuel, in a week I leave the island. Shall I go alone?"

"No, Pauline."

He understood her now. She saw it in the sudden paleness that fell on him, heard it in the rapid beating of his heart, felt it in the strong grasp that fastened on her hand, and knew that the first step was won. A regretful pang smote her, but the dark mood which had taken possession of her stifled the generous warnings of her better self and drove her on.

"Listen, Manuel. A strange spirit rules me tonight, but I will have no reserves from you, all shall be told; then, if you will come, be it so; if not, I shall go my way as solitary as I came. If you think that this loss has broken my heart, undeceive yourself, for such as I live years in an hour and show no sign. I have shed no tears, uttered no cry, asked no comfort; yet, since I read that letter, I have suffered more than many suffer in a lifetime. I am not one to lament long over any hopeless sorrow. A single paroxysm, sharp and short, and it is over. Contempt has killed my love, I have buried it, and no power can make it live again, except as a pale ghost that will not rest till Gilbert shall pass through an hour as bitter as the last."

"Is that the task you give yourself, Pauline?"

The savage element that lurks in southern blood leaped up in the boy's heart as he listened, glittered in his eye, and involuntarily found expression in the nervous grip of the hands that folded a fairer one between them. Alas for Pauline that she had roused the sleeping devil, and was glad to see it!

"Yes, it is weak, wicked, and unwomanly; yet I persist as relentlessly as any Indian on a war trail. See me as I am, not the gay girl you have known, but a revengeful woman with but one tender spot now left in her heart, the place you fill. I have been wronged, and I long to right myself at once. Time is too slow; I cannot wait, for that man must be taught that two can play at the game of hearts, taught soon and sharply. I can do this, can wound as I have been wounded, can sting him with contempt, and prove that I too can forget."

"Go on, Pauline. Show me how I am to help you."

"Manuel, I want fortune, rank, splendor, and power; you can give me all these, and a faithful friend beside. I desire to show Gilbert the creature he deserted no longer poor, unknown, unloved, but lifted higher than himself, cherished, honored, applauded, her life one of royal pleasure, herself a happy queen. Beauty, grace, and talent you tell me I possess; wealth gives them luster, rank exalts them, power makes them irresistible. Place these worldly gifts in my hand and that hand is yours. See, I offer it."

She did so, but it was not taken. Manuel had left his seat and now stood before her, awed by the undertone of strong emotion in her calmly spoken words, bewildered by the proposal so abruptly made, longing to ask the natural question hovering on his lips, yet too generous to utter it. Pauline read his thought, and answered it with no touch of pain or pride in the magical voice that seldom spoke in vain.

"I know your wish; it is as just as your silence is generous, and I reply to it in all sincerity. You would ask, 'When I have given all that I possess, what do I receive in return?' This—a wife whose friendship is as warm as many a woman's love; a wife who will give you all the heart still left her, and cherish the hope that time may bring a harvest of real affection to repay you for the faithfulness of years; who, though she takes the retribution of a wrong into her hands and executes it in the face of heaven, never will forget the honorable name you give into her keeping or blemish it by any act of hers. I can promise no more. Will this content you, Manuel?"

Before she ended his face was hidden in his hands, and tears streamed through them as he listened, for like a true child of the south each emotion found free vent and spent itself as swiftly as it rose. The reaction was more than he could bear, for in a moment his life was changed, months of hopeless longing were banished with a word, a blissful yes canceled the hard no that had been accepted as inexorable, and Happiness, lifting her full cup to his lips, bade him drink. A moment he yielded to the natural relief, then dashed his tears away and threw himself at Pauline's feet in that attitude fit only for a race as graceful as impassioned.

"Forgive me! Take all I have—fortune, name, and my poor self; use us as you will, we are proud and happy to be spent for you! No service will be too hard, no trial too long if in the end you learn to love me with one tithe of the affection I have made my life. Do you mean it? Am I to go with you? To be near you always, to call you wife, and know we are each other's until death? What have I ever done to earn a fate like this?"

Fast and fervently he spoke, and very winsome was the glad abandonment of this young lover, half boy, half man, possessing the simplicity of the one, the fervor of the other. Pauline looked and listened with a soothing sense of consolation in the knowledge that this loyal heart was all her own, a sweet foretaste of the devotion which henceforth was to shelter her from poverty, neglect, and wrong, and turn life's sunniest side to one who had so long seen only its most bleak and barren. Still at her feet, his arms about her waist, his face flushed and proud, lifted to hers, Manuel saw the cold mask soften, the stern eyes melt with a sudden dew as Pauline watched him, saying, "Dear Manuel, love me less; I am not worth such ardent and entire faith. Pause and reflect before you take this step. I will not bind you to my fate too soon lest you repent too late. We both stand alone in the world, free to make or mar our future as we will. I have chosen my lot. Recall all it may cost you to share it and be sure the price is not too high a one. Remember I am poor, you the possessor of one princely fortune, the sole heir to another."

"The knowledge of this burdened me before; now I glory in it because I have the more for you."

"Remember, I am older than yourself, and may early lose the beauty you love so well, leaving an old wife to burden your youth."

"What are a few years to me? Women like you grow lovelier with age, and you shall have a strong young husband to lean on all your life."

"Remember, I am not of your faith, and the priests will shut me out from your heaven."

"Let them prate as they will. Where you go I will go; Santa Paula shall be my madonna!"

"Remember, I am a deserted woman, and in the world we are going to my name may become the sport of that man's cruel tongue. Could you bear that patiently, and curb your fiery pride if I desired it?"

"Anything for you, Pauline!"

"One thing more. I give you my liberty; for a time give me forbearance in return, and though wed in haste woo me slowly, lest this sore heart of mine find even your light yoke heavy. Can you promise this, and wait till time has healed my wound, and taught me to be meek?"

"I swear to obey you in all things; make me what you will, for soul and body I am wholly yours henceforth."

"Faithful and true! I knew you would not fail me. Now go, Manuel. Tomorrow do your part resolutely as I shall do mine, and in

a week we will begin the new life together. Ours is a strange be-
trothal, but it shall not lack some touch of tenderness from me. Love,
good night."

Pauline bent till her bright hair mingled with the dark, kissed the
boy on lips and forehead as a fond sister might have done, then put
him gently from her; and like one in a blessed dream he went away
to pace all night beneath her window, longing for the day.

As the echo of his steps died along the corridor, Pauline's eye fell
on the paper lying where her lover flung it. At this sight all the softness vanished, the stern woman reappeared, and, crushing it in her
hand with slow significance, she said low to herself, "This is an old,
old story, but it shall have a new ending."

CHAPTER II

"What jewels will the señora wear tonight?"

"None, Dolores. Manuel has gone for flowers—he likes them
best. You may go."

"But the señora's toilette is not finished; the sandals, the gloves,
the garland yet remain."

"Leave them all; I shall not go down. I am tired of this endless
folly. Give me that book and go."

The pretty Creole obeyed; and careless of Dolores' work, Pauline sank into the deep chair with a listless mien, turned the pages for
a little, then lost herself in thoughts that seemed to bring no rest.

Silently the young husband entered and, pausing, regarded his
wife with mingled pain and pleasure—pain to see her so spiritless,
pleasure to see her so fair. She seemed unconscious of his presence till
the fragrance of his floral burden betrayed him, and looking up to
smile a welcome she met a glance that changed the sad dreamer into
an excited actor, for it told her that the object of her search was found.
Springing erect, she asked eagerly, "Manuel, is he here?"

"Yes."

"Alone?"

"His wife is with him."

"Is she beautiful?"

"Pretty, petite, and petulant."

"And he?"

"Unchanged: the same imposing figure and treacherous face, the same restless eye and satanic mouth. Pauline, let me insult him!"

"Not yet. Were they together?"

"Yes. He seemed anxious to leave her, but she called him back imperiously, and he came like one who dared not disobey."

"Did he see you?"

"The crowd was too dense, and I kept in the shadow."

"The wife's name? Did you learn it?"

"Barbara St. Just."

"Ah! I knew her once and will again. Manuel, am I beautiful tonight?"

"How can you be otherwise to me?"

"That is not enough. I must look my fairest to others, brilliant and blithe, a happy-hearted bride whose honeymoon is not yet over."

"For his sake, Pauline?"

"For yours. I want him to envy you your youth, your comeliness, your content; to see the man he once sneered at the husband of the woman he once loved; to recall impotent regret. I know his nature, and can stir him to his heart's core with a look, revenge myself with a word, and read the secrets of his life with a skill he cannot fathom."

"And when you have done all this, shall you be happier, Pauline?"

"Infinitely; our three weeks' search is ended, and the real interest of the plot begins. I have played the lover for your sake, now play the man of the world for mine. This is the moment we have waited for. Help me to make it successful. Come! Crown me with your garland, give me the bracelets that were your wedding gift—none can be too brilliant for tonight. Now the gloves and fan. Stay, my sandals—you shall play Dolores and tie them on."

With an air of smiling coquetry he had never seen before, Pauline stretched out a truly Spanish foot and offered him its dainty covering. Won by the animation of her manner, Manuel forgot his misgivings and played his part with boyish spirit, hovering about his stately wife as no assiduous maid had ever done; for every flower was fastened with a word sweeter than itself, the white arms kissed as the ornaments went on, and when the silken knots were deftly accomplished, the lighthearted bridegroom performed a little dance of triumph about his idol, till she arrested him, beckoning as she spoke.

"Manuel, I am waiting to assume the last best ornament you have given me, my handsome husband." Then, as he came to her laughing with frank pleasure at her praise, she added, "You, too, must look your best and bravest now, and remember you must enact the man tonight. Before Gilbert wear your stateliest aspect, your tenderest to me, your courtliest to his wife. You possess dramatic skill. Use it for my sake, and come for your reward when this night's work is done."

The great hotel was swarming with life, ablaze with light, resonant with the tread of feet, the hum of voices, the musical din of the band, and full of the sights and sounds which fill such human hives at a fashionable watering place in the height of the season. As Manuel led his wife along the grand hall thronged with promenaders, his quick ear caught the whispered comments of the passers-by, and the fragmentary rumors concerning themselves amused him infinitely.

"Mon ami! There are five bridal couples here tonight, and there is the handsomest, richest, and most enchanting of them all. The groom is not yet twenty, they tell me, and the bride still younger. Behold them!"

Manuel looked down at Pauline with a mirthful glance, but she had not heard.

"See, Belle! Cubans; own half the island between them. Splendid, aren't they? Look at the diamonds on her lovely arms, and his ravishing moustache. Isn't he your ideal of Prince Djalma, in *The Wandering Jew?*"

A pretty girl, forgetting propriety in interest, pointed as they passed. Manuel half-bowed to the audible compliment, and the blushing damsel vanished, but Pauline had not seen.

"Jack, there's the owner of the black span you fell into raptures over. My lord and lady look as highbred as their stud. We'll patronize them!"

Manuel muttered a disdainful *"Impertinente!"* between his teeth as he surveyed a brace of dandies with an air that augured ill for the patronage of Young America, but Pauline was unconscious of both criticism and reproof. A countercurrent held them stationary for a moment, and close behind them sounded a voice saying, confidentially, to some silent listener, "The Redmonds are here tonight, and I am curious to see how he bears his disappointment. You know he married for money, and was outwitted in the bargain; for his wife's fortune not only proves to be much less than he was led to believe, but is so tied up that he is entirely dependent upon her, and the bachelor debts he sold himself to liquidate still harass him, with a wife's reproaches to augment the affliction. To be ruled by a spoiled child's whims is a fit punishment for a man whom neither pride nor principle could curb before. Let us go and look at the unfortunate."

Pauline heard now. Manuel felt her start, saw her flush and pale, then her eye lit, and the dark expression he dreaded to see settled on her face as she whispered, like a satanic echo, "Let us also go and look at this unfortunate."

A jealous pang smote the young man's heart as he recalled the past.

"You pity him, Pauline, and pity is akin to love."

"I only pity what I respect. Rest content, my husband."

Steadily her eyes met his, and the hand whose only ornament was a wedding ring went to meet the one folded on his arm with a confiding gesture that made the action a caress.

"I will try to be, yet mine is a hard part," Manuel answered with a sigh, then silently they both paced on.

Gilbert Redmond lounged behind his wife's chair, looking intensely bored.

"Have you had enough of this folly, Babie?"

"No, we have but just come. Let us dance."

"Too late; they have begun."

"Then go about with me. It's very tiresome sitting here."

"It is too warm to walk in all that crowd, child."

"You are so indolent! Tell me who people are as they pass. I know no one here."

"Nor I."

But his act belied the words, for as they passed his lips he rose erect, with a smothered exclamation and startled face, as if a ghost had suddenly confronted him. The throng had thinned, and as his wife followed the direction of his glance, she saw no uncanny apparition to cause such evident dismay, but a woman fair-haired, violet-eyed, blooming and serene, sweeping down the long hall with noiseless grace. An air of sumptuous life pervaded her, the shimmer of bridal snow surrounded her, bridal gifts shone on neck and arms, and bridal happiness seemed to touch her with its tender charm as she looked up at her companion, as if there were but one human being in the world to her. This companion, a man slender and tall, with a face delicately dark as a fine bronze, looked back at her with eyes as eloquent as her own, while both spoke rapidly and low in the melodious language which seems made for lover's lips.

"Gilbert, who are they?"

There was no answer, and before she could repeat the question the approaching pair paused before her, and the beautiful woman offered her hand, saying, with inquiring smiles, "Barbara, have you forgotten your early friend, Pauline?"

Recognition came with the familiar name, and Mrs. Redmond welcomed the newcomer with a delight as unrestrained as if she were still the schoolgirl, Babie. Then, recovering herself, she said, with a pretty attempt at dignity, "Let me present my husband. Gilbert, come and welcome my friend Pauline Valary."

Scarlet with shame, dumb with conflicting emotions, and utterly deserted by self-possession, Redmond stood with downcast eyes and agitated mien, suffering a year's remorse condensed into a moment. A mute gesture was all the greeting he could offer. Pauline slightly bent her haughty head as she answered, in a voice frostily sweet, "Your wife mistakes. Pauline Valary died three weeks ago, and Pauline Laroche rose from her ashes. Manuel, my schoolmate, Mrs. Redmond; Gilbert you already know."

With the manly presence he could easily assume and which was henceforth to be his role in public, Manuel bowed courteously to the lady, coldly to the gentleman, and looked only at his wife. Mrs.

Redmond, though childish, was observant; she glanced from face to face, divined a mystery, and spoke out at once.

"Then you have met before? Gilbert, you have never told me this."

"It was long ago—in Cuba. I believed they had forgotten me."

"I never forget." And Pauline's eye turned on him with a look he dared not meet.

Unsilenced by her husband's frown, Mrs. Redmond, intent on pleasing herself, drew her friend to the seat beside her as she said petulantly, "Gilbert tells me nothing, and I am constantly discovering things which might have given me pleasure had he only chosen to be frank. I've spoken of you often, yet he never betrayed the least knowledge of you, and I take it very ill of him, because I am sure he has not forgotten you. Sit here, Pauline, and let me tease you with questions, as I used to do so long ago. You were always patient with me, and though far more beautiful, your face is still the same kind one that comforted the little child at school. Gilbert, enjoy your friend, and leave us to ourselves until the dance is over."

Pauline obeyed; but as she chatted, skillfully leading the young wife's conversation to her own affairs, she listened to the two voices behind her, watched the two figures reflected in the mirror before her, and felt a secret pride in Manuel's address, for it was evident that the former positions were renewed.

The timid boy who had feared the sarcastic tongue of his guardian's guest, and shrunk from his presence to conceal the jealousy that was his jest, now stood beside his formal rival, serene and self-possessed, by far the manliest man of the two, for no shame daunted him, no fear oppressed him, no dishonorable deed left him at the mercy of another's tongue.

Gilbert Redmond felt this keenly, and cursed the falsehood which had placed him in such an unenviable position. It was vain to assume the old superiority that was forfeited; but too much a man of the world to be long discomforted by any contretemps like this, he rapidly regained his habitual ease of manner, and avoiding the perilous past clung to the safer present, hoping, by some unguarded look or word, to fathom the purpose of his adversary, for such he knew the husband of Pauline must be at heart. But Manuel schooled his features, curbed his tongue, and when his hot blood tempted him to point his smooth speech with a taunt, or offer a silent insult with the eye, he remembered Pauline, looked down on the graceful head below, and forgot all other passions in that of love.

"Gilbert, my shawl. The sea air chills me."

"I forgot it, Babie."

"Allow me to supply the want."

Mindful of his wife's commands, Manuel seized this opportunity to win a glance of commendation from her. And taking the downy mantle that hung upon his arm, he wrapped the frail girl in it with a care that made the act as cordial as courteous. Mrs. Redmond felt the charm of his manner with the quickness of a woman, and sent a reproachful glance at Gilbert as she said plaintively, "Ah! It is evident that my honeymoon is over, and the assiduous lover replaced by the negligent husband. Enjoy your midsummer night's dream while you may, Pauline, and be ready for the awakening that must come."

"Not to her, madame, for our honeymoon shall last till the golden wedding day comes round. Shall it not, *cariña?*"

"There is no sign of waning yet, Manuel," and Pauline looked up into her husband's face with a genuine affection which made her own more beautiful and filled his with a visible content. Gilbert read the glance, and in that instant suffered the first pang of regret that Pauline had foretold. He spoke abruptly, longing to be away.

"Babie, we may dance now, if you will."

"I am going, but not with you—so give me my fan, and entertain Pauline till my return."

He unclosed his hand, but the delicately carved fan fell at his feet in a shower of ivory shreds—he had crushed it as he watched his first love with the bitter thought "It might have been!"

"Forgive me, Babie, it was too frail for use; you should choose a stronger."

"I will next time, and a gentler hand to hold it. Now, Monsieur Laroche, I am ready."

Mrs. Redmond rose in a small bustle of satisfaction, shook out her flounces, glanced at the mirror, then Manuel led her away; and the other pair were left alone. Both felt a secret agitation quicken their breath and thrill along their nerves, but the woman concealed it best. Gilbert's eye wandered restlessly to and fro, while Pauline fixed her own on his as quietly as if he were the statue in the niche behind him. For a moment he tried to seem unconscious of it, then essayed to meet and conquer it, but failed signally and, driven to his last resources by that steady gaze, resolved to speak out and have all over before his wife's return. Assuming the seat beside her, he said, impetuously, "Pauline, take off your mask as I do mine—we are alone now, and may see each other as we are."

Leaning deep into the crimson curve of the couch, with the indolent grace habitual to her, yet in strong contrast to the vigilant gleam of her eye, she swept her hand across her face as if obeying him, yet no change followed, as she said with a cold smile, "It is off; what next?"

"Let me understand you. Did my letter reach your hands?"

"A week before my marriage."

He drew a long breath of relief, yet a frown gathered as he asked, like one loath and eager to be satisfied, "Your love died a natural death, then, and its murder does not lie at my door?"

Pointing to the shattered toy upon the ground, she only echoed his own words. "It was too frail for use—I chose a stronger."

It wounded, as she meant it should; and the evil spirit to whose guidance she had yielded herself exulted to see his self-love bleed, and pride vainly struggle to conceal the stab. He caught the expression in her averted glance, bent suddenly a fixed and scrutinizing gaze upon her, asking, below his breath, "Then why are you here to tempt me with the face that tempted me a year ago?"

"I came to see the woman to whom you sold yourself. I have seen her, and am satisfied."

Such quiet contempt iced her tones, such pitiless satisfaction shone through the long lashes that swept slowly down, after her eye had met and caused his own to fall again, that Gilbert's cheek burned as if the words had been a blow, and mingled shame and anger trembled in his voice.

"Ah, you are quick to read our secret, for you possess the key.

Have you no fear that I may read your own, and tell the world you sold your beauty for a name and fortune? Your bargain is a better one than mine, but I know you too well, though your fetters are diamonds and your master a fond boy."

She had been prepared for this, and knew she had a shield in the real regard she bore her husband, for though sisterly, it was sincere. She felt its value now, for it gave her courage to confront the spirit of retaliation she had roused, and calmness to answer the whispered taunt with an unruffled mien, as lifting her white arm she let its single decoration drop glittering to her lap.

"You see my 'fetters' are as loose as they are light, and nothing binds me but my will. Read my heart, if you can. You will find there contempt for a love so poor that it feared poverty; pity for a man who dared not face the world and conquer it, as a girl had done before him, and gratitude that I have found my 'master' in a truehearted boy, not a falsehearted man. If I am a slave, I never know it. Can you say as much?"

Her woman's tongue avenged her, and Gilbert owned his defeat. Pain quenched the ire of his glance, remorse subdued his pride, self-condemnation compelled him to ask, imploringly, "Pauline, when may I hope for pardon?"

"Never."

The stern utterance of the word dismayed him, and, like one shut out from hope, he rose, as if to leave her, but paused irresolutely, looked back, then sank down again, as if constrained against his will by a longing past control. If she had doubted her power this action set the doubt at rest, as the haughtiest nature she had known confessed it by a bittersweet complaint. Eyeing her wistfully, tenderly, Gilbert murmured, in the voice of long ago, "Why do I stay to wound and to be wounded by the hand that once caressed me? Why do I find more pleasure in your contempt than in another woman's praise, and feel myself transported into the delights of that irrecoverable past, now grown the sweetest, saddest memory of my life? Send me away, Pauline, before the old charm asserts its power, and I forget that I am not the happy lover of a year ago."

"Leave me then, Gilbert. Good night."

Half unconsciously, the former softness stole into her voice as it lingered on his name. The familiar gesture accompanied the words, the old charm did assert itself, and for an instant changed the cold woman into the ardent girl again. Gilbert did not go but, with a hasty glance down the deserted hall behind him, captured and kissed the hand he had lost, passionately whispering, "Pauline, I love you still, and that look assures me that you have forgiven, forgotten, and kept a place for me in that deep heart of yours. It is too late to deny it. I have seen the tender eyes again, and the sight has made me the proudest, happiest man that walks the world tonight, slave though I am."

Over cheek and forehead rushed the treacherous blood as the violet eyes filled and fell before his own, and in the glow of mingled pain and fear that stirred her blood, Pauline, for the first time, owned the peril of the task she had set herself, saw the dangerous power she possessed, and felt the buried passion faintly moving in its grave. Indignant at her own weakness, she took refuge in the memory of her wrong, controlled the rebel color, steeled the front she showed him, and with feminine skill mutely conveyed the rebuke she would not trust herself to utter, by stripping the glove from the hand he had touched and dropping it disdainfully as if unworthy of its place. Gilbert had not looked for such an answer, and while it baffled him it excited his man's spirit to rebel against her silent denial. With a bitter laugh he snatched up the glove.

"I read a defiance in your eye as you flung this down. I accept the challenge, and will keep gage until I prove myself the victor. I have asked for pardon. You refuse it. I have confessed my love. You scorn it. I have possessed myself of your secret, yet you deny it. Now we will try our strength together, and leave those children to their play."

"We are the children, and we play with edge tools. There has been enough of this, there must be no more." Pauline rose with her haughtiest mien, and the brief command, "Take me to Manuel."

Silently Gilbert offered his arm, and silently she rejected it.

"Will you accept nothing from me?"

"Nothing."

Side by side they passed through the returning throng till Mrs.

Redmond joined them, looking blithe and bland with the exhilaration of gallantry and motion. Manuel's first glance was at Pauline, his second at her companion; there was a shadow upon the face of each, which seemed instantly to fall upon his own as he claimed his wife with a masterful satisfaction as novel as becoming, and which prompted her to whisper, "You enact your role to the life, and shall enjoy a foretaste of your reward at once. I want excitement; let us show these graceless, frozen people the true art of dancing, and electrify them with the life and fire of a Cuban valse."

Manuel kindled at once, and Pauline smiled stealthily as she glanced over her shoulder from the threshold of the dancing hall, for her slightest act, look, and word had their part to play in that night's drama.

"Gilbert, if you are tired I will go now."

"Thank you, I begin to find it interesting. Let us watch the dancers."

Mrs. Redmond accepted the tardy favor, wondering at his unwonted animation, for never had she seen such eagerness in his countenance, such energy in his manner as he pressed through the crowd and won a place where they could freely witness one of those exhibitions of fashionable figurante which are nightly to be seen at such resorts. Many couples were whirling around the white hall, but among them one pair circled with slowly increasing speed, in perfect time to the inspiring melody of trumpet, flute, and horn, that seemed to sound for them alone. Many paused to watch them, for they gave to the graceful pastime the enchantment which few have skill enough to lend it, and made it a spectacle of life-enjoying youth, to be remembered long after the music ceased and the agile feet were still.

Gilbert's arm was about his little wife to shield her from the pressure of the crowd, and as they stood his hold unconsciously tightened, till, marveling at this unwonted care, she looked up to thank him with a happy glance and discovered that his eye rested on a single pair, kindling as they approached, keenly scanning every gesture as they floated by, following them with untiring vigilance through the many-colored mazes they threaded with such winged steps, while his breath quickened, his hand kept time, and every sense seemed to own the intoxication of the scene. Sorrowfully she too watched this pair, saw their grace, admired their beauty, envied their happiness; for, short as her wedded life had been, the thorns already pierced her through the roses, and with each airy revolution of those figures, dark and bright, her discontent increased, her wonder deepened, her scrutiny grew keener, for she knew no common interest held her husband there, fascinated, flushed, and excited as if his heart beat responsive to the rhythmic rise and fall of that booted foot and satin slipper. The music ended with a crash, the crowd surged across the floor, and the spell was broken. Like one but half disenchanted, Gilbert stood a moment, then remembered his wife, and looking down met brown eyes, full of tears, fastened on his face.

"Tired so soon, Babie? Or in a pet because I cannot change myself into a thistledown and float about with you, like Manuel and Pauline?"

"Neither; I was only wishing that you loved me as he loves her, and hoping he would never tire of her, they are so fond and charming now. How long have you known them—and where?"

"I shall have no peace until I tell you. I passed a single summer with them in a tropical paradise, where we swung half the day in hammocks, under tamarind and almond trees; danced half the night to music, of which this seems but a faint echo; and led a life of luxurious delight in an enchanted climate, where all is so beautiful and brilliant that its memory haunts a life as pressed flowers sweeten the leaves of a dull book."

"Why did you leave it then?"

"To marry you, child."

"That was a regretful sigh, as if I were not worth the sacrifice. Let us go back and enjoy it together."

"If you were dying for it, I would not take you to Cuba. It would be purgatory, not paradise, now."

"How stern you look, how strangely you speak. Would you not go to save your own life, Gilbert?"

"I would not cross the room to do that much, less the sea."

"Why do you both love and dread it? Don't frown, but tell me. I have a right to know."

"Because the bitterest blunder of my life was committed there—a blunder that I never can repair in this world, and may be damned for in the next. Rest satisfied with this, Babie, lest you prove like Bluebeard's wife, and make another skeleton in my closet, which has enough already."

Strange regret was in his voice, strange gloom fell upon his face; but though rendered doubly curious by the change, Mrs. Redmond dared not question further and, standing silent, furtively scanned the troubled countenance beside her. Gilbert spoke first, waking out of his sorrowful reverie with a start.

"Pauline is coming. Say adieu, not au revoir, for tomorrow we must leave this place."

His words were a command, his aspect one of stern resolve, though the intensest longing mingled with the dark look he cast on the approaching pair. The tone, the glance displeased his willful wife, who loved to use her power and exact obedience where she had failed to win affection, often ruling imperiously when a tender word would have made her happy to submit.

"Gilbert, you take no thought for my pleasures though you pursue your own at my expense. Your neglect forces me to find solace and satisfaction where I can, and you have forfeited your right to command or complain. I love Pauline, I am happy with her, therefore I shall stay until we tire of one another. I am a burden to you; go if you will."

"You know I cannot without you, Babie. I ask it as a favor. For my sake, for your own, I implore you to come away."

"Gilbert, do you love her?"

She seized his arm and forced an answer by the energy of her sharply whispered question. He saw that it was vain to dissemble, yet replied with averted head, "I did and still remember it."

"And she? Did she return your love?"

"I believed so; but she forgot me when I went. She married Manuel and is happy. Babie, let me go!"

"No! you shall stay and feel a little of the pain I feel when I look into your heart and find I have no place there. It is this which has stood between us and made all my efforts vain. I see it now and despise you for the falsehood you have shown me, vowing you loved no one but me until I married you, then letting me so soon discover that I was only an encumbrance to your enjoyment of the fortune I possessed. You treat me like a child, but I suffer like a woman, and you shall share my suffering, because you might have spared me, and you did not. Gilbert, you shall stay."

"Be it so, but remember I have warned you."

An exultant expression broke through the gloom of her husband's face as he answered with the grim satisfaction of one who gave restraint to the mind, and stood ready to follow whatever impulse should sway him next. His wife trembled inwardly at what she had done, but was too proud to recall her words and felt a certain bitter pleasure in the excitement of the new position she had taken, the new interest given to her listless life.

Pauline and Manuel found them standing silently together, for a moment had done the work of years and raised a barrier between them never to be swept away.

Mrs. Redmond spoke first, and with an air half resentful, half triumphant:

"Pauline, this morose husband of mine says we must leave tomorrow. But in some things I rule; this is one of them. Therefore we remain and go with you to the mountains when we are tired of the gay life here. So smile and submit, Gilbert, else these friends will count your society no favor. Would you not fancy, from the aspect he thinks proper to assume, that I had sentenced him to a punishment, not a pleasure?"

"Perhaps you have unwittingly, Babie. Marriage is said to cancel the follies of the past, but not those of the future, I believe; and, as there are many temptations to an idle man in a place like this, doubtless your husband is wise enough to own that he dares not stay but finds discretion the better part of valor."

Nothing could be softer than the tone in which these words were uttered, nothing sharper than the hidden taunt conveyed, but Gilbert only laughed a scornful laugh as he fixed his keen eyes full upon her and took her bouquet with the air of one assuming former rights.

"My dear Pauline, discretion is the last virtue I should expect to be accused of by you; but if valor consists in daring all things, I may lay claim to it without its 'better part,' for temptation is my delight—the stronger the better. Have no fears for me, my friend. I gladly accept Babie's decree and, ignoring the last ten years, intend to begin life anew, having discovered a *sauce piquante* which will give the stalest pleasures a redoubled zest. I am unfortunate tonight, and here is a second wreck; this I can rebuild happily. Allow me to do so, for I remember you once praised my skill in floral architecture."

With an air of eager gallantry in strange contrast to the malign expression of his countenance, Gilbert knelt to regather the flowers which a careless gesture of his own had scattered from their jeweled holder. His wife turned to speak to Manuel, and, yielding to the unconquerable anxiety his reckless manner awoke, Pauline whispered below her breath as she bent as if to watch the work, "Gilbert, follow your first impulse, and go tomorrow."

"Nothing shall induce me to."

"I warn you harm will come of it."

"Let it come; I am past fear now."

"Shun me for Babie's sake, if not for your own."

"Too late for that; she is headstrong—let her suffer."

"Have you no power, Gilbert?"

"None over her, much over you."

"We will prove that!"

"We will!"

Rapidly as words could shape them, these questions and answers fell, and with their utterance the last generous feeling died in Pauline's breast; for as she received the flowers, now changed from a love token to a battle gage, she saw the torn glove still crushed in Gilbert's hand, and silently accepted his challenge to the tournament so often held between man and woman—a tournament where the keen tongue is the lance, pride the shield, passion the fiery steed, and the hardest heart the winner of the prize, which seldom fails to prove a barren honor, ending in remorse.

CHAPTER III

For several days the Cubans were almost invisible, appearing only for a daily drive, a twilight saunter on the beach, or a brief visit to the ballroom, there to enjoy the excitement of the pastime in which they both excelled. Their apartments were in the quietest wing of the hotel, and from the moment of their occupancy seemed to acquire all the charms of home. The few guests admitted felt the atmosphere of poetry and peace that pervaded the nest which Love, the worker of miracles, had built himself even under that tumultuous roof. Strollers in the halls or along the breezy verandas often paused to listen to the music of instrument or voice which came floating out from these sequestered rooms. Frequent laughter and the murmur of conversation proved that ennui was unknown, and a touch of romance inevitably enhanced the interest wakened by the beautiful young pair, always together, always happy, never weary of the *dolce far niente* of this summer life.

In a balcony like a hanging garden, sheltered from the sun by blossoming shrubs and vines that curtained the green nook with odorous shade, Pauline lay indolently swinging in a gaily fringed hammock as she had been wont to do in Cuba, then finding only pleasure in the luxury of motion which now failed to quiet her unrest. Manuel had put down the book to which she no longer listened and, leaning his head upon his hand, sat watching her as she swayed to and fro with thoughtful eyes intent upon the sea, whose murmurous voice possessed a charm more powerful than his own. Suddenly he spoke:

"Pauline, I cannot understand you! For three weeks we hurried east and west to find this man, yet when found you shun him and seem content to make my life a heaven upon earth. I sometimes fancy that you have resolved to let the past sleep, but the hope dies as soon as born, for in moments like this I see that, though you devote yourself to me, the old purpose is unchanged, and I marvel why you pause."

Her eyes came back from their long gaze and settled on him full of an intelligence which deepened his perplexity. "You have not learned to know me yet; death is not more inexorable or time more tireless than I. This week has seemed one of indolent delight to you. To me it has been one of constant vigilance and labor, for scarcely a look, act, or word of mine has been without effect. At first I secluded myself that Gilbert might contrast our life with his and, believing us all and all to one another, find impotent regret his daily portion. Three days ago accident placed an unexpected weapon in my hand which I have used in silence, lest in spite of promises you should rebel and end his trial too soon. Have you no suspicion of my meaning?"

"None. You are more mysterious than ever, and I shall, in truth, believe you are the enchantress I have so often called you if your spells work invisibly."

"They do not, and I use no supernatural arts, as I will prove to you. Take my lorgnette that lies behind you, part the leaves where the green grapes hang thickest, look up at the little window in the shadowy angle of the low roof opposite, and tell me what you see."

"Nothing but a half-drawn curtain."

"Ah! I must try the ruse that first convinced me. Do not show yourself, but watch, and if you speak, let it be in Spanish."

Leaving her airy cradle, Pauline bent over the balcony as if to gather the climbing roses that waved their ruddy clusters in the wind. Before the third stem was broken Manuel whispered, "I see the curtain move; now comes the outline of a head, and now a hand, with some bright object in it. Santo Pablo! It is a man staring at you as coolly as if you were a lady in a balcony. What prying rascal is it?"

"Gilbert."

"Impossible! He is a gentleman."

"If gentlemen play the traitor and the spy, then he is one. I am not mistaken; for since the glitter of his glass first arrested me I have watched covertly, and several trials as successful as the present have confirmed the suspicion which Babie's innocent complaints of his long absences aroused. Now do you comprehend why I remained in these rooms with the curtains seldom drawn? Why I swung the hammock here and let you sing and read to me while I played with your hair or leaned upon your shoulder? Why I have been all devotion and made this balcony a little stage for the performance of our version of the honeymoon for one spectator?"

Still mindful of the eager eyes upon her, Pauline had been fastening the roses in her bosom as she spoke, and ended with a silvery laugh that made the silence musical with its heartsome sound. As she paused, Manuel flung down the lorgnette and was striding past her with ireful impetuosity, but the white arms took him captive, adding another figure to the picture framed by the green arch as she whispered decisively, "No farther! There must be no violence. You promised obedience and I exact it. Do you think detection to a man so lost to honor would wound as deeply as the sights which make his daily watch a torment? Or that a blow would be as hard to bear as the knowledge that his own act has placed you where you are and made him what he is? Silent contempt is the law now, so let this insult pass, unclench your hand and turn that defiant face to me, while I console you for submission with a kiss."

He yielded to the command enforced by the caress but drew her jealously from sight, and still glanced rebelliously through the leaves, asking with a frown, "Why show me this if I may not resent it? How long must I bear with this man? Tell me your design, else I shall mar it in some moment when hatred of him conquers love of you."

"I will, for it is time, because though I have taken the first step you must take the second. I showed you this that you might find action pleasanter than rest, and you must bear with this man a little longer for my sake, but I will give you an amusement to beguile the time. Long ago you told me that Gilbert was a gambler. I would not believe it then, now I can believe anything, and you can convince the world of this vice of his as speedily as you will."

"Do you wish me to become a gambler that I may prove him one? I also told you that he was suspected of dishonorable play—shall I load the dice and mark the cards to catch him in his own snares?"

Manuel spoke bitterly, for his high spirit chafed at the task assigned him; womanly wiles seemed more degrading than the masculine method of retaliation, in which strength replaces subtlety and speedier vengeance brings speedier satisfaction. But Pauline, fast learning to play upon that mysterious instrument, the human heart, knew when to stimulate and when to soothe.

"Do not reproach me that I point out a safer mode of operation than your own. You would go to Gilbert and by a hot word, a rash act, put your life and my happiness into his hands, for though dueling is forbidden here, he would not hesitate to break all laws, human or divine, if by so doing he could separate us. What would you gain by it? If you kill him he is beyond our reach forever, and a crime remains to be atoned for. If he kill you your blood will be upon my head, and where should I find consolation for the loss of the one heart always true and tender?"

With the inexplicable prescience which sometimes foreshadows coming ills, she clung to him as if a vision of the future dimly swept before her, but he only saw the solicitude it was a sweet surprise to find he had awakened, and in present pleasure forgot past pain.

"You shall not suffer from this man any grief that I can shield you from, rest assured of that, my heart. I will be patient, though your ways are not mine, for the wrong was yours, and the retribution shall be such as you decree."

"Then hear your task and see the shape into which circumstances have molded my design. I would have you exercise a self-restraint that shall leave Gilbert no hold upon you, accept all invitations like that which you refused when we passed him on the threshold of the billiard room an hour ago, and seem to find in such amusements the same fascination as himself. Your skill in games of chance excels his, as you proved at home where these pastimes lose their disreputable aspect by being openly enjoyed. Therefore I would have you whet this appetite of his by losing freely at first—he will take a grim delight in lessening the fortune he covets—then exert all your skill till he is deeply in your debt. He has nothing but what is doled out to him by Babie's father, I find; he dare not ask help there for such a purpose; other resources have failed else he would not have married; and if the sum be large enough, it lays him under an obligation which will be a thorn in his flesh, the sharper for your knowledge of his impotence to draw it out. When this is done, or even while it is in progress, I would have you add the pain of a new jealousy to the old. He neglects this young wife of his, and she is eager to recover the affections she believes she once possessed. Help her, and teach Gilbert the value of what he now despises. You are young, comely, accomplished, and possessed of many graces more attractive than you are conscious of; your southern birth and breeding gift you with a winning warmth of manners in strong contrast to the colder natures around you; and your love for me lends an almost tender deference to your intercourse with all womankind. Amuse, console this poor girl, and show her husband what he should be; I have no fear of losing your heart nor need you fear for hers; she is one of those spaniel-like creatures who love the hand that strikes them and fawn upon the foot that spurns them."

"Am I to be the sole actor in the drama of deceit? While I woo Babie, what will you do, Pauline?"

"Let Gilbert woo me—have patience till you understand my meaning; he still loves me and believes I still return that love. I shall not undeceive him yet, but let silence seem to confess what I do not own in words. He fed me with false promises, let me build my life's happiness on baseless hopes, and rudely woke me when he could delude no longer, leaving me to find I had pursued a shadow. I will do the same. He shall follow me undaunted, undeterred by all obstacles, all ties; shall stake his last throw and lose it, for when the crowning moment comes I shall show him that through me he is made bankrupt in love, honor, liberty, and hope, tell him I am yours entirely and forever, then vanish like an *ignis-fatuus,* leaving him to the darkness of despair and defeat. Is not this a better retribution than the bullet that would give him peace at once?"

Boy, lover, husband though he was, Manuel saw and stood aghast at the baleful spirit which had enslaved this woman, crushing all generous impulses, withering all gentle charities, and making her the saddest spectacle this world can show—one human soul rebelling against Providence, to become the nemesis of another. Involuntarily he recoiled from her, exclaiming, "Pauline! Are you possessed of a devil?"

"Yes! One that will not be cast out till every sin, shame, and sorrow mental ingenuity can conceive and inflict has been heaped on that man's head. I thought I should be satisfied with one accusing look, one bitter word; I am not, for the evil genii once let loose cannot be recaptured. Once I ruled it, now it rules me, and there is no turning back. I have come under the law of fate, and henceforth the powers I possess will ban, not bless, for I am driven to whet and wield them as weapons which may win me success at the price of my salvation. It is not yet too late for you to shun the spiritual contagion I bear about me. Choose now, and abide by that choice without a shadow of turning, as I abide by mine. Take me as I am; help me willingly and unwillingly; and in the end receive the promised gift— years like the days you have called heaven upon earth. Or retract the vows you plighted, receive again the heart and name you gave me, and live unvexed by the stormy nature time alone can tame. Here is the ring. Shall I restore or keep it, Manuel?"

Never had she looked more beautiful as she stood there, an image of will, daring, defiant, and indomitable, with eyes darkened by intensity of emotion, voice half sad, half stern, and outstretched hand on which the wedding ring no longer shone. She felt her power, yet was wary enough to assure it by one bold appeal to the strongest element of her husband's character: passions, not principles, were the allies she desired, and before the answer came she knew that she had gained them at the cost of innocence and self-respect.

As Manuel listened, an expression like a dark reflection of her own settled on his face; a year of youth seemed to drop away; and with the air of one who puts fear behind him, he took the hand, replaced the ring, resolutely accepted the hard conditions, and gave all to love, only saying as he had said before, "Soul and body, I belong to you; do with me as you will."

A fortnight later Pauline sat alone, waiting for her husband. Under the pretext of visiting a friend, she had absented herself a week, that Manuel might give himself entirely to the distasteful task she set him. He submitted to the separation, wrote daily, but sent no tidings of his progress, told her nothing when they met that night, and had left her an hour before asking her to have patience till he could show his finished work. Now, with her eye upon the door, her ear alert to catch the coming step, her mind disturbed by contending hopes and fears, she sat waiting with the vigilant immobility of an Indian on the watch. She had not long to look and listen. Manuel entered hastily, locked the door, closed the windows, dropped the curtains, then paused in the middle of the room and broke into a low, triumphant laugh as he eyed his wife with an expression she had never seen in those dear eyes before. It startled her, and, scarcely knowing what to desire or dread, she asked eagerly, "You are come to tell me you have prospered."

"Beyond your hopes, for the powers of darkness seem to help us, and lead the man to his destruction faster than any wiles of ours can do. I am tired, let me lie here and rest. I have earned it, so when I have told all say, 'Love, you have done well,' and I am satisfied."

He threw himself along the couch where she still sat and laid his head in her silken lap, her cool hand on his hot forehead, and continued in a muffled voice.

"You know how eagerly Gilbert took advantage of my willingness to play, and soon how recklessly he pursued it, seeming to find the satisfaction you foretold, till, obeying your commands, I ceased losing and won sums which surprised me. Then you went, but I was not idle, and in the effort to extricate himself, Gilbert plunged deeper into debt; for my desire to please you seemed to gift me with redoubled skill. Two days ago I refused to continue the unequal conflict, telling him to give himself no uneasiness, for I could wait. You were right in thinking it would oppress him to be under any obligation to me, but wrong in believing he would endure, and will hardly be prepared for the desperate step he took to free himself. That night he played falsely, was detected, and though his opponent generously promised silence for Babie's sake, the affair stole out—he is shunned and this resource has failed. I thought he had no other, but yesterday he came to me with a strange expression of relief, discharged the debt to the last farthing, then hinted that my friendship with his wife was not approved by him and must cease. This proves that I have obeyed you in all things, though the comforting of Babie was an easy task, for, both loving you, our bond of sympathy and constant theme has been Pauline and her perfections."

"Hush! No praise—it is a mockery. I am what one man's perfidy has made; I may yet learn to be worthy of another man's devotion. What more, Manuel?"

"I thought I should have only a defeat to show you, but today has given me a strange success. At noon a gentleman arrived and asked for Gilbert. He was absent, but upon offering information relative to the time of his return, which proved my intimacy with him, this Seguin entered into conversation with me. His evident desire to avoid Mrs. Redmond and waylay her husband interested me, and when he questioned me somewhat closely concerning Gilbert's habits and movements of late, my suspicions were roused; and on mentioning the debt so promptly discharged, I received a confidence that startled me. In a moment of despair Gilbert had forged the name of his former friend, whom he believed abroad, had drawn the money and freed himself from my power, but not for long. The good fortune which has led him safely through many crooked ways seems to have deserted him in this strait. For the forgery was badly executed, inspection raised doubts, and Seguin, just returned, was at his banker's an hour after Gilbert, to prove the fraud; he came hither at once to accuse him of it and made me his confidant. What would you have had me do, Pauline? Time was short, and I could not wait for you."

"How can I tell at once? Why pause to ask? What did you do?"

"Took a leaf from your book and kept accusation, punishment, and power in my own hands, to be used in your behalf. I returned the money, secured the forged check, and prevailed on Seguin to leave the matter in my hands, while he departed as quietly as he had come. Babie's presence when we met tonight prevented my taking you into my counsels. I had prepared this surprise for you and felt a secret pride in working it out alone. An hour ago I went to watch for Gilbert. He came, I took him to his rooms, told him what I had done, added that compassion for his wife had actuated me. I left him saying the possession of the check was a full equivalent for the money, which I now declined to receive from such dishonorable hands. Are you satisfied, Pauline?"

With countenance and gestures full of exultation she sprang up to pace the room, exclaiming, as she seized the forged paper, "Yes, that stroke was superb! How strangely the plot thickens. Surely the powers of darkness are working with us and have put this weapon in our hands when that I forged proved useless. By means of this we have a hold upon him which nothing can destroy unless he escape by death. Will he, Manuel?"

"No; there was more wrath than shame in his demeanor when I

accused him. He hates me too much to die yet, and had I been the only possessor of this fatal fact, I fancy it might have gone hard with me; for if ever there was murder in a man's heart it was in his when I showed him that paper and then replaced it next the little poniard you smile at me for wearing. This is over. What next, my queen?"

There was energy in the speaker's tone but none in attitude or aspect, as, still lying where she had left him, he pillowed his head upon his arm and turned toward her a face already worn and haggard with the feverish weariness that had usurped the blithe serenity which had been his chiefest charm a month ago. Pausing in her rapid walk, as if arrested by the change that seemed to strike her suddenly, she recalled her thoughts from the dominant idea of her life and, remembering the youth she was robbing of its innocent delights, answered the wistful look which betrayed the hunger of a heart she had never truly fed, as she knelt beside her husband and, laying her soft cheek to his, whispered in her tenderest accents, "I am not wholly selfish or ungrateful, Manuel. You shall rest now while I sing to you, and tomorrow we will go away among the hills and leave behind us for a time the dark temptation which harms you through me."

"No! Finish what you have begun. I will have all or nothing, for if we pause now you will bring me a divided mind, and I shall possess only the shadow of a wife. Take Gilbert and Babie with us, and end this devil's work without delay. Hark! What is that?"

Steps came flying down the long hall, a hand tried the lock, then beat impetuously upon the door, and a low voice whispered with shrill importunity, "Let me in! Oh, let me in!"

Manuel obeyed the urgent summons, and Mrs. Redmond, half dressed, with streaming hair and terror-stricken face, fled into Pauline's arms, crying incoherently, "Save me! Keep me! I never can go back to him; he said I was a burden and a curse, and wished I never had been born!"

"What has happened, Babie? We are your friends. Tell us, and let us comfort and protect you if we can."

But for a time speech was impossible, and the poor girl wept with a despairing vehemence sad to see, till their gentle efforts soothed her;

and, sitting by Pauline, she told her trouble, looking oftenest at Manuel, who stood before them, as if sure of redress from him.

"When I left here an hour or more ago I found my rooms still empty, and, though I had not seen my husband since morning, I knew he would be displeased to find me waiting, so I cried myself to sleep and dreamed of the happy time when he was kind, till the sound of voices woke me. I heard Gilbert say, 'Babie is with your wife, her maid tells me; therefore we are alone here. What is this mysterious affair, Laroche?' That tempted me to listen, and then, Manuel, I learned all the shame and misery you so generously tried to spare me. How can I ever repay you, ever love and honor you enough for such care of one so helpless and forlorn as I?"

"I am repaid already. Let that pass, and tell what brings you here with such an air of fright and fear?"

"When you were gone he came straight to the inner room in search of something, saw me, and knew I must have heard all he had concealed from me so carefully. If you have ever seen him when that fierce temper of his grows ungovernable, you can guess what I endured. He said such cruel things I could not bear it, and cried out that I would come to you, for I was quite wild with terror, grief, and shame, that seemed like oil to fire. He swore I should not, and oh, Pauline, he struck me! See, if I do not tell the living truth!"

Trembling with excitement, Mrs. Redmond pushed back the wide sleeve of her wrapper and showed the red outline of a heavy hand. Manuel set his teeth and stamped his foot into the carpet with an indignant exclamation and the brief question, "Then you left him, Babie?"

"Yes, although he locked me in my room, saying the law gave him the right to teach obedience. I flung on these clothes, crept noiselessly along the balcony till the hall window let me in, and then I ran to you. He will come for me. Can he take me away? Must I go back to suffer any more?"

In the very act of uttering the words, Mrs. Redmond clung to Manuel with a cry of fear, for on the threshold stood her husband. A comprehensive glance seemed to stimulate his wrath and lend the hardihood wherewith to confront the three, saying sternly as he beck-oned, "Babie, I am waiting for you."

She did not speak, but still clung to Manuel as if he were her only hope. A glance from Pauline checked the fiery words trembling on his lips, and he too stood silent while she answered with a calmness that amazed him:

"Your wife has chosen us her guardians, and I think you will scarcely venture to use force again with two such witnesses as these to prove that you have forfeited your right to her obedience and justify the step she has taken."

With one hand she uncovered the discolored arm, with the other held the forgery before him. For a moment Gilbert stood daunted by these mute accusations, but just then his ire burned hottest against Manuel; and believing that he could deal a double blow by wounding Pauline through her husband, he ignored her presence and, turning to the young man, asked significantly, "Am I to understand that you refuse me my wife, and prefer to abide by the consequences of such an act?"

Calmed by Pauline's calmness, Manuel only drew the trembling creature closer, and answered with his haughtiest mien, "I do; spare yourself the labor of insulting me, for having placed yourself beyond the reach of a gentleman's weapon, I shall accept no challenge from a——"

A soft hand at his lips checked the opprobrious word, as Babie, true woman through it all, whispered with a broken sob, "Spare him, for I loved him once."

Gilbert Redmond had a heart, and, sinful though it was, this generous forbearance wrung it with a momentary pang of genuine remorse, too swiftly followed by a selfish hope that all was not lost if through his wife he could retain a hold upon the pair which now possessed for him the strong attraction of both love and hate. In that brief pause this thought came, was accepted and obeyed, for, as if yielding to an uncontrollable impulse of penitent despair, he stretched his arms to his wife, saying humbly, imploringly, "Babie, come back to me, and teach me how I may retrieve the past. I freely confess I bitterly repent my manifold transgressions, and submit to your decree alone; but in executing justice, oh, remember mercy! Remember that I was too early left fatherless, motherless, and went astray for want of some kind heart to guide and cherish me. There is still time. Be compassionate and save me from myself. Am I not punished enough? Must death be my only comforter? Babie, when all others cast me off, will you too forsake me?"

"No, I will not! Only love me, and I can forgive, forget, and still be happy!"

Pauline was right. The spaniel-like nature still loved the hand that struck it, and Mrs. Redmond joyfully returned to the arms from which she had so lately fled. The tenderest welcome she had ever received from him welcomed the loving soul whose faith was not yet dead, for Gilbert felt the value this once neglected possession had suddenly acquired, and he held it close; yet as he soothed with gentle touch and tone, could not forbear a glance of triumph at the spectators of the scene.

Pauline met it with that inscrutable smile of hers, and a look of intelligence toward her husband, as she said, "Did I not prophesy truly, Manuel? Be kind to her, Gilbert, and when next we meet show us a happier wife than the one now sobbing on your shoulder. Babie, good night and farewell, for we are off to the mountains in the morning."

"Oh, let us go with you as you promised! You know our secret, you pity me and will help Gilbert to be what he should. I cannot live at home, and places like this will seem so desolate when you and Manuel are gone. May we, can we be with you a little longer?"

"If Gilbert wishes it and Manuel consents, we will bear and forbear much for your sake, my poor child."

Pauline's eye said, "Dare you go?" and Gilbert's answered, "Yes," as the two met with a somber fire in each; but his lips replied, "Anywhere with you, Babie," and Manuel took Mrs. Redmond's hand with a graceful warmth that touched her deeper than his words.

"Your example teaches me the beauty of compassion, and Pauline's friends are mine."

"Always so kind to me! Dear Manuel, I never can forget it, though I have nothing to return but this," and, like a grateful child, she lifted up her innocent face so wistfully he could only bend his tall head to receive the kiss she offered.

Gilbert's black brows lowered ominously at the sight, but he never spoke; and, when her good-nights were over, bowed silently and carried his little wife away, nestling to him as if all griefs and pains were banished by returning love.

"Poor little heart! She should have a smoother path to tread. Heaven grant she may hereafter; and this sudden penitence prove no sham." Manuel paused suddenly, for as if obeying an unconquerable impulse, Pauline laid a hand on either shoulder and searched his face with an expression which baffled his comprehension, though he bore it steadily till her eyes fell before his own, when he asked smilingly:

"Is the doubt destroyed, *cariña?*"

"No; it is laid asleep."

Then as he drew her nearer, as if to make his peace for his un-known offense, she turned her cheek away and left him silently. Did she fear to find Babie's kiss upon his lips?

CHAPTER IV

The work of weeks is soon recorded, and when another month was gone these were the changes it had wrought. The four so strangely bound together by ties of suffering and sin went on their way, to the world's eye, blessed with every gracious gift, but below the tranquil surface rolled that undercurrent whose mysterious tides ebb and flow in human hearts unfettered by race or rank or time. Gilbert was a good actor, but, though he curbed his fitful temper, smoothed his mien, and sweetened his manner, his wife soon felt the vanity of hoping to recover that which never had been hers. Silently she accepted the fact and, uttering no complaint, turned to others for the fostering warmth without which she could not live. Conscious of a hunger like her own, Manuel could offer her sincerest sympathy, and soon learned to find a troubled pleasure in the knowledge that she loved him and her husband knew it, for his life of the emotions was rapidly maturing the boy into the man, as the fierce ardors of his native skies quicken the growth of wondrous plants that blossom in a night. Mrs. Redmond, as young in character as in years, felt the attraction of a nature generous and sweet, and yielded to it as involuntarily as an unsupported vine yields to the wind that blows it to the strong arms of a tree, still unconscious that a warmer sentiment than gratitude made his companionship the sunshine of her life. Pauline saw this, and sometimes owned within herself that she had evoked spirits which she could not rule, but her purpose drove her on, and in it she found a charm more perilously potent than before. Gilbert watched the three with a smile darker than a frown, yet no reproach warned his wife of the danger which she did not see; no jealous demonstration roused Manuel to rebel against the oppression of a presence so distasteful to him; no rash act or word gave Pauline power to banish him, though the one desire of his soul became the discovery of the key to the inscrutable expression of her eyes as they followed the young pair, whose growing friendship left their mates alone. Slowly her manner softened toward him, pity seemed to bridge across the gulf that lay between them, and in rare moments time appeared to have retraced its steps, leaving the tender woman of a year ago. Nourished by such unexpected hope, the early passion throve and strengthened until it became the mastering ambition of his life, and, only pausing to make assurance doubly sure, he waited the advent of the hour when he could "put his fortune to the touch and win or lose it all."

"Manuel, are you coming?"

He was lying on the sward at Mrs. Redmond's feet, and, waking from the reverie that held him, while his companion sang the love lay he was teaching her, he looked up to see his wife standing on the green slope before him. A black lace scarf lay over her blonde hair as Spanish women wear their veils, below it the violet eyes shone clear, the cheek glowed with the color fresh winds had blown upon their paleness, the lips parted with a wistful smile, and a knot of bright-hued leaves upon her bosom made a mingling of snow and fire in the dress, whose white folds swept the grass. Against a background of hoary cliffs and somber pines, this figure stood out like a picture of blooming womanhood, but Manuel saw three blemishes upon it—

Gilbert had sketched her with that shadowy veil upon her head, Gilbert had swung himself across a precipice to reach the scarlet nosegay for her breast, Gilbert stood beside her with her hand upon his arm; and troubled by the fear that often haunted him since Pauline's manner to himself had grown so shy and sad, Manuel leaned and looked forgetful of reply, but Mrs. Redmond answered blithely:

"He is coming, but with me. You are too grave for us, so go your ways, talking wisely of heaven and earth, while we come after, enjoying both as we gather lichens, chase the goats, and meet you at the waterfall. Now señor, put away guitar and book, for I have learned my lesson; so help me with this unruly hair of mine and leave the Spanish for today."

They looked a pair of lovers as Manuel held back the long locks blowing in the wind, while Babie tied her hat, still chanting the burthen of the tender song she had caught so soon. A voiceless sigh stirred the ruddy leaves on Pauline's bosom as she turned away, but Gilbert embodied it in words, "They are happier without us. Let us go."

Neither spoke till they reached the appointed tryst. The others were not there, and, waiting for them, Pauline sat on a mossy stone, Gilbert leaned against the granite boulder beside her, and both silently surveyed a scene that made the heart glow, the eye kindle with delight as it swept down from that airy height, across valleys dappled with shadow and dark with untrodden forests, up ranges of majestic mountains, through gap after gap, each hazier than the last, far out into that sea of blue which rolls around all the world. Behind them roared the waterfall swollen with autumn rains and hurrying to pour itself into the rocky basin that lay boiling below, there to leave its legacy of shattered trees, then to dash itself into a deeper chasm, soon to be haunted by a tragic legend and go glittering away through forest, field, and intervale to join the river rolling slowly to the sea. Won by the beauty and the grandeur of the scene, Pauline forgot she was not alone, till turning, she suddenly became aware that while she scanned the face of nature her companion had been scanning hers. What he saw there she could not tell, but all restraint had vanished from his manner, all reticence from his speech, for with the old ardor in his eye, the old impetuosity in his voice, he said, leaning down as if to read her heart, "This is the moment I have waited for so long. For now you see what I see, that both have made a bitter blunder, and may yet repair it. Those children love each other; let them love, youth mates them, fortune makes them equals, fate brings them together that we may be free. Accept this freedom as I do, and come out into the world with me to lead the life you were born to enjoy."

With the first words he uttered Pauline felt that the time had come, and in the drawing of a breath was ready for it, with every sense alert, every power under full control, every feature obedient to the art which had become a second nature. Gilbert had seized her hand, and she did not draw it back; the sudden advent of the instant which must end her work sent an unwonted color to her cheek, and she did avert it; the exultation which flashed into her eyes made it unsafe to meet his own, and they drooped before him as if in shame or fear, her whole face woke and brightened with the excitement that stirred her blood. She did not seek to conceal it, but let him cheat himself with the belief that love touched it with such light and warmth, as she softly answered in a voice whose accents seemed to assure his hope.

"You ask me to relinquish much. What do you offer in return, Gilbert, that I may not for a second time find love's labor lost?"

It was a wily speech, though sweetly spoken, for it reminded him how much he had thrown away, how little now remained to give, but her mien inspired him, and nothing daunted, he replied more ardently than ever:

"I can offer you a heart always faithful in truth though not in seeming, for I never loved that child. I would give years of happy life to undo that act and be again the man you trusted. I can offer you a name which shall yet be an honorable one, despite the stain an hour's madness cast upon it. You once taunted me with cowardice because I dared not face the world and conquer it. I dare do that now; I long to escape from this disgraceful servitude, to throw myself into the press, to struggle and achieve for your dear sake. I can offer you strength, energy, devotion—three gifts worthy any woman's acceptance who possesses power to direct, reward, and enjoy them as you do, Pauline. Because with your presence for my inspiration, I feel that I can retrieve my faultful past, and with time become God's noblest work—an honest man. Babie never could exert this influence over me. You can, you will, for now my earthly hope is in your hands, my soul's salvation in your love."

If that love had not died a sudden death, it would have risen up to answer him as the one sincere desire of an erring life cried out to her for help, and this man, as proud as sinful, knelt down before her with a passionate humility never paid at any other shrine, human or divine. It seemed to melt and win her, for he saw the color ebb and flow, heard the rapid beating of her heart, felt the hand tremble in his own, and received no denial but a lingering doubt, whose removal was a keen satisfaction to himself.

"Tell me, before I answer, are you sure that Manuel loves Babie?"

"I am; for every day convinces me that he has outlived the brief delusion, and longs for liberty, but dares not ask it. Ah! that pricks pride! But it is so. I have watched with jealous vigilance and let no sign escape me; because in his infidelity to you lay my chief hope. Has he not grown melancholy, cold, and silent? Does he not seek Babie and, of late, shun you? Will he not always yield his place to me without a token of displeasure or regret? Has he ever uttered reproach, warning, or command to you, although he knows I was and am your lover? Can you deny these proofs, or pause to ask if he will refuse to break the tie that binds him to a woman, whose superiority in all things keeps him a subject where he would be a king? You do not know the heart of man if you believe he will not bless you for his freedom."

Like the cloud which just then swept across the valley, blotting out its sunshine with a gloomy shadow, a troubled look flitted over Pauline's face. But if the words woke any sleeping fear she cherished, it was peremptorily banished, for scarcely had the watcher seen it than it was gone. Her eyes still shone upon the ground, and still she prolonged the bittersweet delight at seeing this humiliation of both soul and body by asking the one question whose reply would complete her sad success.

"Gilbert, do you believe I love you still?"

"I know it! Can I not read the signs that proved it to me once? Can I forget that, though you followed me to pity and despise, you have remained to pardon and befriend? Am I not sure that no other power could work the change you have wrought in me? I was learning to be content with slavery, and slowly sinking into that indolence of will which makes submission easy. I was learning to forget you, and be resigned to hold the shadow when the substance was gone, but you came, and with a look undid my work, with a word destroyed my hard-won peace, with a touch roused the passion which was not dead but sleeping, and have made this month of growing certainty to be the sweetest in my life—for I believed all lost, and you showed me that all was won. Surely that smile is propitious! and I may hope to hear the happy confirmation of my faith from lips that were formed to say 'I love!' "

She looked up then, and her eyes burned on him, with an expression which made his heart leap with expectant joy, as over cheek and forehead spread a glow of womanly emotion too genuine to be feigned, and her voice thrilled with the fervor of that sentiment which blesses life and outlives death.

"Yes, I love; not as of old, with a girl's blind infatuation, but with the warmth and wisdom of heart, mind, and soul—love made up of honor, penitence and trust, nourished in secret by the better self which lingers in the most tried and tempted of us, and now ready to blossom and bear fruit, if God so wills. I have been once deceived, but faith still endures, and I believe that I may yet earn this crowning gift of a woman's life for the man who shall make my happiness as I make his—who shall find me the prouder for past coldness, the humbler for past pride—whose life shall pass serenely loving. And that beloved is—my husband."

If she had lifted her white hand and stabbed him, with that smile upon her face, it would not have shocked him with a more pale dismay than did those two words as Pauline shook him off and rose up, beautiful and stern as an avenging angel. Dumb with an amazement too fathomless for words, he knelt there motionless and aghast. She did not speak. And, passing his hand across his eyes as if he felt himself the prey to some delusion, he rose slowly, asking, half incredulously, half imploringly, "Pauline, this is a jest?"

"To me it is; to you—a bitter earnest."

A dim foreboding of the truth fell on him then, and with it a strange sense of fear; for in this apparition of human judgment he seemed to receive a premonition of the divine. With a sudden gesture of something like entreaty, he cried out, as if his fate lay in her hands, "How will it end? how will it end?"

"As it began—in sorrow, shame and loss."

Then, in words that fell hot and heavy on the sore heart made desolate, she poured out the dark history of the wrong and the atonement wrung from him with such pitiless patience and inexorable will. No hard fact remained unrecorded, no subtle act unveiled, no hint of her bright future unspared to deepen the gloom of his. And when the final word of doom died upon the lips that should have awarded pardon, not punishment, Pauline tore away the last gift he had given, and dropping it to the rocky path, set her foot upon it, as if it were the scarlet badge of her subjection to the evil spirit which had haunted her so long, now cast out and crushed forever.

Gilbert had listened with a slowly gathering despair, which deepened to the blind recklessness that comes to those whose passions are their masters, when some blow smites but cannot subdue. Pale to his very lips, with the still white wrath, so much more terrible to witness than the fiercest ebullition of the ire that flames and feeds like a sudden fire, he waited till she ended, then used the one retaliation she had left him. His hand went to his breast, a tattered glove flashed white against the cliff as he held it up before her, saying, in a voice that rose gradually till the last words sounded clear above the waterfall's wild song:

"It was well and womanly done, Pauline, and I could wish Manuel a happy life with such a tender, frank, and noble wife; but the future which you paint so well never shall be his. For, by the Lord that hears me! I swear I will end this jest of yours in a more bitter earnest than you prophesied. Look; I have worn this since the night you began the conflict, which has ended in defeat to me, as it shall to you. I do not war with women, but you shall have one man's blood upon your soul, for I will goad that tame boy to rebellion by flinging this in his face and taunting him with a perfidy blacker than my own. Will that rouse him to forget your commands and answer like a man?"

"Yes!"

The word rang through the air sharp and short as a pistol shot, a slender brown hand wrenched the glove away, and Manuel came between them. Wild with fear, Mrs. Redmond clung to him. Pauline sprang before him, and for a moment the two faced each other, with a year's smoldering jealousy and hate blazing in fiery eyes, trembling in clenched hands, and surging through set teeth in defiant speech.

"This is the gentleman who gambles his friend to desperation, and skulks behind a woman, like the coward he is," sneered Gilbert.

"Traitor and swindler, you lie!" shouted Manuel, and, flinging his wife behind him, he sent the glove, with a stinging blow, full in his opponent's face.

Then the wild beast that lurks in every strong man's blood leaped up in Gilbert Redmond's, as, with a single gesture of his sinewy right arm he swept Manuel to the verge of the narrow ledge, saw him hang poised there one awful instant, struggling to save the living weight that weighed him down, heard a heavy plunge into the black pool below, and felt that thrill of horrible delight which comes to murderers alone.

So swift and sure had been the act it left no time for help. A rush, a plunge, a pause, and then two figures stood where four had been—a man and woman staring dumbly at each other, appalled at the dread silence that made high noon more ghostly than the deepest night. And with that moment of impotent horror, remorse, and woe, Pauline's long punishment began.

V. V.: or, Plots and Counterplots

✦✦✦

*O*n the greenroom of a Parisian theater a young man was pacing to and fro, evidently waiting with impatience for some expected arrival.

The room was empty, for the last performance of a Grand Spectacle was going on, and the entire strength of the company in demand. Frequent bursts of barbaric music had filled the air; but now a brief lull had fallen, broken only by the soft melody of flutes and horns. Standing motionless, the young man listened with a sudden smile, an involuntary motion of the head, as if in fancy he saw and followed some object of delight. A storm of applause broke in on the last notes of the air. Again and again was it repeated, and when at length it died away, trumpet, clarion, and drum resumed their martial din, and the enchanting episode seemed over.

Suddenly, framed in the dark doorway, upon which the young man's eyes were fixed, appeared an apparition well worth waiting for. A sylph she seemed, costumed in fleecy white and gold; the star that glittered on her forehead was less brilliant than her eyes; the flowers that filled her graceful arms were outrivaled by the blooming face that smiled above them; the ornaments she wore were forgotten in admiration of the long blond tresses that crowned her spirited little head; and when the young man welcomed her she crossed the room as if borne by the shining wings upon her shoulders.

"My Virginie, how long they kept you," began the lover, as this beautiful girl leaned against him, flushed and panting, but radiant with the triumphs of the hour.

"Yes, for they recalled me many times; and see—not one bouquet without a *billet-doux* or gift attached!"

"I have much to say, Virginie, and you give me no time but this. Where is Victor?"

"Safe for many minutes; he is in the 'Pas des Enfers,' and then we are together in the 'Pas des Déesses.' Behold! Another offer from the viscount. Shall I accept?"

While speaking she had been rifling the flowers of their attractive burdens, and now held up a delicately scented note with an air half serious, half gay. Her lover crushed the paper in his hand and answered hotly, "You will refuse, or I shall make the viscount a different sort of offer. His devotion is an insult, for you are mine!"

"Not yet, monsieur. Victor has the first claim. And see, he has set his mark upon me."

Pushing up a bracelet, she showed two dark letters stamped or tattooed on the white flesh.

"And you permitted him to disfigure you? When, Virginie, and why?"

"Ah, that was years ago when I cared nothing for beauty, and clung to Victor as my only friend, letting him do what he would, quite content to please him, for he was very kind, and I, poor child, was nothing but a burden. A year ago we were betrothed, and next year he hopes to marry—for we do well now, and I shall then be eighteen."

"You will not marry him. Then why deceive him, Virginie?"

"Yes, but I may if no one else will offer me a name as he does. I do not love him, but he is useful; he guards me like a dragon, works for me, cherishes me, and keeps me right when from mere youth and gaiety of heart I might go astray. What then? I care nothing for lovers; they are false and vain, they annoy me, waste my time, keep Victor savage, and but for the éclat it gives me, I would banish all but—"
She finished the sentence with a caress more eloquent than any words and, before he could speak, added half tenderly, half reproachfully,

while the flowers strayed down upon the ground, "Not one of all these came from you. I thought you would remember me on this last night."

Passionately kissing the red lips so near his own, the lover answered, "I did remember you, but kept my gift to offer when we were alone."

"That is so like you! A thousand thanks. Now give it to me."

With a pretty gesture of entreaty she held out her little hand, and the young man put his own into it, saying earnestly, "I offer this in all sincerity, and ask you to be my wife."

A brilliant smile flashed over her face, and something like triumph shone in her eyes as she clasped the hand in both her own, exclaiming with mingled delight and incredulity, "You ask that of me, the *danseuse,* friendless, poor and humble? Do you mean it, Allan? Shall I go with you to Scotland, be 'my lady' by-and-by? *Ciel!* It is incredible."

"Yes, I mean it. Passion has conquered pride, and for love's sake I can forgive, forget anything but degradation. That you shall never know; and I thank Victor that his jealous vigilance has kept you innocent through all the temptation of a life like yours. The viscount offers you an establishment and infamy; I offer you an honorable name and a home with my whole heart. Which shall it be, Virginie?"

She looked at him keenly—saw a young and comely face, now flushed and kindled with the ardor of a first love. She had seen many such waiting for her smile; but beyond this she saw truth in the honest eyes, read a pride on the forehead that no dishonor could stain, and knew that she might trust one whose promises were never broken. With a little cry of joy and gratitude she laid her face down on the generous hand that gave so much, and thanked heaven that the desire of her life was won. Gathering her close, Allan whispered, with a soft cheek against his own, "My darling, we must be married at once, or Victor will discover and betray us. All is arranged, and this very night we may quit Paris for a happy honeymoon in Italy. Say yes, and leave the rest to me."

"It is impossible! I cannot leave my possessions behind me; I must prepare a little. Wait till tomorrow, and give me time to think."

She spoke resolutely; the young man saw that his project would fail unless he yielded the point, and controlling his impatience, he modified his plan and won her by the ease of that concession.

"I will not hurry you, but, Virginie, we must be married tonight, because all is prepared, and delay may ruin us. Once mine, Victor has no control over you, and my friends will have no power to part us. Grant me this boon, and you shall leave Paris when you will."

She smiled and agreed to it, but did not confess that the chief reason of her reluctance to depart so suddenly was a desire to secure the salary which on the morrow would be paid her for a most successful but laborious season. Mercenary, vain, and hollow-hearted as she was, there was something so genuine in the perfect confidence, the ardent affection of her lover, that it won her respect and seemed to gift the rank which she aspired to attain with a redoubled charm.

"Now tell me your plan, and tell me rapidly, lest Victor should divine that we are plotting and disturb us," she said, with the look of exultation still gleaming in her eyes.

"It is this. Your engagement ends tonight, and you have made no new one. You have spoken of going into the country to rest, and when you vanish people will believe that you have gone suddenly to rusticate. Victor is too proud to complain, and we will leave a penitent confession behind us to appease him."

"He will be terrible, Allan."

"You have a right to choose, I to protect you. Have no fear; we shall be far beyond his reach when he discovers his mistake. I asked you of him honorably once, and he refused with anger."

"He never told me that. We are requited, so let him rave. What next?"

"When your last dance is over, change your dress quickly, and instead of waiting here for your cousin, as usual, slip out by the private door. I shall be there with a carriage, and while Victor is detained searching for you, we will be married, and I shall take you home to gather up those precious possessions of yours. You will do this, Virginie?"

"Yes."

"Your courage will not fail when I am gone, and some fear of Victor keep you?"

"Bah! I fear nothing now."

"Then I am sure of you, and I swear you never shall regret your confidence; for as soon as my peace is made at home, you shall be received there as my honored wife."

"Are you very sure that you *will* be forgiven?" she asked anxiously, as if weighing possibilities even then.

"I *am* sure of pardon after the first anger is over, for they love me too much to disinherit or banish me, and they need only see you to be won at once."

"This marriage, Allan—it will be a true one? You will not deceive me; for if I leave Victor I shall have no friend in the wide world but you."

The most disloyal lover could not have withstood the pleading look, the gesture of appeal which accompanied her words, and this one, who harbored no treachery, assured her with solemn protestations and the most binding vows.

A few moments were spent in maturing their plan, and Virginie was just leaving him with the word "Tomorrow" on her lips when an animated flame of fire seemed to dart into the room. It was a youth whose scarlet-and-silver costume glowed and glittered in the light, as with one marvelous bound he crossed the room and stood before them. Supple, sinewy, and slight was the threatening figure which they saw; dark and defiant the face, with fierce black eyes, frowning brows, and the gleam of set teeth between lips parted by a muttered malediction. Lovely as the other apparition had been, this was far more striking, for it seemed full of the strong grace and beauty of the fallen angel whom it represented. The pose was magnificent; a flaming crown shone in the dark hair, and filmy pinions of scarlet flecked with silver drooped from shoulder to heel. So fiery and fierce he looked, it was little wonder that one lover drew back and the other uttered an exclamation of surprise. Instantly recovering herself, however, Virginie broke into a blithe laugh, and airily twirled away beyond the reach of Victor's outstretched hand.

"It is late; you are not dressed—you will be disgraced by a failure. Go!" he said, with an air of command.

"Au revoir, monsieur; I leave Paris with you." And as she uttered the words with a glance that pointed their double meaning, Virginie vanished.

Turning to the long mirror behind him, the young gentleman replaced his hat, resettled in his buttonhole the flower just given him, tranquilly drew on his gloves, saying, as he strolled toward the door, "I shall return to my box to witness this famous 'Pas des Déesses.' Virginie, Lucille, and Clotilde, upon my word, Paris, you will find it difficult to decide upon which of the three goddesses to bestow the golden apple."

Not a word spoke Victor, till the sounds of steps died away. Then he departed to his dressing room, moodily muttering as he went, "Tomorrow, she said. They intend to meet somewhere. Good! I will prevent *that*. There has been enough of this—it must end and Virginie shall keep her promise. I will stand guard tonight and watch them well tomorrow."

Three hours later, breathless and pale with fatigue and rage, Victor sprang up the steps leading to his cousin's chamber in the old house by the Seine. A lamp burned in a niche beside her door; a glass of wine and a plate of fruit stood there also, waiting as usual for him. As his eye fell upon these objects a long sigh of relief escaped him.

"Thank heaven, she has come home then. Yet hold! It may be but a ruse to prevent my discovering her absence. Virginie! Cousin! Are you there?"

He struck upon the door, lightly at first, then vehemently, and to his great joy a soft, sleepy voice replied, "Who calls?"

"It is Victor. I missed you, searched for you, and grew anxious when I found you gone. Why did you not wait, as usual?"

"Mlle. Clotilde offered me a seat in her carriage, and I gladly accepted it. She was set down first, and it is a long distance there and back, you know. Now let me rest; I am very tired."

"Good night, my heart," answered Victor, adding, in a tone of pain and tenderness, as he turned away, *"mon Dieu!* How I love that girl, and how she tortures me! Rest well, my cousin; I shall guard your sleep."

Hour after hour passed, and still a solitary figure paced to and fro with noiseless feet along the narrow terrace that lay between the ancient house and the neglected garden sloping to the river. Dawn was slowly breaking in the east when the window of Virginie's chamber opened cautiously, and her charming head appeared. The light was very dim, and shadows still lay dark upon the house; but Victor, coming from the water gate whither he had been drawn by the sound of a passing boat, heard the soft movement, glided behind a group of shrubs, and eyed the window keenly, remembering that now it was "tomorrow." For a moment the lovely face leaned out, looking anxiously across terrace, street, and garden. The morning air seemed to strike cold on her uncovered shoulders, and with a shiver she was drawing back when a man's hand laid a light cloak about her, and a man's head appeared beside her own.

"Imprudent! Go quickly, or Victor will be stirring. At noon I shall be ready," she said half aloud, and as she withdrew the curtain fell.

With the bound of a wounded tiger, Victor reached the terrace, and reckless of life or limb, took the short road to his revenge. The barred shutters of a lower window, the carved ornaments upon the wall, and the balcony that hung above, all offered foot- and handhold for an agile climber like himself, as, creeping upward like a stealthy shadow, he peered in with a face that would have appalled the lovers had they seen it. They did not, for standing near the half-opened door, they were parting as Romeo and Juliet parted, heart to heart, cheek to cheek, and neither saw nor heard the impending doom until the swift stroke fell. So sure, so sudden was it that Virginie knew nothing, till, with a stifled cry, her lover started, swayed backward from her arms, and dyeing her garments with his blood, fell at her feet stabbed through the heart.

An awful silence followed, for Virginie uttered no cry of alarm, made no gesture of flight, showed no sign of guilt; but stood white and motionless as if turned to stone.

Soon Victor grasped her arm and hissed into her ear, "Traitress!

I could find it in my heart to lay you there beside him. But no, you shall live to atone for your falsehood to me and mourn your lover."

Something in the words or tone seemed to recall her scattered senses and rouse her to a passionate abhorrence of him and of his deed. She wrenched herself from his hold, saying vehemently, though instinctively below her breath, "No; it is you who shall atone! He was my husband, not my lover. Look if I lie!"

He did look as a trembling hand was stretched toward him over that dead form. On it he saw a wedding ring, and in it the record of the marriage which in a single night had made her wife and widow. With an ejaculation of despair he snatched the paper as if to tear and scatter it; but some sudden thought flashed into his mind, and putting the record in his bosom, he turned to Virginie with an expression that chilled her by its ominous resolve.

"Listen," he said, "and save yourself while you may; for I swear, if you raise your voice, lift your hand against me, or refuse to obey me now, that I will denounce you as the murderer of that man. You were last seen with him, were missed by others besides me last night. There lies his purse; here is the only proof of your accursed marriage; and if I call in witnesses, which of us looks most like an assassin, you or I?"

She listened with a terror-stricken face, glanced at her bloody garments, knew that she was in the power of a relentless man, and clasped her hands with a gesture of mute supplication and submission.

"You are wise," he said. "Apart, we are both in danger; together we may be strong and safe. I have a plan—hear it and help me to execute it, for time is life now. You have spoken to many of going into the country; it shall be so, but we will give our departure the appearance of a sudden thought, a lover's flight. Leave everything behind you but money and jewels. That purse will more than pay you the sum you cannot claim. While I go to fling this body into the river, to tell no tales till we are safe, destroy all traces of the deed, prepare yourself for traveling, and guard the room in silence until I come. Remember! One sign of treachery, one cry for help, and I denounce you where my word will have much weight and yours none."

She gave him her hand upon the dark bargain, and covering up her face to hide the tragic spectacle, she heard Victor leave the room with his awful burden.

When he returned, she was nearly ready, for though moving like one in a ghastly dream, bewildered by the sudden loss of the long coveted, just won prize, and daunted by the crime whose retribution a word might bring upon herself, she still clung to life and its delights with the tenacity of a selfish nature, a shallow heart. While she finished her hasty preparations, Victor set the room in order, saw that the red witnesses of the crime were burnt, and dashed off a gay note to a friend, enclosing money for all obligations, explaining their sudden flight as an innocent ruse to escape congratulations on their hasty marriage, and promising to send soon for such possessions as were left behind. Then, leaving the quiet room to be forever haunted by the memory of a night of love, and sin, and death, like two pale ghosts they vanished in the dimness of the dawn.

CHAPTER II. EARL'S MYSTERY

Four ladies sat in the luxurious privacy of Lady Lennox's boudoir, whiling away the listless hour before dinner with social chat. Dusk was deepening, but firelight filled the room with its warm glow, flickering on mirrors, marbles, rich hues, and graceful forms, and bathing the four faces with unwonted bloom.

Stately Diana Stuart leaned on the high back of the chair in which sat her aunt and chaperon, the Honorable Mrs. Berkeley. On the opposite side of the wide hearth a slender figure lounged in the deep corner of a couch, with a graceful abandon which no Englishwoman could hope to imitate. The face was hidden by a hand-screen, but a pair of ravishing feet were visible, and a shower of golden hair shone against the velvet pillow. Directly before the fire sat Lady Lennox, a comely, hospitable matron who was never so content as when she could gather her female guests about her and refresh herself with a little good-natured gossip. She had evidently been discussing some subject which interested her hearers, for all were intently listening, and all looked eager for more, when she said, with a significant nod:

"Yes, I assure you there is a mystery in that family. Lady Carrick has known them all her life, and from what she has dropped from time to time, I quite agree with her in believing that something has gone wrong."

"Dear Lady Lennox, pray go on! There is nothing so charming as a family mystery when the narrator can give a clue to her audience, as I am sure you can," exclaimed the lady on the couch, in a persuasive voice which had a curious ring to it despite its melody.

"That is just what I cannot do, Mrs. Vane. However, I will gladly tell you all I know. This is in strict confidence, you understand."

"Certainly!" "Upon my honor!" "Not a word shall pass my lips!" murmured the three listeners, drawing nearer, as Lady Lennox fixed her eyes upon the fire and lowered her voice.

"It is the custom in ancient Scottish families for the piper of the house, when dying, to put the pipes into the hand of the heir to name or title. Well, when old Dougal lay on his deathbed, he called for Earl, the fourth son—"

"What a peculiar name!" interrupted Mrs. Berkeley.

"It was not his proper name, but they called him so because of his strong resemblance to the pictures of the great earl, Black Douglass. They continued to call him so to this day, and I really don't know whether his name is Allan, Archie, or Alex, for they are all family names, and one cannot remember which belongs to whom. Now the eldest son was Robert, and Dougal should have called for him, because the title and the fortune always go to the eldest son of the eldest son. But no, Earl must come; and into his hands the pipes were put, with a strange prophecy that no heir would enjoy the title but a year until it came to him."

"Was the prediction fulfilled?" asked Diana.

"To the letter. This was five or six years ago, and not one year has passed without a death, till now a single feeble life is all that stands between Earl and the title. Nor was this all. When his father died, though he had lain insensible for days, he rose up in his bed at the last and put upon Earl's hand the iron ring which is their most precious heirloom, because it belonged to the ancient earl. This, too, should have gone to Robert; but the same gift of second sight seemed given to the father as to the servant, and these strange things made a deep impression upon the family, as you may suppose."

"That is the mystery, then?" said Mrs. Vane, with an accent of disappointment in her voice.

"Only a part of it. I am not superstitious, so the prediction and all the rest of it don't trouble me much, but what occurred afterward does. When Earl was one-and-twenty he went abroad, was gone a year, and came home so utterly and strangely changed that everyone was amazed at the alteration. The death of a cousin just then drew people's attention from him, and when that stir was over the family seemed to be reconciled to the sad change in him. Nothing was said, nothing ever transpired to clear up the matter; and to this day he has remained a cold, grave, peculiar man, instead of the frank, gay fellow he once was."

"He met with some loss in an affair of the heart, doubtless. Such little tragedies often mar a young man's peace for years—perhaps for life."

As Mrs. Vane spoke she lowered her screen, showing a pair of wonderfully keen and brilliant eyes fixed full upon Diana. The young lady was unconscious of this searching glance as she intently regarded Lady Lennox, who said:

"That is my opinion, though Lady Carrick never would confirm it, being hampered by some promise to the family, I suspect, for they are almost as high and haughty now as in the olden time. There was a vague rumor of some serious entanglement at Paris, but it was hushed up at once, and few gave it credence. Still, as year after year passed, and Earl remains unmarried, I really begin to fear there was some truth in what I fancied an idle report."

Something in this speech seemed to ruffle Mrs. Berkeley; a look of intelligence passed between her and her niece as she drew herself up, and before Diana could speak, the elder lady exclaimed, with an air of mystery, "Your ladyship does Mr. Douglas great injustice, and a few months, weeks, perhaps, will quite change your opinion. We saw a good deal of him last season before my poor brother's death took us from town, and I assure you that he is free to address any lady in England. More I am not at liberty to say at present."

Lady Lennox looked politely incredulous, but Diana's eyes fell and a sudden color bathed her face in a still deeper bloom than that which the firelight shed over it. A slight frown contracted Mrs. Vane's beautiful brows as she watched the proud girl's efforts to conceal the secret of her heart. But the frown faded to a smile of intelligent compassion as she said, with a significant glance that stung Diana like an insult, "Dear Miss Stuart, pray take my screen. This glowing fire is ruining your complexion."

"Thank you, I need no screens of any sort."

There was a slight emphasis upon the "I," and a smile of equal significance curled her lips. If any taunt was intended it missed its mark, for Mrs. Vane only assumed a more graceful pose, saying with a provoking little air of superior wisdom, "There you are wrong, for our faces are such traitors, that unless we have learned the art of self-control, it is not best for us to scorn such harmless aids as fans, screens, and veils. Emotions are not well-bred, and their demonstrations are often as embarrassing to others as to ourselves."

"That, doubtless, is the reason why you half conceal your face behind a cloud of curls. It certainly is a most effectual mask at times," replied Diana, pushing back her own smooth bands of hair.

"Thanks for the suggestion. I wonder it never occurred to me before," sweetly answered Mrs. Vane, adding, as she gathered up the disheveled locks, "my poor hair is called a great ornament, but indeed it is a trial both to Gabrielle and to myself."

Lady Lennox touched a long tress that rolled down the pillow, saying with motherly admiration, "My dear, I promised Mrs. Berkeley she should see this wonderful hair of yours, for she could not believe my account of it. The dressing bell will ring directly, so you may gratify us without making more work for Gabrielle."

"Willingly, dear Lady Lennox; anything for you!"

As she spoke with affectionate goodwill, Mrs. Vane rose, drew out a comb or two, and a stream of golden hair rippled far below her knee. Mrs. Berkeley exclaimed, and Diana praised, while watching with a very natural touch of envy the charming picture the firelight showed her. In its full glow stood Mrs. Vane; against the deep purple of her dress glittered the golden mass, and a pair of lovely hands parted the shining veil from a face whose beauty was as peculiar and alluring as the mingled spirit and sweetness of her smile.

"A thousand pardons! I thought your ladyship was alone." A deep voice broke the momentary silence, and a tall figure paused upon the threshold of the softly opened door. All started, and with a little cry of pleasure and surprise, Lady Lennox hurried forward to greet her guest.

"My dear Earl, this is a most inhospitable welcome. George should have apprised me of your arrival."

"He is a lazy fellow, as he bade me find you here. I tapped, but receiving no reply, fancied the room empty and peeped to make sure. Pray accept my apologies, and put me out if I intrude."

The voice of Mr. Douglas was remarkably calm, his manner stately yet cordial, and his dark eyes went rapidly from face to face with a glance that seemed to comprehend the scene at once.

"Not in the least," said Lady Lennox heartily. "Let me present you to Mrs. Berkeley, Miss Stuart, and—why, where is she? The poor little woman has run away in confusion, and must receive your apologies by-and-by."

"We must run away also, for it is quite time to dress." And with a most gracious smile Mrs. Berkeley led her niece away before the gentleman should have time to note her flushed face and telltale eyes.

"You did not mention the presence of those ladies in your ladyship's letter," began Douglas, as his hostess sat down and motioned him to do likewise.

"They came unexpectedly, and you have met before, it seems. You never mentioned that fact, Earl," said Lady Lennox, with a sharp glance.

"Why should I? We only met a few times last winter, and I quite forgot that you knew them. But pray tell me who was the fair one with golden locks, whom I frightened away?"

"The widow of Colonel Vane."

"My dear lady, do you mean to tell me that child is a widow?"

"Yes; and a very lovely one, I assure you. I invited you here expressly to fall in love with her, for George and Harry are too young."

"Thank you. Now be so kind as to tell me all about her, for I knew Vane before he went to India."

"I can only tell you that he married this lady when she was very young, took her to India, and in a year she returned a widow."

"I remember hearing something of an engagement, but fancied it was broken off. Who was the wife?"

"A Montmorenci; noble but poor, you know. The family lost everything in the revolution, and never regained their former grandeur. But one can see at a glance that she is of high birth—high enough to suit even a Douglas."

"Ah, you know our weakness, and I must acknowledge that the best blood in France is not to be despised by the best blood in Scotland. How long have you known her?"

"Only a few months; that charming Countess Camareena brought her from Paris, and left her when she returned. Mrs. Vane seemed lonely for so young a thing; her family are all gone, and she made herself so agreeable, seemed so grateful for any friendship, that I asked her here. She went into very little society in London, and was really suffering for change and care."

"Poor young lady! I will do my best to aid your friendly purpose—for Vane's sake, if not for her own," said Douglas, evidently continuing the subject, lest her ladyship should revert to the former one.

"That reminds me to give you one warning: Never speak to her or before her of the colonel. He died three or four years ago; but when I mentioned him, she implored me to spare her all allusion to that unhappy past, and I have done so. It is my belief that he was not all she believed him to be, and she may have suffered what she is too generous to complain of or confess."

"I doubt that; for when I knew him, though weak on some points, Vane was an excellent fellow. She wears no weeds, I observe."

"You have a quick eye, to discover that in such an instant," replied Lady Lennox, smiling.

"I could scarcely help looking longest at the most striking figure of the group."

"I forgive you for it. She left off her weeds by my advice, for the somber colors seemed to oppress and sadden her. Three or four years are long enough to mourn one whom she did not wholly love, and she is too young to shroud herself in sables for a lifetime."

"Has she fortune?"

"The colonel left her something handsome, I suspect, for she keeps both man and maid, and lives as becomes her rank. I ask no questions, but I feel deeply for the poor child, and do my best for her. Now tell me about home, and your dear mother."

Earl obeyed, and entertained his hostess till the dressing bell rang.

CHAPTER III. THE IRON RING

When Douglas entered the drawing rooms, he was instantly seized upon by Major Mansfield, and while he stood listening with apparent interest to that gentleman's communications, he took a survey of the party before him. The elder ladies were not yet down; Harry Lennox was worshiping Diana with all the frank admiration of a lad of eighteen, and Mrs. Vane was pacing up and down the rooms on the arm of George Lennox, the young master of the house. Few little women would have appeared to advantage beside the tall guardsman; but Mrs. Vane moved with a dignity that seemed to add many inches to her almost fairylike stature, and make her a fit companion for her martial escort. Everything about her was peculiar and piquant. Her dress was of that vivid silvery green which is so ruinous to any but the purest complexion, so ravishing when worn by one whose bloom defies all hues. The skirt swept long behind her, and the Pompadour waist, with its flowing sleeves, displayed a neck and arms of dazzling fairness, half concealed by a film of costly lace. No jewels but an antique opal ring, attached by a slender chain to a singular bracelet, or wide band of enchased gold. A single deep-hued flower glowed on her bosom, and in that wonderful hair of hers a chaplet of delicate ferns seemed to gather back the cloud of curls, and encircle coil upon coil of glossy hair, that looked as if it burdened her small head.

The young man watched her so intently that the major soon observed his preoccupation, and paused in the middle of his account of a review to ask good-naturedly, "Well, what do you think of the bewitching widow?"

"She reminds me of a little green viper," replied Douglas coolly.

"The deuce she does! What put such an odd fancy into your head?" asked the major.

"The color of her gown, her gliding gait, her brilliant eyes, and poor George's evident fascination."

"Faith! I see the resemblance, and you've expressed my feeling exactly. Do you know I've tried to fall in love with that woman, and, upon my soul, I can't do it!"

"She does not care to fascinate you, perhaps."

"Neither does she care to charm George, as I happen to know; yet you see what a deuce of a state he's getting into."

"His youth prevents his seeing the danger before it is too late; and there you have the advantage, Major."

"We shall see how you will prosper, Douglas; for you are not a lad of twenty, like George, or an old fellow of forty, like me, and, if rumor does not lie, you have had 'experiences,' and understand womankind."

Though he spoke in a tone of raillery, the major fixed a curious eye upon his companion's countenance. But the dark handsome face remained inscrutably calm, and the only answer he received was a low—

"Hush! they are coming. Present me, and I'll see what I can make of her."

Now Douglas was undoubtedly the best *parti* of the season, and he knew it. He was not a vain man, but an intensely proud one—proud of his ancient name, his honorable race, his ancestral home, his princely fortune; and he received the homage of both men and women as his due. Great, therefore, was his surprise at the little scene which presently occurred, and very visible was his haughty displeasure.

Lennox and his fair companion approached, the one bending his tall head to listen ardently, the other looking up with a most tempting face, as she talked rapidly, after softening a hard English phrase by an entrancing accent. The major presented his friend with much *em-*

pressement, and Douglas was prepared to receive the gracious greeting which women seldom failed to give him. But scarcely pausing in her progress, Mrs. Vane merely glanced at him, as his name was mentioned, returned his bow with a slight inclination, and rustled on as if quite oblivious that a direct descendant of the great Scotch earl had been presented to her.

The major stifled an irrepressible laugh at this unexpected rebuff, and took a malicious pleasure in watching his friend's eye kindle, his attitude become more stately as he talked on, and deigned to take no notice of an act which evidently much annoyed and amazed him. Just then Lady Lennox entered, and dinner was announced. George beckoned, and Douglas reluctantly joined him.

"As host, I am obliged to take Mrs. Berkeley down; Harry has monopolized Miss Stuart, and the major belongs to my mother—so I must reluctantly relinquish Mrs. Vane to you."

Being a well-bred man, Douglas could only bow, and offer his arm. Mrs. Vane made George happy by a smile, as he left her, then turned to Douglas with a "May I trouble you?" as she gave him her fan and handkerchief to hold, while she gathered up her train and took his arm, as unconcernedly as if he had been a footman. Though rather piqued by her nonchalance, Douglas found something half amusing, half captivating in her demeanor; for, much as he had been courted and admired, few women were quite at ease with the high-born gentleman, whose manners were so coldly charming, whose heart seemed so invulnerable. It was a new sensation to be treated like other men, and set to serve an imperious lady, who leaned upon his arm as if she needed its support, and tranquilly expected the small courtesies which hitherto had been left to his own goodwill and pleasure to offer.

Whatever the secret of his past might be, and however well he might conceal his real self behind a grave demeanor, Douglas had not yet lost his passion for beautiful women, and though no word was spoken during the short transit from drawing room to dinner table, the power of loveliness and womanhood made itself felt beyond a doubt. The touch of a fair hand upon his arm, the dazzle of white shoulders at his side, the soft scent of violets shaken from the folds of lace and cambric which he held, the glimpse of a dainty foot, and the glance of a vivacious eye, all made the little journey memorable. When they took their places, the hauteur had melted from his manner, the coldness from his face, and with his courtliest air he began a conversation which soon became absorbing—for Mrs. Vane talked with the grace of a French woman, and the intelligence of an English woman.

When the gentlemen rejoined the ladies, they were found examining some antique jewels, which Lady Lennox had been prevailed upon to show.

"How well those diamonds look in Diana's dark hair. Ah, my dear, a coronet becomes you vastly. Does it not?" said Mrs. Berkeley, appealing to Douglas, who was approaching.

"So well that I hope you will soon see one rightfully there, madam," he answered, with a glance that made Diana's eyes fall, and Mrs. Berkeley look radiant.

Mrs. Vane saw the look, divined its meaning, and smiled a strange smile, as she looked down upon the jewels that strewed her lap.

Mrs. Berkeley mistook her attitude for one of admiration and envy, and said, "You wear no ornaments but flowers, I observe; from choice, doubtless, for, as you are the last of your race, you must possess many of the family relics."

Mrs. Vane looked up, and answered with an indescribable mixture of simplicity and dignity, "I wear flowers because I have no other ornaments. My family paid the price of loyalty with both life and fortune; but I possess one jewel which I value above all these—a noble name."

A banished princess might have so looked, so spoken, as, gathering up the glittering mass in her white hands, she let it fall again, with an air of gentle pride. Douglas gave her a glance of genuine admiration, and Diana took the diamonds from her hair, as if they burdened her. Mrs. Berkeley saw that her shot had failed, but tried again, only to be more decidedly defeated.

"Very prettily done, my dear; but I really thought you were going to say that your most valuable jewel was the peculiar bracelet you wear. Is there any charming legend or mystery concerning it? I fancied so, because you never take it off, however out of taste it may be; and otherwise your dress is always perfect."

"I wear it in fulfillment of a vow, and the beauty of the ring atones for the ugliness of the bracelet. Does it not?"

As she spoke, Mrs. Vane extended an exquisitely molded arm and hand to Douglas, who answered with most unusual gallantry, "The beauty of the arm would render any fetter an ornament."

He bent to examine the jewel as he spoke, and Mrs. Vane whispered, below her breath, "You have offended Diana; pray make your peace. I should be desolated to think my poor arm had estranged you, even for an hour."

So entirely was he thrown off his guard by this abrupt address, that he whispered eagerly, "Do my actions interest her? Have I any cause for hope? Does she—"

There he paused, recovered his self-possession, but not his countenance—for an angry flush stained his dark cheek, and he fixed a look upon Mrs. Vane that would have daunted any other woman. She did not seem to see it, for her head drooped till her face was hidden, and she sat absently playing with the little chain that shone against her hand. George Lennox looked fiercely jealous; Diana turned pale; Mrs. Berkeley frowned; and good, unconscious Lady Lennox said blandly, "Apropos to heirlooms and relics, I was telling these ladies about your famous iron ring, Earl. I wish you had it here to show them."

"I am happy to be able to gratify your ladyship's wish. I never leave without it, for I use it as my seal. I will ring for it."

Mrs. Vane lifted her head with an air of interest as Douglas gave an order, and his servant presently put a small steel-bound case into his hand. Opening this with a key that hung upon his watch guard, he displayed the famous relic. Antique, rusty, and massive it was, and on its shield the boar's head and the motto of the house.

"You say you use this as a signet ring; why do you not have your arms cut on some jewel, and set in a more graceful setting? This device is almost effaced, and the great ring anything but ornamental to one's hand or chatelaine," said Mrs. Vane, curiously examining the ring as it was passed to her.

"Because I am superstitious and believe that an especial virtue lies in this ancient bit of iron. The legend goes that no harm can befall its possessor, and as I have gone scatheless so far, I hold fast to the old faith."

As Douglas turned to hear and answer Mrs. Vane's question, Harry Lennox, with the freedom of a boy, had thrown back the lid of the case, which had been opened with peculiar care, and, lifting several worn papers, disclosed two objects that drew exclamations of surprise from several of the party. A satin slipper, of fairylike proportions, with a dull red stain upon its sole, and what looked like a ring of massive gold, till the lad lifted it, when coil after coil unwound, till a long curl of human hair touched the ground.

"My faith! That is the souvenir of the beautiful *danseuse* Virginie Varens, about whom you bored me with questions when you showed me that several years ago," said the major, staring with all his eyes.

Mrs. Vane had exclaimed with the rest, but her color faded perceptibly, her eye grew troubled, and when Harry leaned toward her to compare the long tress with her own, she shrank back with a shudder. Diana caught a muttered ejaculation from Douglas, saw Mrs. Vane's discomposure, and fixed a scrutinizing gaze upon her. But in a moment those obedient features resumed their former calm, and, with a little gesture of contrition, Mrs. Vane laid the long curl beside one of her own, saying tranquilly:

"Pardon, that I betrayed an instinctive shrinking from anything plebeian. The hair of the dancer is lighter than mine, you see; for this is pure gold, and mine is fast deepening to brown. Let me atone for my rudeness thus; and believe me, I can sympathize, for I, too, have loved and lost."

While speaking, she had refolded the lock, and, tying it together with a little knot of ribbon from her dress, she laid it back into its owner's hand, with a soft glance and a delicate dropping of the voice at the last words.

If it was a bit of acting, it was marvelously well done, and all believed it to be a genuine touch of nature. Diana looked consumed with curiosity, and Douglas answered hastily, "Thanks for the pity, but I need none. I never saw this girl, and as for love—"

He paused there, as if words unfit for time and place were about to pass his lips. His eye grew fierce, and his black brows lowered heavily, leaving no doubt on the mind of any observer that hate, not love, was the sentiment with which he now regarded the mysterious *danseuse.* An uncomfortable pause followed as Douglas relocked the case and put it in his pocket, forgetting, in his haste, the ring he had slipped upon his finger.

Feeling that some unpleasant theme had been touched upon, Lady Lennox asked for music. Diana coldly declined, but Mrs. Vane readily turned to the piano. The two elder ladies and the major went to chat by the fire; Lennox took his brother aside to administer a reproof; and Douglas, after a moment of moody thoughtfulness, placed himself beside Diana on the couch which stood just behind Mrs. Vane. She had begun with a brilliant overture, but suddenly passed to a softer movement, and filled the room with the whispering melody of a Venetian barcarole. This seeming caprice was caused by an intense desire to overhear the words of the pair behind her. But though she strained her keen ear to the utmost, she caught only broken fragments of their low-toned conversation, and these fragments filled her with disquiet.

"Why so cold, Miss Stuart? One would think you had forgotten me."

"I fancied the forgetfulness was yours."

"I never shall forget the happiest hours of my life. May I hope that you recall those days with pleasure?"

There was no answer, and a backward glance showed Mrs. Vane Diana's head bent low, and Douglas watching the deepening color on her half-averted cheek with an eager, ardent glance. More softly murmured the boat song, and scarcely audible was the whispered entreaty:

"I have much to say; you will hear me tomorrow, early, in the park?"

A mute assent was given, and, with the air of a happy lover, Douglas left her, as if fearing to say more, lest their faces should betray them. Then the barcarole ended as suddenly as it had begun, and Mrs. Vane resumed the stormy overture, playing as if inspired by a musical frenzy. So pale was she when she left the instrument that no one doubted the fact of her needing rest, as, pleading weariness, she sank into a deep chair, and leaning her head upon her hand, sat silent for an hour.

As they separated for the night, and Douglas stood listening to his young host's arrangements for the morrow, a singular-looking man appeared at the door of an anteroom and, seeing them, paused where he stood, as if waiting for them to precede him.

"Who is that, George? What does he want?" said Douglas, drawing his friend's attention to the dark figure, whose gleaming eyes belied his almost servile posture of humility and respect.

"Oh, that is Mrs. Vane's man, Jitomar. He was one of the colonel's Indian servants, I believe. Deaf and dumb, but harmless, devoted, and invaluable—*she* says. A treacherous-looking devil, to my mind," replied Lennox.

"He looks more like an Italian than an Indian, in spite of his Eastern costume and long hair. What is he after now?" asked Earl.

"Going to receive the orders of his mistress. I would gladly change places with him, heathen as he is, for the privilege of serving her. Good night."

As George spoke, they parted, and while the dark servant watched Douglas going up the wide oaken stairs, he shook his clenched hand after the retreating figure, and his lips moved as if he muttered something low between his teeth.

A few moments afterward, as Earl sat musing over his fire, there came a tap at his door. Having vainly bidden the knocker to enter, he answered the summons, and saw Jitomar obsequiously offering a handkerchief. Douglas examined it, found the major's name, and, pointing out that gentleman's room, farther down the corridor, he returned the lost article with a nod of thanks and dismissal. While he had been turning the square of cambric in his hands, the man's keen eyes had explored every corner of the room. Nothing seemed to escape them, from the ashes on the hearth, to a flower which Diana had worn, now carefully preserved in water; and once a gleam of satisfaction glittered in them, as if some desired object had met their gaze. Making a low obeisance, he retired, and Douglas went to bed, to dream waking dreams till far into the night.

The great hall clock had just struck one, and sleep was beginning to conquer love, when something startled him wide awake. What it was he could not tell, but every sense warned him of impending danger. Sitting up in his bed, he pushed back the curtains and looked out. The night lamp burned low, the fire had faded, and the room was full of dusky shadows. There were three doors: one led to the dressing room, one to the corridor, and the third was locked on the outside. He knew that it opened upon a flight of narrow stairs that communicated with the library, having been built for the convenience of a studious Lennox long ago.

As he gazed about him, to his great amazement the door was seen to move. Slowly, noiselessly it opened, with no click of lock, no creak of hinge. Almost sure of seeing some ghostly visitant enter, he waited mute and motionless. A muffled hand and arm appeared and, stretching to their utmost, seemed to take something from the writing table that stood near this door. It was a human hand, and with a single leap Douglas was halfway across the room. But the door closed rapidly, and as he laid his hand upon it, the key turned in the lock. He demanded who was there, but not a sound replied; he shook the door, but the lock held fast; he examined the table, but nothing seemed gone, till, with an ominous thrill, he missed the iron ring. On reaching his chamber, he had taken it off, meaning to restore it to its place; had laid it down, to put Diana's rose in water; had forgotten it, and now it was gone!

Flinging on dressing gown and slippers, and taking a pistol from his traveling case, he left his room. The house was quiet as a tomb, the library empty, and no sign of intruders visible, till, coming to the door itself, he found that the rusty lock had been newly oiled, for the rusty key turned noiselessly, and the hinges worked smoothly, though the dust that lay thickly everywhere showed that this passage was still unused. Stepping into his room, Douglas gave a searching glance about him, and in an instant an expression of utter bewilderment fell upon his face, for there, on the exact spot which had been empty five minutes ago, there lay the iron ring!

CHAPTER IV. A SHRED OF LACE

Long before any of the other guests were down, Diana stole into the garden on her way to the park. Hope shone in her eyes, smiles sat on her lips, and her heart sang for joy. She had long loved in secret; had believed and despaired alternately; and now her desire was about to be fulfilled, her happiness assured by a lover's voice. Hurrying through the wilderness of autumn flowers, she reached the shrubbery that divided park and garden. Pausing an instant to see if anyone awaited her beyond, she gave a great start, and looked as if she had encountered a ghost.

It was only Mrs. Vane; she often took early strolls in the park, followed by her man; Diana knew this, but had forgotten it in her new bliss. She was alone now, and as she seemed unconscious of her presence, Diana would have noiselessly withdrawn, if a glimpse of Mrs. Vane's face had not arrested and detained her. As if she had thrown herself down in a paroxysm of distress, sat Mrs. Vane, with both hands tightly clasped; her white lips were compressed, and in her eyes was a look of mingled pain, grief, and despair. The most careless observer would have detected the presence of some great anxiety or sorrow, and Diana, made generous by the assurance of her own happiness, for the first time felt a touch of pity for the woman of whom she had been both envious and jealous. Forgetting herself, she hastened forward, saying kindly, "Are you suffering, Mrs. Vane? What can I do for you?"

Mrs. Vane started as if she had been shot, sprang to her feet, and putting out her hands as if to keep the other off, cried, almost incoherently, "Go back! Go back, and save yourself! For me you can do nothing—it is too late!"

"Indeed, I hope not. Tell me your trouble, and let me help you if I can," urged Diana, shocked yet not alarmed by the wildness of Mrs. Vane's look and manner.

But she only clasped her hands before her face, saying despairingly, "You can help both of us—but at what a price!"

"No price will be too costly, if I can honorably pay it. I have been unjust, unkind; forgive it, and confide in me; for indeed, I pity you."

"Ah, if I dared!" sighed Mrs. Vane. "It seems impossible, and yet I ought—for you, not I, will suffer most from my enforced silence."

She paused an instant, seemed to calm herself by strong effort, and, fixing her mournful eyes upon Diana, she said, in a strangely solemn and impressive manner, "Miss Stuart, if ever a woman needed help and pity, it is I. You have misjudged, distrusted, and disliked me; I freely forgive this, and long to save you, as I alone can do. But a sacred promise fetters me—I dare not break it; yet if you will pledge your word to keep this interview secret, I will venture to give you one hint, one warning, which may save you from destroying your peace forever. Will you give me this assurance?"

Diana shrank back, disturbed and dismayed by the appeal and the requirement. Mrs. Vane saw her hesitation, and wrung her hands together in an agony of impotent regret.

"I knew it—I feared it. You will not trust me—you will not let me ease my conscience by trying to save another woman from the fate that darkens all my life. Go your way, then, and when the bitter hour comes, remember that I tried to save you from it, and you would not hear me."

"Stay, Mrs. Vane! I do trust you—I will listen; and I give you my word that I will conceal this interview. Speak quickly—I must go," cried Diana, won to compliance even against her wishes.

"Stoop to me—not even the air must hear what I breathe. Ask Allan Douglas the mystery of his life before you marry him, else you will rue the hour that you became his wife."

"Allan Douglas! You know his name? You know the secret of his past?" exclaimed Diana, lost in wonder.

"My husband knew him, and I—Hush! Someone is coming. Quick! Escape into the park, or your face will betray you. I can command myself; I will meet and accost whoever comes."

Before the rapid whisper ended, Diana was gone, and when

Douglas came hastening to his tryst, he too found Mrs. Vane alone—and he too paused a moment, surprised to see her there. But the picture he saw was a very different one from that which arrested Diana. Great indeed must have been Mrs. Vane's command of countenance, for no trace of agitation was visible, and never had she looked more lovely than now, as she stood with a handful of flowers in the white skirt of her dress, her bright hair blowing in the wind, her soft eyes fixed on vacancy, while a tranquil smile proved that her thoughts were happy ones.

So young, so innocent, so blithe she looked that Douglas involuntarily thought, with a touch of self-reproach: "Pretty creature! What injustice my ungallant smile did her last night! I ask her pardon." Then aloud, as he approached, "Good morning, Mrs. Vane. I am off for an early stroll."

With the shy grace, the artless glance of a child, she looked up at him, offering a flower, and saying, as she smilingly moved on, "May it be a pleasant one."

It was not a pleasant one, however; and perhaps Mrs. Vane's wish had been sweetly ironical. Diana greeted her lover coldly, listened to his avowal with an air of proud reserve, that contrasted strangely with the involuntary betrayals of love and joy that escaped her. Entirely laying aside the chilly gravity, the lofty manner, which was habitual to him, Douglas proved that he could woo ardently, and forget the pride of the man in the passion of the lover. But when he sued for a verbal answer to his prayer, although he thought he read the assent in the crimson cheek half turned away, the downcast eyes, that would not meet his own, and the quick flutter of the heart that beat under his hand, he was thunderstruck at the change which passed over Diana. She suddenly grew colorless and calm as any statue, and freeing herself from his hold, fixed a searching look upon him, while she said slowly and distinctly, "When you have told me the mystery of your life, I will give my answer to your love—not before."

"The mystery of my life!" he echoed, falling back a step or two, with such violent discomposure in face and manner that Diana's heart sank within her, though she answered steadily:

"Yes; I must know it, before I link my fate with yours."

"Who told you that I had one?" he demanded.

"Lady Lennox. I had heard the rumor before, but never gave it thought till she confirmed it. Now I wait for your explanation."

"It is impossible to give it; but I swear to you, Diana, that I am innocent of any act that could dishonor my name, or mar your peace, if it were known. The secret is not mine to tell; I have promised to keep it, and I cannot forfeit my word, even for your sake. Be generous; do not let mere curiosity or pique destroy my hopes, and make you cruel when you should be kind."

So earnestly he spoke, so tenderly he pleaded, that Diana's purpose wavered, and would have failed her, had not the memory of Mrs. Vane's strange warning returned to her, bringing with it other memories of other mysterious looks, hints, and acts which had transpired since Douglas came. These recollections hardened her heart, confirmed her resolution, and gave her power to appear inexorable to the last.

"You mistake my motive, sir. Neither curiosity nor pique influenced me, but a just and natural desire to assure myself that in trusting my happiness to your keeping, I am not entailing regret upon myself, remorse upon you. I must know all your past, before I endanger my future; clear yourself from the suspicions which have long clung to you, and I am yours; remain silent, and we are nothing to each other from this day forth."

Her coldness chilled his passion, her distrust irritated his pride; all the old hauteur returned fourfold, his eye grew hard, his voice bitter, and his whole manner showed that his will was as inflexible as hers.

"Are you resolved on making this unjust, ungenerous test of my affection, Miss Stuart?"

"I am."

"You have no faith in my honor, then? No consideration for the hard strait in which my promise places me? No compassion for the loss I must sustain in losing the love, respect, and confidence of the woman dearest to me?"

"Assure me that you are worthy of love, respect, confidence, and I gladly accord them to you."

"I cannot, in the way you demand. Will nothing else satisfy you?"

"Nothing!"

"Then, in your words, we are nothing to one another from this day forth. Farewell, Diana!"

With an involuntary impulse, she put out her hand to detain him as he turned away. He took it, and bending, kissed it, with a lingering fondness that nearly conquered her. The act, the look that accompanied it, the tremor of the lips that performed it, touched the poor girl's heart, and words of free acceptance were rising to her lips, when, as he bent, a miniature, suspended by a chain of mingled hair and gold, swung forward from its hiding place in his breast, and though she saw no face, the haste with which he replaced it roused all her suspicions again, and redoubled all her doubts. Scorning herself for her momentary weakness, the gesture of recall was changed to one of dismissal, as she withdrew her hand, and turned from him, with a quiet "Farewell, then, forever!"

"One moment," he pleaded. "Do not let us destroy the peace of both our lives by an unhappy secret which in no way but this can do us harm. Bear with me for a few days, Diana; think over this interview, remember my great love for you, let your own generous nature appeal to your pride, and perhaps time may show you that it is possible to love, trust, and pardon me."

Glad of any delay which should spare her the pain of an immediate separation, she hesitated a moment, and then, with feigned reluctance, answered, "My visit was to have ended with the coming week; I will not shorten it, but give you till then to reconsider your decision, and by a full confession secure your happiness and my own."

Then they parted—not with the lingering adieus of happy lovers, but coldly, silently, like estranged friends—and each took a different way back, instead of walking blissfully together, as they had thought to do.

"Why so *triste,* Diana? One would think you had seen a ghost in the night, you look so pale and solemn. And, upon my word, Mr. Douglas looks as if he had seen one also," said Mrs. Berkeley, as they all gathered about the breakfast table two hours later.

"I did see one," answered Douglas, generously distracting general attention from Diana, who could ill sustain it.

"Last night?" exclaimed Mrs. Berkeley, full of interest at once.

"Yes, madam—at one o'clock last night."

"How charming! Tell us all about it; I dote upon ghosts, yet never saw one," said Mrs. Vane.

Douglas narrated his adventure. The elder ladies looked disturbed, Diana incredulous; and Mrs. Vane filled the room with her silvery laughter, as Harry protested that no ghost belonged to the house, and George explained the mystery as being the nightmare.

"I never have it; neither do I walk in my sleep, and seldom dream," replied Douglas. "I perfectly remember rising, partially dressing, and going down to the library, up the private stairs, and examining the door. This may be proved by the key, now changed to my side of the lock, and the train of wax which dropped from my candle as I hurried along."

"What woke you?" asked Mrs. Vane.

"I cannot tell; some slight sound, probably, although I do not remember hearing any, and fancy it was an instinctive sense of danger."

"That door could not have been opened without much noise, for the key was rusted in the lock. We tried to turn it the other day, and could not, so were forced to go round by the great gallery to reach that room."

Diana spoke, and for the first time since they parted in the park, Douglas looked at and addressed her.

"You have explored the private passage then, and tried the door? May I ask when?"

"Harry was showing us the house; anything mysterious pleased us, so we went up, tried the rusty key, and finding it immovable, we came down again."

"Of whom was the party composed?"

"My aunt, Mrs. Vane, and myself, accompanied by Harry."

"Then I must accuse Harry of the prank, for both key and lock have been newly oiled, and the door opens easily and noiselessly, as you may prove if you like. He must have had an accomplice among the housemaids, for it was a woman's hand that took the ring. She doubtless passed it to him, and while I was preparing to sally forth, both ran away—one to hide, the other to wait till I left my room, when he slipped in and restored the ring. Was that it, Hal?"

As Douglas spoke, all looked at Harry; but the boy shook his head, and triumphantly replied to his brother:

"George will tell you that your accusation is entirely unjust; and as he sat up till dawn, writing poetry, I could not have left him without his knowledge."

"True, Hal—you had nothing to do with it, I know. Did you distinctly see the hand that purloined your ring, Earl?" asked Lennox, anxious to divert attention from the revelation of his poetical amusements.

"No; the room was dusky, and the hand muffled in something dark. But it was no ghostly hand, for as it was hastily withdrawn when I sprang up, the wrapper slipped aside, and I saw white human flesh, and the outlines of a woman's arm."

"Was it a beautiful arm?" asked Lennox, with his eyes upon Mrs. Vane's, which lay like a piece of sculptured marble against the red velvet cushion of her chair.

"Very beautiful, I should say; for in that hasty glimpse it looked too fair to belong to any servant, and when I found this hanging to the lock, I felt assured that my spirit was a lady, for housemaids do not wear anything like this, I fancy," and Douglas produced a shred of black lace, evidently torn from some costly flounce or scarf.

The ladies put their heads together over the scrap, and all pronounced it quite impossible for any dressing maid to have come honestly by such expensive trimming as this must have been.

"It looks as if it had belonged to a deeply scalloped flounce," said Mrs. Vane. "Who of us wears such? Miss Stuart, you are in black; have I not seen you with a trimming like this?"

"You forget—I wear no trimming but crepe. This never was a part of a flounce. It is the corner of a shawl. You see how unequally rounded the two sides are; and no flounce was ever scalloped so deeply as this," returned Diana.

"How acute you are, Di! It is so, I really believe. See how exactly this bit compares with the corner of my breakfast shawl, made to imitate lace. Who wears a black lace shawl? Neither Di nor myself," said Mrs. Berkeley.

"Mrs. Vane often wears one."

Diana uttered the name with significance, and Douglas stirred a little, as if she put into words some vague idea of his own. Mrs. Vane shrugged her shoulders, sipped her coffee, and answered tranquilly, "So does Lady Lennox; but I will bear all the suspicions of phantom folly, and when I dress for dinner will put on every rag of lace I possess, so that you may compare this bit, and prove me guilty if it gives you pleasure. Though what object I could have in running about in the dark, oiling door locks, stealing rings, and frightening gentlemen is not as clear to me as it appears to be to you—probably because I am not as much interested in the sufferer."

Diana looked embarrassed, Lady Lennox grave, and, as if weary of the subject, Douglas thrust the shred of lace into his waistcoat pocket, and proposed a riding party. Miss Stuart preferred driving her aunt in the pony carriage, but Mrs. Vane accepted the invitation, and made George Lennox wretched by accepting the loan of one of Earl's horses in preference to his own, which she had ridden the day before. When she appeared, ready for the expedition, glances of admiration shone in the eyes of all the gentlemen, even the gloomy Douglas, as he watched her, wondering if the piquant figure before him could be the same that he had seen in the garden, looking like a lovely, dreaming child. Her black habit, with its velvet facings, set off her little lithe figure to a charm; her hair shone like imprisoned sunshine through the scarlet net that held it, and her face looked bewilderingly brilliant and arch in the shadow of a cavalier hat, with its graceful plume.

As Douglas bent to offer his hand in mounting her, she uttered an exclamation of pain, and caught at his arm to keep herself from falling. Involuntarily he sustained her, and for an instant she leaned upon him, with her face hidden in his breast, as if to conceal some convulsion of suffering.

"My dear Mrs. Vane, what is it? Let me take you in—shall I call for help?" began Douglas, much alarmed.

But she interrupted him and, looking up with a faint smile, answered quietly, as she attempted to stand alone, "It is nothing but the cramp in my foot. It will be over in a moment; Gabrielle fastened my boot too tightly—let me sit down, and I will loosen it."

"Allow me; lean on my shoulder; it's but a moment."

Down knelt Douglas; and, with one hand lightly touching his shoulder to steady herself, the other still closely folded, as if not yet out of pain, Mrs. Vane stood glancing from under her long lashes at Diana, who was waiting in the hall for her aunt, and observing the scene in the avenue with ill-concealed anxiety. The string was in a knot, and Douglas set about his little service very leisurely, for the foot and ankle before him were the most perfect he had ever seen. While so employed, Jitomar, Mrs. Vane's man, appeared, and, tossing him the gloves she had taken off, she signed to him to bid her maid bring her another pair, as some slight blemish in these had offended her fastidious taste. He comprehended with difficulty, it seemed, for words were useless to a deaf-mute, and the motions of his mistress's hands appeared at first without meaning to him. The idea came with a flash, and bowing, he bounded into the house, with his white robes streaming, and his scarlet slippers taking him along as if enchanted, while the grooms wondered, and Mrs. Vane laughed.

Jitomar hurried to his lady's room, delivered his message, and while Gabrielle went down with a fresh pair of gloves, he enacted a curious little scene in the deserted chamber. Carefully unfolding the discarded gloves, he took from the inside of one of them the shred of lace that Douglas had put into his waistcoat pocket at the breakfast table. He examined it with a peculiar smile; then going to a tiger-skin rug that lay beside the bed, he lifted it and produced a black lace shawl, which seemed to have been hastily hidden there. One corner was gone; but laying the torn bit in its place, it fitted exactly, and, as if satisfied, Jitomar refolded both, put them in his pocket, glided to his own room, prepared himself for going out, and, unobserved by anyone, took the next train to London. Mrs. Vane meanwhile had effaced the memory of her first failure by mounting her horse alone, with an elasticity and grace that filled her escort with astonishment and admiration. Laughing her enchanting laugh, she settled herself in the saddle, touched her hat to Lady Lennox, and cantered away with

Douglas, while Harry followed far behind, for George had suddenly remembered that an engagement would prevent his joining them, having no mind to see Mrs. Vane absorbed by another.

As they climbed a long hill, Mrs. Vane suddenly paused in her witty badinage, and after a thoughtful moment, and a backward glance at Harry, who followed apparently out of earshot, she said, earnestly yet timidly, "Mr. Douglas, I desire to ask a favor of you— not for myself, but for the sake of one who is dear to both of us."

"Mrs. Vane can ask no favor that I shall not be both proud and happy to grant for her own sake," returned Earl, eyeing her with much surprise.

"Well, then, I shall be most grateful if you will shun me for a few days; ignore my presence as far as possible, and so heal the breach which I fear I may unconsciously have caused between Miss Stuart and yourself."

"I assure you that you are mistaken regarding the cause of the slight coolness between us, and it is impossible to ignore the existence of Mrs. Vane, having once had the happiness of seeing her."

"Ah, you take refuge in evasion and compliments, as I feared you would; but it is my nature to be frank, and I shall compass my end by leaving you no subterfuge and no power to deny me. I met you both this morning, and read a happy secret in your faces; I hoped when next I saw you to find your mutual happiness secured. But no—I found you grave and cold; saw trouble in your eyes, jealousy and pain in Diana's. I have seen the latter sentiment in her eyes before, and could not but think that I was the unhappy cause of this estrangement. She is peculiar; she does not like me, will not let me love her, and wounds me in many ways. I easily forgive her, for she is not happy, and I long to help her, even against her will—therefore I speak to you."

"Again I assure you that you are wrong. Diana is jealous, but not of you alone, and she has placed me in a cruel strait. I, too, will be frank, and confess that she will not listen to me, unless I betray a secret that is not my own."

"You will not do this, having sworn to keep it?"

"Never! A Douglas cannot break his word."

"I comprehend now," said Mrs. Vane. "Diana wishes to test her power, and you rebel. It is not natural in both; yet I beseech you not to try her too much, because at a certain point she will become unmanageable. She comes of an unhappy race, and desperate things have been done in her family. Guard your secret, for honor demands it, but take my warning and shun me, that you may add nothing to the trouble she has brought upon herself."

"I have no wish to do so; but she also must beware of testing her power too severely, for I am neither a patient nor a humble man, and my will is inflexible when once I am resolved. She should see this, should trust me, and let us both be happy."

"Ah, if she truly loved, she would; for then one believes blindly, can think no ill, fear no wrong, desire no confidence that is not freely given. She does not know the bliss of loving with one's whole heart and soul, and asking no happier fate than to live for a man whose affection makes a heaven anywhere."

They had paused on the brow of the hill to wait for Harry, and as she spoke, Mrs. Vane's face kindled with a glow that made it doubly beautiful; for voice, eyes, lips, and gestures all betrayed how well *she* could love. Douglas regarded her with a curious consciousness of attraction and repulsion, feeling that had he met her before he saw and loved Diana, he never should have given his peace into the keeping of that exacting girl. An involuntary sigh escaped him; Mrs. Vane brightened instantly, saying:

"Nay, do not fall back into your gloomy mood again, or I shall think that I have increased, not lessened, your anxiety. I came to cheer you if I could, for though I have done with love myself, it gives me sincerest satisfaction to serve those who are just beginning to know its pleasant pain."

She was smiling as she spoke, but the lovely eyes lifted to her companion's face were full of tears. Remembering her loneliness, her loss, and with a grateful sense of all she desired to do for him, Douglas ungloved and offered her his hand, with an impulsive gesture, saying warmly, "You are very kind; I thank you, and feel already comforted by the thought that though I may have lost a lover, I have gained a friend."

Here Harry came up brimful of curiosity, for he had seen and heard more than they knew. After this they all rode on together, and when Douglas dismounted Mrs. Vane she whispered, "Remember, you are to shun me, no matter how pointedly. I shall forgive you, and she will be happier for our little ruse."

This speech, as well as the first uttered by Mrs. Vane when their serious conversation began, was overheard by Harry, and when Diana carelessly asked him if he had enjoyed his ride, he repeated the two remarks, hoping to gain some explanation of them before he told his brother, whose cause he heartily espoused. He knew nothing of Miss Stuart's love, and made her his confidante without a suspicion of the pang he was inflicting. She bade him forget what he had heard, but could not do so herself, and all that day those two sentences rang through her mind unceasingly.

Pausing that evening in the hall to examine one of the ancient portraits hanging there, Douglas heard a soft rustle, and turning, saw Mrs. Vane entering, as if from a moonlight stroll on the balcony. The night was cool, and over her head was drawn a corner of the black lace shawl that drooped from her shoulders. Her dress of violet silk was trimmed with a profusion of black lace, and wonderingly becoming to white skin and golden hair was the delicate tint and its rich decoration. Douglas went to her, saying, as he offered his hand, "You see how well I keep my word; now let me reward myself by taking you in. But, first, pray tell me if this is a picture of Sir Lionel."

He led her to the portrait that had excited his curiosity, and while she told him some little legend of it, he still lingered, held as much by the charm of the living voice as by the exploits of the dead knight. Standing thus, arm in arm, alone and engrossed in one another, neither, apparently, saw Diana pausing on the threshold of the library with an expression of deep displeasure in her face. Douglas did not see her; Mrs. Vane did, though not a sign betrayed it, except that in an instant her whole expression changed. As Douglas looked up at the picture, she looked up at him with love, grief, pain, and pity visibly contending in her beautiful face; then suddenly withdrawing her arm, she said, "I forgot, we are strangers now. Let me enter alone." And gliding from him with bent head, she passed into the drawing room.

Much amazed at her abrupt flight, Earl looked after her, saw Diana watching him, and inexpressibly annoyed by the contretemps, he started, colored, bowed coldly, and followed Mrs. Vane without a word. For a moment, Diana lingered with her head in her hands, thinking disconsolately: "What secret lies between them? She leaned and looked as if she had a right there. He is already more at ease with her than me, although they met but yesterday. Have they not met before? She asked some favor 'for the sake of one dear to both.' Who is it? He must shun her that someone may be happy, though deceived. Is that me? She knows his mystery, has a part in it, and I am to be kept blind. Wait a little! I too can plot, and watch, and wait. I can read faces, fathom actions, and play a part, though my heart breaks in doing it."

All that evening she watched them; saw that Douglas did not shun Mrs. Vane; also that he feigned unconsciousness of her own keen scrutiny, and seemed endeavoring to chase from her mind the memory of the morning's interview, or the evening's discovery. She saw Mrs. Vane act surprise, pique, and displeasure at his seeming desertion, and console herself by making her peace with Lennox. To others, Diana appeared unusually animated and carefree, but never had an evening seemed so interminable, and never had she so gladly hailed the hour of separation.

She was standing by Lady Lennox when Mrs. Vane came up to say good night. Her ladyship did not like Diana, and did both love and pity the lonely little widow, who had endeared herself in so many ways. As she swept a curtsy, with the old-fashioned reverence that her hostess liked, Lady Lennox drew her nearer and kissed her with motherly affection, saying playfully as she did so, "No pranks tonight among the spirits, my dear, else these friends will think you and I are witches in good earnest."

"That reminds me, I have kept my promise, and Mr. Douglas can compare his telltale bit with my mother's, and, as you see, very precious in every respect."

Gravely exploring one pocket after another, Earl presently announced, with some chagrin, that the bit was lost, blown away while riding, probably. So nothing could be done, and Mrs. Vane was acquitted of lending her laces to the household ghost. Diana looked disappointed, and taking up a corner of the shawl, said, as she examined it narrowly, "As I remember the shred, it matched this pattern exactly. It is a peculiar one, and I observed it well. I wish the bit was not lost, for if people play such games with your clothes, they may take equal liberties with mine."

Seeing suspicion in her eyes, Mrs. Vane gathered the four corners of the shawl together, and with great care spread each over her violet skirt before Diana. Not a fracture appeared, and when she had done the same with every atom of trimming on her dress, she drew her slender figure up with an air of proud dignity, asking almost sternly, "Am I acquitted of this absurd charge, Miss Stuart?"

Entirely disconcerted by the quickness with which her distrust had been seen and exposed, Diana could only look guilty, apologize, and find herself convicted of an unjust suspicion. Mrs. Vane received her atonement graciously, and wrapping her shawl about her, went away to bed, with a mischievous smile shining in her eyes as she bowed to Douglas, whose glance followed her till the last glimpse of the violet dress disappeared.

CHAPTER V. TREASON

The week passed gaily enough, externally, but to several of the party it was a very dreary and very memorable week. George Lennox basked in the light of Mrs. Vane's smiles, and his mother began to hope that Douglas would not take her at her word, but leave her son to woo and win the bonny widow, if he could. Earl watched and waited for Diana to relent, pleading with his eyes, though never a word of submission or appeal passed his lips. And poor Diana, hoping to conquer him, silenced the promptings of her reason, and stood firm, when a yielding look, a tender word, would have overcome his pride, and healed the breach. She suffered much, but told no one her pain till the last day came. Then, driven by the thought that a few hours would seal her fate, she resolved to appeal to Mrs. Vane. She knew the mystery; she professed to pity her. She was a woman, and to her this humiliation would not be so hard, this confession so impossible.

Diana haunted the hall and drawing rooms all that morning, hoping to find Mrs. Vane alone. At last, just before lunch, she caught her playing with Earl's spaniel, while she waited for Lennox to bring her hat from the garden seat where she had left it.

"Be so kind as to take a turn with me on the balcony, Mrs. Vane. I wish much to say a few words to you," began Diana, with varying color and anxious eyes, as she met her at the great hall door.

"With pleasure. Give me your arm, and let us have our little chat quite comfortably together. Can I do anything for you, my dear Miss Stuart? Pray speak freely, and, believe me, I desire to be your friend."

So kind, so cordial was the tone, the look, that poor Diana felt comforted at once; and bending her stately head to the bright one at her side, she said, with a sad humility, which proved how entirely her love had subdued her pride, "I hope so, Mrs. Vane, for I need a friend. You, and you alone, can help me. I humble myself to you; I forget not my own misgivings. I endeavor to see in you only a woman younger, yet wiser than myself, who, knowing my sore necessity, will help me by confessing the share she bears in the secret that is destroying my peace."

"I wish I could! I wish I dared! I have thought of it often; have longed to do it at all costs; and then remembering my vow, I have held my peace!"

"Assure me of one thing and I will submit. I will ask Allan to forgive me, and I will be happy in my ignorance, if I can. He told me that this mystery would not stain his honor, or mar my peace if it were known. Mrs. Vane, is this true?" asked Diana solemnly.

"No; a man's honor is not tarnished in his eyes by treachery to a woman, and he believes that a woman's peace will not be marred by the knowledge that in God's sight she is not his wife, although she may be in the eyes of the world."

"Mrs. Vane, I conjure you to tell me what you mean! I have a right to know; it is your duty to save me from sin and sorrow if you can, and I will make any promise you exact to keep eternally secret whatever you may tell me. If you fear Douglas, he shall never know that you have broken your vow, whether I marry or discard him. Have pity upon me, I implore you, for this day must make or mar my life!"

Few women could have withstood the desperate urgency of Diana's prayer; Mrs. Vane did not. A moment she stood, growing paler as some purpose took shape in her mind, then drew her companion onward, saying hurriedly, as George Lennox appeared in the avenue, "Invite me to drive out alone with you after lunch, and then you shall know all. But, O Miss Stuart, remember that you bring the sorrow upon yourself if you urge this disclosure. I cannot think it right to see you give yourself to this man without a protest; but you may curse me for destroying your faith in him, while powerless to kill your love. Go now, and if you retract your wish, be silent; I shall know."

They parted, and when Lennox came up, the balcony was deserted.

"My love, you get so pale and spiritless that I am quite reconciled to our departure; for the air here does not suit you, and we must try the seashore," said Mrs. Berkeley, as they rose from the table after lunch.

"I shall be myself again soon, Aunt. I need more exercise, and if Mrs. Vane will allow me, I should enjoy a long drive with her this afternoon," returned Diana, growing still paler as she spoke.

Mrs. Vane bowed her acceptance, and as she left the room a curious shiver seemed to shake her from head to foot as she pressed her hands together and hurried to her chamber.

The two ladies drove in silence, till Diana said abruptly, "I am ready, Mrs. Vane; tell me all, and spare nothing."

"Your solemn oath first, that living or dying, you will never reveal to any human soul what I shall tell you." And as she spoke, Mrs. Vane extended her hand.

Diana gave her own, and took the oath which the other well knew she would keep inviolate.

"I shall not torture you by suspense," Mrs. Vane began, "but show you at once why I would save you from a greater suffering than the loss of love. Miss Stuart, read that, and learn the mystery of your lover's life."

With a sudden gesture, she took from her bosom a worn paper, and unfolding it, held before the other's eyes the marriage record of Allan Douglas and Virginie Varens.

Not a word passed Diana's lips, but with the moan of a broken heart she covered up her face, and slowly, tremulously, the voice at her side went on, "You see here the date of that mysterious journey to Paris, from which he returned an altered man. There, too, is his private seal. That long lock of hair, that stained slipper, belonged to Virginie; and though he said he had never seen her, the lie cost him an effort, and well it might, for I sat there before him, and I am Virginie."

Diana's hands dropped from her pallid face, as she shrank away from her companion, yet gazed at her like one fascinated by an awful spell.

"Hear my story, and then judge between us," the voice continued, so melancholy, yet so sweet that tears came to the listener's eyes, as the sad story was unfolded. "I am of a noble family, but was left so poor, so friendless, that but for a generous boy I should have perished in the streets of Paris. He was a dancer, his poor earnings could not support us both. I discovered this, and in my innocence, thought no labor degrading that lessened my great debt to him. I, too, had become a dancer. I had youth, beauty, health, and a grateful heart to help me on. I made money. I had many lovers, but Victor kept me safe, for he, too, loved, but in secret, till he was sure I could give him love, not gratitude. Then Allan came, and I forgot the world about me; for I loved as only a girl of seventeen can love the first man who has touched her heart. He offered me his hand and honorable name, for I was as wellborn as himself, and even in my seeming degradation, he respected me. We were married, and for a year I was as happy as an angel. Then my boy was born, and for a time I lost my beauty. That cooled Allan's waning passion. Some fear of consequences, some later regret for his rash act, came over him, and made him very bitter to me when I most needed tenderness. He told me that our marriage had been without witnesses, that our faith was different, and that vows pronounced before a Catholic priest alone were not binding upon him. That he was weary of me, and having been recalled to Scotland, he desired to return as free as he went. If I would promise solemnly to conceal the truth, he would support the boy and me abroad, until I chose to marry; that I must destroy the record of the deed, and never claim him, or he would denounce me as an impostor, and take away the boy. Miss Stuart, I was very ignorant and young; my heart was broken, and I believed myself dying. For the child's sake, I promised all things, and he left me; but remorse haunted him, and his peace was poisoned from that hour."

"And you? You married Colonel Vane?" whispered Diana, holding her breath to listen.

"No, I have never married, for in my eyes that ceremony made me Allan's wife, and I shall be so till I die. When I was most forlorn, Colonel Vane found me. He was Allan's friend; he had seen me with him, and when we met again, he pitied me; and finding that I longed to hide myself from the world, he took me to India under an assumed name, as the widow of a friend. My boy went with me, and for a time I was as happy as a desolate creature could be. Colonel Vane desired to marry me; for, though I kept my promise, he suspected that I had been deceived and cruelly deserted, and longed to atone for his friend's perfidy by his own devotion. I would not marry him; but when he was dying, he begged me to take his name as a shield against a curious world, to take his fortune, and give my son the memory of a father when his own had cast him off. I did so; and no one knew me there except under my false name. It was believed that I had married him too soon after my husband's death to care to own it at once, and when I came to England, no one denied me the place I chose to fill."

"Oh, why did you come?" cried Diana, with a tearless sob.

"I came because I longed to know if Allan had forgotten me, if he had married, and left his poor boy fatherless. I saw him last winter, saw that you loved him, feared that he would love you, and when I learned that both were coming here, I resolved to follow. It was evident that Allan had not forgotten me, that he had suffered as well as I; and perhaps if he could bring himself to brave the pity, curiosity, and criticism of the world, he might yet atone for his deceit, and make me happy. We had met in London; he had told me to remember my vow; had confessed that he still loved me, but dared not displease his haughty family by owning me; had seen his boy, and reiterated his promise to provide for us as long as we were silent. I saw him no more till we met here, and this explains all that has seemed so strange to you. It was I who entered his room, but not to juggle with the ring. He invented that tale to account for the oiled lock, and whatever stir might have been overheard. I went to implore him to pause before he pledged himself to you. He would not yield, having gone too far to retract with honor, he said. Then I was in despair; for well I knew that if ever the knowledge of this passage in his life should come to you, you would feel as I feel, and regard that first marriage as sacred in God's eye, whatever the world might say. I gave him one more opportunity to spare you by the warning I whispered in the park. That has delayed the wrong, but you would have yielded had not other things roused suspicion of me. I had decided to say no more, but let you two tangle your fates as you would. Your appeal this morning conquered me, and I have broken every vow, dared every danger, to serve and save you. Have I done all this in vain?"

"No; let me think, let me understand—then I will act."

For many minutes they rolled on silently, two pale, stern-faced women, sitting side by side looking out before them, with fixed eyes that saw nothing but a hard task performed, a still harder one yet to be done. Diana spoke first, asking, "Do you intend to proclaim your wrong, and force your husband to do you justice?"

"No, I shall not ask that of him again, but I shall do my best to prevent any other woman from blindly sacrificing her happiness by marrying him, unconscious of my claim. For the boy's sake I have a right to do this."

"You have. I thank you for sparing me the affliction of discovering that man's perfidy too late. Where is your boy, Mrs. Douglas?"

Steadily she spoke; and when her lips pronounced the name she had hoped to make her own, a stern smile passed across her white face, and left a darker shadow behind. Mrs. Vane touched her lips with a warning gesture, saying pitifully, yet commandingly: "Never call me that until he gives me the right to bear it openly. You ask for my boy; will you come and see him? He is close by; I cannot be parted from him long, yet must conceal him, for the likeness to his father would betray him at once, if we were seen together."

Turning down a grassy lane, Mrs. Vane drove on till the way became too narrow for the carriage. Here they alighted, and climbing a wooded path, came to a lonely cottage in a dell.

"My faithful Jitomar found this safe nook for me, and brings me tidings of my darling every day," whispered Mrs. Vane, as she stole along the path that wound round the house.

Turning a sharp corner, a green, lawnlike bit of ground appeared. On a vine-covered seat sat an old French *bonne,* knitting as she nodded in the sun. But Diana saw nothing but a little figure tossing buttercups into the air, and catching them as they fell with peals of childish laughter. A three-year-old boy it was, with black curls blowing round a bold bright face, where a healthful color glowed through the dark skin, and brilliant eyes sparkled under a brow so like that other that she could not doubt that this was Allan's son. Just then the boy spied his mother, and with a cry of joy ran to her, to be gathered close, and covered with caresses.

There was no acting here, for genuine mother love transformed Mrs. Vane from her usual inexplicable self into a simple woman, whose heart was bound up in the little creature whom she loved with the passionate fondness of an otherwise cold and superficial nature.

Waving off the old *bonne* when she would have approached, Mrs. Vane turned to Diana, asking, "Are you satisfied?"

"Heaven help me, yes!"

"Is he not like his father? See, the very shape of his small hands, the same curve to his baby mouth. Stay, you shall hear him speak. Darling, who am I?"

"Mamma, my dear mamma," replied the little voice.

"And who is this?" asked Mrs. Vane, showing a miniature of Douglas.

"Oh, Papa! When will he come again?"

"God only knows, my poor baby. Now kiss Mamma, and go and make a pretty daisy chain against I come next time. See, love, here are bonbons and new toys; show them to Babette. Quick, let us slip away, Miss Stuart."

As the boy ran to his nurse the ladies vanished, and in silence regained the carriage. Only one question and answer passed between them, as they drove rapidly homeward.

"Diana, what will you do?"

"Go tomorrow, and in silence. It is all over between us, forever. Mrs. Vane, I envy you, I thank you, and I could almost *hate* you for the kind yet cruel deed you have done this day."

A gloomy darkness settled down on her altered face; despair sat in her eyes, and death itself could not have stricken hope, energy, and vitality out of it more utterly than the bitter truth which she had wrung from her companion.

George Lennox and Douglas were waiting at the door, and both ran down to help them alight. Diana dragged her veil over her face, while Mrs. Vane assumed an anxious, troubled air as the carriage stopped, and both gentlemen offered a hand to Miss Stuart. Putting Earl's aside with what seemed almost rude repugnance, she took George's arm, hurried up the steps, and as her foot touched the threshold of the door, she fell heavily forward in a swoon.

Douglas was springing toward her, when a strong grasp detained him, and Mrs. Vane whispered, as she clung to his arm tremblingly, "Do not touch her; she must not see you; it will kill her."

"Good heavens! What is the cause of this?" he asked, as Lennox carried Diana in, and help came flocking at his call.

"O Mr. Douglas, I have had an awful drive! She terrified me so by her wild conversation, her fierce threats of taking her own life, that I drove home in agony. You saw how she repulsed you, and rushed away to drop exhausted in the hall; imagine what it all means, and spare me the pain of telling you."

She spoke breathlessly, and glanced nervously about her, as if still in fear. Earl listened, half bewilderingly at first, then, as her meaning broke upon him, his dark cheek whitened, and he looked aghast.

"You do not mean that she is mad?" he whispered, recalling her fierce gesture, and the moody silence she had preserved for days.

"No, oh, no, I dare not say that *yet;* but I fear that her mind is unsettled by long brooding over one unhappy thought, and that the hereditary taint may be upon the point of showing itself. Poor girl!"

"Am I the cause of this outbreak? Is our disagreement the unhappy thought that has warped her reason? What shall I, what ought I to do?" Earl asked in great distress, as Diana's senseless body was carried up the stairs, and her aunt stood wringing her hands, while Lady Lennox dispatched a servant for medical help.

"Do nothing but avoid her, for she says your presence tortures her. She will go tomorrow. Let her leave quietly, and when absence has restored her, take any steps toward a reconciliation that you think best. Now I must go to her; do not repeat what I have said. It escaped me in my agitation, and may do her harm if she learns that her strange behavior is known."

Pressing his hand with a sympathizing glance, Mrs. Vane hurried in, and for an hour busied herself about Diana so skillfully that the physician sent all the rest away and gave directions to her alone. When recovered from her faint, Diana lay like one dead, refusing to speak or move, yet taking obediently whatever Mrs. Vane offered her, as if a mutual sorrow linked them together with a secret bond. At dusk she seemed to fall asleep, and leaving Gabrielle to watch beside her, Mrs. Vane went down to join the others at a quiet meal.

CHAPTER VI. A DARK DEATH

The party separated early. Diana was still sleeping, and leaving her own maid to watch in the dressing room between their chambers, Mrs. Berkeley went to bed. As he passed them down the gallery to his apartment, Earl heard Mrs. Vane say to the maid, "If anything happens in the night, call me." The words made him anxious, and instead of going to bed, he sat up writing letters till very late. It was past midnight when the sound of a closing door broke the long silence that had filled the house. Stepping into the gallery, he listened. All was still, and nothing stirred but the heavy curtain before the long window at the end of the upper hall; this swayed to and fro in the strong current of air that swept in. Fearing that the draft might slam other doors and disturb Diana, he went to close it.

Pausing a moment to view the gloomy scene without, Douglas was startled by an arm flung violently about his neck, lips pressed passionately to his own, and a momentary glimpse of a woman's figure dimly defined on the dark curtain that floated backward from his hand. Silently and suddenly as it came, the phantom went, leaving Douglas so amazed that for an instant he could only stare dumbly before him, half breathless, and wholly bewildered by the ardor of that mysterious embrace. Then he sprang forward to discover who the woman was and whither she had gone. But, as if blown outward by some counterdraft, the heavy curtain wrapped him in its fold, and when he had freed himself, neither ghost nor woman was visible.

Earl was superstitious, and for a moment he fancied the spirit of Diana had appeared to him, foretelling her death. But a second thought assured him that it was a human creature, and no wraith, for the soft arms had no deathly chill in them, the lips were warm, living breath had passed across his face, and on his cheek he felt a tear that must have fallen from human eyes. The light had been too dim to reveal the partially shrouded countenance, or more than a tall and shadowy outline, but with a thrill of fear he thought, "It was Diana, and she is mad!"

Taking his candle, he hurried to the door of the dressing room, tapped softly, and when the sleepy maid appeared, inquired if Miss Stuart still slept.

"Yes, sir, like a child, it does one's heart good to see her."

"You are quite sure she is asleep?"

"Bless me, yes, sir, I've just looked at her, and she hasn't stirred since I looked an hour ago."

"Does she ever walk in her sleep, Mrs. Mason?"

"Dear, no, sir."

"I thought I saw her just now in the upper gallery. I went to shut the great window, lest the wind should disturb her, and someone very like her certainly stood for a moment at my side."

"Lord, sir! You make my blood run cold. It couldn't have been her, for she never left her bed, much less her room."

"Perhaps so; never mind; just look again, and tell me if you see her, then I shall be at ease."

Mrs. Mason knew that her young lady loved the gentleman before her, and never doubted that he loved her, and so considering his anxiety quite natural and proper, she nodded, crept away, and soon returned, saying, with a satisfied air, "She's all right, sir, sleeping beautifully. I didn't speak, for once when I looked at her, she said, quite fierce, 'Go away, and let me be until I call you.' So I've only peeped through the curtain since. I see her lying with her face to the wall, and the coverlet drawn comfortably round her." "Thank God! She is safe. Excuse my disturbing you, Mrs. Mason, but I was very anxious. Be patient and faithful in your care of her; I shall remember it. Good night."

"Handsome creeter; how fond he is of her, and well he may be, for she dotes on him, and they'll make a splendid couple. Now I'll finish my nap, and then have a cup of tea."

With a knowing look and a chilly shiver, Mrs. Mason resettled herself in a luxurious chair, and was soon dozing.

Douglas meanwhile returned to his room, after a survey of the house, and went to bed, thinking with a smile and frown that if all spirits came in such an amicable fashion, the fate of a ghost seer was not a hard one.

In the dark hour just before the dawn, a long shrill cry rent the silence, and brought every sleeper under that roof out of his bed, trembling and with fright. The cry came from Diana's room, and in a moment the gallery, dressing room, and chamber were filled with pale faces and half-dressed figures, as ladies and gentlemen, men and maids came flocking in, asking breathlessly, "What is it? Oh, what is it?"

Mrs. Berkeley lay on the floor in strong hysterics, and Mrs. Mason, instead of attending to her, was beating her hands distractedly together, and running wildly about the room, as if searching for something she had lost. Diana's bed was empty, with the clothes flung one way and the pillows another, and every sign of strange disorder, but its occupant was nowhere to be seen.

"Where is she?" "What has happened?" "Why don't you speak?" cried the terrified beholders.

A sudden lull fell upon the excited group, as Mrs. Vane, white, resolute, and calm, made her way through the crowd, and laying her hand on Mrs. Mason's shoulder, commanded her to stand still and explain the mystery. The poor soul endeavored to obey, but burst into tears, and dropping on her knees, poured out her story in a passion of penitent despair.

"You left her sleeping, ma'am, and I sat as my lady bid me, going now and then to look at Miss. The last time I drew the curtain, she looked up and said, sharp and short, 'Let me be in peace, and don't disturb me till I call you.' After that, I just peeped through the crack, and she seemed quiet. You know I told you so, sir, when you came to ask, and oh, my goodness me, it wasn't her at all, sir, and she's gone! She's gone!"

"Hush! Stop sobbing, and tell me how you missed her. Gabrielle and Justine, attend to Mrs. Berkeley; Harry, go at once and search the house. Now, Mrs. Mason."

Mrs. Vane's clear, calm voice seemed to act like a spell on the agitation of all about her, and the maids obeyed; Harry, with the menservants, hurried away, and Mrs. Mason more coherently went on:

"Well, ma'am, when Mr. Douglas came to the door asking if Miss was here, thinking he saw her in the hall, I looked again, and thought she lay as I'd left her an hour before. But oh, ma'am, it wasn't her, it was the pillow that she'd fixed like herself, with the coverlet pulled round it, like she'd pulled it round her own head and shoulders when she spoke last. It looked all right, the night lamp being low, and me so sleepy, and I went back to my place, after setting Mr. Douglas's mind at rest. I fell asleep, and when I woke, I ran in here to make sure she was safe, for I'd had a horrid dream about seeing her laid out, dead and dripping, with weeds in her hair, and her poor feet all covered with red clay, as if she'd fallen into one of them pits over yonder. I ran in here, pulled up the curtain, and was just going to say, 'Thank the Lord,' when, as I stooped down to listen if she slept easy, I saw she wasn't there. The start took my wits away, and I don't know what I did, till my lady came running in, as I was tossing the pillows here and there to find her, and when I told what had happened, my lady gave one dreadful scream, and went off in a fit."

There was a dead silence for a moment, as Mrs. Mason relapsed into convulsive sobbing, and everyone looked into each other's frightened face. Douglas leaned on Lennox, as if all the strength had gone out of him, and George stood aghast. Mrs. Vane alone seemed self-possessed, though an awful anxiety blanched her face, and looked out at her haggard eyes.

"What did you see in the hall?" she asked of Douglas. Briefly he told the incident, and Lady Lennox clasped her hands in despair, exclaiming, "She has destroyed herself, and that was her farewell."

"Your ladyship is mistaken, I hope, for among the wild things she said this afternoon was a longing to go home at once, as every hour here was torture to her. She may have attempted this in her delirium. Look in her wardrobe, Mrs. Mason, and see what clothes are gone. That will help us in our search. Be calm, I beg of you, my lady; I am sure we shall find the poor girl soon."

"It's no use looking, ma'am; she's gone in the clothes she had on, for she wouldn't let me take 'em off her. It was a black silk with crepe trimmings, and her black mantle's gone, and the close crepe bonnet. Here's her gloves just where they dropped when we laid her down in her faint."

"Is her purse gone?" asked Mrs. Vane.

"It's always in her pocket, ma'am; when she drives out, she likes to toss a bit of money to the little lads that open gates, or hold the ponies while she gets flowers, and such like. She was so generous, so kind, poor dear!"

Here Harry came in, saying that no trace of the lost girl was visible in the house. But as he spoke, Jitomar's dark face and glittering eyes looked over his shoulder with an intelligent motion, which his mistress understood, and put into words.

"He says that one of the long windows in the little breakfast room is unfastened and ajar. Go, gentlemen, at once, and take him with you; he is as keen as a hound, and will do good service. It is just possible that she may have remembered the one o'clock mail train, and taken it. Inquire, and if you find any trace of her, let us know without delay."

In an instant they were gone, and the anxious watchers left be-

hind traced their progress by the glimmer of the lantern, which Jitomar carried low, that he might follow the print her flying feet had left
here and there in the damp earth.

A long hour passed, then Harry and the Indian returned, bringing the good news that a tall lady in black had been seen at the station
alone, had not been recognized, being veiled, and had taken the mail
train to London. Douglas and Lennox had at once ordered horses,
and gone with all speed to catch an early train that left a neighboring
town in an hour or two. They would trace and discover the lost girl,
if she was in London.

"There can be no doubt that it was she, no lady would be traveling alone at such an hour, and the station people say that she seemed
in great haste. Now let us compose ourselves, hope for the best, and
comfort her poor aunt."

As Mrs. Vane spoke, Harry frankly looked his admiration of the
cheerful, courageous little woman, and his mother took her arm, saying affectionately, "My dear, what should we do without you? For
you have the nerves of a man, the quick wit of a woman, and presence of mind enough for us all."

The dreary day dawned, and slowly wore away. A dull rain fell, and a
melancholy wind sighed among the yellowing leaves. All occupations
flagged, all failed, except the one absorbing hope. The servants loitered, unreproved, and gossiped freely among themselves about the
sad event. The ladies sat in Mrs. Berkeley's room, consoling her distress, while Harry haunted the station, waiting for an arrival or a
telegram. At noon the letter came.

"The lady in black not Diana. On another scent now. If that fails,
home at night."

No one knew how much they leaned upon this hope, until it
failed and all was uncertainty again. Harry searched house, garden,
park, and riverside, but found no trace of the lost girl beyond the
point where her footprints ended on the hard gravel of the road. So
the long afternoon wore on, and at dusk the gentlemen returned,
haggard, wet, and weary, bringing no tidings of good cheer. The lady
in black proved to be a handsome young governess, called suddenly to

town by her father's dangerous illness. The second search was equally fruitless, and nowhere had Diana been seen.

Their despondent story was scarcely ended when the bell rang. Every servant in the house sprang to answer it, and every occupant of the drawing room listened breathlessly. A short parley followed the ring; then an astonished footman showed in a little farmer lad, with a bundle under his arm.

"He wants to see my lady, and would come in," said the man, lingering, as all eyes were fixed on the newcomer.

The boy looked important, excited, and frightened, but when Lady Lennox bade him to do his errand without fear, he spoke up briskly, though his voice shook a little, and he now and then gave a nervous clutch at the bundle under his arm.

"Please, my lady, Mother told me to come up as soon as ever I got home, so I ran off right away, knowing you'd be glad to hear something, even if it weren't good."

"Something about Miss Stuart, you mean?"

"Yes, my lady, I know where she is."

"Where? Speak quickly, you shall be paid for your tidings."

"In that pit, my lady," and the boy began to cry.

"No!"

Douglas spoke, and turned on the lad a face that stopped his crying, and sent the words to his lips faster than he could utter them, so full of mute entreaty was its glance of anguish.

"You see, sir, I was here this noon, and heard about it. Mrs. Mason's dream scared me, because my brother was drowned in the pit. I couldn't help thinking of it all the afternoon, and when work was done, I went home that way. The first thing I saw were tracks in the red clay, coming from the lodge way. The pit has overflowed and made a big pool, but just where it's deepest, the tracks stopped, and there I found these."

With a sudden gesture of the arm, he shook out the bundle; a torn mantle, heavily trimmed, and a crushed crepe bonnet dropped upon the floor. Lady Lennox sank back in her chair, and George covered up his face with a groan; but Earl stood motionless, and Mrs.

Vane looked as if the sight of these relics had confirmed some wordless fear.

"Perhaps she is not there, however," she said below her breath. "She may have wandered on and lost herself. Oh, let us look!"

"She *is* there, ma'am, I see her sperrit," and the boy's eyes dilated as they glanced fearfully about him while he spoke. "I was awful scared when I see them things, but she was good to me, and I loved her, so I took 'em up and went on round the pool, meaning to strike off by the great ditch. Just as I got to the bit of brush that grows down by the old clay pits, something flew right up before me, something like a woman, all black but a white face and arms. It gave a strange screech, and seemed to go out of sight all in a minute, like as if it vanished in the pits. I know it warn't a real woman, it flew so, and looked so awful when it wailed, as Granny says the sperrits do."

The boy paused, till Douglas beckoned solemnly, and left the room with the one word "Come."

The brothers went, the lad followed, Mrs. Vane hid her face in Lady Lennox's lap, and neither stirred nor spoke for one long dreadful hour.

"They are coming," whispered Mrs. Vane, when at length her quick ear caught the sound of many approaching feet. Slowly, steadily they came on, across the lawn, up the steps through the hall; then there was a pause.

"Go and see if she is found, I cannot," implored Lady Lennox, spent and trembling with the long suspense.

There was no need to go, for as she spoke, the wail of women's voices filled the air, and Lennox stood in the doorway with a face that made all question needless.

He beckoned, and Mrs. Vane went to him as if her feet could hardly bear her, while her face might have been that of a dead woman, so white and stony had it grown. Drawing her outside, he said, "My mother must not see her yet. Mrs. Mason can do all that is necessary, if you will give her orders, and spare my mother the first sad duties. Douglas bade me come for you, for you are always ready."

"I will come; where is she?"

"In the library. Send the servants away, in pity to poor Earl. Harry can't bear it, and it kills me to see her look so."

"You found her there?"

"Yes, quite underneath the deepest water of the pool. That dream was surely sent by heaven. Are you faint? Can you bear it?"

"I can bear anything. Go on."

Poor Diana! There she lay, a piteous sight, with stained and dripping garments, slimy weeds entangled in her long hair, a look of mortal woe stamped on her dead face, for the blue lips were parted, as if by the passage of the last painful breath, and the glassy eyes seemed fixed imploringly upon some stern specter, darker and more dreadful even than the most desperate death she had sought and found.

A group of awestricken men and sobbing women stood about her. Harry leaned upon the high arm of the couch where they had laid her, with his head down upon his arm, struggling to control himself, for he had loved her with a boy's first love, and the horror of her end unmanned him. Douglas sat at the head of the couch, holding the dead hand, and looking at her with a white tearless anguish, which made his face old and haggard, as with the passage of long and heavy years.

With an air of quiet command, and eyes that never once fell on the dead girl, Mrs. Vane gave a few necessary orders, which cleared the room of all but the gentlemen and herself. Laying her hand softly on Earl's shoulder, she said, in a tone of tenderest compassion, "Come with me, and let me try to comfort you, while George and Harry take the poor girl to her room, that these sad tokens of her end may be removed, and she made beautiful for the eyes of those who loved her."

He heard, but did not answer in words, for waving off the brothers, Earl took his dead love in his arms, and carrying her to her own room, laid her down tenderly, kissed her pale forehead with one lingering kiss, and then without a word shut himself into his own apartment.

Mrs. Vane watched him go with a dark glance, followed him upstairs, and when his door closed, muttered low to herself, "He loved her better than I knew, but she has made my task easier than I dared to hope it would be, and now I can soon teach him to forget."

A strange smile passed across her face as she spoke, and still, without a glance at the dead face, left the chamber for her own, whither Jitomar was soon summoned, and where he long remained.

CHAPTER VII. THE FOOTPRINT BY THE POOL

Three sad and solemn days had passed, and now the house was still again. Mr. Berkeley had removed his wife, and the remains of his niece, and Lennox had gone with him. Mrs. Vane devoted herself to her hostess, who had been much affected by the shock, and to Harry, who was almost ill with the excitement and the sorrow. Douglas had hardly been seen except by his own servant, who reported that he was very quiet, but in a stern and bitter mood, which made solitude his best comforter. Only twice had he emerged during those troubled days. Once, when Mrs. Vane's sweet voice came up from below singing a sacred melody in the twilight, he came out and paced to and fro in the long gallery, with a softer expression than his face had worn since the night of Diana's passionate farewell. The second time was in answer to a tap at his door, on opening which he saw Jitomar, who with the graceful reverence of his race, bent on one knee, as with dark eyes full of sympathy, he delivered a lovely bouquet of the flowers Diana most loved, and oftenest wore. The first tears that had been seen there softened Earl's melancholy eyes, as he took the odorous gift, and with a grateful impulse stretched his hand to the giver. But Jitomar drew back with a gesture which signified that his mistress sent the offering, and glided away. Douglas went straight to the drawing room, found Mrs. Vane alone, and inexpressibly touched by her tender thought of him, he thanked her warmly, let her detain him for an hour with her soothing conversation, and left her, feeling that comfort was possible when such an angel administered it.

On the third day, impelled by an unconquerable wish to revisit the lonely spot hereafter, and forever to be haunted by the memory of that tragic death, he stole out, unperceived, and took his way to the pool. It lay there dark and still under a gloomy sky, its banks

trampled by many hasty feet; and in one spot the red clay still bore
the impress of the pale shape drawn from the water on that memorable night. As he stood there, he remembered the lad's story of the
spirit which he believed he had seen. With a dreary smile at the super-
stition of the boy, he followed his tracks along the bank as they
branched off toward the old pits, now half-filled with water by recent
rains. Pausing where the boy had passed when the woman's figure
sprang up before him with its old-witch cry, Douglas looked keenly
all about, wondering if it were possible for any human being to vanish
as the lad related. Several yards from the clump of bushes and coarse
grass at his feet lay the wide pit; between it and the spot where he
stood stretched a smooth bed of clay, unmarked by the impress of any
step, as he first thought. A second and more scrutinizing glance
showed him the print of a human foot on the very edge of the pit.
Stepping lightly forward, he examined it. Not the boy's track, for he
had not passed the bushes, but turned and fled in terror, when the
phantom seemed to vanish. It was a child's footprint, apparently, or
that of a very small woman; probably the latter, for it was a slender,
shapely print, cut deep into the yielding clay, as if by the impetus of a
desperate spring. But whither had she sprung? Not across the pit, for
that was impossible to any but a very active man, or a professional
gymnast of either sex. Douglas took the leap, and barely reached the
other side, though a tall agile man. Nor did he find any trace of the
other leaper, though the grass that grew to the very edge of that side
might have concealed a lighter, surer tread than his own.

With a thrill of suspicion and dread, he looked down into the
turbid water of the pit, asking himself if it were possible that two
women had found their death so near together on that night. The
footprint was not Diana's; hers was larger, and utterly unlike; whose
was it, then? With a sudden impulse he cut a long, forked pole, and
searched the depths of the pit. Nothing was found; again and again
he plunged in the pole and drew it carefully up, after sweeping the
bottom in all directions. A dead branch, a fallen rod, a heavy stone
were all he found.

As he stood pondering over the mysterious mark, having re-
crossed the pit, some sudden peculiarity in it seemed to give it a

familiar aspect. Kneeling down, he examined it minutely, and as he looked, an expression of perplexity came into his face, while he groped for some recollection in the dimness of the past, the gloom of the present.

"Where have I seen a foot like this, so dainty, so slender, yet so strong, for the tread was firm here, the muscles wonderfully elastic to carry this unknown woman over that wide gap? Stay! It was not a foot, but a shoe that makes this mark so familiar. Who wears a shoe with a coquettish heel like this stamped here in the clay? A narrow sole, a fairylike shape, a slight pressure downward at the top, as if the wearer walked well and lightly, yet danced better than she walked? Good heavens! Can it be? That word 'danced' makes it clear to me—but it is impossible—unless—can she have discovered me, followed me, wrought me fresh harm, and again escaped me? I will be satisfied at all hazards, and if I find her, Virginie shall meet a double vengeance for a double wrong."

Up he sprang, as these thoughts swept through his mind, and like someone bent on some all-absorbing purpose, he dashed homeward through bush and brake, park and garden, till, coming to the lawn, he restrained his impetuosity, but held on his way, turning neither to the right nor the left, till he stood in his own room. Without pausing for breath, he snatched the satin slipper from the case, put it in his breast, and hurried back to the pool. Making sure that no one followed him, he cautiously advanced, and bending, laid the slipper in the mold of that mysterious foot. It fitted exactly! Outline, length, width, even the downward pressure at the toe corresponded, and the sole difference was to the depth of heel, as if the walking boot or shoe had been thicker than the slipper.

Bent on assuring himself, Douglas pressed the slipper carefully into the smooth clay beside the other print, and every slight peculiarity was repeated with wonderful accuracy.

"I am satisfied," he muttered, adding, as he carefully effaced both the little tracks, "no one must follow this out but myself. I have sworn to find her and her accomplice, and henceforth it shall be my life business to keep my vow."

A few moments he stood buried in dark thoughts and memories,

then putting up the slipper, he bent his steps toward the home of little
Wat, the farmer's lad. He was watering horses at the spring, his
mother said, and Douglas strolled that way, saying he desired to give
the boy something for the intelligence he brought three days before.
Wat lounged against the wall, while the tired horses slowly drank
their fill, but when he saw the gentleman approaching, he looked
troubled, for his young brain had been sadly perplexed by the late
events.

"I want to ask you a few questions, Wat; answer me truly, and I
will thank you in a way you will like better than words," began
Douglas, as the boy pulled off his hat and stood staring.

"I'm ready; what will I say, sir?" he asked.

"Tell me just what sort of a thing or person the spirit looked like
when you saw it by the pit."

"A woman, sir, all black but her face and arms."

"Did she resemble the person we were searching for?"

"No, sir; leastways, I never saw Miss looking so; of course she
wouldn't when she was alive, you know."

"Did the spirit look like the lady afterward? When we found her,
I mean?"

The boy pondered a minute, seemed perplexed, but answered
slowly, as he grew a little pale, "No, sir, then she looked awful, but
the spirit seemed scared like, and screamed as any woman would if
frightened."

"And she vanished in the pit, you say?"

"She couldn't go nowhere else, sir, 'cause she didn't turn."

"Did you see her go down into the water, Wat?"

"No, sir, I only see her fly up out of the bushes, looking at me
over her shoulder, and giving a great leap, as light and easy as if she
hadn't no body. But it started me, so that I fell over backward, and
when I got up, she was gone."

"I thought so. Now tell me, was the spirit large or small?"

"I didn't mind, but I guess it wasn't very big, or them few bushes
wouldn't have hid it from me."

"Was its hair black or light?"

"Don't know, sir, a hood was all over its head, and I only see the face."

"Did you mind the eyes?"

"They looked big and dark, and scared me horridly."

"You said the face was handsome but white, I think?"

"I didn't say anything about handsome, sir; it was too dark to make out much, but it was white, and when she threw up her arms, they looked like snow. I never see any live lady with such white ones."

"You did not go down to the edge of the pit to leap after her, did you?"

"Lord, no, sir. I just scud the other way, and never looked back till I see the lodge."

"Is there any strange lady down at the inn, or staying anywhere in the village?"

"Not as I know, sir. I'm down there every day, and guess I'd hear of it if there was. Do you want to find anyone, sir?"

"No, I thought your spirit might have been some live woman, whom you frightened as much as she did you. Are you quite sure it was not?"

"I shouldn't be sure, if she hadn't flown away so strange, for no woman could go over the pit, and if she'd fell in, I'd have heard the splash."

"So you would. Well, let the spirit go, and keep away from the pit and the pool, lest you see it again. Here is a golden thank-you, my boy, so good-bye."

"Oh, sir, that's a deal too much! I'm heartily obliged. Be you going to leave these parts, please, sir?"

"Not yet; I've much to do before I go."

Satisfied with his inquiries, Douglas went on, and Wat, pulling on his torn hat as the gentleman disappeared, fell to examining the bit of gold that had been dropped into his brown palm.

"Do you want another, my lad?" said a soft voice behind him, and turning quickly, he saw a man leaning over the wall, just below the place where he had lounged a moment before.

The man was evidently a gypsy; long brown hair hung about a

brown face with black eyes, a crafty mouth, and glittering teeth. His costume was picturesquely ragged and neglected, and in his hand he held a stout staff. Bending farther over, he eyed the boy with a nod, repeating his words in a smooth low tone, as he held up a second half-sovereign between his thumb and finger.

"Yes, I do," answered Wat sturdily, as he sent his horses trotting homeward with a chirrup and a cut of his long whip.

"Tell me what the gentleman said, and you shall have it," whispered the gypsy.

"You might have heard for yourself, if you'd been where you are a little sooner," returned Wat, edging toward the road—for there was something about the swarthy-faced fellow that he did not like, in spite of his golden offer.

"I was there," said the man with a laugh, "but you spoke so low I couldn't catch it all."

"What do you want to know for?" demanded Wat.

"Why, perhaps I know something about that spirit woman he seemed to be asking about, and if I do, he'd be glad to hear it, wouldn't he? Now I don't want to go and tell him myself, for fear of getting into trouble, but I might tell you, and you could do it. Only I must know what he said, first; perhaps he has found out for himself what I could tell him."

"What are you going to give me that for, then?" asked Wat, much reassured.

"Because you are a clever little chap, and were good to some of my people here once upon a time. I'm rich, though I don't look it, and I'd like to pay for the news you give me. Out with it, and then here's another yellow boy for you."

Wat was entirely conquered by the grateful allusion to a friendly act of his own on the previous day, and willingly related his conversation with Douglas, explaining as he went on. The gypsy questioned and cross-questioned, and finished the interview by saying, with a warning glance, "He's right; you'd better not tell anyone you saw the spirit—it's a bad sign, and if it's known, you'll find it hard to get on in the world. Now here's your money; catch it, and then I'll tell you my story."

The coin came ringing through the air, and fell into the road not far from Wat's feet. He ran to pick it up, and when he turned to thank the man, he was gone as silently and suddenly as he had come. The lad stared in amaze, listened, searched, but no gypsy was heard or seen, and poor bewildered Wat scampered home as fast as his legs could carry him, believing that he was bewitched.

That afternoon Douglas wrote a long letter, directed it to "M. Antoine Duprès, Rue Saint Honoré, Paris," and was about to seal it when a servant came to tell him that Mrs. Vane desired her adieus, as she was leaving for town by the next train. Anxious to atone for his seeming negligence, not having seen her that day, and therefore being in ignorance of her intended departure, he hastily dropped a splash of wax on his important letter, and leaving it upon his table hurried down to see her off. She was already in the hall, having bidden Lady Lennox farewell in her boudoir—for her ladyship was too poorly to come down. Harry was giving directions about the baggage, and Gabrielle chattering her adieus in the housekeeper's room.

"My dear Mrs. Vane, forgive my selfish sorrow; when you are settled in town let me come to thank you for the great kindness you have shown me through these dark days."

Douglas spoke warmly; he pressed the hand she gave him in both his own, and gratitude flushed his pale face with a glow that restored all its lost comeliness.

Mrs. Vane dropped her beautiful eyes, and answered, with a slight quiver of the lips that tried to smile, "I have suffered for you, if not with you, and I need no thanks for the sympathy that was involuntary. Here is my address; come to me when you will, and be assured that you will always find a welcome."

He led her to the carriage, assiduously arranging all things for her comfort, and when she waved a last adieu, he seized the little hand, regardless of Harry, who accompanied her, and kissed it warmly as he said, "I shall not forget, and shall see you soon."

The carriage rolled away, and Douglas watched it, saying to the groom, who was just turning stableward, "Does not Jitomar go with his mistress?"

"No, sir; he's to take some plants my lady gave Mrs. Vane, so he's to go in a later train—and good riddance to the sly devil, I say," added the man, under his breath, as he walked off.

Had he turned his head a moment afterward, he would have been amazed at the strange behavior of the gentleman he had left behind him. Happening to glance downward, Douglas gave a start, stooped suddenly, examining something on the ground, and as he rose, struck his hands together like one in great perplexity or exultation, while his face assumed a singular expression of mingled wonder, pain, and triumph. Well it might, for there, clearly defined in the moist earth, was an exact counterpart of the footprint by the pool.

CHAPTER VIII. ON THE TRAIL

The packet from Havre was just in. It had been a stormy trip, and all the passengers hurried ashore, as if glad to touch English soil. Two gentlemen lingered a moment, before they separated to different quarters of the city. One was a stout, gray-haired Frenchman, perfectly dressed, blandly courteous, and vivaciously grateful, as he held the other's hand, and poured out a stream of compliments, invitations, and thanks. The younger man was evidently a Spaniard, slight, dark, and dignified, with melancholy eyes, a bronzed, bearded face, and a mien as cool and composed as if he had just emerged from some elegant retreat, instead of the cabin of an overcrowded packet, whence he had been tossing about all day.

"It is a thousand pities we do not go on together; but remember I am under many obligations to Señor Arguelles, and I implore that I may be allowed to return them during my stay. I believe you have my card; now *au revoir,* and my respectful compliments to Madame your friend."

"Adieu, Monsieur Dupont—we shall meet again."

The Frenchman waved his hand, the Spaniard raised his hat, and they separated.

Antoine Duprès, for it was he, drove at once to a certain hotel, asked for M. Douglas, sent up his name, and was at once heartily welcomed by his friend, with whom he sat in deep consultation till very late.

Arguelles was set down at the door of a lodging house in a quiet street, and admitting himself by means of a latchkey, he went noiselessly upstairs and looked about him. The scene was certainly a charming one, though somewhat peculiar. A bright fire filled the room with its ruddy light; several lamps added their milder shine; and the chamber was a flush of color, for carpet, chairs, and tables were strewn with brilliant costumes. Wreaths of artificial flowers strewed the floor; mock jewels glittered here and there; a lyre, a silver bow and arrow, a slender wand of many colors, a pair of ebony castanets; a gaily decorated tambourine lay on the couch; little hats, caps, bodices, jackets, skirts, boots, slippers, and clouds of rosy, blue, white, and green tulle were heaped, hung, and scattered everywhere. In the midst of this gay confusion stood a figure in perfect keeping with it. A slight blooming girl of eighteen she looked, evidently an actress—for though busily sorting the contents of two chests that stood before her, she was *en costume,* as if she had been reviewing her wardrobe, and had forgotten to take off the various parts of different suits which she had tried on. A jaunty hat of black velvet, turned up with a white plume, was stuck askew on her blond head; scarlet boots with brass heels adorned her feet; a short white satin skirt was oddly contrasted with a blue-and-silver hussar jacket; and a flame-colored silk domino completed her piquant array.

A smile of tenderest joy and admiration lighted up the man's dark features, as he leaned in, watching the pretty creature purse up her lips and bend her brows, in deep consideration, over a faded pink-and-black Spanish dress, just unfolded.

"Madame, it is I."

He closed the door behind him, as he spoke, and advanced with open arms.

The girl dropped the garment she held, turned sharply, and surveyed the newcomer with little surprise but much amazement, for suddenly clapping her hands, she broke into a peal of laughter, exclaiming, as she examined him, "My faith! You are superb. I admire you thus; the melancholy is becoming, the beard ravishing, and the *tout ensemble* beyond my hopes. I salute you, Señor Arguelles."

"Come, then, and embrace me. So long away, and no tenderer welcome than this, my heart?"

She shrugged her white shoulders, and submitted to be drawn close, kissed, and caressed with ardor, by her husband or lover, asking a multitude of questions the while, and smoothing the petals of a crumpled camellia, quite unmoved by the tender names showered upon her, the almost fierce affection that glowed in her companion's face, and lavished itself in demonstrations of delight at regaining her.

"But tell me, darling, why do I find you at such work? Is it wise or needful?"

"It is pleasant, and I please myself now. I have almost lived here since you have been gone. At my aunt's in the country, they say, at the other place. The rooms there were dull; no one came, and at last I ran away. Once here, the old mania returned; I was mad for the gay life I love, and while I waited, I played at carnival."

"Were you anxious for my return? Did you miss me, *carina?*"

"That I did, for I needed you, my Juan," she answered, with a laugh. "Do you know we must have money? I am deciding which of my properties I will sell, though it breaks my heart to part with them. Mother Ursule will dispose of them, and as I shall never want them again, they must go."

"Why will you never need them again? There may be no course but that in the end."

"My husband will never let me dance, except for my own plea- sure," she answered, dropping a half-humble, half-mocking curtsy, and glancing at him with a searching look.

Juan eyed her gloomily, as she waltzed away clinking her brass heels together, and humming a gay measure in time to her graceful steps. He shook his head, threw himself wearily into a chair, and leaned his forehead upon his hand. The girl watched him over her shoulder, paused, shook off her jaunty hat, dropped the red domino, and stealing toward him, perched herself upon his knee, peering under his hand with a captivating air of penitence, as she laid her arm about his neck and whispered in his ear, "I meant you, *mon ami,* and

I will keep my promise by-and-by when all is as we would have it. Believe me, and be gay again, because I do not love you when you are grim and grave, like an Englishman."

"Do you ever love me, my—"

She stopped his mouth with a kiss, and answered, as she smoothed the crisp black curls off his forehead, "You shall see how well I love you, by-and-by."

"Ah, it is always 'by-and-by,' never now. I have a feeling that I never shall possess you, even if my long service ends this year. You are so cold, so treacherous, I have no faith in you, though I adore you, and shall until I die."

"Have I ever broken the promise made so long ago?"

"You dare not; you know the penalty of treason is death."

"Death for you, not for me. I am wiser now; I do not fear you, but I need you, and at last I think—I love you."

As she added the last words, the black frown that had darkened the man's face lifted suddenly, and the expression of intense devotion returned to make it beautiful. He turned that other face upward, scanned it with those magnificent eyes of his, now soft and tender, and answered with a sigh, "It would be death to me to find that after all I have suffered, done, and desired for you, there was no reward but falsehood and base ingratitude. It must not be so; and in that thought I will find patience to work on for one whom I try to love for your sake."

A momentary expression of infinite love and longing touched the girl's face, and filled her eyes with tenderness. But it passed, and settling herself more comfortably, she asked, "How have you prospered since you wrote? Well, I know, else I should have read it at the first glance."

"Beyond my hopes. We crossed together; we are friends already, and shall meet as such. It was an inspiration of yours, and has worked like a charm. Monsieur from the country has not yet appeared, has he?"

"He called when I was out. I did not regret it, for I feel safer when you are by, and it is as well to whet his appetite by absence."

"How is this to end? As we last planned?"

"Yes; but not yet. We must be sure, and that we only can be through himself. Leave it to me. I know him well, and he is willing to be led, I fancy. Now I shall feed you, for it occurs to me that you are fasting. See, I am ready for you."

She left him and ran to and fro, preparing a dainty little supper, but on her lips still lay a smile of conscious power, and in the eyes that followed her still lurked a glance of disquiet and distrust.

Mrs. Vane was driving in the park—not in her own carriage, for she kept none—but having won the hearts of several amiable dowagers, their equipages were always at her command. In one of the most elegant of these she was reclining, apparently unconscious of the many glances of curiosity and admiration fixed upon the lovely face enshrined in the little black tulle bonnet, with its frill of transparent lace to heighten her blond beauty.

Two gentlemen were entering the great gate as she passed by for another turn; one of them pronounced her name, and sprang forward. She recognized the voice, ordered the carriage to stop, and when Douglas came up, held out her hand to him, with a smile of welcome. He touched it, expressed his pleasure of meeting her, and added, seeing her glance at his companion, "Permit me to present my friend, M. Dupont, just from Paris, and happy in so soon meeting a country-woman."

Duprès executed a superb bow, and made his compliments in his mother tongue.

Mrs. Vane listened with an air of pretty perplexity, and answered, in English, while she gave him her most beaming look, "Monsieur must pardon me that I have forgotten my native language so sadly that I dare not venture to use it in his presence. My youth was spent in Spain, and since then England or India has been my home; but to this dear country I must cordially welcome any friend of M. Douglas."

As she turned to Earl, and listened to his tidings of Lady Lennox, Duprès fixed a searching glance upon her. His keen eyes ran over her from head to foot, and nothing seemed to escape his scrutiny. Her figure was concealed by a great mantle of black velvet; her hair waved plainly away under her bonnet; the heavy folds of her dress flowed over her feet; and her delicately gloved hands lay half buried in the deep lace of her handkerchief. She was very pale, her eyes were languid, her lips sad even in smiling, and her voice had lost its lightsome ring. She looked older, graver, more pensive and dignified than when Douglas last saw her.

"You have been ill, I fear?" he said, regarding her with visible solicitude, while his friend looked down, yet marked every word she uttered.

"Yes, quite ill; I have been through so much in the last month that I can hardly help betraying it in my countenance. A heavy cold, with fever, has kept me a prisoner till these few days past, when I have driven out, being still too feeble to walk."

Earl was about to express his sorrow when Duprès cried, "Behold! It is he—the friend who so assuaged the tortures of that tempestuous passage. Let me reward him by a word from M. Douglas, and a smile from Madame. Is it permitted?"

Scarcely waiting for an assent, the vivacious gentleman darted forward and arrested the progress of a gentleman who was bending at the moment to adjust his stirrup. A few hasty words and emphatic gestures prepared the stranger for the interview, and with the courtesy of a Spaniard, he dismounted and advanced bareheaded, to be presented to Madame. It was Arguelles; and even Douglas was struck with his peculiar beauty, and the native pride that was but half veiled by the Southern softness of his manners. He spoke English well, but when Mrs. Vane addressed him in Spanish, he answered with a flash of pleasure that proved how grateful to him was the sound of his own melodious tongue.

Too well-bred to continue the conversation in a language which excluded the others, Mrs. Vane soon broke up the party by inviting Douglas and his friend to call upon her that evening, adding, with a glance toward the Spaniard, "It will gratify me to extend the hospitalities of an English home to Señor Arguelles, if he is a stranger here, and to enjoy again the familiar sound of the language which is dearer to me than my own."

Three hats were lifted, and three grateful gentlemen expressed their thanks with smiles of satisfaction; then the carriage rolled on, the *señor* galloped off, looking very like some knightly figure from a romance, and Douglas turned to his companion with an eager "Tell me, is it she?"

"No; Virginie would be but one-and-twenty, and this woman must be thirty if she is a day, ungallant that I am to say so of the charming creature."

"You have not seen her to advantage, Antoine. Wait till you meet her again tonight in full toilet, and then pronounce. She has been ill; even I perceive the great change this short time has wrought, for we parted only ten days ago," said Douglas, disappointed, yet not convinced.

"It is well; we will go; I will study her, and if it be that lovely devil, we will cast her out, and so avenge the past."

At nine o'clock, a cab left Douglas at the door of a handsome house in a West End square. A servant in livery admitted him, and passing up one flight of stairs, richly carpeted, softly lighted, and decorated with flowers, he entered a wide doorway, hung with curtains of blue damask, and found himself in a charming room. Directly opposite hung a portrait of Colonel Vane, a handsome, soldierly man, with such a smile upon his painted lips that his friend involuntarily smiled in answer and advanced as if to greet him.

"Would that he were here to welcome you."

The voice was at his side, and there stood Mrs. Vane. But not the woman whom he met in Lady Lennox's drawing room; that was a young and blooming creature, festally arrayed—this a pale, sad-eyed widow, in her weeds. Never, surely, had weeds been more becoming, for the black dress, in spite of its nunlike simplicity, had an air of elegance that many a balldress lacks, and the widow's cap was a mere froth of tulle, encircling the fair face, and concealing all the hair but two plain bands upon the forehead. Not an ornament was visible but a tiny pearl brooch which Douglas himself had given his friend long ago, and a wedding ring upon the hand that once had worn the opal also. She, too, was looking upward toward the picture, and for an instant a curious pause fell between them.

The apartment was an entire contrast to the gay and brilliant drawing rooms he had been accustomed to see. Softly lighted by the pale flame of antique lamps, the eye was relieved from the glare of gas, while the graceful blending of blue and silver, in furniture, hangings, and decorations, pleased one as a change from the more garish colors so much in vogue. A few rare pictures leaned from the walls; several statues stood cool and still in remote recesses; from the curtained entrance of another door was blown the odorous breath of flowers; and the rustle of leaves, the drip of falling water, betrayed the existence of a conservatory close at hand.

"No wonder you were glad to leave the country, for a home like this," said Douglas, as she paused.

"Yes, it is pleasant to be here; but I should tell you that it is not my own. My kind friend Lady Leigh is in Rome for the winter, and knowing that I was a homeless little creature, she begged me to stay here, and keep both servants and house in order till she came again. I was very grateful, for I dread the loneliness of lodgings, and having arranged matters to suit my taste, I shall nestle here till spring tempts me to the hills again."

She spoke quite simply, and seemed as thankful for kindness as a solitary child. Despite his suspicions, and all the causes for distrust— nay, even hatred, if his belief was true—Douglas could not resist the wish that she might be proved innocent, and somewhere find the safe home her youth and beauty needed. So potent was the fascination of her presence that when with her his doubts seemed unfounded, and so great was the confusion into which his mind was thrown by these conflicting impressions that his native composure quite deserted him at times.

It did so then, for, leaning nearer, as they sat together on the couch, he asked almost abruptly, "Why do I find you so changed, in all respects, that I scarcely recognize my friend just now?"

"You mean this?" and she touched her dress. "As you have honored me with the name of friend, I will speak frankly, and explain my seeming caprice. At the desire of Lady Lennox, I laid aside my weeds, and found that I could be a gay young girl again. But with that discovery came another, which made me regret the change, and resolve to return to my sad garb."

"You mean that you found that the change made you too beautiful for George's peace? Poor lad—I knew his secret, and now I understand your sacrifice," Earl said, as she paused, too delicate to betray her young lover, who had asked and been denied.

She colored beautifully, and sat silent; but Douglas was possessed by an irresistible desire to probe her heart as deeply as he dared, and quite unconscious that interest lent his voice and manner an unusual warmth, he asked, thinking only of poor George, "Was it not possible to spare both yourself and him? You see I use a friend's privilege to the utmost."

She still looked down, and the color deepened visibly in her smooth cheek as she replied, "It was not possible, nor will it ever be, for him."

"You have not vowed yourself to an eternal widowhood, I trust?"

She looked up suddenly, as if to rebuke the persistent questioner, but something in his eager face changed her own expression of displeasure into one of half-concealed confusion.

"No, it is so sweet to be beloved that I have not the courage to relinquish the hope of retasting the happiness so quickly snatched from me before."

Douglas rose suddenly, and paced down the room, as if attracted by a balmy gust that just then came floating in. But in truth he fled from the siren by his side, for despite the bitter past, the late loss, the present distrust, something softer than pity, warmer than regard, seemed creeping into his heart, and the sight of the beautiful blushing face made his own cheek burn with a glow such as his love for Diana had never kindled. Indignant at his own weakness, he paused halfway down the long room, wheeled about, and came back, saying, with his accustomed tone of command disguised by a touch of pity, "Come and do the honors of your little paradise. I am restless tonight, and the splash of that fountain has a soothing sound that tempts me to draw nearer."

She went with him, and standing by the fountain's brim talked tranquilly of many things, till the sound of voices caused them to look toward the drawing room. Two gentlemen were evidently coming to join them, and Earl said with a smile, "You have not asked why I came alone; yet your invitation included Arguelles and Dupont."

Again the blush rose to her cheek, and she answered hastily, as she advanced to meet her guests, "I forgot them, now I must atone for my rudeness."

Down the green vista came the gentlemen—the stout French-man tripping on before, the dark Spaniard walking behind, with a dignity of bearing that made his companion's gait more ludicrous by comparison. Compliments were exchanged, and then, as the guests expressed a desire to linger in the charming spot, Mrs. Vane led them on, doing the honors with her accustomed grace.

Busied in translating the names of remarkable plants into Spanish for Arguelles, they were somewhat in advance of the other pair; and after a sharp glance or two at Douglas, Duprès paused behind a young orange tree, saying, in a low whisper, "You are going fast, Earl. Finish this business soon, or it will be too late for anything but flight."

"No fear; but what can *I* do? I protest I never was so bewildered in my life. Help me, for heaven's sake, and do it at once!" replied Douglas, with a troubled and excited air.

"Chut! You English have no idea of *finesse;* you bungle sadly. See, now, how smoothly I will discover all I wish to know." Then aloud, as he moved on, "I assure you, *mon ami,* it is an orange, not a lemon tree. Madame shall decide the point, and award me yonder fine flower if I am right."

"Monsieur is correct, and here is the prize."

As she spoke, Mrs. Vane lifted her hand to break the flower which grew just above her. As she stretched her arm upward, her sleeve slipped back, and on her white wrist shone the wide bracelet once attached to the opal ring. As if annoyed by its exposure, she shook down her sleeve with a quick gesture, and before either gentle-man could assist her, she stepped on a low seat, gathered the azalea, and turned to descend. Her motion was sudden, the seat frail; it broke as she turned, and she would have fallen, had not Arguelles sprung forward and caught her hands. She recovered herself instantly, and apologizing for her awkwardness, presented the flower with a playful speech. To Earl's great surprise, Duprès received it without his usual flow of compliments, and bowing, silently settled it in his buttonhole, with such a curious expression that his friend fancied he had made some unexpected discovery. He had—but not what Douglas imagined, as he lifted his brows inquiringly when Mrs. Vane and her escort walked on.

"Hush!" breathed Duprès in answer. "Ask her where Jitomar is, in some careless way."

"Why?" asked Earl, recollecting the man for the first time.

But his question received no reply, and the entrance of a servant with refreshments offered the desired pretext for the inquiry.

"Where is your handsome Jitomar? His Oriental face and costume would give the finishing touch to this Eastern garden of palms and lotus flowers," said Douglas, as he offered his hostess a glass of wine, when they paused at a rustic table by the fountain.

"Poor Jitomar—I have lost him!" she replied.

"Dead?" exclaimed Earl.

"Oh, no; and I should have said happy Jitomar, for he is on his way home to his own palms and lotus flowers. He dreaded another winter here so much that when a good opportunity offered for his return, I let him go, and have missed him sadly ever since—for he was a faithful servant to me."

"Let us drink the health of the good and faithful servant, and wish him a prosperous voyage to the torrid land where he belongs," cried Duprès, as he touched his glass to that of Arguelles, who looked somewhat bewildered both by the odd name and the new ceremony.

By some mishap, as Duprès turned to replace his glass upon the table, it slipped from his hand and fell into the fountain, with a splash that caused a little wave to break over the basin's edge, and wet Mrs. Vane's foot with an unexpected bath.

"Great heavens—what carelessness! A thousand pardons! Madame, permit me to repair the damage, although it is too great an honor for me, *maladroit* that I am," exclaimed the Frenchman, with a gesture of despair.

Mrs. Vane shook her dress and assured him that no harm was done; but nothing could prevent the distressed gentleman from going down upon his knees, and with his perfumed handkerchief removing several drops of water from the foot of his hostess—during which process he discovered that, being still an invalid, she wore quilted black silk boots, with down about the tops; also that though her foot was a very pretty one, it was by no means as small as that of Virginie Varens.

When this small stir was over, Mrs. Vane led the way back to the saloon, and here Douglas was more than ever mystified by Duprès's behavior. Entirely ignoring Madame's presence, he devoted himself to Arguelles, besetting him with questions regarding Spain, his own family, pursuits, and tastes; on all of which points the Spaniard satisfied him, and accepted his various invitations for the coming days, looking much at their fair hostess the while, who was much engrossed with Douglas, and seemed quite content.

Arguelles was the first to leave, and his departure broke up the party. As Earl and Duprès drove off together, the former exclaimed, in a fever of curiosity, "Are you satisfied?"

"Entirely."

"She is not Virginie, then?"

"On the contrary, she *is* Virginie, I suspect."

"You suspect? I thought you were entirely satisfied."

"On another point, I am. She baffles me somewhat, I confess, with her woman's art in dress. But I shall discover her yet, if you let me conduct the affair in my own way. I adore mystery; to fathom a secret, trace a lie, discover a disguise, is my delight. I should make a superb detective. Apropos to that, promise me that you will not call in the help of your blundering constabulary, police, or whatever you name them, until I give the word. They will destroy the éclat of the *dénouement,* and annoy me by their stupidity."

"I leave all to you, and regret that the absence of this Jitomar should complicate the affair. What deviltry is he engaged in now, do you think? Not traveling to India, of course, though she told it very charmingly."

His companion whispered three words in his ear.

Earl fell back and stared at him, exclaiming presently, "It is impossible!"

"Nothing is impossible to me," returned the other, with an air of conviction. "That point is clear to my mind; one other remains, and being more difficult, I must consider it. But have no fear; this brain of mine is fertile in inventions, and by morning will have been inspired with a design which will enchant you by its daring, its acuteness, its romance."

CHAPTER IX. MIDNIGHT

For a week the three gentlemen haunted the house of the widow, and were much together elsewhere. Duprès was still enthusiastic in praise of his new-made friend, but Douglas was far less cordial, and merely courteous when they met. To outside observers this seemed but natural, for the world knew nothing of his relations to Diana, nor the sad secret that existed between himself and Mrs. Vane. And when it was apparent that the Spaniard was desperately in love with that lady, Douglas could not but look coldly upon him as a rival, for according to rumor the latter gentleman was also paying court to the bewitching widow. It was soon evident which was the favored lover, for despite the dark glances and jealous surveillance of Arguelles, Mrs. Vane betrayed, by unmistakable signs, that Douglas possessed a power over her which no other man had ever attained. It was impossible to conceal it, for when the great passion for the first time possessed her heart, all her art was powerless against this touch of nature, and no timid girl could have been more harassed by the alternations of hope and fear, and the effort to hide her passion.

Going to their usual rendezvous somewhat earlier than usual one evening, Duprès stopped a moment in an anteroom to exchange a word with Gabrielle, the coquettish maid, who was apt to be in the way when the Frenchman appeared. Douglas went on to the drawing room, expecting to find Mrs. Vane alone. The apartment was empty, but the murmur of voices was audible in the conservatory, and going to the curtained arch, he was about to lift the drapery that had fallen from its fastening, when through a little crevice in the middle he saw two figures that arrested him, and, in spite of certain honorable scruples, held him motionless where he stood.

Mrs. Vane and the Spaniard were beside the fountain; both

looked excited. Arguelles talked vehemently; she listened with a hard, scornful expression, and made brief answers that seemed to chafe and goad him bitterly. Both spoke Spanish, and even if they had not, so low and rapid were their tones that nothing was audible but the varied murmur rising or falling as the voices alternated. From his gestures, the gentleman seemed by turns to reproach, entreat, command; the lady to recriminate, refuse, and defy. Once she evidently announced some determination that filled her companion with despair; then she laughed, and in a paroxysm of speechless wrath he broke from her, hurrying to the farthest limits of the room, as if unconscious whither he went, and marking with scattered leaves and flowers the passage of his reckless steps.

As he turned from her, Mrs. Vane dipped her hands in the basin and laid them on her forehead, as if to cool some fever of the brain, while such a weight of utter weariness came over her that in an instant ten years seemed to be added to her age. Her eyes roved restlessly to and fro, as if longing to discover some method of escape from the danger or the doubt that oppressed her.

A book from which Douglas had read to her lay on the rustic table at her side, and as her eye fell on it, all her face changed beautifully, hope, bloom, and youth returned, as she touched the volume with a lingering touch, and smiled a smile in which love and exultation blended. A rapid step announced the Spaniard's return; she caught her hand away, mused a moment, and when he came back to her, she spoke in a softer tone, while her eyes betrayed that now she pleaded for some boon, and did not plead in vain. Seizing both her hands in a grasp more firm than tender, Arguelles seemed to extort some promise from her with sternest aspect. She gave it reluctantly; he looked but half satisfied, even though she drew his tall head down and sealed her promise with a kiss; and when she bade him go, he left her with a gloomy air, and some dark purpose stamped upon his face.

So rapidly had this scene passed, so suddenly was it ended, that Douglas had barely time to draw a few paces back before the curtain was pushed aside and Arguelles stood in the arch. Unused to the dishonorable practices to which he had lent himself for the completion of a just work, Earl's face betrayed him.

The Spaniard saw that the late interview had not been without a witness, and forgetting that they had spoken in an unknown tongue, for a moment he looked perfectly livid with fear and fury. Some recollection suddenly seemed to reassure him, but the covert purpose just formed appeared to culminate in action, for, with ungovernable hatred flaming up in his eyes, he said, in a suppressed voice that scarcely parted his white lips, "Eavesdropper and spy! I spit upon you!" And advancing one step struck Douglas full in the face.

It had nearly been his last act, for, burning with scorn and detestation, Earl took him by the throat, and was about to execute swift retribution for both the old wrong and the new when Duprès came between them, whispering, as he wrenched Earl's arm away, "Hold! Remember where you are. Come away, señor, I am your friend in this affair. It shall be arranged. Douglas, remain here, I entreat you."

As he spoke, Duprès gave Earl a warning glance, and drew Arguelles swiftly from the house. Controlling a desperate desire to follow, Douglas remembered his promise to let his friend conduct the affair in his own way, and by a strong effort composed himself, though his cheek still tingled with the blow, and his blood burned within him. The whole encounter had passed noiselessly, and when after a brief pause Douglas entered the conservatory, Mrs. Vane still lingered by the fountain, unconscious of the scene which had just transpired. She turned to greet the newcomer with extended hand, and it was with difficulty that he restrained the rash impulse to strike it from him. The very effort to control this desire made the pressure of his own hand almost painful as he took that other, and the strong grasp sent a thrill of joy to Mrs. Vane's heart, as she smiled and glowed under his glance like a flower at the coming of the sun. The inward excitement, which it was impossible to wholly subdue, manifested itself in Earl's countenance and manner more plainly than he knew, and would have excited some of ill in his companion's mind had not love blinded her, and left none but prophecies of good. A little tremble of delight agitated her, and the eyes that once were so coldly bright and penetrating now were seldom lifted to the face that she had studied so carefully, not long ago. After the first greetings, she waited for him to speak, for words would not come at her will when with him; but he stood thoughtfully, dipping his hand into the fountain as she had done, and laying the wet palm against his cheek, lest its indignant color should betray the insult he had just received.

"Did you meet Señor Arguelles as you came in?" she asked presently, as the pause was unbroken.

"He passed me, and went out."

"You do not fancy him, I suspect."

"I confess it, Mrs. Vane."

"And why?"

"Need I tell *you?*"

The words escaped him involuntarily, and had she seen his face just then, her own would have blanched with fear. But she was looking down, and as he spoke the traitorous color rose to her forehead, though she ignored the betrayal by saying, with an accent of indifference, "He will not annoy you long. Tomorrow he fulfills some engagement with a friend in the country, and in the evening will take leave of me."

"He is about to return to Spain, then?"

"I believe so. I did not question him."

"You will not bid him adieu without regret?"

"With the greatest satisfaction, I assure you, for underneath that Spanish dignity of manner lurks fire, and I have no desire to be consumed." And the sigh of relief that accompanied her words was the most sincere expression of feeling that had escaped her for weeks.

Anxious to test his power to the utmost, Douglas pursued the subject, though it was evidently distasteful to her. Assuming an air of loverlike anxiety, he half timidly, half eagerly inquired, "Then when he comes again to say farewell, you will not consent to go with him to occupy the 'castle in Spain' which he has built up for himself during this short week?"

He thought to see some demonstration of pleasure at the jealous fear his words implied, but her color faded suddenly, and she shivered as if a chilly gust had blown over her, while she answered briefly, with a little gesture of the hand as she set the topic decidedly aside, "No, he will go alone."

There was a momentary pause, and in it something like pity

knocked at the door of Earl's heart, for with all his faults he was a generous man, and as he saw this woman sitting there, so unconscious of impending danger, so changed and beautiful by one true sentiment, his purpose wavered, a warning word rose to his lips, and with an impetuous gesture he took her hand, and turned away with an abrupt "Pardon me—it is too soon—I will explain hereafter."

The entrance of a servant with coffee seemed to rouse him into sudden spirits and activity, for begging Mrs. Vane to sit and rest, he served her with assiduous care.

"Here is your own cup of violet and gold; you see I know your fancy even in trifles. Is it right? I took such pains to have it as you like it," he said, as he presented the cup with an air of tender solicitude.

"It does not matter, but one thing you have forgotten, I take no sugar," she answered, smiling as she tasted.

"I knew it, yet the line 'Sweets to the sweet' was running in my head, and so I unconsciously spoiled your draft. Let me retrieve the error?"

"By no means. I drink to you." And lifting the tiny cup to her lips, she emptied it with a look which proved that his words had already retrieved the error.

He received the cup with a peculiar smile, looked at his watch, and exclaimed, "It is late, and I should go, yet—"

"No, not yet; stay and finish the lines you began yesterday. I find less beauty in them when I read them to myself," she answered, detaining him.

Glad of an excuse to prolong his stay, Earl brought the book, and sitting near her, lent to the poem the sonorous music of his voice.

The last words came all too soon, and when Douglas rose, Mrs. Vane bade him good night with a dreamy softness in her eyes which caused a gleam of satisfaction to kindle in his own. As he passed through the anteroom, Gabrielle met him with a look of anxious though mute inquiry in her face. He answered it with a significant nod, a warning gesture, and she let him out, wearing an aspect of the deepest mystery.

Douglas hurried to his rooms, and there found Duprès with

Major Mansfield, who had been put in possession of the secret, and the part he was expected to play in its unraveling.

"What in heaven's name did you mean by taking the wrong side of the quarrel, and forcing me to submit quietly to such an indignity?" demanded Earl, giving vent to the impatience which had only been curbed till now, that he might perform the portion of the plot allotted to him.

"Tell me first, have you succeeded?" said Duprès.

"I have."

"You are sure?"

"Beyond a doubt."

"It is well; I applaud your dexterity. Behold the major, he knows all, he is perfect in his role. Now hear yours. You will immediately write a challenge."

"It is impossible! Antoine, you are a daft to ask me to meet that man."

"Bah! I ask you to meet, but not to honor him by blowing his brains out. He is a dead shot, and thirsts for your blood, but look you, he will be disappointed. We might arrest him this instant, but he will confess nothing, and that clever creature will escape us. No, my little arrangement suits me better."

"Time flies, Duprès, and so perhaps may this crafty hind that you are about to snare," said the major, whose slow British wits were somewhat confused by the Frenchman's *finesse*.

"It is true; see then, my Earl. In order that our other little affair may come smoothly off without interference from our friend, I propose to return to the *señor*, whom I have lately left writing letters, and amuse myself by keeping him at home to receive your challenge, which the major will bring about twelve. Then we shall arrange the affair to take place at sunrise, in some secluded spot out of town. You will be back here by that time, you will agree to our plans, and present yourself at the appointed time, when the grand *dénouement* will take place with much éclat."

"Am I not to know more?" asked Douglas.

"It would be well to leave all to me, for you will act your part better if you do not know the exact program, because you do not perform so well with Monsieur as with Madame. But if you must know, the major will tell you, while you wait for Hyde and the hour. I have seen him, he has no scruples; I have ensured his safety, and he will not fail us. Now the charming *billet* to the *señor,* and I go to my post."

Douglas wrote the challenge; Duprès departed in buoyant spirits; and while Earl waited for the stranger, Hyde, the major enlightened him upon the grand finale.

The city clocks were striking twelve as two men, masked and cloaked, passed up the steps of Mrs. Vane's house and entered noiselessly. No light beamed in the hall, but scarcely had they closed the door behind them when a glimmer shone from above, and at the stairhead appeared a woman beckoning. Up they stole, as if shod with velvet, and the woman flitted like a shadow before them, till they reached a door to the second story. Opening this, she motioned them to enter, and as they passed in, she glided up another flight, as if to stand guard over her sleeping fellow servants.

One of the men was tall and evidently young, the other a bent and withered little man, whose hands trembled slightly as he adjusted his mask, and peered about him. It was a large still room, lighted by a night lamp, burning behind its shade, richly furnished, and decorated with warm hues, that produced the effect of mingled snow and fire. A luxurious nest it seemed, and a fit inmate of it looked the beautiful woman asleep in the shadow of the crimson-curtained bed. One white arm pillowed her head; from the little cap that should have confined it flowed a mass of golden hair over neck and shoulders; the long lashes lay dark against her cheek; the breath slept upon her lips; and perfect unconsciousness lent its reposeful charm to both face and figure.

Noiselessly advancing, the taller man looked and listened for a moment, as if to assure himself that this deep slumber was not feigned; then he beckoned the other to bring the lamp. It flickered as the old man took it up, but he trimmed the wick, removed the shade, and a clear light shone across the room. Joining his companion, he too looked at the sleeping beauty, shook his gray head, and seemed to deplore some fact that marred the pretty picture in his sight.

"Is there no danger of her waking, sir?" he whispered, as the light fell on her face.

"It is impossible for an hour yet. The bracelet is on that wrist; we must move her, or you cannot reach it," returned the other; and with a gentle touch drew the left arm from underneath her head.

She sighed in her sleep, knit her brows, as if a dream disturbed her, and turning on her pillow, all the bright hair fell about her face, but could not hide the glitter of the chain about her neck. Drawing it forth, the taller man started, uttered an exclamation, dragged from his own bosom a duplicate of the miniature hanging from that chain, and compared the two with trembling intentness. Very like they were, those two young faces, handsome, frank and full of boyish health, courage, and blithesomeness. One might have been taken a year after the other, for the brow was bolder, the mouth graver, the eye more steadfast, but the same charm of expression appeared in both, making the ivory oval more attractive even to a stranger's eye than the costly setting, or the initial letters *A. D.* done in pearls upon the back. A small silver key hung on the chain the woman wore, and as if glad to tear his thoughts from some bitter reminiscence, the man detached this key, and glanced about the room, as if to discover what lock it would be.

His action seemed to remind the other of his own task, for setting down the lamp on the little table where lay a prayer book, a bell, and a rosary, he produced a case of delicate instruments and a bunch of tiny keys, and bending over the bracelet, examined the golden padlock that fastened it. While he carefully tried key after key upon that miniature lock, the chief of this mysterious inspection went to and fro with the silver key, attempting larger locks. Nowhere did it fit, till in passing the toilet table his foot brushed its draperies aside, disclosing a quaint foreign-looking casket of ebony and silver. Quick as thought it was drawn out and opened, for here the key did its work. In the upper tray lay the opal ring in its curiously thick setting, beside it a seal, rudely made from an impression in wax of his own iron ring, and a paper bearing its stamp. The marriage record was in hand, and he longed to keep or destroy it, but restrained the impulse; and lifting the tray, found below two or three relics of his friend Vane, and some childish toys, soiled and broken, but precious still.

"A child! Good God! What have I done?" he said to himself, as the lid fell from his hand.

"Hush, come and look, it is off," whispered the old man, and hastily restoring all things to their former order, the other relocked and replaced the casket, and obeyed the call.

For a moment a mysterious and striking picture might have been seen in that quiet room. Under the crimson canopy lay the fair figure of the sleeping woman, her face half hidden by the golden shadow of her hair, her white arm laid out on the warm-hued coverlet, and bending over it, the two masked men, one holding the lamp nearer, the other pointing to something just above the delicate wrist, now freed from the bracelet, which lay open beside it. Two distinctly traced letters were seen, *V. V.*, and underneath a tiny true-lover's knot, in the same dark lines.

The man who held the lamp examined the brand with minutest care, then making a gesture of satisfaction, he said, "It is enough, I am sure now. Put on the bracelet, and come away; there is nothing more to be done tonight."

The old man skillfully replaced the hand, while the other put back locket and key, placed the lamp where they found it; and with a last look at the sleeper, whose unconscious helplessness appealed to them for mercy, both stole away as noiselessly as they had come. The woman reappeared the instant they left the room, lighted them to the hall door, received some reward that glittered as it passed from hand to hand, and made all fast behind them, pausing a moment in a listening attitude, till the distant roll of a carriage assured her that the maskers were safely gone.

CHAPTER X. IN THE SNARE

The first rays of the sun fell on a group of five men, standing together on a waste bit of ground in the environs of London. Major Mansfield and Duprès were busily loading pistols, marking off the distance, and conferring together with a great display of interest. Douglas conversed tranquilly with the surgeon in attendance, a quiet, unassuming man, who stood with his hand in his pocket, as if ready to produce his case of instruments at a moment's notice. The Spaniard was alone, and a curious change seemed to have passed over him. The stately calmness of his demeanor was gone, and he paced to and fro with restless steps, like a panther in his cage. A look of almost savage hatred lowered on his swarthy face; desperation and despair alternately glowed and gloomed in his fierce eye; and the whole man wore a look of one who after long restraint yields himself utterly to the dominion of some passion, dauntless and indomitable as death.

Once he paused, drew from his pocket an ill-spelled, rudely written letter, which had been put into his hand by a countryman as he left his hotel, reread the few lines it contained, and thrust it back into his bosom, muttering, "All things favor me; this was the last tie that bound her; now we must stand or fall together."

"Señor, we are prepared," called Duprès, advancing, pistol in hand, to place his principal, adding, as Arguelles dropped hat and cloak, "our custom may be different from yours, but give heed, and at the word 'Three,' fire."

"I comprehend, monsieur," and a dark smile passed across the Spaniard's face as he took his place and stretched his hand to receive the weapon.

But Duprès drew back a step—and with a sharp metallic click, around that extended wrist snapped a handcuff. A glance showed Arguelles that he was lost, for on his right stood the counterfeit surgeon, with the well-known badge now visible on his blue coat, behind him Major Mansfield, armed, before him Douglas, guarding the nearest outlet of escape, and on his left Duprès, radiant with satisfaction, exclaiming, as he bowed with grace, "A thousand pardons, Monsieur Victor Varens, but this little ruse was inevitable."

Quick as a flash that freed left hand snatched the pistol from Duprès, aimed it at Douglas, and it would have accomplished its work had not the Frenchman struck up the weapon. But the ball was sped, and as the pistol turned in his hand, the bullet lodged in Victor's breast, sparing him the fate he dreaded more than death. In an instant all trace of passion vanished, and with a melancholy dignity that nothing could destroy, he offered his hand to receive the fetter, saying calmly, while his lips whitened, and a red stain dyed the linen on his breast, "I am tired of my life; take it."

They laid him down, for as he spoke, consciousness ebbed away. A glance assured the major that the wound was mortal, and carefully conveying the senseless body to the nearest house, Douglas and the detective remained to tend and guard the prisoner, while the other gentlemen posted to town to bring a genuine surgeon and necessary help, hoping to keep life in the man till his confession had been made.

At nightfall, Mrs. Vane, or Virginie, as we may now call her, grew anxious for the return of Victor, who was to bring her tidings of the child, because she dared not visit him just now herself.

When dressed for the evening, she dismissed Gabrielle, opened the antique casket, and put on the opal ring, carefully attaching the little chain that fastened it securely to her bracelet, for the ring was too large for the delicate hand that wore it. Then with steady feet she went down to the drawing room to meet her lover and her victim.

But some reproachful memory seemed to start up and haunt the present with a vision of the past. She passed her hand across her eyes, as if she saw again the little room, where in the gray dawn she had left her husband lying dead, and she sank into a seat, groaning half aloud, "Oh, if I could forget!"

A bell rang from below, but she did not hear it; steps came through the drawing room, yet she did not heed them; and Douglas stood before her, but she did not see him till he spoke. So great was her surprise, that with all her power of dissimulation she would have found difficulty in concealing it, had not the pale gravity of the newcomer's face afforded a pretext for alarm.

"You startled me at first, and now you look as if you brought ill news," she said, with a vain effort to assume her usual gaiety.

"I do" was the brief reply.

"The señor? Is he with you? I am waiting for him."

"Wait no longer, he will never come."

"Where is he?"

"Quiet in his shroud."

He thought to see her shrink and pale before the blow, but she did neither; she grasped his arm, searched his face, and whispered, with a look of relief, not terror, in her own, "You have killed him?"

"No, his blood is not upon my head; he killed himself."

She covered up her face, and from behind her hands he heard her murmur, "Thank God, he did not come! I am spared that."

While he pondered over the words, vainly trying to comprehend them, she recovered herself, and turning to him said, quite steadily though very pale, "This is awfully sudden; tell me how it came to pass. I am not afraid to hear."

"I will tell you, for you have a right to know. Sit, Mrs. Vane; it is a long tale, and one that will try your courage to the utmost.

"Six years ago I went abroad to meet my cousin Allan," Douglas began, speaking slowly, almost sternly. "He was my senior by a year, but we so closely resembled each other that we were often taken for twin brothers. Alike in person, character, temper, and tastes, we were never so happy as when together, and we loved one another as tenderly as women love. For nearly a year we roamed east and west, then our holiday was over, for we had promised to return. One month more remained; I desired to revisit Switzerland, Allan to remain in Paris, so we parted for a time, each to our own pleasures, appointing to meet on a certain day at a certain place. I never saw him again, for when I reached the spot where he should have met me, I found only a letter, saying that he had been called from Paris suddenly, but that I should receive further intelligence before many days. I waited, but not long. Visiting the Morgue that very week, I found my poor Allan waiting for me there. His body had been taken from the river, and the deep wound in his breast showed that foul play was at the bottom of the mystery. Night and day I labored to clear up the mystery, but labored secretly, lest publicity should warn the culprits, or bring dishonor upon our name, for I soon found that Allan had led a wild life in my absence, and I feared to make some worse discoveries than a young man's follies. I did so; for it appeared that he had been captivated by a singularly beautiful girl, a *danseuse,* had privately married her, and both had disappeared with a young cousin of her own. Her apartments were searched, but all her possessions had been removed, and nothing remained but a plausible letter, which would have turned

suspicion from the girl to the cousin, had not the marriage been discovered, and in her room two witnesses against them. The handle of
a stiletto, half consumed in the ashes, which fitted the broken blade
entangled in the dead man's clothes, and, hidden by the hangings of
the bed, a woman's slipper, with a bloodstain on the sole. Ah, you
may well shudder, Mrs. Vane; it is an awful tale."

"Horrible! Why tell it?" she asked, pressing her hand upon her
eyes, as if to shut out some image too terrible to look upon.

"Because it concerns our friend Arguelles, and explains his
death," replied Earl, in the same slow stern voice. She did not look
up, but he saw that she listened breathlessly, and grew paler still behind her hand.

"Nothing more was discovered then. My cousin's body was sent
home, and none but our two families ever knew the truth. It was
believed by the world that he died suddenly of an affection of the
heart—poor lad! it was the bitter truth—and whatever rumors were
about regarding his death, and the change it wrought in me, were
speedily silenced at the time, and have since died away. Over the dead
body of my dearest friend, I vowed a solemn vow to find his murderer and avenge his death. I have done both."

"Where? How?"

Her hand dropped, and she looked at him with a face that was
positively awful in its unnatural calmness.

"Arguelles was Victor Varens. I suspected, watched, ensnared
him, and would have let the law avenge Allan's death, but the murderer escaped by his own hand."

"Well for him it was so. May his sins be forgiven. Now let us go
elsewhere, and forget this dark story and its darker end."

She rose as she spoke, and a load seemed lifted off her heart; but
it fell again, as Douglas stretched his hand to detain her, saying, "Stay,
the end is not yet told. You forget the girl."

"She was innocent—why should she suffer?" returned the other,
still standing as if defying both fear and fate.

"She was *not* innocent—for she lured that generous boy to marry
her, because she coveted his rank and fortune, not his heart, and,
when he lay dead, left him to the mercies of wind and wave, while

she fled away to save herself. But that cruel cowardice availed her nothing, for though I have watched and waited long, at length I have found her, and at this moment her life lies in my hand—for you and Virginie are one!"

Like a hunted creature driven to bay, she turned on him with an air of desperate audacity, saying haughtily, "Prove it!"

"I will."

For a moment they looked at one another. In his face she saw pitiless resolve; in hers he read passionate defiance.

"Sit down, Virginie, and hear the story through. Escape is impossible—the house is guarded, Duprès waits in yonder room, and Victor can no longer help you with quick wit or daring hand. Submit quietly, and do not force me to forget that you are my cousin's— wife."

She obeyed him, and as the last words fell from his lips a new hope sprang up within her, the danger seemed less imminent, and she took heart again, remembering the child, who might yet plead for her, if her own eloquence should fail.

"You ask me to prove that fact, and evidently doubt my power to do it; but well as you have laid your plots, carefully as you have erased all traces of your former self, and skillfully as you have played your new part, the truth has come to light, and through many winding ways I have followed you, till my labors end here. When you fled from Paris, Victor, whose mother was a Spaniard, took you to Spain, and there, among his kindred, your boy was born."

"Do you know that, too?" she cried, lost in wonder at the quiet statement of what she believed to be known only to herself, her dead cousin, and those far-distant kindred who had succored her in her need.

"I know everything," Earl answered, with an expression that made her quail; then a daring spirit rose up in her, as she remembered more than one secret, which she now felt to be hers alone.

"Not everything, my cousin; you are keen and subtle, but I excel you, though you win this victory, it seems."

So cool, so calm she seemed, so beautifully audacious she looked,

that Earl could only resent the bold speech with a glance, and proceed
to prove the truth of his second assertion with the first.

"You suffered the sharpest poverty, but Victor respected your
helplessness, forgave your treachery, supplied your wants as far as possible, and when all other means failed, left you there, while he went
to earn bread for you and your boy. Virginie, I never can forgive him
my cousin's death, but for his faithful, long-suffering devotion to you,
I honor him, sinner though he was."

She shrugged her shoulders, with an air of indifference or displeasure, took off the widow's cap, no longer needed for a disguise,
and letting loose the cloud of curls that seemed to cluster round her
charming face, she lay back in her chair with all her former graceful
ease, saying, as she fixed her lustrous eyes upon the man she meant to
conquer yet, "I let him love me, and he was content. What more
could I do, for I never loved *him?*"

"Better for him that you did not, and better for poor Allan that
he never lived to know it was impossible for you to love."

Earl spoke bitterly, but Virginie bent her head till her face was
hidden, as she murmured, "Ah, if it were impossible, this hour would
be less terrible, the future far less dark."

He heard the soft lament, divined its meaning, but abruptly continued his story, as if he ignored the sorrowful fact which made her
punishment heavier from his hand than from any other.

"While Victor was away, you wearied of waiting, you longed for
the old life of gaiety and excitement, and, hoping to free yourself
from him, you stole away, and for a year were lost to him. Your plan
was to reach France, and under another name dance yourself into
some other man's heart and home, making him your shield against all
danger. You did reach France, but weary, ill, poor, and burdened with
the child, you failed to find help, till some evil fortune threw Vane in
your way. You had heard of him from Allan, knew his chivalrous
nature, his passion for relieving pain or sorrow, at any cost to himself,
and you appealed to him for charity. A piteous story of a cruel husband, desertion, suffering, and destitution you told him; he believed
it, and being on the point of sailing for India, offered you the place
of companion to a lady sailing with him. Your tale was plausible, your

youth made it pathetic, your beauty lent it power, and the skill with which you played the part of a sad gentlewoman won all hearts, and served your end successfully. Vane loved you, wished to marry you, and would have done so had not death prevented. He died suddenly; you were with him, and though his last act was to make generous provision for you and the boy, some devil prompted you to proclaim yourself his wife, as soon as he was past denying it. His love for you was well-known among those with whom you lived, and your statement was believed."

"You are a magician," she said suddenly. "I have thought so before; now I am sure of it, for you must have transported yourself to India, to make these discoveries."

"No—India came to me in the person of a Hindoo, and from him I learned these facts," replied Douglas, slow to tell her of Victor's perfidy, lest he should put her on her guard, and perhaps lose some revelation which in her ignorance she might make. Fresh bewilderment seemed to fall upon her, and with intensest interest she listened, as that ruthless voice went on.

"Your plan was this: From Vane you had learned much of Allan's family, and the old desire to be 'my lady' returned more strongly than before. Once in England, you hoped to make your way as Colonel Vane's widow, and if no safe, sure opportunity appeared of claiming your boy's right, you resolved to gain your end by wooing and winning another Douglas. You were on the point of starting with poor Vane's fortune in your power (for he left no will, and you were prepared to produce forged papers, if your possession was questioned in England), when Victor found you. He had traced you with the instinct of a faithful dog, though his heart was nearly broken by your cruel desertion. You saw that he could not serve you; you appeased his anger and silenced his reproaches by renewed promises to be his when the boy was acknowledged, if he would aid you in that project. At the risk of his life, this devoted slave consented, and disguised as an Indian servant came with you to England. On the way, you met and won the good graces of the Countess Camareena; she introduced you to the London world, and you began your career as a lady under the best auspices. Money, beauty, art served you well, and as an unfortunate descendant of the noble house of Montmorenci, you were received by those who would have shrunk from you as you once did from the lock of hair of the plebeian French *danseuse,* found in Allan's bosom."

"I *am* noble," she cried, with an air that proved it, "for though my mother was a peasant, my father was a prince, and better blood than that of the Montmorencis flows in my veins."

He only answered with a slight bow, which might be intended as a mocking obeisance in honor of her questionable nobility, or a grave dismissal of the topic.

"From this point the tale is unavoidably egotistical," he said, "for through Lady Lennox you heard of me, learned that I was the next heir to the title, and began at once to weave the web in which I was to be caught. You easily understood what was the mystery of my life, as it was called among the gossips, and that knowledge was a weapon in your hands, which you did not fail to use. You saw that Diana loved me, soon learned my passion for her, and set yourself to separate us, without one thought of the anguish it would bring us, one fear of the consequences of such wrong to yourself. You bade her ask of me a confession that I could not make, having given my word to Allan's mother that her son's name should not be tarnished by the betrayal of the rash act that cost his life. That parted us; then you told her a tale of skillfully mingled truth and falsehood, showed her the marriage record on which a name and date appeared to convict me, took her to the boy whose likeness to his father, and therefore to myself, completed the cruel deception, and drove that high-hearted girl to madness and to death."

"I did not kill her! On my soul, I never meant it! I was terror-stricken when we missed her, and knew no peace or rest till she was found. Of that deed I am innocent—I swear it to you on my knees."

The haunting horror of that night seemed again to overwhelm her; she fell down upon her knees before him, enforcing her denial with clasped hands, imploring eyes, and trembling voice. But Douglas drew back with a gesture of repugnance that wounded her more deeply than his sharpest word, and from that moment all traces of compassion vanished from his countenance, which wore the relentless aspect of a judge who resolves within himself no longer to temper justice with mercy.

"Stand up," he said. "I will listen to no appeal, believe no oath, let no touch of pity soften my heart, for your treachery, your craft, your sin deserve nothing but the heavy retribution you have brought upon yourself. Diana's death lies at your door, as much as if you had stabbed her with the same dagger that took Allan's life. It may yet be proved that you beguiled her to that fatal pool, for you were seen there, going to remove all traces of her, perhaps. But in your hasty flight you left traces of yourself behind you, as you sprang away with an agility that first suggested to me the suspicion of Virginie's presence. I tried your slipper to the footprint, and it fitted too exactly to leave me in much doubt of the truth of my wild conjecture. I had never seen you. Antoine Duprès knew both Victor and yourself. I sent for him, but before the letter went, Jitomar, your spy, read the address, feared that some peril menaced you both, and took counsel with you how to delude the newcomer, if any secret purpose lurked behind our seeming friendliness. You devised a scheme that would have baffled us, had not accident betrayed Victor. In the guise of Arguelles he met Duprès in Paris, returned with him, and played his part so well that the Frenchman was entirely deceived, never dreaming of being sought by the very man who would most desire to shun him. You, too, disguised yourself, with an art that staggered my own senses, and perplexed Duprès, for our masculine eye could not fathom the artifices of costume, cosmetics, and consummate acting. We feared to alarm you by any open step, and resolved to oppose craft to craft, treachery to treachery. Duprès revels in such intricate affairs, and I yielded, against my will, till the charm of success drew me on with increasing eagerness and spirit. The day we first met here, in gathering a flower you would have fallen, had not the Spaniard sprung forward to save you; that involuntary act betrayed him, for the momentary attitude he assumed recalled to Duprès the memory of a certain pose which the dancer Victor often assumed. It was too peculiar to be accidental, too striking to be easily forgotten, and the entire unconsciousness of its actor was a proof that it was so familiar as to be quite natural. From that instant Duprès devoted himself to

the Spaniard; this first genuine delusion put Victor off his guard with
Antoine; and Antoine's feigned friendship was so adroitly assumed
that no suspicion woke in Victor's mind till the moment when, instead of offering him a weapon with which to take my life, he took
him prisoner."

"He is not dead, then? You lie to me; you drive me wild with
your horrible recitals of the past, and force me to confess against my
will. Who told you these things? The dead alone could tell you what
passed between Diana and myself."

Still on the ground, as if forgetful of everything but the bewilderment of seeing plot after plot unfolded before her, she had looked up
and listened with dilated eyes, lips apart, and both hands holding back
the locks that could no longer hide her from his piercing glance. As
she spoke, she paled and trembled with a sudden fear that clutched
her heart, that Diana was not dead, for even now she clung to her
love with a desperate hope that it might save her.

Calm and cold as a man of marble, Douglas looked down upon
her, so beautiful in all her abasement, and answered steadily, "You
forget Victor. To him all your acts, words, and many of your secret
thoughts were told. Did you think his love would endure forever, his
patience never tire, his outraged heart never rebel, his wild spirit
never turn and rend you? All day I have sat beside him, listening to
his painful confessions, painfully but truthfully made, and with his last
breath he cursed you as the cause of a wasted life, and ignominious
death. Virginie, this night your long punishment begins, and that
curse is a part of it."

"Oh, no, no! You will have mercy, remembering how young,
how friendless I am? For Allan's sake you will pity me; for his boy's
sake you will save me; for your own sake you will hide me from the
world's contempt?"

"What mercy did you show poor Diana? What love for Allan?
What penitence for your child's sake? What pity for my grief? I tell
you, if a word would save you, my lips should not utter it!"

He spoke passionately now, and passionately she replied, clinging
to him, though he strove to tear his hands away.

"You have heard Victor's confession, now hear mine. I *have* longed to repent; I did hope to make my life better, for my baby's sake; and oh, I did pity you, till my cold heart softened and grew warm. I should have given up my purpose, repaid Victor's fidelity, and gone away to grow an honest, happy, humble woman, if I had not loved *you*. That made me blind, when I should have been more keen-sighted than ever; that kept me here to be deceived, betrayed, and that should save me now."

"It will not; and the knowledge that I detest and despise you is to add bitterness to your threefold punishment; the memory of Allan, Victor, and Diana is another part of it; and here is the heaviest blow which heaven inflicts as a retribution that will come home to you."

As he spoke, Douglas held to her a crumpled paper, stained with a red stain, and torn with the passage of a bullet that ended Victor's life. She knew the writing, sprang up to seize it, read the few lines, and when the paper fluttered to the ground, the white anguish of her face betrayed that the last blow *had* crushed her as no other could have done. She dropped into a seat, with the wail of tearless woe that breaks from a bereaved mother's heart as she looks on the dead face of the child who has been her idol, and finds no loving answer.

"My baby gone—and I not there to say good-bye! Oh, my darling, I could have borne anything but this!"

So utterly broken did she seem, so wild and woeful did she look, that Douglas had not the heart to add another pang to her sharp grief by any word of explanation or compassion. Silently he poured out a glass of wine and placed it nearer, then resumed his seat and waited till she spoke. Soon she lifted up her head, and showed him the swift and subtle blight that an hour had brought upon her. Life, light, and beauty seemed to have passed away, and a pale shadow of her former self alone remained. Some hope or some resolve had brought her an unnatural calmness, for her eyes were tearless, her face expressionless, her voice tranquil, as if she had done with life, and neither pain nor passion could afflict her now.

"What next?" she said, and laid her hand upon the glass, but did not lift it to her lips, as if the former were too tremulous, or the latter incapable of receiving the draft.

"Only this," he answered, with a touch of pity in his voice. "I

will not have my name handed from mouth to mouth, in connection
with an infamous history like this. For Allan's sake, and for Diana's, I
shall keep it secret, and take your punishment into my hands. Victor
I leave to a wiser judge than any human one; the innocent child is
safe from shame and sorrow; but you must atone for the past with the
loss of liberty and your whole future. It is a more merciful penalty
than the law would exact, were the truth known, for you are spared
public contempt, allowed time for repentance, and deprived of nothing but the liberty which you have so cruelly abused."

"I thank you. Where is my prison to be?"

She took the glass into her hand, yet still held it suspended, as
she waited for his answer, with an aspect of stony immobility which
troubled him.

"Far away in Scotland I own a gray old tower, all that now remains of an ancient stronghold. It is built on the barren rock, where
it stands like a solitary eagle's eyrie, with no life near it but the sound
of the wind, the scream of the gulls, the roll of the sea that foams
about it. There with my faithful old servants you shall live, cut off
from all the world, but not from God, and when death comes to you,
may it find you ready and glad to go, a humble penitent, more fit to
meet your little child than now."

A long slow tremor shook her from head to foot, as word by
word her merciful yet miserable doom was pronounced, leaving no
hope, no help but the submission and repentance which it was not in
her nature to give. For a moment she bowed her head, while her pale
lips moved, and her hands, folded above the glass, were seen to tremble as if some fear mingled even in her prayers. Then she sat erect,
and fixing on him a glance in which love, despair, and defiance mingled, she said, with all her former pride and spirit, as she slowly drank
the wine, "Death cannot come too soon; I go to meet it."

Her look, her tone, awed Douglas, and for a moment he regarded her in silence, as she sat there, leaning her bright head against
the dark velvet of the cushioned chair. Her eyes were on him still
brilliant and brave, in spite of all that had just passed; a disdainful smile
curved her lips, and one fair arm lay half extended on the table, as it
fell when she put the glass away. On this arm the bracelet shone; he

pointed to it, saying, with a meaning glance, "I know that secret, as I know all the rest."

"Not all; there is one more you have not discovered—yet."

She spoke very slowly, and her lips seemed to move reluctantly, while a strange pallor fell on her face, and the fire began to die out of her eyes, leaving them dim, but tender.

"You mean the mystery of the iron ring; but I learned that last night, when, with an expert companion, I entered your room, where you lay buried in the deep sleep produced by the drugged coffee which I gave you. I saw my portrait on your neck, as I wear Allan's, ever since we gave them to each other, long ago, and beside the miniature, the silver key that opened your quaint treasure casket. I found the wax impression of my signet, taken, doubtless, on the night when, as a ghost, you haunted my room; I found the marriage record, stamped with that counterfeit seal, to impose upon Diana; I found relics of Vane, and of your child; and when Hyde called me, I saw and examined the two letters on your arm, which he had uncovered by removing the bracelet from it."

He paused there, expecting some demonstration. None appeared; she leaned and listened, with the same utter stillness of face and figure, the same fixed look and deathly pallor. He thought her faint and spent with the excitement of the hour, and hastened to close the interview, which had been so full of contending emotions to them both.

"Go now, and rest," he said. "I shall make all necessary arrangements here, all proper explanations to Lady Leigh. Gabrielle will prepare for your departure in the morning; but let me warn you not to attempt to bribe her, or to deceive me by any new ruse, for now escape is impossible."

"I have escaped!"

The words were scarcely audible, but a glance of exultation flashed from her eyes, then faded, and the white lids fell, as if sleep weighed them down. A slight motion of the nerveless hand that lay upon the table drew Earl's attention, and with a single look those last words were explained. The opal ring was turned inward on her finger, and some unsuspected spring had been touched when she laid her hands together; for now in the deep setting appeared a tiny cavity, which had evidently contained some deadly poison. The quick and painless death that was to have been Victor's had fallen to herself, and, unable to endure the fate prepared for her, she had escaped, when the net seemed most securely drawn about her. Horror-stricken, Douglas called for help; but all human aid was useless, and nothing of the fair, false Virginie remained but a beautiful, pale image of repose.

Behind a Mask: or, A Woman's Power

⊹⊹⊹

CHAPTER I. JEAN MUIR

*H*as she come?"

"No, Mamma, not yet."

"I wish it were well over. The thought of it worries and excites me. A cushion for my back, Bella."

And poor, peevish Mrs. Coventry sank into an easy chair with a nervous sigh and the air of a martyr, while her pretty daughter hovered about her with affectionate solicitude.

"Who are they talking of, Lucia?" asked the languid young man lounging on a couch near his cousin, who bent over her tapestry work with a happy smile on her usually haughty face.

"The new governess, Miss Muir. Shall I tell you about her?"

"No, thank you. I have an inveterate aversion to the whole tribe. I've often thanked heaven that I had but one sister, and she a spoiled child, so that I have escaped the infliction of a governess so long."

"How will you bear it now?" asked Lucia.

"Leave the house while she is in it."

"No, you won't. You're too lazy, Gerald," called out a younger and more energetic man, from the recess where he stood teasing his dogs.

"I'll give her a three days' trial; if she proves endurable I shall not disturb myself; if, as I am sure, she is a bore, I'm off anywhere, anywhere out of her way."

"I beg you won't talk in that depressing manner, boys. I dread the coming of a stranger more than you possibly can, but Bella *must* not be neglected; so I have nerved myself to endure this woman, and Lucia is good enough to say she will attend to her after tonight."

"Don't be troubled, Mamma. She is a nice person, I dare say, and when once we are used to her, I've no doubt we shall be glad to have her, it's so dull here just now. Lady Sydney said she was a quiet, accomplished, amiable girl, who needed a home, and would be a help to poor stupid me, so try to like her for my sake."

"I will, dear, but isn't it getting late? I do hope nothing has happened. Did you tell them to send a carriage to the station for her, Gerald?"

"I forgot it. But it's not far, it won't hurt her to walk" was the languid reply.

"It was indolence, not forgetfulness, I know. I'm very sorry; she will think it so rude to leave her to find her way so late. Do go and see to it, Ned."

"Too late, Bella, the train was in some time ago. Give your orders to me next time. Mother and I'll see that they are obeyed," said Edward.

"Ned is just at an age to make a fool of himself for any girl who comes in his way. Have a care of the governess, Lucia, or she will bewitch him."

Gerald spoke in a satirical whisper, but his brother heard him and answered with a good-humored laugh.

"I wish there was any hope of your making a fool of yourself in that way, old fellow. Set me a good example, and I promise to follow it. As for the governess, she is a woman, and should be treated with common civility. I should say a little extra kindness wouldn't be amiss, either, because she is poor, and a stranger."

"That is my dear, good-hearted Ned! We'll stand by poor little Muir, won't we?" And running to her brother, Bella stood on tiptoe to offer him a kiss which he could not refuse, for the rosy lips were pursed up invitingly, and the bright eyes full of sisterly affection.

"I do hope she has come, for, when I make an effort to see anyone, I hate to make it in vain. Punctuality is *such* a virtue, and I know this woman hasn't got it, for she promised to be here at seven, and now it is long after," began Mrs. Coventry, in an injured tone.

Before she could get breath for another complaint, the clock struck seven and the doorbell rang.

"There she is!" cried Bella, and turned toward the door as if to go and meet the newcomer.

But Lucia arrested her, saying authoritatively, "Stay here, child. It is her place to come to you, not yours to go to her."

"Miss Muir," announced a servant, and a little black-robed figure stood in the doorway. For an instant no one stirred, and the governess had time to see and be seen before a word was uttered. All looked at her, and she cast on the household group a keen glance that impressed them curiously; then her eyes fell, and bowing slightly she walked in. Edward came forward and received her with the frank cordiality which nothing could daunt or chill.

"Mother, this is the lady whom you expected. Miss Muir, allow me to apologize for our apparent neglect in not sending for you. There was a mistake about the carriage, or, rather, the lazy fellow to whom the order was given forgot it. Bella, come here."

"Thank you, no apology is needed. I did not expect to be sent for." And the governess meekly sat down without lifting her eyes.

"I am glad to see you. Let me take your things," said Bella, rather shyly, for Gerald, still lounging, watched the fireside group with languid interest, and Lucia never stirred. Mrs. Coventry took a second survey and began:

"You were punctual, Miss Muir, which pleases me. I'm a sad invalid, as Lady Sydney told you, I hope; so that Miss Coventry's lessons will be directed by my niece, and you will go to her for directions, as she knows what I wish. You will excuse me if I ask you a few questions, for Lady Sydney's note was very brief, and I left everything to her judgment."

"Ask anything you like, madam," answered the soft, sad voice.

"You are Scotch, I believe."

"Yes, madam."

"Are your parents living?"

"I have not a relation in the world."

"Dear me, how sad! Do you mind telling me your age?"

"Nineteen." And a smile passed over Miss Muir's lips, as she folded her hands with an air of resignation, for the catechism was evidently to be a long one.

"So young! Lady Sydney mentioned five-and-twenty, I think, didn't she, Bella?"

"No, Mamma, she only said she thought so. Don't ask such questions. It's not pleasant before us all," whispered Bella.

A quick, grateful glance shone on her from the suddenly lifted eyes of Miss Muir, as she said quietly, "I wish I was thirty, but, as I am not, I do my best to look and seem old."

Of course, every one looked at her then, and all felt a touch of pity at the sight of the pale-faced girl in her plain black dress, with no ornament but a little silver cross at her throat. Small, thin, and color-less she was, with yellow hair, gray eyes, and sharply cut, irregular, but very expressive features. Poverty seemed to have set its bond stamp upon her, and life to have had for her more frost than sunshine. But something in the lines of the mouth betrayed strength, and the clear, low voice had a curious mixture of command and entreaty in its varying tones. Not an attractive woman, yet not an ordinary one; and, as she sat there with her delicate hands lying in her lap, her head bent, and a bitter look on her thin face, she was more interesting than many a blithe and blooming girl. Bella's heart warmed to her at once, and she drew her seat nearer, while Edward went back to his dogs that his presence might not embarrass her.

"You have been ill, I think," continued Mrs. Coventry, who considered this fact the most interesting of all she had heard concern-ing the governess.

"Yes, madam, I left the hospital only a week ago."

"Are you quite sure it is safe to begin teaching so soon?"

"I have no time to lose, and shall soon gain strength here in the country, if you care to keep me."

"And you are fitted to teach music, French, and drawing?"

"I shall endeavor to prove that I am."

"Be kind enough to go and play an air or two. I can judge by your touch; I used to play finely when a girl."

Miss Muir rose, looked about her for the instrument, and seeing it at the other end of the room went toward it, passing Gerald and Lucia as if she did not see them. Bella followed, and in a moment forgot everything in admiration. Miss Muir played like one who loved music and was perfect mistress of her art. She charmed them all by the magic of this spell; even indolent Gerald sat up to listen, and Lucia put down her needle, while Ned watched the slender white fingers as they flew, and wondered at the strength and skill which they possessed.

"Please sing," pleaded Bella, as a brilliant overture ended.

With the same meek obedience Miss Muir complied, and began a little Scotch melody, so sweet, so sad, that the girl's eyes filled, and Mrs. Coventry looked for one of her many pocket-handkerchiefs. But suddenly the music ceased, for, with a vain attempt to support herself, the singer slid from her seat and lay before the startled listeners, as white and rigid as if struck with death. Edward caught her up, and, ordering his brother off the couch, laid her there, while Bella chafed her hands, and her mother rang for her maid. Lucia bathed the poor girl's temples, and Gerald, with unwonted energy, brought a glass of wine. Soon Miss Muir's lips trembled, she sighed, then murmured, tenderly, with a pretty Scotch accent, as if wandering in the past, "Bide wi' me, Mither, I'm sae sick an sad here all alone."

"Take a sip of this, and it will do you good, my dear," said Mrs. Coventry, quite touched by the plaintive words.

The strange voice seemed to recall her. She sat up, looked about her, a little wildly, for a moment, then collected herself and said, with a pathetic look and tone, "Pardon me. I have been on my feet all day, and, in my eagerness to keep my appointment, I forgot to eat since morning. I'm better now; shall I finish the song?"

"By no means. Come and have some tea," said Bella, full of pity and remorse.

"Scene first, very well done," whispered Gerald to his cousin.

Miss Muir was just before them, apparently listening to Mrs. Coventry's remarks upon fainting fits; but she heard, and looked over her shoulders with a gesture like Rachel. Her eyes were gray, but at that instant they seemed black with some strong emotion of anger, pride, or defiance. A curious smile passed over her face as she bowed, and said in her penetrating voice, "Thanks. The last scene shall be still better."

Young Coventry was a cool, indolent man, seldom conscious of any emotion, any passion, pleasurable or otherwise; but at the look, the tone of the governess, he experienced a new sensation, indefinable, yet strong. He colored and, for the first time in his life, looked abashed. Lucia saw it, and hated Miss Muir with a sudden hatred; for, in all the years she had passed with her cousin, no look or word of hers had possessed such power. Coventry was himself again in an instant, with no trace of that passing change, but a look of interest in his usually dreamy eyes, and a touch of anger in his sarcastic voice.

"What a melodramatic young lady! I shall go tomorrow."

Lucia laughed, and was well pleased when he sauntered away to bring her a cup of tea from the table where a little scene was just taking place. Mrs. Coventry had sunk into her chair again, exhausted by the flurry of the fainting fit. Bella was busied about her; and Edward, eager to feed the pale governess, was awkwardly trying to make the tea, after a beseeching glance at his cousin which she did not choose to answer. As he upset the caddy and uttered a despairing exclamation, Miss Muir quietly took her place behind the urn, saying with a smile, and a shy glance at the young man, "Allow me to assume my duty at once, and serve you all. I understand the art of making people comfortable in this way. The scoop, please. I can gather this up quite well alone, if you will tell me how your mother likes her tea."

Edward pulled a chair to the table and made merry over his mishaps, while Miss Muir performed her little task with a skill and grace that made it pleasant to watch her. Coventry lingered a moment after she had given him a steaming cup, to observe her more nearly, while he asked a question or two of his brother. She took no more notice of him than if he had been a statue, and in the middle of the one remark he addressed to her, she rose to take the sugar basin to Mrs. Coventry, who was quite won by the modest, domestic graces of the new governess.

"Really, my dear, you are a treasure; I haven't tasted such tea since my poor maid Ellis died. Bella never makes it good, and Miss Lucia always forgets the cream. Whatever you do you seem to do well, and that is *such* a comfort."

"Let me always do this for you, then. It will be a pleasure, madam." And Miss Muir came back to her seat with a faint color in her cheek which improved her much.

"My brother asked if young Sydney was at home when you left," said Edward, for Gerald would not take the trouble to repeat the question.

Miss Muir fixed her eyes on Coventry, and answered with a slight tremor of the lips, "No, he left home some weeks ago."

The young man went back to his cousin, saying, as he threw himself down beside her, "I shall not go tomorrow, but wait till the three days are out."

"Why?" demanded Lucia.

Lowering his voice he said, with a significant nod toward the governess, "Because I have a fancy that she is at the bottom of Sydney's mystery. He's not been himself lately, and now he is gone without a word. I rather like romances in real life, if they are not too long, or difficult to read."

"Do you think her pretty?"

"Far from it, a most uncanny little specimen."

"Then why fancy Sydney loves her?"

"He is an oddity, and likes sensations and things of that sort."

"What do you mean, Gerald?"

"Get the Muir to look at you, as she did at me, and you will understand. Will you have another cup, Juno?"

"Yes, please." She liked to have him wait upon her, for he did it to no other woman except his mother.

Before he could slowly rise, Miss Muir glided to them with another cup on the salver; and, as Lucia took it with a cold nod, the girl said under her breath, "I think it honest to tell you that I possess a quick ear, and cannot help hearing what is said anywhere in the room. What you say of me is of no consequence, but you may speak of things which you prefer I should not hear; therefore, allow me to warn you." And she was gone again as noiselessly as she came.

"How do you like that?" whispered Coventry, as his cousin sat looking after the girl, with a disturbed expression.

"What an uncomfortable creature to have in the house! I am very sorry I urged her coming, for your mother has taken a fancy to her, and it will be hard to get rid of her," said Lucia, half angry, half amused.

"Hush, she hears every word you say. I know it by the expression of her face, for Ned is talking about horses, and she looks as haughty as ever you did, and that is saying much. Faith, this is getting interesting."

"Hark, she is speaking; I want to hear," and Lucia laid her hand on her cousin's lips. He kissed it, and then idly amused himself with turning the rings to and fro on the slender fingers.

"I have been in France several years, madam, but my friend died and I came back to be with Lady Sydney, till—" Muir paused an instant, then added, slowly, "till I fell ill. It was a contagious fever, so I went of my own accord to the hospital, not wishing to endanger her."

"Very right, but are you sure there is no danger of infection now?" asked Mrs. Coventry anxiously.

"None, I assure you. I have been well for some time, but did not leave because I preferred to stay there, than to return to Lady Sydney."

"No quarrel, I hope? No trouble of any kind?"

"No quarrel, but—well, why not? You have a right to know, and I will not make a foolish mystery out of a very simple thing. As your family, only, is present, I may tell the truth. I did not go back on the young gentleman's account. Please ask no more."

"Ah, I see. Quite prudent and proper, Miss Muir. I shall never allude to it again. Thank you for your frankness. Bella, you will be careful not to mention this to your young friends; girls gossip sadly, and it would annoy Lady Sydney beyond everything to have this talked of."

"Very neighborly of Lady S. to send the dangerous young lady here, where there are *two* young gentlemen to be captivated. I wonder why she didn't keep Sydney after she had caught him," murmured Coventry to his cousin.

"Because she had the utmost contempt for a titled fool." Miss Muir dropped the words almost into his ear, as she bent to take her shawl from the sofa corner.

"How the deuce did she get there?" ejaculated Coventry, looking as if he had received another sensation. "She has spirit, though, and upon my word I pity Sydney, if he did try to dazzle her, for he must have got a splendid dismissal."

"Come and play billiards. You promised, and I hold you to your word," said Lucia, rising with decision, for Gerald was showing too much interest in another to suit Miss Beaufort.

"I am, as ever, your most devoted. My mother is a charming woman, but I find our evening parties slightly dull, when only my own family are present. Good night, Mamma." He shook hands with his mother, whose pride and idol he was, and, with a comprehensive nod to the others, strolled after his cousin.

"Now they are gone we can be quite cozy, and talk over things, for I don't mind Ned any more than I do his dogs," said Bella, settling herself on her mother's footstool.

"I merely wish to say, Miss Muir, that my daughter has never had a governess and is sadly backward for a girl of sixteen. I want you to pass the mornings with her, and get her on as rapidly as possible. In the afternoon you will walk or drive with her, and in the evening sit with us here, if you like, or amuse yourself as you please. While in the country we are very quiet, for I cannot bear much company, and when my sons want gaiety, they go away for it. Miss Beaufort oversees the servants, and takes my place as far as possible. I am very delicate and keep my room till evening, except for an airing at noon. We will try each other for a month, and I hope we shall get on quite comfortably together."

"I shall do my best, madam."

One would not have believed that the meek, spiritless voice which uttered these words was the same that had startled Coventry a few minutes before, nor that the pale, patient face could ever have kindled with such sudden fire as that which looked over Miss Muir's shoulder when she answered her young host's speech.

Edward thought within himself, Poor little woman! She has had a hard life. We will try and make it easier while she is here; and began his charitable work by suggesting that she might be tired. She acknowledged she was, and Bella led her away to a bright, cozy room, where with a pretty little speech and a good-night kiss she left her.

When alone Miss Muir's conduct was decidedly peculiar. Her first act was to clench her hands and mutter between her teeth, with passionate force, "I'll not fail again if there is power in a woman's wit and will!" She stood a moment motionless, with an expression of almost fierce disdain on her face, then shook her clenched hand as if menacing some unseen enemy. Next she laughed, and shrugged her shoulders with a true French shrug, saying low to herself, "Yes, the last scene *shall* be better than the first. *Mon dieu,* how tired and hungry I am!"

Kneeling before the one small trunk which held her worldly possessions, she opened it, drew out a flask, and mixed a glass of some ardent cordial, which she seemed to enjoy extremely as she sat on the carpet, musing, while her quick eyes examined every corner of the room.

"Not bad! It will be a good field for me to work in, and the harder the task the better I shall like it. *Merci,* old friend. You put heart and courage into me when nothing else will. Come, the curtain is down, so I may be myself for a few hours, if actresses ever are themselves."

Still sitting on the floor she unbound and removed the long abundant braids from her head, wiped the pink from her face, took out several pearly teeth, and slipping off her dress appeared herself indeed, a haggard, worn, and moody woman of thirty at least. The metamorphosis was wonderful, but the disguise was more in the expression she assumed than in any art of costume or false adornment. Now she was alone, and her mobile features settled into their natural expression, weary, hard, bitter. She had been lovely once, happy, innocent, and tender; but nothing of all this remained to the gloomy woman who leaned there brooding over some wrong, or loss, or disappointment which had darkened all her life. For an hour she sat so, sometimes playing absently with the scanty locks that hung about her face, sometimes lifting the glass to her lips as if the fiery draught warmed her cold blood; and once she half uncovered her breast to eye with a terrible glance the scar of a newly healed wound. At last she rose and crept to bed, like one worn out with weariness and mental pain.

CHAPTER II. A GOOD BEGINNING

Only the housemaids were astir when Miss Muir left her room next morning and quietly found her way into the garden. As she walked, apparently intent upon the flowers, her quick eye scrutinized the fine old house and its picturesque surroundings.

"Not bad," she said to herself, adding, as she passed into the adjoining park, "but the other may be better, and I will have the best."

Walking rapidly, she came out at length upon the wide green lawn which lay before the ancient hall where Sir John Coventry lived in solitary splendor. A stately old place, rich in oaks, well-kept shrubberies, gay gardens, sunny terraces, carved gables, spacious rooms, liveried servants, and every luxury befitting the ancestral home of a rich and honorable race. Miss Muir's eyes brightened as she looked, her step grew firmer, her carriage prouder, and a smile broke over her face; the smile of one well pleased at the prospect of the success of some cherished hope. Suddenly her whole air changed, she pushed back her hat, clasped her hands loosely before her, and seemed absorbed in girlish admiration of the fair scene that could not fail to charm any beauty-loving eye. The cause of this rapid change soon appeared. A hale, handsome man, between fifty and sixty, came through the little gate leading to the park, and, seeing the young stranger, paused to examine her. He had only time for a glance, however; she seemed conscious of his presence in a moment, turned with a startled look, uttered an exclamation of surprise, and looked as if hesitating whether to speak or run away. Gallant Sir John took off his hat and said, with the old-fashioned courtesy which became him well,

"I beg your pardon for disturbing you, young lady. Allow me to atone for it by inviting you to walk where you will, and gather what flowers you like. I see you love them, so pray make free with those about you."

With a charming air of maidenly timidity and artlessness, Miss Muir replied, "Oh, thank you, sir! But it is I who should ask pardon for trespassing. I never should have dared if I had not known that Sir John was absent. I always wanted to see this fine old place, and ran over the first thing, to satisfy myself."

"And *are* you satisfied?" he asked, with a smile.

"More than satisfied—I'm charmed; for it is the most beautiful spot I ever saw, and I've seen many famous seats, both at home and abroad," she answered enthusiastically.

"The Hall is much flattered, and so would its master be if he heard you," began the gentleman, with an odd expression.

"I should not praise it to him—at least, not as freely as I have to you, sir," said the girl, with eyes still turned away.

"Why not?" asked her companion, looking much amused.

"I should be afraid. Not that I dread Sir John; but I've heard so many beautiful and noble things about him, and respect him so highly, that I should not dare to say much, lest he should see how I admire and—"

"And what, young lady? Finish, if you please."

"I was going to say, love him. I will say it, for he is an old man, and one cannot help loving virtue and bravery."

Miss Muir looked very earnest and pretty as she spoke, standing there with the sunshine glinting on her yellow hair, delicate face, and downcast eyes. Sir John was not a vain man, but he found it pleasant to hear himself commended by this unknown girl, and felt redoubled curiosity to learn who she was. Too well-bred to ask, or to abash her by avowing what she seemed unconscious of, he left both discoveries to chance; and when she turned, as if to retrace her steps, he offered her the handful of hothouse flowers which he held, saying, with a gallant bow, "In Sir John's name let me give you my little nosegay, with thanks for your good opinion, which, I assure you, is not entirely deserved, for I know him well."

Miss Muir looked up quickly, eyed him an instant, then dropped her eyes, and, coloring deeply, stammered out, "I did not know—I beg your pardon—you are too kind, Sir John."

He laughed like a boy, asking, mischievously, "Why call me Sir John? How do you know that I am not the gardener or the butler?"

"I did not see your face before, and no one but yourself would say that any praise was undeserved," murmured Miss Muir, still overcome with girlish confusion.

"Well, well, we will let that pass, and the next time you come we will be properly introduced. Bella always brings her friends to the Hall, for I am fond of young people."

"I am not a friend. I am only Miss Coventry's governess." And Miss Muir dropped a meek curtsy. A slight change passed over Sir John's manner. Few would have perceived it, but Miss Muir felt it at once, and bit her lips with an angry feeling at her heart. With a curious air of pride, mingled with respect, she accepted the still offered bouquet, returned Sir John's parting bow, and tripped away, leaving the old gentleman to wonder where Mrs. Coventry found such a piquant little governess.

"That is done, and very well for a beginning," she said to herself as she approached the house.

In a green paddock close by fed a fine horse, who lifted up his head and eyed her inquiringly, like one who expected a greeting. Following a sudden impulse, she entered the paddock and, pulling a handful of clover, invited the creature to come and eat. This was evidently a new proceeding on the part of a lady, and the horse careered about as if bent on frightening the newcomer away.

"I see," she said aloud, laughing to herself. "I am not your master, and you rebel. Nevertheless, I'll conquer you, my fine brute."

Seating herself in the grass, she began to pull daisies, singing idly the while, as if unconscious of the spirited prancings of the horse. Presently he drew nearer, sniffing curiously and eyeing her with surprise. She took no notice, but plaited the daisies and sang on as if he was not there. This seemed to pique the petted creature, for, slowly approaching, he came at length so close that he could smell her little foot and nibble at her dress. Then she offered the clover, uttering caressing words and making soothing sounds, till by degrees and with much coquetting, the horse permitted her to stroke his glossy neck and smooth his mane.

It was a pretty sight—the slender figure in the grass, the high-spirited horse bending his proud head to her hand. Edward Coventry, who had watched the scene, found it impossible to restrain himself any longer and, leaping the wall, came to join the group, saying, with mingled admiration and wonder in countenance and voice, "Good morning, Miss Muir. If I had not seen your skill and courage proved before my eyes, I should be alarmed for your safety. Hector is a wild, wayward beast, and has damaged more than one groom who tried to conquer him."

"Good morning, Mr. Coventry. Don't tell tales of this noble creature, who has not deceived my faith in him. Your grooms did not know how to win his heart, and so subdue his spirit without breaking it."

Miss Muir rose as she spoke, and stood with her hand on Hector's neck while he ate the grass which she had gathered in the skirt of her dress.

"You have the secret, and Hector is your subject now, though heretofore he has rejected all friends but his master. Will you give him his morning feast? I always bring him bread and play with him before breakfast."

"Then you are not jealous?" And she looked up at him with eyes so bright and beautiful in expression that the young man wondered he had not observed them before.

"Not I. Pet him as much as you will; it will do him good. He is a solitary fellow, for he scorns his own kind and lives alone, like his master," he added, half to himself.

"Alone, with such a happy home, Mr. Coventry?" And a softly compassionate glance stole from the bright eyes.

"That was an ungrateful speech, and I retract it for Bella's sake. Younger sons have no position but such as they can make for themselves, you know, and I've had no chance yet."

"Younger sons! I thought—I beg pardon." And Miss Muir paused, as if remembering that she had no right to question.

Edward smiled and answered frankly, "Nay, don't mind me. You thought I was the heir, perhaps. Whom did you take my brother for last night?"

"For some guest who admired Miss Beaufort. I did not hear his name, nor observe him enough to discover who he was. I saw only your kind mother, your charming little sister, and—"

She stopped there, with a half-shy, half-grateful look at the young man which finished the sentence better than any words. He was still a boy, in spite of his one-and-twenty years, and a little color came into his brown cheek as the eloquent eyes met his and fell before them.

"Yes, Bella is a capital girl, and one can't help loving her. I know you'll get her on, for, really, she is the most delightful little dunce. My mother's ill health and Bella's devotion to her have prevented our attending to her education before. Next winter, when we go to town, she is to come out, and must be prepared for that great event, you know," he said, choosing a safe subject.

"I shall do my best. And that reminds me that I should report myself to her, instead of enjoying myself here. When one has been ill and shut up a long time, the country is so lovely one is apt to forget duty for pleasure. Please remind me if I am negligent, Mr. Coventry."

"That name belongs to Gerald. I'm only Mr. Ned here," he said as they walked toward the house, while Hector followed to the wall and sent a sonorous farewell after them.

Bella came running to meet them, and greeted Miss Muir as if she had made up her mind to like her heartily. "What a lovely bouquet you have got! I never can arrange flowers prettily, which vexes me, for Mamma is so fond of them and cannot go out herself. You have charming taste," she said, examining the graceful posy which Miss Muir had much improved by adding feathery grasses, delicate ferns, and fragrant wild flowers to Sir John's exotics.

Putting them into Bella's hand, she said, in a winning way, "Take them to your mother, then, and ask her if I may have the pleasure of making her a daily nosegay; for I should find real delight in doing it, if it would please her."

"How kind you are! Of course it would please her. I'll take them to her while the dew is still on them." And away flew Bella, eager to give both the flowers and the pretty message to the poor invalid.

Edward stopped to speak to the gardener, and Miss Muir went up the steps alone. The long hall was lined with portraits, and pacing slowly down it she examined them with interest. One caught her eye, and, pausing before it, she scrutinized it carefully. A young, beautiful, but very haughty female face. Miss Muir suspected at once who it was, and gave a decided nod, as if she saw and caught at some unexpected chance. A soft rustle behind her made her look around, and, seeing Lucia, she bowed, half turned, as if for another glance at the picture, and said, as if involuntarily, "How beautiful it is! May I ask if it is an ancestor, Miss Beaufort?"

"It is the likeness of my mother" was the reply, given with a softened voice and eyes that looked up tenderly.

"Ah, I might have known, from the resemblance, but I scarcely saw you last night. Excuse my freedom, but Lady Sydney treated me as a friend, and I forget my position. Allow me."

As she spoke, Miss Muir stooped to return the handkerchief which had fallen from Lucia's hand, and did so with a humble mien which touched the other's heart; for, though a proud, it was also a very generous one.

"Thank you. Are you better, this morning?" she said, graciously. And having received an affirmative reply, she added, as she walked on, "I will show you to the breakfast room, as Bella is not here. It is a very informal meal with us, for my aunt is never down and my cousins are very irregular in their hours. You can always have yours when you like, without waiting for us if you are an early riser."

Bella and Edward appeared before the others were seated, and Miss Muir quietly ate her breakfast, feeling well satisfied with her hour's work. Ned recounted her exploit with Hector, Bella delivered her mother's thanks for the flowers, and Lucia more than once recalled, with pardonable vanity, that the governess had compared her to her lovely mother, expressing by a look as much admiration for the living likeness as for the painted one. All kindly did their best to make the pale girl feel at home, and their cordial manner seemed to warm and draw her out; for soon she put off her sad, meek air and entertained them with gay anecdotes of her life in Paris, her travels in Russia when governess in Prince Jermadoff's family, and all manner of witty stories that kept them interested and merry long after the meal was over. In the middle of an absorbing adventure, Coventry came in, nodded lazily, lifted his brows, as if surprised at seeing the governess there, and began his breakfast as if the ennui of another day had already taken possession of him. Miss Muir stopped short, and no entreaties could induce her to go on.

"Another time I will finish it, if you like. Now Miss Bella and I should be at our books." And she left the room, followed by her pupil, taking no notice of the young master of the house, beyond a graceful bow in answer to his careless nod.

"Merciful creature! she goes when I come, and does not make life unendurable by moping about before my eyes. Does she belong to the moral, the melancholy, the romantic, or the dashing class, Ned?" said Gerald, lounging over his coffee as he did over everything he attempted.

"To none of them; she is a capital little woman. I wish you had seen her tame Hector this morning." And Edward repeated his story.

"Not a bad move on her part," said Coventry in reply. "She must be an observing as well as an energetic young person, to discover your chief weakness and attack it so soon. First tame the horse, and then the master. It will be amusing to watch the game, only I shall be under the painful necessity of checkmating you both, if it gets serious."

"You needn't exert yourself, old fellow, on my account. If I was not above thinking ill of an inoffensive girl, I should say you were the prize best worth winning, and advise you to take care of your own heart, if you've got one, which I rather doubt."

"I often doubt it, myself; but I fancy the little Scotchwoman will not be able to satisfy either of us upon that point. How does your highness like her?" asked Coventry of his cousin, who sat near him.

"Better than I thought I should. She is well-bred, unassuming, and very entertaining when she likes. She has told us some of the wittiest stories I've heard for a long time. Didn't our laughter wake you?" replied Lucia.

"Yes. Now atone for it by amusing me with a repetition of these witty tales."

"That is impossible; her accent and manner are half the charm," said Ned. "I wish you had kept away ten minutes longer, for your appearance spoilt the best story of all."

"Why didn't she go on?" asked Coventry, with a ray of curiosity.

"You forget that she overheard us last night, and must feel that you consider her a bore. She has pride, and no woman forgets speeches like those you made," answered Lucia.

"Or forgives them, either, I believe. Well, I must be resigned to languish under her displeasure then. On Sydney's account I take a slight interest in her; not that I expect to learn anything from her, for a woman with a mouth like that never confides or confesses anything. But I have a fancy to see what captivated him; for captivated he was, beyond a doubt, and by no lady whom he met in society. Did you ever hear anything of it, Ned?" asked Gerald.

"I'm not fond of scandal or gossip, and never listen to either." With which remark Edward left the room.

Lucia was called out by the housekeeper a moment after, and Coventry left to the society most wearisome to him, namely his own. As he entered, he had caught a part of the story which Miss Muir had been telling, and it had excited his curiosity so much that he found himself wondering what the end could be and wishing that he might hear it.

What the deuce did she run away for, when I came in? he thought. If she *is* amusing, she must make herself useful; for it's intensely dull, I own, here, in spite of Lucia. Hey, what's that?

It was a rich, sweet voice, singing a brilliant Italian air, and singing it with an expression that made the music doubly delicious. Stepping out of the French window, Coventry strolled along the sunny terrace, enjoying the song with the relish of a connoisseur. Others followed, and still he walked and listened, forgetful of weariness or time. As one exquisite air ended, he involuntarily applauded. Miss Muir's face appeared for an instant, then vanished, and no more music followed, though Coventry lingered, hoping to hear the voice again. For music was the one thing of which he never wearied, and neither

Lucia nor Bella possessed skill enough to charm him. For an hour he loitered on the terrace or the lawn, basking in the sunshine, too indolent to seek occupation or society. At length Bella came out, hat in hand, and nearly stumbled over her brother, who lay on the grass.

"You lazy man, have you been dawdling here all this time?" she said, looking down at him.

"No, I've been very busy. Come and tell me how you've got on with the little dragon."

"Can't stop. She bade me take a run after my French, so that I might be ready for my drawing, and so I must."

"It's too warm to run. Sit down and amuse your deserted brother, who has had no society but bees and lizards for an hour."

He drew her down as he spoke, and Bella obeyed; for, in spite of his indolence, he was one to whom all submitted without dreaming of refusal.

"What have you been doing? Muddling your poor little brains with all manner of elegant rubbish?"

"No, I've been enjoying myself immensely. Jean is *so* interesting, so kind and clever. She didn't bore me with stupid grammar, but just talked to me in such pretty French that I got on capitally, and like it as I never expected to, after Lucia's dull way of teaching it."

"What did you talk about?"

"Oh, all manner of things. She asked questions, and I answered, and she corrected me."

"Questions about our affairs, I suppose?"

"Not one. She don't care two sous for us or our affairs. I thought she might like to know what sort of people we were, so I told her about Papa's sudden death, Uncle John, and you, and Ned; but in the midst of it she said, in her quiet way, 'You are getting too confidential, my dear. It is not best to talk too freely of one's affairs to strangers. Let us speak of something else.'"

"What were you talking of when she said that, Bell?"

"You."

"Ah, then no wonder she was bored."

"She was tired of my chatter, and didn't hear half I said; for she was busy sketching something for me to copy, and thinking of something more interesting than the Coventrys."

"How do you know?"

"By the expression of her face. Did you like her music, Gerald?"

"Yes. Was she angry when I clapped?"

"She looked surprised, then rather proud, and shut the piano at once, though I begged her to go on. Isn't Jean a pretty name?"

"Not bad; but why don't you call her Miss Muir?"

"She begged me not. She hates it, and loves to be called Jean, alone. I've imagined such a nice little romance about her, and some-day I shall tell her, for I'm sure she has had a love trouble."

"Don't get such nonsense into your head, but follow Miss Muir's well-bred example and don't be curious about other people's affairs. Ask her to sing tonight; it amuses me."

"She won't come down, I think. We've planned to read and work in my boudoir, which is to be our study now. Mamma will stay in her room, so you and Lucia can have the drawing room all to yourselves."

"Thank you. What will Ned do?"

"He will amuse Mamma, he says. Dear old Ned! I wish you'd stir about and get him his commission. He is so impatient to be doing something and yet so proud he won't ask again, after you have ne-glected it so many times and refused Uncle's help."

"I'll attend to it very soon; don't worry me, child. He will do very well for a time, quietly here with us."

"You always say that, yet you know he chafes and is unhappy at being dependent on you. Mamma and I don't mind; but he is a man, and it frets him. He said he'd take matters into his own hands soon, and then you may be sorry you were so slow in helping him."

"Miss Muir is looking out of the window. You'd better go and take your run, else she will scold."

"Not she. I'm not a bit afraid of her, she's so gentle and sweet. I'm fond of her already. You'll get as brown as Ned, lying here in the sun. By the way, Miss Muir agrees with me in thinking him hand-somer than you."

"I admire her taste and quite agree with her."

"She said he was manly, and that was more attractive than beauty in a man. She does express things so nicely. Now I'm off." And away danced Bella, humming the burden of Miss Muir's sweetest song.

" 'Energy is more attractive than beauty in a man.' She is right, but how the deuce *can* a man be energetic, with nothing to expend his energies upon?" mused Coventry, with his hat over his eyes.

A few moments later, the sweep of a dress caught his ear. Without stirring, a sidelong glance showed him Miss Muir coming across the terrace, as if to join Bella. Two stone steps led down to the lawn. He lay near them, and Miss Muir did not see him till close upon him. She started and slipped on the last step, recovered herself, and glided on, with a glance of unmistakable contempt as she passed the recumbent figure of the apparent sleeper. Several things in Bella's report had nettled him, but this look made him angry, though he would not own it, even to himself.

"Gerald, come here, quick!" presently called Bella, from the rustic seat where she stood beside her governess, who sat with her hand over her face as if in pain.

Gathering himself up, Coventry slowly obeyed, but involuntarily quickened his pace as he heard Miss Muir say, "Don't call him; *he* can do nothing"; for the emphasis on the word "he" was very significant.

"What is it, Bella?" he asked, looking rather wider awake than usual.

"You startled Miss Muir and made her turn her ankle. Now help her to the house, for she is in great pain; and don't lie there anymore to frighten people like a snake in the grass," said his sister petulantly.

"I beg your pardon. Will you allow me?" And Coventry offered his arm.

Miss Muir looked up with the expression which annoyed him and answered coldly, "Thank you, Miss Bella will do as well."

"Permit me to doubt that." And with a gesture too decided to be resisted, Coventry drew her arm through his and led her into the house. She submitted quietly, said the pain would soon be over, and when settled on the couch in Bella's room dismissed him with the briefest thanks. Considering the unwonted exertion he had made, he thought she might have been a little more grateful, and went away to Lucia, who always brightened when he came.

No more was seen of Miss Muir till teatime; for now, while the family were in retirement, they dined early and saw no company. The governess had excused herself at dinner, but came down in the evening a little paler than usual and with a slight limp in her gait. Sir John was there, talking with his nephew, and they merely acknowledged her presence by the sort of bow which gentlemen bestow on governesses. As she slowly made her way to her place behind the urn, Coventry said to his brother, "Take her a footstool, and ask her how she is, Ned." Then, as if necessary to account for his politeness to his uncle, he explained how he was the cause of the accident.

"Yes, yes. I understand. Rather a nice little person, I fancy. Not exactly a beauty, but accomplished and well-bred, which is better for one of her class."

"Some tea, Sir John?" said a soft voice at his elbow, and there was Miss Muir, offering cups to the gentlemen.

"Thank you, thank you," said Sir John, sincerely hoping she had overheard him.

As Coventry took his, he said graciously, "You are very forgiving, Miss Muir, to wait upon me, after I have caused you so much pain."

"It is my duty, sir" was her reply, in a tone which plainly said, "but not my pleasure." And she returned to her place, to smile, and chat, and be charming, with Bella and her brother.

Lucia, hovering near her uncle and Gerald, kept them to herself, but was disturbed to find that their eyes often wandered to the cheerful group about the table, and that their attention seemed distracted by the frequent bursts of laughter and fragments of animated conversation which reached them. In the midst of an account of a tragic affair which she endeavored to make as interesting and pathetic as possible, Sir John burst into a hearty laugh, which betrayed that he had been listening to a livelier story than her own. Much annoyed, she said hastily, "I knew it would be so! Bella has no idea of the proper manner in which to treat a governess. She and Ned will forget the difference of rank and spoil that person for her work. She is inclined to be presumptuous already, and if my aunt won't trouble herself to give Miss Muir a hint in time, I shall."

"Wait till she has finished that story, I beg of you," said Coventry, for Sir John was already off.

"If you find that nonsense so entertaining, why don't you follow Uncle's example? I don't need you."

"Thank you. I will." And Lucia was deserted.

But Miss Muir had ended and, beckoning to Bella, left the room, as if quite unconscious of the honor conferred upon her or the dullness she left behind her. Ned went up to his mother, Gerald returned to make his peace with Lucia, and, bidding them good-night, Sir John turned homeward. Strolling along the terrace, he came to the lighted window of Bella's study, and wishing to say a word to her, he half pushed aside the curtain and looked in. A pleasant little scene. Bella working busily, and near her in a low chair, with the light falling on her fair hair and delicate profile, sat Miss Muir, reading aloud. "Novels!" thought Sir John, and smiled at them for a pair of romantic girls. But pausing to listen a moment before he spoke, he found it was no novel, but history, read with a fluency which made every fact interesting, every sketch of character memorable, by the dramatic effect given to it. Sir John was fond of history, and failing eyesight often curtailed his favorite amusement. He had tried readers, but none suited him, and he had given up the plan. Now as he listened, he thought how pleasantly the smoothly flowing voice would wile away his evenings, and he envied Bella her new acquisition.

A bell rang, and Bella sprang up, saying, "Wait for me a minute. I must run to Mamma, and then we will go on with this charming prince."

Away she went, and Sir John was about to retire as quietly as he came, when Miss Muir's peculiar behavior arrested him for an instant. Dropping the book, she threw her arms across the table, laid her head down upon them, and broke into a passion of tears, like one who could bear restraint no longer. Shocked and amazed, Sir John stole away; but all that night the kindhearted gentleman puzzled his brains with conjectures about his niece's interesting young governess, quite unconscious that she intended he should do so.

CHAPTER III. PASSION AND PIQUE

For several weeks the most monotonous tranquillity seemed to reign at Coventry House, and yet, unseen, unsuspected, a storm was gathering. The arrival of Miss Muir seemed to produce a change in everyone, though no one could have explained how or why. Nothing could be more unobtrusive and retiring than her manners. She was devoted to Bella, who soon adored her, and was only happy when in her society. She ministered in many ways to Mrs. Coventry's comfort, and that lady declared there never was such a nurse. She amused, interested and won Edward with her wit and womanly sympathy. She made Lucia respect and envy her for her accomplishments, and piqued indolent Gerald by her persistent avoidance of him, while Sir John was charmed with her respectful deference and the graceful little attentions she paid him in a frank and artless way, very winning to the lonely old man. The very servants liked her; and instead of being, what most governesses are, a forlorn creature hovering between superiors and inferiors, Jean Muir was the life of the house, and the friend of all but two.

Lucia disliked her, and Coventry distrusted her; neither could exactly say why, and neither owned the feeling, even to themselves. Both watched her covertly yet found no shortcoming anywhere. Meek, modest, faithful, and invariably sweet-tempered—they could complain of nothing and wondered at their own doubts, though they could not banish them.

It soon came to pass that the family was divided, or rather that two members were left very much to themselves. Pleading timidity, Jean Muir kept much in Bella's study and soon made it such a pleasant little nook that Ned and his mother, and often Sir John, came in to enjoy the music, reading, or cheerful chat which made the evenings so gay. Lucia at first was only too glad to have her cousin to herself, and he too lazy to care what went on about him. But presently he wearied of her society, for she was not a brilliant girl, and possessed few of those winning arts which charm a man and steal into his heart. Rumors of the merrymakings that went on reached him and made him curious to share them; echoes of fine music went sounding through the house, as he lounged about the empty drawing room; and peals of laughter reached him while listening to Lucia's grave discourse.

She soon discovered that her society had lost its charm, and the more eagerly she tried to please him, the more signally she failed. Before long Coventry fell into a habit of strolling out upon the terrace of an evening, and amusing himself by passing and repassing the window of Bella's room, catching glimpses of what was going on and reporting the result of his observations to Lucia, who was too proud to ask admission to the happy circle or to seem to desire it.

"I shall go to London tomorrow, Lucia," Gerald said one evening, as he came back from what he called "a survey," looking very much annoyed.

"To London?" exclaimed his cousin, surprised.

"Yes, I must bestir myself and get Ned his commission, or it will be all over with him."

"How do you mean?"

"He is falling in love as fast as it is possible for a boy to do it. That girl has bewitched him, and he will make a fool of himself very soon, unless I put a stop to it."

"I was afraid she would attempt a flirtation. These persons always do, they are such a mischief-making race."

"Ah, but there you are wrong, as far as little Muir is concerned. She does not flirt, and Ned has too much sense and spirit to be caught by a silly coquette. She treats him like an elder sister, and mingles the most attractive friendliness with a quiet dignity that captivates the boy. I've been watching them, and there he is, devouring her with his eyes, while she reads a fascinating novel in the most fascinating style. Bella and Mamma are absorbed in the tale, and see nothing; but Ned makes himself the hero, Miss Muir the heroine, and lives the love scene with all the ardor of a man whose heart has just waked up. Poor lad! Poor lad!"

Lucia looked at her cousin, amazed by the energy with which he spoke, the anxiety in his usually listless face. The change became him, for it showed what he might be, making one regret still more what he was. Before she could speak, he was gone again, to return presently, laughing, yet looking a little angry.

"What now?" she asked.

" 'Listeners never hear any good of themselves' is the truest of proverbs. I stopped a moment to look at Ned, and heard the following flattering remarks. Mamma is gone, and Ned was asking little Muir to sing that delicious barcarole she gave us the other evening.

" 'Not now, not here,' she said.

" 'Why not? You sang it in the drawing room readily enough,' said Ned, imploringly.

" 'That is a very different thing,' and she looked at him with a little shake of the head, for he was folding his hands and doing the passionate pathetic.

" 'Come and sing it there then,' said innocent Bella. 'Gerald likes your voice so much, and complains that you will never sing to him.'

" 'He never asks me,' said Muir, with an odd smile.

" 'He is too lazy, but he wants to hear you.'

" 'When he asks me, I will sing—if I feel like it.' And she shrugged her shoulders with a provoking gesture of indifference.

" 'But it amuses him, and he gets so bored down here,' began stupid little Bella. 'Don't be shy or proud, Jean, but come and entertain the poor old fellow.'

" 'No, thank you. I engaged to teach Miss Coventry, not to amuse Mr. Coventry' was all the answer she got.

" 'You amuse Ned, why not Gerald? Are you afraid of him?' asked Bella.

"Miss Muir laughed, such a scornful laugh, and said, in that peculiar tone of hers, 'I cannot fancy anyone being *afraid* of your elder brother.'

" 'I am, very often, and so would you be, if you ever saw him angry.' And Bella looked as if I'd beaten her.

" 'Does he ever wake up enough to be angry?' asked that girl, with an air of surprise. Here Ned broke into a fit of laughter, and they are at it now, I fancy, by the sound."

"Their foolish gossip is not worth getting excited about, but I certainly would send Ned away. It's no use trying to get rid of 'that girl,' as you say, for my aunt is as deluded about her as Ned and Bella, and she really does get the child along splendidly. Dispatch Ned, and then she can do no harm," said Lucia, watching Coventry's altered face as he stood in the moonlight, just outside the window where she sat.

"Have you no fears for me?" he asked smiling, as if ashamed of his momentary petulance.

"No, have you for yourself?" And a shade of anxiety passed over her face.

"I defy the Scotch witch to enchant me, except with her music," he added, moving down the terrace again, for Jean was singing like a nightingale.

As the song ended, he put aside the curtain, and said, abruptly, "Has anyone any commands for London? I am going there to-morrow."

"A pleasant trip to you," said Ned carelessly, though usually his brother's movements interested him extremely.

"I want quantities of things, but I must ask Mamma first." And Bella began to make a list.

"May I trouble you with a letter, Mr. Coventry?"

Jean Muir turned around on the music stool and looked at him with the cold keen glance which always puzzled him.

He bowed, saying, as if to them all, "I shall be off by the early train, so you must give me your orders tonight."

"Then come away, Ned, and leave Jean to write her letter."

And Bella took her reluctant brother from the room.

"I will give you the letter in the morning," said Miss Muir, with a curious quiver in her voice, and the look of one who forcibly suppressed some strong emotion.

"As you please." And Coventry went back to Lucia, wondering who Miss Muir was going to write to. He said nothing to his brother of the purpose which took him to town, lest a word should produce the catastrophe which he hoped to prevent; and Ned, who now lived in a sort of dream, seemed to forget Gerald's existence altogether.

With unwonted energy Coventry was astir at seven next morning. Lucia gave him his breakfast, and as he left the room to order the carriage, Miss Muir came gliding downstairs, very pale and heavy-eyed (with a sleepless, tearful night, he thought) and, putting a delicate little letter into his hand, said hurriedly, "Please leave this at Lady Sydney's, and if you see her, say 'I have remembered.' "

Her peculiar manner and peculiar message struck him. His eye involuntarily glanced at the address of the letter and read young Sydney's name. Then, conscious of his mistake, he thrust it into his pocket with a hasty "Good morning," and left Miss Muir standing with one hand pressed on her heart, the other half extended as if to recall the letter.

All the way to London, Coventry found it impossible to forget the almost tragical expression of the girl's face, and it haunted him through the bustle of two busy days. Ned's affair was put in the way of being speedily accomplished, Bella's commissions were executed, his mother's pet delicacies provided for her, and a gift for Lucia, whom the family had given him for his future mate, as he was too lazy to choose for himself.

Jean Muir's letter he had not delivered, for Lady Sydney was in the country and her townhouse closed. Curious to see how she would receive his tidings, he went quietly in on his arrival at home. Everyone had dispersed to dress for dinner except Miss Muir, who was in the garden, the servant said.

"Very well, I have a message for her"; and, turning, the "young master," as they called him, went to seek her. In a remote corner he saw her sitting alone, buried in thought. As his step roused her, a look of surprise, followed by one of satisfaction, passed over her face, and, rising, she beckoned to him with an almost eager gesture. Much amazed, he went to her and offered the letter, saying kindly, "I regret that I could not deliver it. Lady Sydney is in the country, and I did not like to post it without your leave. Did I do right?"

"Quite right, thank you very much—it is better so." And with an air of relief, she tore the letter to atoms, and scattered them to the wind.

More amazed than ever, the young man was about to leave her when she said, with a mixture of entreaty and command, "Please stay a moment. I want to speak to you."

He paused, eyeing her with visible surprise, for a sudden color dyed her cheeks, and her lips trembled. Only for a moment, then she was quite self-possessed again. Motioning him to the seat she had left, she remained standing while she said, in a low, rapid tone full of pain and of decision:

"Mr. Coventry, as the head of the house I want to speak to you, rather than to your mother, of a most unhappy affair which has occurred during your absence. My month of probation ends today; your mother wishes me to remain; I, too, wish it sincerely, for I am happy here, but I ought not. Read this, and you will see why."

She put a hastily written note into his hand and watched him intently while he read it. She saw him flush with anger, bite his lips, and knit his brows, then assume his haughtiest look, as he lifted his eyes and said in his most sarcastic tone, "Very well for a beginning. The boy has eloquence. Pity that it should be wasted. May I ask if you have replied to this rhapsody?"

"I have."

"And what follows? He begs you 'to fly with him, to share his fortunes, and be the good angel of his life.' Of course you consent?"

There was no answer, for, standing erect before him, Miss Muir regarded him with an expression of proud patience, like one who expected reproaches, yet was too generous to resent them. Her manner had its effect. Dropping his bitter tone, Coventry asked briefly, "Why do you show me this? What can I do?"

"I show it that you may see how much in earnest 'the boy' is, and how open I desire to be. You can control, advise, and comfort your brother, and help me to see what is my duty."

"You love him?" demanded Coventry bluntly.

"No!" was the quick, decided answer.

"Then why make him love you?"

"I never tried to do it. Your sister will testify that I have endeavored to avoid him as I—" And he finished the sentence with an unconscious tone of pique, "As you have avoided me."

She bowed silently, and he went on:

"I will do you the justice to say that nothing can be more blameless than your conduct toward myself; but why allow Ned to haunt you evening after evening? What could you expect of a romantic boy who had nothing to do but lose his heart to the first attractive woman he met?"

A momentary glisten shone in Jean Muir's steel-blue eyes as the last words left the young man's lips; but it was gone instantly, and her voice was full of reproach, as she said, steadily, impulsively, "If the 'romantic boy' had been allowed to lead the life of a man, as he longed to do, he would have had no time to lose his heart to the first sorrowful girl whom he pitied. Mr. Coventry, the fault is yours. Do not blame your brother, but generously own your mistake and retrieve it in the speediest, kindest manner."

For an instant Gerald sat dumb. Never since his father died had anyone reproved him; seldom in his life had he been blamed. It was a new experience, and the very novelty added to the effect. He saw his fault, regretted it, and admired the brave sincerity of the girl in telling him of it. But he did not know how to deal with the case, and was forced to confess not only past negligence but present incapacity. He was as honorable as he was proud, and with an effort he said frankly, "You are right, Miss Muir. I *am* to blame, yet as soon as I saw the danger, I tried to avert it. My visit to town was on Ned's account; he will have his commission very soon, and then he will be sent out of harm's way. Can I do more?"

"No, it is too late to send him away with a free and happy heart. He must bear his pain as he can, and it may help to make a man of him," she said sadly.

"He'll soon forget," began Coventry, who found the thought of gay Ned suffering an uncomfortable one.

"Yes, thank heaven, that is possible, for men."

Miss Muir pressed her hands together, with a dark expression on her half-averted face. Something in her tone, her manner, touched Coventry; he fancied that some old wound bled, some bitter memory awoke at the approach of a new lover. He was young, heart-whole, and romantic, under all his cool nonchalance of manner. This girl, who he fancied loved his friend and who was beloved by his brother, became an object of interest to him. He pitied her, desired to help her, and regretted his past distrust, as a chivalrous man always regrets injustice to a woman. She was happy here, poor, homeless soul, and she should stay. Bella loved her, his mother took comfort in her, and when Ned was gone, no one's peace would be endangered by her winning ways, her rich accomplishments. These thoughts swept through his mind during a brief pause, and when he spoke, it was to say gently:

"Miss Muir, I thank you for the frankness which must have been painful to you, and I will do my best to be worthy of the confidence which you repose in me. You were both discreet and kind to speak only to me. This thing would have troubled my mother extremely, and have done no good. I shall see Ned, and try and repair my long neglect as promptly as possible. I know you will help me, and in return let me beg of you to remain, for he will soon be gone."

She looked at him with eyes full of tears, and there was no coolness in the voice that answered softly, "You are too kind, but I had better go; it is not wise to stay."

"Why not?"

She colored beautifully, hesitated, then spoke out in the clear, steady voice which was her greatest charm, "If I had known there were sons in this family, I never should have come. Lady Sydney spoke only of your sister, and when I found two gentlemen, I was troubled, because—I am so unfortunate—or rather, people are so kind as to like me more than I deserve. I thought I could stay a month, at least, as your brother spoke of going away, and you were already affianced, but—"

"I am not affianced."

Why he said that, Coventry could not tell, but the words passed his lips hastily and could not be recalled. Jean Muir took the announcement oddly enough. She shrugged her shoulders with an air of extreme annoyance, and said almost rudely, "Then you should be; you will be soon. But that is nothing to me. Miss Beaufort wishes me gone, and I am too proud to remain and become the cause of disunion in a happy family. No, I will go, and go at once."

She turned away impetuously, but Edward's arm detained her, and Edward's voice demanded, tenderly, "Where will you go, my Jean?"

The tender touch and name seemed to rob her of her courage and calmness, for, leaning on her lover, she hid her face and sobbed audibly.

"Now don't make a scene, for heaven's sake," began Coventry impatiently, as his brother eyed him fiercely, divining at once what had passed, for his letter was still in Gerald's hand and Jean's last words had reached her lover's ear.

"Who gave you the right to read that, and to interfere in my affairs?" demanded Edward hotly.

"Miss Muir" was the reply, as Coventry threw away the paper.

"And you add to the insult by ordering her out of the house," cried Ned with increasing wrath.

"On the contrary, I beg her to remain."

"The deuce you do! And why?"

"Because she is useful and happy here, and I am unwilling that your folly should rob her of a home which she likes."

"You are very thoughtful and devoted all at once, but I beg you will not trouble yourself. Jean's happiness and home will be my care now."

"My dear boy, do be reasonable. The thing is impossible. Miss Muir sees it herself; she came to tell me, to ask how best to arrange matters without troubling my mother. I've been to town to attend to your affairs, and you may be off now very soon."

"I have no desire to go. Last month it was the wish of my heart. Now I'll accept nothing from you." And Edward turned moodily away from his brother.

"What folly! Ned, you *must* leave home. It is all arranged and cannot be given up now. A change is what you need, and it will make a man of you. We shall miss you, of course, but you will be where you'll see something of life, and that is better for you than getting into mischief here."

"Are you going away, Jean?" asked Edward, ignoring his brother entirely and bending over the girl, who still hid her face and wept. She did not speak, and Gerald answered for her.

"No, why should she if you are gone?"

"Do you mean to stay?" asked the lover eagerly of Jean.

"I wish to remain, but—" She paused and looked up. Her eyes went from one face to the other, and she added, decidedly, "Yes, I must go, it is not wise to stay even when you are gone."

Neither of the young men could have explained why that hurried glance affected them as it did, but each felt conscious of a willful desire to oppose the other. Edward suddenly felt that his brother loved Miss Muir, and was bent on removing her from his way. Gerald had a vague idea that Miss Muir feared to remain on his account, and he longed to show her that he was quite safe. Each felt angry, and each showed it in a different way, one being violent, the other satirical.

"You are right, Jean, this is not the place for you; and you must let me see you in a safer home before I go," said Ned, significantly.

"It strikes me that this will be a particularly safe home when your dangerous self is removed," began Coventry, with an aggravating smile of calm superiority.

"And *I* think that I leave a more dangerous person than myself behind me, as poor Lucia can testify."

"Be careful what you say, Ned, or I shall be forced to remind you that I am master here. Leave Lucia's name out of this disagreeable affair, if you please."

"You *are* master here, but not of me, or my actions, and you have no right to expect obedience or respect, for you inspire neither. Jean, I asked you to go with me secretly; now I ask you openly to share my fortune. In my brother's presence I ask, and *will* have an answer."

He caught her hand impetuously, with a defiant look at Coventry, who still smiled, as if at boy's play, though his eyes were kindling and his face changing with the still, white wrath which is more terrible than any sudden outburst. Miss Muir looked frightened; she shrank away from her passionate young lover, cast an appealing glance at Gerald, and seemed as if she longed to claim his protection yet dared not.

"Speak!" cried Edward, desperately. "Don't look to him, tell me truly, with your own lips, do you, can you love me, Jean?"

"I have told you once. Why pain me by forcing another hard

reply," she said pitifully, still shrinking from his grasp and seeming to appeal to his brother.

"You wrote a few lines, but I'll not be satisfied with that. You shall answer; I've seen love in your eyes, heard it in your voice, and I know it is hidden in your heart. You fear to own it; do not hesitate, no one can part us—speak, Jean, and satisfy me."

Drawing her hand decidedly away, she went a step nearer Coventry, and answered, slowly, distinctly, though her lips trembled, and she evidently dreaded the effect of her words, "I will speak, and speak truly. You have seen love in my face; it is in my heart, and I do not hesitate to own it, cruel as it is to force the truth from me, but this love is not for you. Are you satisfied?"

He looked at her with a despairing glance and stretched his hand toward her beseechingly. She seemed to fear a blow, for suddenly she clung to Gerald with a faint cry. The act, the look of fear, the protecting gesture Coventry involuntarily made were too much for Edward, already excited by conflicting passions. In a paroxysm of blind wrath, he caught up a large pruning knife left there by the gardener, and would have dealt his brother a fatal blow had he not warded it off with his arm. The stroke fell, and another might have followed had not Miss Muir with unexpected courage and strength wrested the knife from Edward and flung it into the little pond near by. Coventry dropped down upon the seat, for the blood poured from a deep wound in his arm, showing by its rapid flow that an artery had been severed. Edward stood aghast, for with the blow his fury passed, leaving him overwhelmed with remorse and shame.

Gerald looked up at him, smiled faintly, and said, with no sign of reproach or anger, "Never mind, Ned. Forgive and forget. Lend me a hand to the house, and don't disturb anyone. It's not much, I dare say." But his lips whitened as he spoke, and his strength failed him. Edward sprang to support him, and Miss Muir, forgetting her terrors, proved herself a girl of uncommon skill and courage.

"Quick! Lay him down. Give me your handkerchief, and bring some water," she said, in a tone of quiet command. Poor Ned obeyed and watched her with breathless suspense while she tied the handkerchief tightly around the arm, thrust the handle of his riding whip underneath, and pressed it firmly above the severed artery to stop the dangerous flow of blood.

"Dr. Scott is with your mother, I think. Go and bring him here" was the next order; and Edward darted away, thankful to do anything to ease the terror which possessed him. He was gone some minutes, and while they waited Coventry watched the girl as she knelt beside him, bathing his face with one hand while with the other she held the bandage firmly in its place. She was pale, but quite steady and self-possessed, and her eyes shone with a strange brilliancy as she looked down at him. Once, meeting his look of grateful wonder, she smiled a reassuring smile that made her lovely, and said, in a soft, sweet tone never used to him before, "Be quiet. There is no danger. I will stay by you till help comes."

Help did come speedily, and the doctor's first words were "Who improvised that tourniquet?"

"She did," murmured Coventry.

"Then you may thank her for saving your life. By Jove! It was capitally done"; and the old doctor looked at the girl with as much admiration as curiosity in his face.

"Never mind that. See to the wound, please, while I run for bandages, and salts, and wine."

Miss Muir was gone as she spoke, so fleetly that it was in vain to call her back or catch her. During her brief absence, the story was told by repentant Ned and the wound examined.

"Fortunately I have my case of instruments with me," said the doctor, spreading on the bench a long array of tiny, glittering implements of torture. "Now, Mr. Ned, come here, and hold the arm in that way, while I tie the artery. Hey! That will never do. Don't tremble so, man, look away and hold it steadily."

"I can't!" And poor Ned turned faint and white, not at the sight but with the bitter thought that he had longed to kill his brother.

"I will hold it," and a slender white hand lifted the bare and bloody arm so firmly, steadily, that Coventry sighed a sigh of relief, and Dr. Scott fell to work with an emphatic nod of approval.

It was soon over, and while Edward ran in to bid the servants beware of alarming their mistress, Dr. Scott put up his instruments and Miss Muir used salts, water, and wine so skillfully that Gerald was able to walk to his room, leaning on the old man, while the girl supported the wounded arm, as no sling could be made on the spot. As he entered the chamber, Coventry turned, put out his left hand, and with much feeling in his fine eyes said simply, "Miss Muir, I thank you."

The color came up beautifully in her pale cheeks as she pressed the hand and without a word vanished from the room. Lucia and the housekeeper came bustling in, and there was no lack of attendance on the invalid. He soon wearied of it, and sent them all away but Ned, who remorsefully haunted the chamber, looking like a comely young Cain and feeling like an outcast.

"Come here, lad, and tell me all about it. I was wrong to be domineering. Forgive me, and believe that I care for your happiness more sincerely than for my own."

These frank and friendly words healed the breach between the two brothers and completely conquered Ned. Gladly did he relate his love passages, for no young lover ever tires of that amusement if he has a sympathizing auditor, and Gerald *was* sympathetic now. For an hour did he lie listening patiently to the history of the growth of his brother's passion. Emotion gave the narrator eloquence, and Jean Muir's character was painted in glowing colors. All her unsuspected kindness to those about her was dwelt upon; all her faithful care, her sisterly interest in Bella, her gentle attentions to their mother, her sweet forbearance with Lucia, who plainly showed her dislike, and most of all, her friendly counsel, sympathy, and regard for Ned himself.

"She would make a man of me. She puts strength and courage into me as no one else can. She is unlike any girl I ever saw; there's no sentimentality about her; she is wise, and kind, and sweet. She says what she means, looks you straight in the eye, and is as true as steel. I've tried her, I know her, and—ah, Gerald, I love her so!"

Here the poor lad leaned his face into his hands and sighed a sigh that made his brother's heart ache.

"Upon my soul, Ned, I feel for you; and if there was no obstacle on her part, I'd do my best for you. She loves Sydney, and so there is nothing for it but to bear your fate like a man."

"Are you sure about Sydney? May it not be some one else?" and Ned eyed his brother with a suspicious look.

Coventry told him all he knew and surmised concerning his friend, not forgetting the letter. Edward mused a moment, then seemed relieved, and said frankly, "I'm glad it's Sydney and not you. I can bear it better."

"Me!" ejaculated Gerald, with a laugh.

"Yes, you; I've been tormented lately with a fear that you cared for her, or rather, she for you."

"You jealous young fool! We never see or speak to one another scarcely, so how could we get up a tender interest?"

"What do you lounge about on that terrace for every evening? And why does she get fluttered when your shadow begins to come and go?" demanded Edward.

"I like the music and don't care for the society of the singer, that's why I walk there. The fluttering is all your imagination; Miss Muir isn't a woman to be fluttered by a man's shadow." And Coventry glanced at his useless arm.

"Thank you for that, and for not saying 'little Muir,' as you generally do. Perhaps it was my imagination. But she never makes fun of you now, and so I fancied she might have lost her heart to the 'young master.' Women often do, you know."

"She used to ridicule me, did she?" asked Coventry, taking no notice of the latter part of his brother's speech, which was quite true nevertheless.

"Not exactly, she was too well-bred for that. But sometimes when Bella and I joked about you, she'd say something so odd or witty that it was irresistible. You're used to being laughed at, so you don't mind, I know, just among ourselves."

"Not I. Laugh away as much as you like," said Gerald. But he did mind, and wanted exceedingly to know what Miss Muir had said, yet was too proud to ask. He turned restlessly and uttered a sigh of pain.

"I'm talking too much; it's bad for you. Dr. Scott said you must be quiet. Now go to sleep, if you can."

Edward left the bedside but not the room, for he would let no one take his place. Coventry tried to sleep, found it impossible, and after a restless hour called his brother back.

"If the bandage was loosened a bit, it would ease my arm and then I could sleep. Can you do it, Ned?"

"I dare not touch it. The doctor gave orders to leave it till he came in the morning, and I shall only do harm if I try."

"But I tell you it's too tight. My arm is swelling and the pain is intense. It can't be right to leave it so. Dr. Scott dressed it in a hurry and did it too tight. Common sense will tell you that," said Coventry impatiently.

"I'll call Mrs. Morris; she will understand what's best to be done." And Edward moved toward the door, looking anxious.

"Not she, she'll only make a stir and torment me with her chatter. I'll bear it as long as I can, and perhaps Dr. Scott will come tonight. He said he would if possible. Go to your dinner, Ned. I can ring for Neal if I need anything. I shall sleep if I'm alone, perhaps."

Edward reluctantly obeyed, and his brother was left to himself. Little rest did he find, however, for the pain of the wounded arm grew unbearable, and, taking a sudden resolution, he rang for his servant.

"Neal, go to Miss Coventry's study, and if Miss Muir is there, ask her to be kind enough to come to me. I'm in great pain, and she understands wounds better than anyone else in the house."

With much surprise in his face, the man departed and a few moments after the door noiselessly opened and Miss Muir came in. It had been a very warm day, and for the first time she had left off her plain black dress. All in white, with no ornament but her fair hair, and a fragrant posy of violets in her belt, she looked a different woman from the meek, nunlike creature one usually saw about the house. Her face was as altered as her dress, for now a soft color glowed in her cheeks, her eyes smiled shyly, and her lips no longer wore the firm look of one who forcibly repressed every emotion. A fresh, gentle, and charming woman she seemed, and Coventry found the dull room suddenly brightened by her presence. Going straight to him, she said simply, and with a happy, helpful look very comforting to see, "I'm glad you sent for me. What can I do for you?"

He told her, and before the complaint was ended, she began loosening the bandages with the decision of one who understood what was to be done and had faith in herself.

"Ah, that's relief, that's comfort!" ejaculated Coventry, as the last tight fold fell away. "Ned was afraid I should bleed to death if he touched me. What will the doctor say to us?"

"I neither know nor care. I shall say to him that he is a bad surgeon to bind it so closely, and not leave orders to have it untied if necessary. Now I shall make it easy and put you to sleep, for that is what you need. Shall I? May I?"

"I wish you would, if you can."

And while she deftly rearranged the bandages, the young man watched her curiously. Presently he asked, "How came you to know so much about these things?"

"In the hospital where I was ill, I saw much that interested me, and when I got better, I used to sing to the patients sometimes."

"Do you mean to sing to me?" he asked, in the submissive tone men unconsciously adopt when ill and in a woman's care.

"If you like it better than reading aloud in a dreamy tone," she answered, as she tied the last knot.

"I do, much better," he said decidedly.

"You are feverish. I shall wet your forehead, and then you will be quite comfortable." She moved about the room in the quiet way which made it a pleasure to watch her, and, having mingled a little cologne with water, bathed his face as unconcernedly as if he had been a child. Her proceedings not only comforted but amused Coventry, who mentally contrasted her with the stout, beer-drinking matron who had ruled over him in his last illness.

"A clever, kindly little woman," he thought, and felt quite at his ease, she was so perfectly easy herself.

"There, now you look more like yourself," she said with an approving nod as she finished, and smoothed the dark locks off his forehead with a cool, soft hand. Then seating herself in a large chair near by, she began to sing, while tidily rolling up the fresh bandages which had been left for the morning. Coventry lay watching her by the dim light that burned in the room, and she sang on as easily as a bird, a dreamy, low-toned lullaby, which soothed the listener like a spell. Presently, looking up to see the effect of her song, she found the young man wide awake, and regarding her with a curious mixture of pleasure, interest, and admiration.

"Shut your eyes, Mr. Coventry," she said, with a reproving shake of the head, and an odd little smile.

He laughed and obeyed, but could not resist an occasional covert glance from under his lashes at the slender white figure in the great velvet chair. She saw him and frowned.

"You are very disobedient; why won't you sleep?"

"I can't, I want to listen. I'm fond of nightingales."

"Then I shall sing no more, but try something that has never failed yet. Give me your hand, please."

Much amazed, he gave it, and, taking it in both her small ones, she sat down behind the curtain and remained as mute and motionless as a statue. Coventry smiled to himself at first, and wondered which would tire first. But soon a subtle warmth seemed to steal from the soft palms that enclosed his own, his heart beat quicker, his breath grew unequal, and a thousand fancies danced through his brain. He sighed, and said dreamily, as he turned his face toward her, "I like this." And in the act of speaking, seemed to sink into a soft cloud which encompassed him about with an atmosphere of perfect repose. More than this he could not remember, for sleep, deep and dreamless, fell upon him, and when he woke, daylight was shining in between the curtains, his hand lay alone on the coverlet, and his fair-haired enchantress was gone.

CHAPTER IV. A DISCOVERY

For several days Coventry was confined to his room, much against his will, though everyone did their best to lighten his irksome captivity. His mother petted him, Bella sang, Lucia read, Edward was devoted, and all the household, with one exception, were eager to serve the young master. Jean Muir never came near him, and Jean Muir alone seemed to possess the power of amusing him. He soon tired of the others, wanted something new; recalled the piquant character of the girl and took a fancy into his head that she would lighten his ennui. After some hesitation, he carelessly spoke of her to Bella, but nothing came of it, for Bella only said Jean was well, and very busy doing something lovely to surprise Mamma with. Edward complained that he never saw her, and Lucia ignored her existence altogether. The only intelligence the invalid received was from the gossip of two housemaids over their work in the next room. From them he learned that the governess had been "scolded" by Miss Beaufort for going to Mr. Coventry's room; that she had taken it very sweetly and kept herself carefully out of the way of both young gentlemen, though it was plain to see that Mr. Ned was dying for her.

Mr. Gerald amused himself by thinking over this gossip, and quite annoyed his sister by his absence of mind.

"Gerald, do you know Ned's commission has come?"

"Very interesting. Read on, Bella."

"You stupid boy! You don't know a word I say," and she put down the book to repeat her news.

"I'm glad of it; now we must get him off as soon as possible— that is, I suppose he will want to be off as soon as possible." And Coventry woke up from his reverie.

"You needn't check yourself, I know all about it. I think Ned was very foolish, and that Miss Muir has behaved beautifully. It's quite impossible, of course, but I wish it wasn't, I do so like to watch lovers. You and Lucia are so cold you are not a bit interesting."

"You'll do me a favor if you'll stop all that nonsense about Lucia and me. We are not lovers, and never shall be, I fancy. At all events, I'm tired of the thing, and wish you and Mamma would let it drop, for the present at least."

"Oh Gerald, you know Mamma has set her heart upon it, that Papa desired it, and poor Lucia loves you so much. How can you speak of dropping what will make us all so happy?"

"It won't make me happy, and I take the liberty of thinking that

this is of some importance. I'm not bound in any way, and don't
intend to be till I am ready. Now we'll talk about Ned."

Much grieved and surprised, Bella obeyed, and devoted herself
to Edward, who very wisely submitted to his fate and prepared to
leave home for some months. For a week the house was in a state of
excitement about his departure, and everyone but Jean was busied for
him. She was scarcely seen; every morning she gave Bella her lessons,
every afternoon drove out with Mrs. Coventry, and nearly every evening went up to the Hall to read to Sir John, who found his wish
granted without exactly knowing how it had been done.

The day Edward left, he came down from bidding his mother
good-bye, looking very pale, for he had lingered in his sister's little
room with Miss Muir as long as he dared.

"Good-bye, dear. Be kind to Jean," he whispered as he kissed
his sister.

"I will, I will," returned Bella, with tearful eyes.

"Take care of Mamma, and remember Lucia," he said again, as
he touched his cousin's beautiful cheek.

"Fear nothing. I will keep them apart," she whispered back, and
Coventry heard it.

Edward offered his hand to his brother, saying, significantly, as
he looked him in the eye, "I trust you, Gerald."

"You may, Ned."

Then he went, and Coventry tired himself with wondering what
Lucia meant. A few days later he understood.

Now Ned is gone, little Muir will appear, I fancy, he said to
himself; but "little Muir" did not appear, and seemed to shun him
more carefully than she had done her lover. If he went to the drawing
room in the evening hoping for music, Lucia alone was there. If he
tapped at Bella's door, there was always a pause before she opened it,
and no sign of Jean appeared though her voice had been audible when
he knocked. If he went to the library, a hasty rustle and the sound of
flying feet betrayed that the room was deserted at his approach. In the
garden Miss Muir never failed to avoid him, and if by chance they
met in hall or breakfast room, she passed him with downcast eyes and
the briefest, coldest greeting. All this annoyed him intensely, and the

more she eluded him, the more he desired to see her—from a spirit
of opposition, he said, nothing more. It fretted and yet it entertained
him, and he found a lazy sort of pleasure in thwarting the girl's little
maneuvers. His patience gave out at last, and he resolved to know
what was the meaning of this peculiar conduct. Having locked and
taken away the key of one door in the library, he waited till Miss
Muir went in to get a book for his uncle. He had heard her speak to
Bella of it, knew that she believed him with his mother, and smiled
to himself as he stole after her. She was standing in a chair, reaching
up, and he had time to see a slender waist, a pretty foot, before he
spoke.

"Can I help you, Miss Muir?"

She started, dropped several books, and turned scarlet, as she said
hurriedly, "Thank you, no; I can get the steps."

"My long arm will be less trouble. I've got but one, and that is
tired of being idle, so it is very much at your service. What will you
have?"

"I—I—you startled me so I've forgotten." And Jean laughed,
nervously, as she looked about her as if planning to escape.

"I beg your pardon, wait till you remember, and let me thank
you for the enchanted sleep you gave me ten days ago. I've had no
chance yet, you've shunned me so pertinaciously."

"Indeed I try not to be rude, but—" She checked herself, and
turned her face away, adding, with an accent of pain in her voice, "It
is not my fault, Mr. Coventry. I only obey orders."

"Whose orders?" he demanded, still standing so that she could
not escape.

"Don't ask; it is one who has a right to command where you are
concerned. Be sure that it is kindly meant, though it may seem folly
to us. Nay, don't be angry, laugh at it, as I do, and let me run away,
please."

She turned, and looked down at him with tears in her eyes, a
smile on her lips, and an expression half sad, half arch, which was
altogether charming. The frown passed from his face, but he still
looked grave and said decidedly, "No one has a right to command in

this house but my mother or myself. Was it she who bade you avoid me as if I was a madman or a pest?"

"Ah, don't ask. I promised not to tell, and you would not have me break my word, I know." And still smiling, she regarded him with a look of merry malice which made any other reply unnecessary. It was Lucia, he thought, and disliked his cousin intensely just then. Miss Muir moved as if to step down; he detained her, saying earnestly, yet with a smile, "Do you consider me the master here?"

"Yes," and to the word she gave a sweet, submissive intonation which made it expressive of the respect, regard, and confidence which men find pleasantest when women feel and show it. Unconsciously his face softened, and he looked up at her with a different glance from any he had ever given her before.

"Well, then, will you consent to obey me if I am not tyrannical or unreasonable in my demands?"

"I'll try."

"Good! Now frankly, I want to say that all this sort of thing is very disagreeable to me. It annoys me to be a restraint upon anyone's liberty or comfort, and I beg you will go and come as freely as you like, and not mind Lucia's absurdities. She means well, but hasn't a particle of penetration or tact. Will you promise this?"

"No."

"Why not?"

"It is better as it is, perhaps."

"But you called it folly just now."

"Yes, it seems so, and yet—" She paused, looking both confused and distressed.

Coventry lost patience, and said hastily, "You women are such enigmas I never expect to understand you! Well, I've done my best to make you comfortable, but if you prefer to lead this sort of life, I beg you will do so."

"I *don't* prefer it; it is hateful to me. I like to be myself, to have my liberty, and the confidence of those about me. But I cannot think it kind to disturb the peace of anyone, and so I try to obey. I've promised Bella to remain, but I will go rather than have another scene with Miss Beaufort or with you."

Miss Muir had burst out impetuously, and stood there with a sudden fire in her eyes, sudden warmth and spirit in her face and voice that amazed Coventry. She was angry, hurt, and haughty, and the change only made her more attractive, for not a trace of her former meek self remained. Coventry was electrified, and still more surprised when she added, imperiously, with a gesture as if to put him aside, "Hand me that book and move away. I wish to go."

He obeyed, even offered his hand, but she refused it, stepped lightly down, and went to the door. There she turned, and with the same indignant voice, the same kindling eyes and glowing cheeks, she said rapidly, "I know I have no right to speak in this way. I restrain myself as long as I can, but when I can bear no more, my true self breaks loose, and I defy everything. I am tired of being a cold, calm machine; it is impossible with an ardent nature like mine, and I shall try no longer. I cannot help it if people love me. I don't want their love. I only ask to be left in peace, and why I am tormented so I cannot see. I've neither beauty, money, nor rank, yet every foolish boy mistakes my frank interest for something warmer, and makes me miserable. It is my misfortune. Think of me what you will, but beware of me in time, for against my will I may do you harm."

Almost fiercely she had spoken, and with a warning gesture she hurried from the room, leaving the young man feeling as if a sudden thunder-gust had swept through the house. For several minutes he sat in the chair she left, thinking deeply. Suddenly he rose, went to his sister, and said, in his usual tone of indolent good nature, "Bella, didn't I hear Ned ask you to be kind to Miss Muir?"

"Yes, and I try to be, but she is so odd lately."

"Odd! How do you mean?"

"Why, she is either as calm and cold as a statue, or restless and queer; she cries at night, I know, and sighs sadly when she thinks I don't hear. Something is the matter."

"She frets for Ned perhaps," began Coventry.

"Oh dear, no; it's a great relief to her that he is gone. I'm afraid that she likes someone very much, and someone don't like her. Can it be Mr. Sydney?"

"She called him a 'titled fool' once, but perhaps that didn't mean anything. Did you ever ask her about him?" said Coventry, feeling rather ashamed of his curiosity, yet unable to resist the temptation of questioning unsuspecting Bella.

"Yes, but she only looked at me in her tragical way, and said, so pitifully, 'My little friend, I hope you will never have to pass through the scenes I've passed through, but keep your peace unbroken all your life.' After that I dared say no more. I'm very fond of her, I want to make her happy, but I don't know how. Can you propose anything?"

"I was going to propose that you make her come among us more, now Ned is gone. It must be dull for her, moping about alone. I'm sure it is for me. She is an entertaining little person, and I enjoy her music very much. It's good for Mamma to have gay evenings; so you bestir yourself, and see what you can do for the general good of the family."

"That's all very charming, and I've proposed it more than once, but Lucia spoils all my plans. She is afraid you'll follow Ned's example, and that is so silly."

"Lucia is a—no, I won't say fool, because she has sense enough when she chooses; but I wish you'd just settle things with Mamma, and then Lucia can do nothing but submit," said Gerald angrily.

"I'll try, but she goes up to read to Uncle, you know, and since he has had the gout, she stays later, so I see little of her in the evening. There she goes now. I think she will captivate the old one as well as the young one, she is so devoted."

Coventry looked after her slender black figure, just vanishing through the great gate, and an uncomfortable fancy took possession of him, born of Bella's careless words. He sauntered away, and after eluding his cousin, who seemed looking for him, he turned toward the Hall, saying to himself, I will see what is going on up here. Such things have happened. Uncle is the simplest soul alive, and if the girl is ambitious, she can do what she will with him.

Here a servant came running after him and gave him a letter, which he thrust into his pocket without examining it. When he reached the Hall, he went quietly to his uncle's study. The door was ajar, and looking in, he saw a scene of tranquil comfort, very pleasant to watch. Sir John leaned in his easy chair with one foot on a cushion. He was dressed with his usual care and, in spite of the gout, looked like a handsome, well-preserved old gentleman. He was smiling as he listened, and his eyes rested complacently on Jean Muir, who sat near him reading in her musical voice, while the sunshine glittered on her hair and the soft rose of her cheek. She read well, yet Coventry thought her heart was not in her task, for once when she paused, while Sir John spoke, her eyes had an absent expression, and she leaned her head upon her hand, with an air of patient weariness.

Poor girl! I did her great injustice; she has no thought of captivating the old man, but amuses him from simple kindness. She is tired. I'll put an end to her task; and Coventry entered without knocking.

Sir John received him with an air of polite resignation, Miss Muir with a perfectly expressionless face.

"Mother's love, and how are you today, sir?"

"Comfortable, but dull, so I want you to bring the girls over this evening, to amuse the old gentleman. Mrs. King has got out the antique costumes and trumpery, as I promised Bella she should have them, and tonight we are to have a merrymaking, as we used to do when Ned was here."

"Very well, sir, I'll bring them. We've all been out of sorts since the lad left, and a little jollity will do us good. Are you going back, Miss Muir?" asked Coventry.

"No, I shall keep her to give me my tea and get things ready. Don't read anymore, my dear, but go and amuse yourself with the pictures, or whatever you like," said Sir John; and like a dutiful daughter she obeyed, as if glad to get away.

"That's a very charming girl, Gerald," began Sir John as she left the room. "I'm much interested in her, both on her own account and on her mother's."

"Her mother's! What do you know of her mother?" asked Coventry, much surprised.

"Her mother was Lady Grace Howard, who ran away with a poor Scotch minister twenty years ago. The family cast her off, and she lived and died so obscurely that very little is known of her except that she left an orphan girl at some small French pension. This is the girl, and a fine girl, too. I'm surprised that you did not know this."

"So am I, but it is like her not to tell. She is a strange, proud creature. Lady Howard's daughter! Upon my word, that is a discovery," and Coventry felt his interest in his sister's governess much increased by this fact; for, like all wellborn Englishmen, he valued rank and gentle blood even more than he cared to own.

"She has had a hard life of it, this poor little girl, but she has a brave spirit, and will make her way anywhere," said Sir John admiringly.

"Did Ned know this?" asked Gerald suddenly.

"No, she only told me yesterday. I was looking in the *Peerage* and chanced to speak of the Howards. She forgot herself and called Lady Grace her mother. Then I got the whole story, for the lonely little thing was glad to make a confidant of someone."

"That accounts for her rejection of Sydney and Ned: she knows she is their equal and will not snatch at the rank which is hers by right. No, she's not mercenary or ambitious."

"What do you say?" asked Sir John, for Coventry had spoken more to himself than to his uncle.

"I wonder if Lady Sydney was aware of this?" was all Gerald's answer.

"No, Jean said she did not wish to be pitied, and so told nothing to the mother. I think the son knew, but that was a delicate point, and I asked no questions."

"I shall write to him as soon as I discover his address. We have been so intimate I can venture to make a few inquiries about Miss Muir, and prove the truth of her story."

"Do you mean to say that you doubt it?" demanded Sir John angrily.

"I beg your pardon, Uncle, but I must confess I have an instinctive distrust of that young person. It is unjust, I dare say, yet I cannot banish it."

"Don't annoy me by expressing it, if you please. I have some penetration and experience, and I respect and pity Miss Muir heartily.

This dislike of yours may be the cause of her late melancholy, hey, Gerald?" And Sir John looked suspiciously at his nephew.

Anxious to avert the rising storm, Coventry said hastily as he turned away, "I've neither time nor inclination to discuss the matter now, sir, but will be careful not to offend again. I'll take your message to Bella, so good-bye for an hour, Uncle."

And Coventry went his way through the park, thinking within himself, The dear old gentleman is getting fascinated, like poor Ned. How the deuce does the girl do it? Lady Howard's daughter, yet never told us; I don't understand that.

CHAPTER V. HOW THE GIRL DID IT

At home he found a party of young friends, who hailed with delight the prospect of a revel at the Hall. An hour later, the blithe company trooped into the great saloon, where preparations had already been made for a dramatic evening.

Good Sir John was in his element, for he was never so happy as when his house was full of young people. Several persons were chosen, and in a few moments the curtains were withdrawn from the first of these impromptu tableaux. A swarthy, darkly bearded man lay asleep on a tiger skin, in the shadow of a tent. Oriental arms and drapery surrounded him; an antique silver lamp burned dimly on a table where fruit lay heaped in costly dishes, and wine shone redly in half-emptied goblets. Bending over the sleeper was a woman robed with barbaric splendor. One hand turned back the embroidered sleeve from the arm which held a scimitar; one slender foot in a scarlet sandal was visible under the white tunic; her purple mantle swept down from snowy shoulders; fillets of gold bound her hair, and jewels shone on neck and arms. She was looking over her shoulder toward the entrance of the tent, with a steady yet stealthy look, so effective that for a moment the spectators held their breath, as if they also heard a passing footstep.

"Who is it?" whispered Lucia, for the face was new to her.

"Jean Muir," answered Coventry, with an absorbed look.

"Impossible! She is small and fair," began Lucia, but a hasty "Hush, let me look!" from her cousin silenced her.

Impossible as it seemed, he was right nevertheless; for Jean Muir it was. She had darkened her skin, painted her eyebrows, disposed some wild black locks over her fair hair, and thrown such an intensity of expression into her eyes that they darkened and dilated till they were as fierce as any southern eyes that ever flashed. Hatred, the deepest and bitterest, was written on her sternly beautiful face, courage glowed in her glance, power spoke in the nervous grip of the slender hand that held the weapon, and the indomitable will of the woman was expressed—even the firm pressure of the little foot half hidden in the tiger skin.

"Oh, isn't she splendid?" cried Bella under her breath.

"She looks as if she'd use her sword well when the time comes," said someone admiringly.

"Good night to Holofernes; his fate is certain," added another.

"He is the image of Sydney, with that beard on."

"Doesn't she look as if she really hated him?"

"Perhaps she does."

Coventry uttered the last exclamation, for the two which preceded it suggested an explanation of the marvelous change in Jean. It was not all art: the intense detestation mingled with a savage joy that the object of her hatred was in her power was too perfect to be feigned; and having the key to a part of her story, Coventry felt as if he caught a glimpse of the truth. It was but a glimpse, however, for the curtain dropped before he had half analyzed the significance of that strange face.

"Horrible! I'm glad it's over," said Lucia coldly.

"Magnificent! Encore! Encore!" cried Gerald enthusiastically.

But the scene was over, and no applause could recall the actress. Two or three graceful or gay pictures followed, but Jean was in none, and each lacked the charm which real talent lends to the simplest part.

"Coventry, you are wanted," called a voice. And to everyone's surprise, Coventry went, though heretofore he had always refused to exert himself when handsome actors were in demand.

"What part am I to spoil?" he asked, as he entered the green room, where several excited young gentlemen were costuming and attitudinizing.

"A fugitive cavalier. Put yourself into this suit, and lose no time asking questions. Miss Muir will tell you what to do. She is in the tableau, so no one will mind you," said the manager pro tem, throwing a rich old suit toward Coventry and resuming the painting of a moustache on his own boyish face.

A gallant cavalier was the result of Gerald's hasty toilet, and when he appeared before the ladies a general glance of admiration was bestowed upon him.

"Come along and be placed; Jean is ready on the stage." And Bella ran before him, exclaiming to her governess, "Here he is, quite splendid. Wasn't he good to do it?"

Miss Muir, in the charmingly prim and puritanical dress of a Roundhead damsel, was arranging some shrubs, but turned suddenly and dropped the green branch she held, as her eye met the glittering figure advancing toward her.

"You!" she said with a troubled look, adding low to Bella, "Why did you ask him? I begged you not."

"He is the only handsome man here, and the best actor if he likes. He won't play usually, so make the most of him." And Bella was off to finish powdering her hair for "The Marriage à la Mode."

"I was sent for and I came. Do you prefer some other person?" asked Coventry, at a loss to understand the half-anxious, half-eager expression of the face under the little cap.

It changed to one of mingled annoyance and resignation as she said, "It is too late. Please kneel here, half behind the shrubs; put down your hat, and—allow me—you are too elegant for a fugitive."

As he knelt before her, she disheveled his hair, pulled his lace collar awry, threw away his gloves and sword, and half untied the cloak that hung about his shoulders.

"That is better; your paleness is excellent—nay, don't spoil it. We are to represent the picture which hangs in the Hall. I need tell you no more. Now, Roundheads, place yourselves, and then ring up the curtain."

With a smile, Coventry obeyed her; for the picture was of two lovers, the young cavalier kneeling, with his arm around the waist of the girl, who tries to hide him with her little mantle, and presses his head to her bosom in an ecstasy of fear, as she glances back at the approaching pursuers. Jean hesitated an instant and shrank a little as his hand touched her; she blushed deeply, and her eyes fell before his. Then, as the bell rang, she threw herself into her part with sudden spirit. One arm half covered him with her cloak, the other pillowed his head on the muslin kerchief folded over her bosom, and she looked backward with such terror in her eyes that more than one chivalrous young spectator longed to hurry to the rescue. It lasted but a moment; yet in that moment Coventry experienced another new sensation. Many women had smiled on him, but he had remained heart-whole, cool, and careless, quite unconscious of the power which a woman possesses and knows how to use, for the weal or woe of man. Now, as he knelt there with a soft arm about him, a slender waist yielding to his touch, and a maiden heart throbbing against his cheek, for the first time in his life he felt the indescribable spell of womanhood, and looked the ardent lover to perfection. Just as his face assumed this new and most becoming aspect, the curtain dropped, and clamorous encores recalled him to the fact that Miss Muir was trying to escape from his hold, which had grown painful in its unconscious pressure. He sprang up, half bewildered, and looking as he had never looked before.

"Again! Again!" called Sir John. And the young men who played the Roundheads, eager to share in the applause begged for a repetition in new attitudes.

"A rustle has betrayed you, we have fired and shot the brave girl, and she lies dying, you know. That will be effective; try it, Miss Muir," said one. And with a long breath, Jean complied.

The curtain went up, showing the lover still on his knees, unmindful of the captors who clutched him by the shoulder, for at his feet the girl lay dying. Her head was on his breast, now, her eyes looked full into his, no longer wild with fear, but eloquent with the love which even death could not conquer. The power of those tender eyes thrilled Coventry with a strange delight, and set his heart beating as rapidly as hers had done. She felt his hands tremble, saw the color flash into his cheek, knew that she had touched him at last, and when she rose it was with a sense of triumph which she found it hard to conceal. Others thought it fine acting; Coventry tried to believe so; but Lucia set her teeth, and, as the curtain fell on that second picture, she left her place to hurry behind the scenes, bent on putting an end to such dangerous play. Several actors were complimenting the mimic lovers. Jean took it merrily, but Coventry, in spite of himself, betrayed that he was excited by something deeper than mere gratified vanity.

As Lucia appeared, his manner changed to its usual indifference; but he could not quench the unwonted fire of his eyes, or keep all trace of emotion out of his face, and she saw this with a sharp pang.

"I have come to offer my help. You must be tired, Miss Muir. Can I relieve you?" said Lucia hastily.

"Yes, thank you. I shall be very glad to leave the rest to you, and enjoy them from the front."

So with a sweet smile Jean tripped away, and to Lucia's dismay Coventry followed.

"I want you, Gerald; please stay," she cried.

"I've done my part—no more tragedy for me tonight." And he was gone before she could entreat or command.

There was no help for it; she must stay and do her duty, or expose her jealousy to the quick eyes about her. For a time she bore it; but the sight of her cousin leaning over the chair she had left and chatting with the governess, who now filled it, grew unbearable, and she dispatched a little girl with a message to Miss Muir.

"Please, Miss Beaufort wants you for Queen Bess, as you are the only lady with red hair. Will you come?" whispered the child, quite unconscious of any hidden sting in her words.

"Yes, dear, willingly though I'm not stately enough for Her Majesty, nor handsome enough," said Jean, rising with an untroubled face, though she resented the feminine insult.

"Do you want an Essex? I'm all dressed for it," said Coventry, following to the door with a wistful look.

"No, Miss Beaufort said *you* were not to come. She doesn't want you both together," said the child decidedly.

Jean gave him a significant look, shrugged her shoulders, and went away smiling her odd smile, while Coventry paced up and down the hall in a curious state of unrest, which made him forgetful of everything till the young people came gaily out to supper.

"Come, bonny Prince Charlie, take me down, and play the lover as charmingly as you did an hour ago. I never thought you had so much warmth in you," said Bella, taking his arm and drawing him on against his will.

"Don't be foolish, child. Where is—Lucia?"

Why he checked Jean's name on his lips and substituted another's, he could not tell; but a sudden shyness in speaking of her possessed him, and though he saw her nowhere, he would not ask for her. His cousin came down looking lovely in a classical costume; but Gerald scarcely saw her, and, when the merriment was at its height, he slipped away to discover what had become of Miss Muir.

Alone in the deserted drawing room he found her, and paused to watch her a moment before he spoke; for something in her attitude and face struck him. She was leaning wearily back in the great chair which had served for a throne. Her royal robes were still unchanged, though the crown was off and all her fair hair hung about her shoulders. Excitement and exertion made her brilliant, the rich dress became her wonderfully, and an air of luxurious indolence changed the meek governess into a charming woman. She leaned on the velvet cushions as if she were used to such support; she played with the jewels which had crowned her as carelessly as if she were born to wear them; her attitude was full of negligent grace, and the expression of her face half proud, half pensive, as if her thoughts were bittersweet.

One would know she was wellborn to see her now. Poor girl, what a burden a life of dependence must be to a spirit like hers! I wonder what she is thinking of so intently. And Coventry indulged in another look before he spoke.

"Shall I bring you some supper, Miss Muir?"

"Supper!" she ejaculated, with a start. "Who thinks of one's body when one's soul is—" She stopped there, knit her brows, and laughed faintly as she added, "No, thank you. I want nothing but advice, and that I dare not ask of anyone."

"Why not?"

"Because I have no right."

"Everyone has a right to ask help, especially the weak of the strong. Can I help you? Believe me, I most heartily offer my poor services."

"Ah, you forget! This dress, the borrowed splendor of these jewels, the freedom of this gay evening, the romance of the part you played, all blind you to the reality. For a moment I cease to be a servant, and for a moment you treat me as an equal."

It was true; he *had* forgotten. That soft, reproachful glance touched him, his distrust melted under the new charm, and he answered with real feeling in voice and face, "I treat you as an equal because you *are* one; and when I offer help, it is not to my sister's governess alone, but to Lady Howard's daughter."

"Who told you that?" she demanded, sitting erect.

"My uncle. Do not reproach him. It shall go no further, if you forbid it. Are you sorry that I know it?"

"Yes."

"Why?"

"Because I will not be pitied!" And her eyes flashed as she made a half-defiant gesture.

"Then, if I may not pity the hard fate which has befallen an innocent life, may I admire the courage which meets adverse fortune so bravely, and conquers the world by winning the respect and regard of all who see and honor it?"

Miss Muir averted her face, put up her hand, and answered hastily, "No, no, not that! Do not be kind; it destroys the only barrier now left between us. Be cold to me as before, forget what I am, and let me go on my way, unknown, unpitied, and unloved!"

Her voice faltered and failed as the last word was uttered, and she bent her face upon her hand. Something jarred upon Coventry in this speech, and moved him to say, almost rudely, "You need have no fears for me. Lucia will tell you what an iceberg I am."

"Then Lucia would tell me wrong. I have the fatal power of reading character; I know you better than she does, and I see—" There she stopped abruptly.

"What? Tell me and prove your skill," he said eagerly.

Turning, she fixed her eyes on him with a penetrating power that made him shrink as she said slowly, "Under the ice I see fire, and warn you to beware lest it prove a volcano."

For a moment he sat dumb, wondering at the insight of the girl; for she was the first to discover the hidden warmth of a nature too proud to confess its tender impulses, or the ambitions that slept till some potent voice awoke them. The blunt, almost stern manner in which she warned him away from her only made her more attractive; for there was no conceit or arrogance in it, only a foreboding fear emboldened by past suffering to be frank. Suddenly he spoke impetuously:

"You are right! I am not what I seem, and my indolent indifference is but the mask under which I conceal my real self. I could be as passionate, as energetic and aspiring as Ned, if I had any aim in life. I have none, and so I am what you once called me, a thing to pity and despise."

"I never said that!" cried Jean indignantly.

"Not in those words, perhaps; but you looked it and thought it, though you phrased it more mildly. I deserved it, but I shall deserve it no longer. I am beginning to wake from my disgraceful idleness, and long for some work that shall make a man of me. Why do you go? I annoy you with my confessions. Pardon me. They are the first I ever made; they shall be the last."

"No, oh no! I am too much honored by your confidence; but is it wise, is it loyal to tell *me* your hopes and aims? Has not Miss Beaufort the first right to be your confidante?"

Coventry drew back, looking intensely annoyed, for the name recalled much that he would gladly have forgotten in the novel excitement of the hour. Lucia's love, Edward's parting words, his own reserve so strangely thrown aside, so difficult to resume. What he would have said was checked by the sight of a half-open letter which fell from Jean's dress as she moved away. Mechanically he took it up to return it, and, as he did so, he recognized Sydney's handwriting. Jean snatched it from him, turning pale to the lips as she cried, "Did you read it? What did you see? Tell me, tell me, on your honor!"

"On my honor, I saw nothing but this single sentence, 'By the love I bear you, believe what I say.' No more, as I am a gentleman. I know the hand, I guess the purport of the letter, and as a friend of Sydney, I earnestly desire to help you, if I can. Is this the matter upon which you want advice?"

"Yes."

"Then let me give it?"

"You cannot, without knowing all, and it is so hard to tell!"

"Let me guess it, and spare you the pain of telling. May I?" And Coventry waited eagerly for her reply, for the spell was still upon him.

Holding the letter fast, she beckoned him to follow, and glided before him to a secluded little nook, half boudoir, half conservatory. There she paused, stood an instant as if in doubt, then looked up at him with confiding eyes and said decidedly, "I will do it; for, strange as it may seem, you are the only person to whom I *can* speak. You know Sydney, you have discovered that I am an equal, you have offered your help. I accept it; but oh, do not think me unwomanly! Remember how alone I am, how young, and how much I rely upon your sincerity, your sympathy!"

"Speak freely. I am indeed your friend." And Coventry sat down beside her, forgetful of everything but the soft-eyed girl who confided in him so entirely.

Speaking rapidly, Jean went on, "You know that Sydney loved me, that I refused him and went away. But you do not know that his importunities nearly drove me wild, that he threatened to rob me of my only treasure, my good name, and that, in desperation, I tried to kill myself. Yes, mad, wicked as it was, I did long to end the life which was, at best, a burden, and under his persecution had become a torment. You are shocked, yet what I say is the living truth. Lady Sydney will confirm it, the nurses at the hospital will confess that it was not a fever which brought me there; and here, though the external wound is healed, my heart still aches and burns with the shame and indignation which only a proud woman can feel."

She paused and sat with kindling eyes, glowing cheeks, and both hands pressed to her heaving bosom, as if the old insult roused her spirit anew. Coventry said not a word, for surprise, anger, incredulity, and admiration mingled so confusedly in his mind that he forgot to speak, and Jean went on, "That wild act of mine convinced him of my indomitable dislike. He went away, and I believed that this stormy love of his would be cured by absence. It is not, and I live in daily fear of fresh entreaties, renewed persecution. His mother promised not to betray where I had gone, but he found me out and wrote to me. The letter I asked you to take to Lady Sydney was a reply to his, imploring him to leave me in peace. You failed to deliver it, and I was glad, for I thought silence might quench hope. All in vain; this is a more passionate appeal than ever, and he vows he will never desist from his endeavors till I give another man the right to protect me. I *can* do this—I am sorely tempted to do it, but I rebel against the cruelty. I love my freedom, I have no wish to marry at this man's bidding. What can I do? How can I free myself? Be my friend, and help me!"

Tears streamed down her cheeks, sobs choked her words, and she clasped her hands imploringly as she turned toward the young man in all the abandonment of sorrow, fear, and supplication. Coventry found it hard to meet those eloquent eyes and answer calmly, for he had no experience in such scenes and knew not how to play his part. It is this absurd dress and that romantic nonsense which makes me feel so unlike myself, he thought, quite unconscious of the dangerous power which the dusky room, the midsummer warmth and fragrance, the memory of the "romantic nonsense," and, most of all, the presence of a beautiful, afflicted woman had over him. His usual self-possession deserted him, and he could only echo the words which had made the strongest impression upon him:

"You *can* do this, you are tempted to do it. Is Ned the man who can protect you?"

"No" was the soft reply.

"Who then?"

"Do not ask me. A good and honorable man; one who loves me well, and would devote his life to me; one whom once it would have been happiness to marry, but now—"

There her voice ended in a sigh, and all her fair hair fell down about her face, hiding it in a shining veil.

"Why not now? This is a sure and speedy way of ending your distress. Is it impossible?"

In spite of himself, Gerald leaned nearer, took one of the little hands in his, and pressed it as he spoke, urgently, compassionately, nay, almost tenderly. From behind the veil came a heavy sigh, and the brief answer, "It is impossible."

"Why, Jean?"

She flung her hair back with a sudden gesture, drew away her hand, and answered, almost fiercely, "Because I do not love him! Why do you torment me with such questions? I tell you I am in a sore strait and cannot see my way. Shall I deceive the good man, and secure peace at the price of liberty and truth? Or shall I defy Sydney and lead a life of dread? If he menaced my life, I should not fear; but he menaces that which is dearer than life—my good name. A look, a word can tarnish it; a scornful smile, a significant shrug can do me more harm than any blow; for I am a woman—friendless, poor, and at the mercy of his tongue. Ah, better to have died, and so have been saved the bitter pain that has come now!"

She sprang up, clasped her hands over her head, and paced despairingly through the little room, not weeping, but wearing an expression more tragical than tears. Still feeling as if he had suddenly stepped into a romance, yet finding a keen pleasure in the part assigned him, Coventry threw himself into it with spirit, and heartily did his best to console the poor girl who needed help so much. Going to her, he said as impetuously as Ned ever did, "Miss Muir—nay, I will say Jean, if that will comfort you—listen, and rest assured that no harm shall touch you if I can ward it off. You are needlessly alarmed. Indignant you may well be, but, upon my life, I think you wrong Sydney. He is violent, I know, but he is too honorable a man to injure you by a light word, an unjust act. He did but threaten, hoping to soften you. Let me see him, or write to him. He is my friend; he will listen to me. Of that I am sure."

"Be sure of nothing. When a man like Sydney loves and is thwarted in his love, nothing can control his headstrong will. Promise me you will not see or write to him. Much as I fear and despise him,

I will submit, rather than any harm should befall you—or your brother. You promise me, Mr. Coventry?"

He hesitated. She clung to his arm with unfeigned solicitude in her eager, pleading face, and he could not resist it.

"I promise; but in return you must promise to let me give what help I can; and, Jean, never say again that you are friendless."

"You are so kind! God bless you for it. But I dare not accept your friendship; *she* will not permit it, and I have no right to mar her peace."

"Who will not permit it?" he demanded hotly.

"Miss Beaufort."

"Hang Miss Beaufort!" exclaimed Coventry, with such energy that Jean broke into a musical laugh, despite her trouble. He joined in it, and, for an instant they stood looking at one another as if the last barrier were down, and they were friends indeed. Jean paused suddenly, with the smile on her lips, the tears still on her cheek, and made a warning gesture. He listened: the sound of feet mingled with calls and laughter proved that they were missed and sought.

"That laugh betrayed us. Stay and meet them. I cannot." And Jean darted out upon the lawn. Coventry followed; for the thought of confronting so many eyes, so many questions, daunted him, and he fled like a coward. The sound of Jean's flying footsteps guided him, and he overtook her just as she paused behind a rose thicket to take breath.

"Fainthearted knight! You should have stayed and covered my retreat. Hark! they are coming! Hide! Hide!" she panted, half in fear, half in merriment, as the gay pursuers rapidly drew nearer.

"Kneel down; the moon is coming out and the glitter of your embroidery will betray you," whispered Jean, as they cowered behind the roses.

"Your arms and hair will betray you. 'Come under my plaiddie,' as the song says." And Coventry tried to make his velvet cloak cover the white shoulders and fair locks.

"We are acting our parts in reality now. How Bella will enjoy the thing when I tell her!" said Jean as the noises died away.

"Do not tell her," whispered Coventry.

"And why not?" she asked, looking up into the face so near her own, with an artless glance.

"Can you not guess why?"

"Ah, you are so proud you cannot bear to be laughed at."

"It is not that. It is because I do not want you to be annoyed by silly tongues; you have enough to pain you without that. I am your friend, now, and I do my best to prove it."

"So kind, so kind! How can I thank you?" murmured Jean. And she involuntarily nestled closer under the cloak that sheltered both.

Neither spoke for a moment, and in the silence the rapid beating of two hearts was heard. To drown the sound, Coventry said softly, "Are you frightened?"

"No, I like it," she answered, as softly, then added abruptly, "But why do we hide? There is nothing to fear. It is late. I must go. You are kneeling on my train. Please rise."

"Why in such haste? This flight and search only adds to the charm of the evening. I'll not get up yet. Will you have a rose, Jean?"

"No, I will not. Let me go, Mr. Coventry, I insist. There has been enough of this folly. You forget yourself."

She spoke imperiously, flung off the cloak, and put him from her. He rose at once, saying, like one waking suddenly from a pleasant dream, "I do indeed forget myself."

Here the sound of voices broke on them, nearer than before. Pointing to a covered walk that led to the house, he said, in his usually cool, calm tone, "Go in that way; I will cover your retreat." And turning, he went to meet the merry hunters.

Half an hour later, when the party broke up, Miss Muir joined them in her usual quiet dress, looking paler, meeker, and sadder than usual. Coventry saw this, though he neither looked at her nor addressed her. Lucia saw it also, and was glad that the dangerous girl had fallen back into her proper place again, for she had suffered much that night. She appropriated her cousin's arm as they went through the park, but he was in one of his taciturn moods, and all her attempts at conversation were in vain. Miss Muir walked alone, singing softly to herself as she followed in the dusk. Was Gerald so silent because he listened to that fitful song? Lucia thought so, and felt her dislike rapidly deepening to hatred.

When the young friends were gone, and the family were exchanging good-nights among themselves, Jean was surprised by Coventry's offering his hand, for he had never done it before, and whispering, as he held it, though Lucia watched him all the while, "I have not given my advice, yet."

"Thanks, I no longer need it. I have decided for myself."

"May I ask how?"

"To brave my enemy."

"Good! But what decided you so suddenly?"

"The finding of a friend." And with a grateful glance she was gone.

CHAPTER VI. ON THE WATCH

"If you please, Mr. Coventry, did you get the letter last night?" were the first words that greeted the "young master" as he left his room next morning.

"What letter, Dean? I don't remember any," he answered, pausing, for something in the maid's manner struck him as peculiar.

"It came just as you left for the Hall, sir. Benson ran after you with it, as it was marked 'Haste.' Didn't you get it, sir?" asked the woman, anxiously.

"Yes, but upon my life, I forgot all about it till this minute. It's in my other coat, I suppose, if I've not lost it. That absurd masquerading put everything else out of my head." And speaking more to himself than to the maid, Coventry turned back to look for the missing letter.

Dean remained where she was, apparently busy about the arrangement of the curtains at the hall window, but furtively watching meanwhile with a most unwonted air of curiosity.

"Not there, I thought so!" she muttered, as Coventry impatiently thrust his hand into one pocket after another. But as she spoke, an expression of amazement appeared in her face, for suddenly the letter was discovered.

"I'd have sworn it wasn't there! I don't understand it, but she's a deep one, or I'm much deceived." And Dean shook her head like one perplexed. but not convinced.

Coventry uttered an exclamation of satisfaction on glancing at the address and, standing where he was, tore open the letter.

Dear C:

I'm off to Baden. Come and join me, then you'll be out of harm's way; for if you fall in love with J. M. (and you can't escape if you stay where she is), you will incur the trifling inconvenience of having your brains blown out by

Yours truly, F. R. Sydney

"The man is mad!" ejaculated Coventry, staring at the letter while an angry flush rose to his face. "What the deuce does he mean by writing to me in that style? Join him—not I! And as for the threat, I laugh at it. Poor Jean! This headstrong fool seems bent on tormenting her. Well, Dean, what are you waiting for?" he demanded, as if suddenly conscious of her presence.

"Nothing, sir; I only stopped to see if you found the letter. Beg pardon, sir."

And she was moving on when Coventry asked, with a suspicious look, "What made you think it was lost? You seem to take an uncommon interest in my affairs today."

"Oh dear, no, sir. I felt a bit anxious, Benson is so forgetful, and it was me who sent him after you, for I happened to see you go out, so I felt responsible. Being marked that way, I thought it might be important so I asked about it."

"Very well, you can go, Dean. It's all right, you see."

"I'm not so sure of that," muttered the woman, as she curtsied respectfully and went away, looking as if the letter had *not* been found.

Dean was Miss Beaufort's maid, a grave, middle-aged woman with keen eyes and a somewhat grim air. Having been long in the family, she enjoyed all the privileges of a faithful and favorite servant. She loved her young mistress with an almost jealous affection. She watched over her with the vigilant care of a mother and resented any attempt at interference on the part of others. At first she had pitied and liked Jean Muir, then distrusted her, and now heartily hated her, as the cause of the increased indifference of Coventry toward his cousin. Dean knew the depth of Lucia's love, and though no man, in her eyes, was worthy of her mistress, still, having honored him with her regard, Dean felt bound to like him, and the late change in his manner disturbed the maid almost as much as it did the mistress. She watched Jean narrowly, causing that amiable creature much amusement but little annoyance, as yet, for Dean's slow English wit was no match for the subtle mind of the governess. On the preceding night, Dean had been sent up to the Hall with costumes and had there seen something which much disturbed her. She began to speak of it while undressing her mistress, but Lucia, being in an unhappy mood, had so sternly ordered her not to gossip that the tale remained untold, and she was forced to bide her time.

Now I'll see how *she* looks after it; though there's not much to be got out of *her* face, the deceitful hussy, thought Dean, marching down the corridor and knitting her black brows as she went.

"Good morning, Mrs. Dean. I hope you are none the worse for last night's frolic. You had the work and we the play," said a blithe voice behind her; and turning sharply, she confronted Miss Muir. Fresh and smiling, the governess nodded with an air of cordiality which would have been irresistible with anyone but Dean.

"I'm quite well, thank you, miss," she returned coldly, as her keen eye fastened on the girl as if to watch the effect of her words. "I had a good rest when the young ladies and gentlemen were at supper, for while the maids cleared up, I sat in the 'little anteroom.' "

"Yes, I saw you, and feared you'd take cold. Very glad you didn't. How is Miss Beaufort? She seemed rather poorly last night" was the tranquil reply, as Jean settled the little frills about her delicate wrists. The cool question was a return shot for Dean's hint that she had been where she could oversee the interview between Coventry and Miss Muir.

"She is a bit tired, as any *lady* would be after such an evening. People who are *used* to *play-acting* wouldn't mind it, perhaps, but Miss Beaufort don't enjoy *romps* as much as *some* do."

The emphasis upon certain words made Dean's speech as impertinent as she desired. But Jean only laughed, and as Coventry's step was heard behind them, she ran downstairs, saying blandly, but with a wicked look, "I won't stop to thank you now, lest Mr. Coventry should bid me good-morning, and so increase Miss Beaufort's indisposition."

Dean's eyes flashed as she looked after the girl with a wrathful face, and went her way, saying grimly, "I'll bide my time, but I'll get the better of her yet."

Fancying himself quite removed from "last night's absurdity," yet curious to see how Jean would meet him, Coventry lounged into the breakfast room with his usual air of listless indifference. A languid nod and murmur was all the reply he vouchsafed to the greetings of cousin, sister, and governess as he sat down and took up his paper.

"Have you had a letter from Ned?" asked Bella, looking at the note which her brother still held.

"No" was the brief answer.

"Who then? You look as if you had received bad news."

There was no reply, and, peeping over his arm, Bella caught sight of the seal and exclaimed, in a disappointed tone, "It is the Sydney crest. I don't care about the note now. Men's letters to each other are not interesting."

Miss Muir had been quietly feeding one of Edward's dogs, but at the name she looked up and met Coventry's eyes, coloring so distressfully that he pitied her. Why he should take the trouble to cover her confusion, he did not stop to ask himself, but seeing the curl of Lucia's lip, he suddenly addressed her with an air of displeasure, "Do you know that Dean is getting impertinent? She presumes too much on her age and your indulgence, and forgets her place."

"What has she done?" asked Lucia coldly.

"She troubles herself about my affairs and takes it upon herself to keep Benson in order."

Here Coventry told about the letter and the woman's evident curiosity.

"Poor Dean, she gets no thanks for reminding you of what you had forgotten. Next time she will leave your letters to their fate, and perhaps it will be as well, if they have such a bad effect upon your temper, Gerald."

Lucia spoke calmly, but there was an angry color in her cheek as she rose and left the room. Coventry looked much annoyed, for on Jean's face he detected a faint smile, half pitiful, half satirical, which disturbed him more than his cousin's insinuation. Bella broke the awkward silence by saying, with a sigh, "Poor Ned! I do so long to hear again from him. I thought a letter had come for some of us. Dean said she saw one bearing his writing on the hall table yesterday."

"She seems to have a mania for inspecting letters. I won't allow it. Who was the letter for, Bella?" said Coventry, putting down his paper.

"She wouldn't or couldn't tell, but looked very cross and told me to ask you."

"Very odd! I've had none," began Coventry.

"But I had one several days ago. Will you please read it, and my reply?" And as she spoke, Jean laid two letters before him.

"Certainly not. It would be dishonorable to read what Ned intended for no eyes but your own. You are too scrupulous in one way, and not enough so in another, Miss Muir." And Coventry offered both the letters with an air of grave decision, which could not conceal the interest and surprise he felt.

"You are right. Mr. Edward's note *should* be kept sacred, for in it the poor boy has laid bare his heart to me. But mine I beg you will read, that you may see how well I try to keep my word to you. Oblige me in this, Mr. Coventry; I have a right to ask it of you."

So urgently she spoke, so wistfully she looked, that he could not refuse and, going to the window, read the letter. It was evidently an answer to a passionate appeal from the young lover, and was written with consummate skill. As he read, Gerald could not help thinking, If this girl writes in this way to a man whom she does *not* love, with what a world of power and passion would she write to one whom she *did* love. And this thought kept returning to him as his eye went over line after line of wise argument, gentle reproof, good counsel, and friendly regard. Here and there a word, a phrase, betrayed what she had already confessed, and Coventry forgot to return the letter, as he stood wondering who was the man whom Jean loved.

The sound of Bella's voice recalled him, for she was saying, half kindly, half petulantly, "Don't look so sad, Jean. Ned will outlive it, I dare say. You remember you said once men never died of love, though women might. In his one note to me, he spoke so beautifully of you, and begged me to be kind to you for his sake, that I try to be with all my heart, though if it was anyone but you, I really think I should hate them for making my dear boy so unhappy."

"You are too kind, Bella, and I often think I'll go away to relieve you of my presence; but unwise and dangerous as it is to stay, I haven't the courage to go. I've been so happy here." And as she spoke, Jean's head dropped lower over the dog as it nestled to her affectionately.

Before Bella could utter half the loving words that sprang to her lips, Coventry came to them with all languor gone from face and mien, and laying Jean's letter before her, he said, with an undertone of deep feeling in his usually emotionless voice, "A right womanly and eloquent letter, but I fear it will only increase the fire it was meant to quench. I pity my brother more than ever now."

"Shall I send it?" asked Jean, looking straight up at him, like one who had entire reliance on his judgment.

"Yes, I have not the heart to rob him of such a sweet sermon upon self-sacrifice. Shall I post it for you?"

"Thank you; in a moment." And with a grateful look, Jean dropped her eyes. Producing her little purse, she selected a penny, folded it in a bit of paper, and then offered both letter and coin to Coventry, with such a pretty air of business, that he could not control a laugh.

"So you won't be indebted to me for a penny? What a proud woman you are, Miss Muir."

"I am; it's a family failing." And she gave him a significant glance, which recalled to him the memory of who she was. He understood her feeling, and liked her the better for it, knowing that he would have done the same had he been in her place. It was a little thing, but if done for effect, it answered admirably, for it showed a quick insight into his character on her part, and betrayed to him the existence of a pride in which he sympathized heartily. He stood by Jean a moment, watching her as she burnt Edward's letter in the blaze of the spirit lamp under the urn.

"Why do you do that?" he asked involuntarily.

"Because it is my duty to forget" was all her answer.

"Can you always forget when it becomes a duty?"

"I wish I could! I wish I could!"

She spoke passionately, as if the words broke from her against her will, and, rising hastily, she went into the garden, as if afraid to stay.

"Poor, dear Jean is very unhappy about something, but I can't discover what it is. Last night I found her crying over a rose, and now she runs away, looking as if her heart was broken. I'm glad I've got no lessons."

"What kind of a rose?" asked Coventry from behind his paper as Bella paused.

"A lovely white one. It must have come from the Hall; we have none like it. I wonder if Jean was ever going to be married, and lost her lover, and felt sad because the flower reminded her of bridal roses."

Coventry made no reply, but felt himself change countenance as he recalled the little scene behind the rose hedge, where he gave Jean the flower which she had refused yet taken. Presently, to Bella's surprise, he flung down the paper, tore Sydney's note to atoms, and rang for his horse with an energy which amazed her.

"Why, Gerald, what has come over you? One would think Ned's restless spirit had suddenly taken possession of you. What are you going to do?"

"I'm going to work" was the unexpected answer, as Coventry turned toward her with an expression so rarely seen on his fine face.

"What has waked you up all at once?" asked Bella, looking more and more amazed.

"You did," he said, drawing her toward him.

"I! When? How?"

"Do you remember saying once that energy was better than beauty in a man, and that no one could respect an idler?"

"I never said anything half so sensible as that. Jean said something like it once, I believe, but I forgot. Are you tired of doing nothing, at last, Gerald?"

"Yes, I neglected my duty to Ned, till he got into trouble, and now I reproach myself for it. It's not too late to do other neglected tasks, so I'm going at them with a will. Don't say anything about it to anyone, and don't laugh at me, for I'm in earnest, Bell."

"I know you are, and I admire and love you for it, my dear old boy," cried Bella enthusiastically, as she threw her arms about his neck and kissed him heartily. "What will you do first?" she asked, as he stood thoughtfully smoothing the bright head that leaned upon his shoulder, with that new expression still clear and steady in his face.

"I'm going to ride over the whole estate, and attend to things as a master should; not leave it all to Bent, of whom I've heard many complaints, but have been too idle to inquire about them. I shall consult Uncle, and endeavor to be all that my father was in his time. Is that a worthy ambition, dear?"

"Oh, Gerald, let me tell Mamma. It will make her so happy. You are her idol, and to hear you say these things, to see you look so like dear Papa, would do more for her spirits than all the doctors in England."

"Wait till I prove what my resolution is worth. When I have really done something, then I'll surprise Mamma with a sample of my work."

"Of course you'll tell Lucia?"

"Not on any account. It is a little secret between us, so keep it till I give you leave to tell it."

"But Jean will see it at once; she knows everything that happens, she is so quick and wise. Do you mind her knowing?"

"I don't see that I can help it if she is so wonderfully gifted. Let her see what she can, I don't mind her. Now I'm off." And with a kiss to his sister, a sudden smile on his face, Coventry sprang upon his horse and rode away at a pace which caused the groom to stare after him in blank amazement.

Nothing more was seen of him till dinnertime, when he came in so exhilarated by his brisk ride and busy morning that he found some difficulty in assuming his customary manner, and more than once astonished the family by talking animatedly on various subjects which till now had always seemed utterly uninteresting to him. Lucia was amazed, his mother delighted, and Bella could hardly control her desire to explain the mystery; but Jean took it very calmly and regarded him with the air of one who said, "I understand, but you will soon tire of it." This nettled him more than he would confess, and he exerted himself to silently contradict that prophecy.

"Have you answered Mr. Sydney's letter?" asked Bella, when they were all scattered about the drawing room after dinner.

"No," answered her brother, who was pacing up and down with restless steps, instead of lounging near his beautiful cousin.

"I ask because I remembered that Ned sent a message for him in my last note, as he thought you would know Sydney's address. Here it is, something about a horse. Please put it in when you write," and Bella laid the note on the writing table nearby.

"I'll send it at once and have done with it," muttered Coventry and, seating himself, he dashed off a few lines, sealed and sent the letter, and then resumed his march, eyeing the three young ladies with three different expressions, as he passed and repassed. Lucia sat apart, feigning to be intent upon a book, and her handsome face looked almost stern in its haughty composure, for though her heart ached, she was too proud to own it. Bella now lay on the sofa, half asleep, a rosy little creature, as unconsciously pretty as a child. Miss Muir sat in the recess of a deep window, in a low lounging chair, working at an embroidery frame with a graceful industry pleasant to see. Of late she had worn colors, for Bella had been generous in gifts, and the pale blue muslin which flowed in soft waves about her was very becoming to her fair skin and golden hair. The close braids were gone, and loose curls dropped here and there from the heavy coil wound around her well-shaped head. The tip of one dainty foot was visible, and a petulant little gesture which now and then shook back the falling sleeve gave glimpses of a round white arm. Ned's great hound lay nearby, the sunshine flickered on her through the leaves, and as she sat smiling to herself, while the dexterous hands shaped leaf and flower, she made a charming picture of all that is most womanly and winning; a picture which few men's eyes would not have liked to rest upon.

Another chair stood near her, and as Coventry went up and down, a strong desire to take it possessed him. He was tired of his thoughts and wished to be amused by watching the changes of the girl's expressive face, listening to the varying tones of her voice, and trying to discover the spell which so strongly attracted him in spite of himself. More than once he swerved from his course to gratify his whim, but Lucia's presence always restrained him, and with a word to the dog, or a glance from the window, as pretext for a pause, he resumed his walk again. Something in his cousin's face reproached him, but her manner of late was so repellent that he felt no desire to resume their former familiarity, and, wishing to show that he did not consider himself bound, he kept aloof. It was a quiet test of the power of each woman over this man; they instinctively felt it, and both tried to conquer. Lucia spoke several times, and tried to speak frankly and affably; but her manner was constrained, and Coventry, having answered politely, relapsed into silence. Jean said nothing, but silently appealed to eye and ear by the pretty picture she made of herself, the snatches of song she softly sang, as if forgetting that she was not alone, and a shy glance now and then, half wistful, half merry, which was more alluring than graceful figure or sweet voice. When she had tormented Lucia and tempted Coventry long enough, she quietly asserted her supremacy in a way which astonished her rival, who knew nothing of the secret of her birth, which knowledge did much to attract and charm the young man. Letting a ball of silk escape from her lap, she watched it roll toward the promenader, who caught and returned it with an alacrity which added grace to the trifling service. As she took it, she said, in the frank way that never failed to win him, "I think you must be tired; but if exercise is necessary, employ your energies to some purpose and put your mother's basket of silks in order. They are in a tangle, and it will please her to know that you did it, as your brother used to do."

"Hercules at the distaff," said Coventry gaily, and down he sat in the long-desired seat. Jean put the basket on his knee, and as he surveyed it, as if daunted at his task, she leaned back, and indulged in a musical little peal of laughter charming to hear. Lucia sat dumb with surprise, to see her proud, indolent cousin obeying the commands of a governess, and looking as if he heartily enjoyed it. In ten minutes she was as entirely forgotten as if she had been miles away; for Jean seemed in her wittiest, gayest mood, and as she now treated the "young master" like an equal, there was none of the former meek timidity. Yet often her eyes fell, her color changed, and the piquant sallies faltered on her tongue, as Coventry involuntarily looked deep into the fine eyes which had once shone on him so tenderly in that mimic tragedy. He could not forget it, and though neither alluded to it, the memory of the previous evening seemed to haunt both and lend a secret charm to the present moment. Lucia bore this as long as she could, and then left the room with the air of an insulted princess; but Coventry did not, and Jean feigned not to see her go. Bella was fast asleep, and before he knew how it came to pass, the young man was listening to the story of his companion's life. A sad tale, told with wonderful skill, for soon he was absorbed in it. The basket slid unobserved from his knee, the dog was pushed away, and, leaning forward, he listened eagerly as the girl's low voice recounted all the hardships, loneliness, and grief of her short life. In the midst of a touching episode she started, stopped, and looked straight before her, with an intent expression which changed to one of intense contempt, and her eye turned to Coventry's, as she said, pointing to the window behind him, "We are watched."

"By whom?" he demanded, starting up angrily.

"Hush, say nothing, let it pass. I am used to it."

"But *I* am not, and I'll not submit to it. Who was it, Jean?" he answered hotly.

She smiled significantly at a knot of rose-colored ribbon, which a little gust was blowing toward them along the terrace. A black frown darkened the young man's face as he sprang out of the long window and went rapidly out of sight, scrutinizing each green nook as he passed. Jean laughed quietly as she watched him, and said softly to herself, with her eyes on the fluttering ribbon, "That was a fortunate accident, and a happy inspiration. Yes, my dear Mrs. Dean, you will find that playing the spy will only get your mistress as well as yourself

into trouble. You would not be warned, and you must take the consequences, reluctant as I am to injure a worthy creature like yourself."

Soon Coventry was heard returning. Jean listened with suspended breath to catch his first words, for he was not alone.

"Since you insist that it was you and not your mistress, I let it
pass, although I still have my suspicions. Tell Miss Beaufort I desire to
see her for a few moments in the library. Now go, Dean, and be
careful for the future, if you wish to stay in my house."

The maid retired, and the young man came in looking both
ireful and stern.

"I wish I had said nothing, but I was startled, and spoke involuntarily. Now you are angry, and I have made fresh trouble for poor
Miss Lucia. Forgive me as I forgive her, and let it pass. I have learned
to bear this surveillance, and pity her causeless jealousy," said Jean,
with a self-reproachful air.

"I will forgive the dishonorable act, but I cannot forget it, and I
intend to put a stop to it. I am not betrothed to my cousin, as I told
you once, but you, like all the rest, seem bent on believing that I am.
Hitherto I have cared too little about the matter to settle it, but now
I shall prove beyond all doubt that I am free."

As he uttered the last word, Coventry cast on Jean a look that
affected her strangely. She grew pale, her work dropped on her lap,
and her eyes rose to his, with an eager, questioning expression, which
slowly changed to one of mingled pain and pity, as she turned her
face away, murmuring in a tone of tender sorrow, "Poor Lucia, who
will comfort her?"

For a moment Coventry stood silent, as if weighing some fateful
purpose in his mind. As Jean's rapt sigh of compassion reached his
ear, he had echoed it within himself, and half repented of his resolution; then his eye rested on the girl before him looking so lonely in
her sweet sympathy for another that his heart yearned toward her.
Sudden fire shot into his eye, sudden warmth replaced the cold stern-
ness of his face, and his steady voice faltered suddenly, as he said, very
low, yet very earnestly, "Jean, I have tried to love her, but I cannot.
Ought I to deceive her, and make myself miserable to please my
family?"

"She is beautiful and good, and loves you tenderly; is there no hope for her?" asked Jean, still pale, but very quiet, though she held one hand against her heart, as if to still or hide its rapid beating.

"None," answered Coventry.

"But can you not learn to love her? Your will is strong, and most men would not find it a hard task."

"I cannot, for something stronger than my own will controls me."

"What is that?" And Jean's dark eyes were fixed upon him, full of innocent wonder.

His fell, and he said hastily, "I dare not tell you yet."

"Pardon! I should not have asked. Do not consult me in this matter; I am not the person to advise you. I can only say that it seems to me as if any man with an empty heart would be glad to have so beautiful a woman as your cousin."

"My heart is not empty," began Coventry, drawing a step nearer, and speaking in a passionate voice. "Jean, I *must* speak; hear me. I cannot love my cousin, because I love you."

"Stop!" And Jean sprang up with a commanding gesture. "I will not hear you while any promise binds you to another. Remember your mother's wishes, Lucia's hopes, Edward's last words, your own pride, my humble lot. You forget yourself, Mr. Coventry. Think well before you speak, weigh the cost of this act, and recollect who I am before you insult me by any transient passion, any false vows."

"I have thought, I do weigh the cost, and I swear that I desire to woo you as humbly, honestly as I would any lady in the land. You speak of my pride. Do I stoop in loving my equal in rank? You speak of your lowly lot, but poverty is no disgrace, and the courage with which you bear it makes it beautiful. I should have broken with Lucia before I spoke, but I could not control myself. My mother loves you, and will be happy in my happiness. Edward must forgive me, for I have tried to do my best, but love is irresistible. Tell me, Jean, is there any hope for me?"

He had seized her hand and was speaking impetuously, with ardent face and tender tone, but no answer came, for as Jean turned her eloquent countenance toward him, full of maiden shame and timid love, Dean's prim figure appeared at the door, and her harsh voice broke the momentary silence, saying, sternly, "Miss Beaufort is waiting for you, sir."

"Go, go at once, and be kind, for my sake, Gerald," whispered Jean, for he stood as if deaf and blind to everything but her voice, her face.

As she drew his head down to whisper, her cheek touched his, and regardless of Dean, he kissed it, passionately, whispering back, "My little Jean! For your sake I can be anything."

"Miss Beaufort is waiting. Shall I say you will come, sir?" demanded Dean, pale and grim with indignation.

"Yes, yes, I'll come. Wait for me in the garden, Jean." And Coventry hurried away, in no mood for the interview but anxious to have it over.

As the door closed behind him, Dean walked up to Miss Muir, trembling with anger, and laying a heavy hand on her arm, she said below her breath, "I've been expecting this, you artful creature. I saw your game and did my best to spoil it, but you are too quick for me. You think you've got him. There you are mistaken; for as sure as my name is Hester Dean, I'll prevent it, or Sir John shall."

"Take your hand away and treat me with proper respect, or you will be dismissed from this house. Do you know who I am?" And Jean drew herself up with a haughty air, which impressed the woman more deeply than her words. "I am the daughter of Lady Howard and, if I choose it, can be the wife of Mr. Coventry."

Dean drew back amazed, yet not convinced. Being a well-trained servant, as well as a prudent woman, she feared to overstep the bounds of respect, to go too far, and get her mistress as well as herself into trouble. So, though she still doubted Jean, and hated her more than ever, she controlled herself. Dropping a curtsy, she assumed her usual air of deference, and said, meekly, "I beg pardon, miss. If I'd known, I should have conducted myself differently, of course, but ordinary governesses make so much mischief in a house, one can't help mistrusting them. I don't wish to meddle or be overbold, but being fond of my dear young lady, I naturally take her part, and must say that Mr. Coventry has not acted like a gentleman."

"Think what you please, Dean, but I advise you to say as little as possible if you wish to remain. I have not accepted Mr. Coventry yet, and if he chooses to set aside the engagement his family made for him, I think he has a right to do so. Miss Beaufort would hardly care to marry him against his will, because he pities her for her unhappy love," and with a tranquil smile, Miss Muir walked away.

CHAPTER VII. THE LAST CHANCE

"She will tell Sir John, will she? Then I must be before her, and hasten events. It will be as well to have all sure before there can be any danger. My poor Dean, you are no match for me, but you may prove annoying, nevertheless."

These thoughts passed through Miss Muir's mind as she went down the hall, pausing an instant at the library door, for the murmur of voices was heard. She caught no word, and had only time for an instant's pause as Dean's heavy step followed her. Turning, Jean drew a chair before the door, and, beckoning to the woman, she said, smiling still, "Sit here and play watchdog. I am going to Miss Bella, so you can nod if you will."

"Thank you, miss. I will wait for my young lady. She may need me when this hard time is over." And Dean seated herself with a resolute face.

Jean laughed and went on; but her eyes gleamed with sudden malice, and she glanced over her shoulder with an expression which boded ill for the faithful old servant.

"I've got a letter from Ned, and here is a tiny note for you," cried Bella as Jean entered the boudoir. "Mine is a very odd, hasty letter, with no news in it, but his meeting with Sydney. I hope yours is better, or it won't be very satisfactory."

As Sydney's name passed Bella's lips, all the color died out of Miss Muir's face, and the note shook with the tremor of her hand. Her very lips were white, but she said calmly, "Thank you. As you are busy, I'll go and read my letter on the lawn." And before Bella could speak, she was gone.

Hurrying to a quiet nook, Jean tore open the note and read the few blotted lines it contained.

I have seen Sydney; he has told me all; and, hard as I found it to believe, it was impossible to doubt, for he has discovered proofs which cannot be denied. I make no reproaches, shall demand no confession or atonement, for I cannot forget that I once loved you. I give you three days to find another home, before I return to tell the family who you are. Go at once, I beseech you, and spare me the pain of seeing your disgrace.

Slowly, steadily she read it twice over, then sat motionless, knitting her brows in deep thought. Presently she drew a long breath, tore up the note, and rising, went slowly toward the Hall, saying to herself, "Three days, only three days! Can it be accomplished in so short a time? It shall be, if wit and will can do it, for it is my last chance. If this fails, I'll not go back to my old life, but end all at once."

Setting her teeth and clenching her hands, as if some memory stung her, she went on through the twilight, to find Sir John waiting to give her a hearty welcome.

"You look tired, my dear. Never mind the reading tonight; rest yourself, and let the book go," he said kindly, observing her worn look.

"Thank you, sir. I am tired, but I'd rather read, else the book will not be finished before I go."

"Go, child! Where are you going?" demanded Sir John, looking anxiously at her as she sat down.

"I will tell you by-and-by, sir." And opening the book, Jean read for a little while.

But the usual charm was gone; there was no spirit in the voice of the reader, no interest in the face of the listener, and soon he said, abruptly, "My dear, pray stop! I cannot listen with a divided mind. What troubles you? Tell your friend, and let him comfort you."

As if the kind words overcame her, Jean dropped the book, covered up her face, and wept so bitterly that Sir John was much alarmed; for such a demonstration was doubly touching in one who usually was all gaiety and smiles. As he tried to soothe her, his words grew tender, his solicitude full of a more than paternal anxiety, and his kind heart overflowed with pity and affection for the weeping girl. As she grew calmer, he urged her to be frank, promising to help and counsel her, whatever the affliction or fault might be.

"Ah, you are too kind, too generous! How can I go away and leave my one friend?" sighed Jean, wiping the tears away and looking up at him with grateful eyes.

"Then you do care a little for the old man?" said Sir John with an eager look, an involuntary pressure of the hand he held.

Jean turned her face away, and answered, very low, "No one ever was so kind to me as you have been. Can I help caring for you more than I can express?"

Sir John was a little deaf at times, but he heard that, and looked well pleased. He had been rather thoughtful of late, had dressed with unusual care, been particularly gallant and gay when the young ladies visited him, and more than once, when Jean paused in the reading to ask a question, he had been forced to confess that he had not been listening; though, as she well knew, his eyes had been fixed upon her. Since the discovery of her birth, his manner had been peculiarly benignant, and many little acts had proved his interest and goodwill. Now, when Jean spoke of going, a panic seized him, and desolation seemed about to fall upon the old Hall. Something in her unusual agitation struck him as peculiar and excited his curiosity. Never had she seemed so interesting as now, when she sat beside him with tearful eyes, and some soft trouble in her heart which she dared not confess.

"Tell me everything, child, and let your friend help you if he can." Formerly he said "father" or "the old man," but lately he always spoke of himself as her "friend."

"I will tell you, for I have no one else to turn to. I must go away because Mr. Coventry has been weak enough to love me."

"What, Gerald?" cried Sir John, amazed.

"Yes; today he told me this, and left me to break with Lucia; so I ran to you to help me prevent him from disappointing his mother's hopes and plans."

Sir John had started up and paced down the room, but as Jean paused he turned toward her, saying, with an altered face, "Then you do not love him? Is it possible?"

"No, I do not love him," she answered promptly.

"Yet he is all that women usually find attractive. How is it that you have escaped, Jean?"

"I love someone else" was the scarcely audible reply.

Sir John resumed his seat with the air of a man bent on getting at a mystery, if possible.

"It will be unjust to let you suffer for the folly of these boys, my little girl. Ned is gone, and I was sure that Gerald was safe; but now that his turn has come, I am perplexed, for he cannot be sent away."

"No, it is I who must go; but it seems so hard to leave this safe and happy home, and wander away into the wide, cold world again. You have all been too kind to me, and now separation breaks my heart."

A sob ended the speech, and Jean's head went down upon her hands again. Sir John looked at her a moment, and his fine old face was full of genuine emotion, as he said slowly, "Jean, will you stay and be a daughter to the solitary old man?"

"No, sir" was the unexpected answer.

"And why not?" asked Sir John, looking surprised, but rather pleased than angry.

"Because I could not be a daughter to you; and even if I could, it would not be wise, for the gossips would say you were not old enough to be the adopted father of a girl like me. Sir John, young as I am, I know much of the world, and am sure that this kind plan is impractical; but I thank you from the bottom of my heart."

"Where will you go, Jean?" asked Sir John, after a pause.

"To London, and try to find another situation where I can do no harm."

"Will it be difficult to find another home?"

"Yes. I cannot ask Mrs. Coventry to recommend me, when I have innocently brought so much trouble into her family; and Lady Sydney is gone, so I have no friend."

"Except John Coventry. I will arrange all that. When will you go, Jean?"

"Tomorrow."

"So soon!" And the old man's voice betrayed the trouble he was trying to conceal.

Jean had grown very calm, but it was the calmness of desperation. She had hoped that the first tears would produce the avowal for which she waited. It had not, and she began to fear that her last chance was slipping from her. Did the old man love her? If so, why did he not speak? Eager to profit by each moment, she was on the alert for any hopeful hint, any propitious word, look, or act, and every nerve was strung to the utmost.

"Jean, may I ask one question?" said Sir John.

"Anything of me, sir."

"This man whom you love—can he not help you?"

"He could if he knew, but he must not."

"If he knew what? Your present trouble?"

"No. My love."

"He does know this, then?"

"No, thank heaven! And he never will."

"Why not?"

"Because I am too proud to own it."

"He loves you, my child?"

"I do not know—I dare not hope it," murmured Jean.

"Can I not help you here? Believe me, I desire to see you safe and happy. Is there nothing I can do?"

"Nothing, nothing."

"May I know the name?"

"No! No! Let me go; I cannot bear this questioning!" And Jean's distressful face warned him to ask no more.

"Forgive me, and let me do what I may. Rest here quietly. I'll write a letter to a good friend of mine, who will find you a home, if you leave us."

As Sir John passed into his inner study, Jean watched him with despairing eyes and wrung her hands, saying to herself, Has all my skill deserted me when I need it most? How can I make him understand, yet not overstep the bounds of maiden modesty? He is so blind, so timid, or so dull he will not see, and time is going fast. What shall I do to open his eyes?

Her own eyes roved about the room, seeking for some aid from inanimate things, and soon she found it. Close behind the couch where she sat hung a fine miniature of Sir John. At first her eye rested on it as she contrasted its placid comeliness with the unusual pallor and disquiet of the living face seen through the open door, as the old man sat at his desk trying to write and casting covert glances at the girlish figure he had left behind him. Affecting unconsciousness of this, Jean gazed on as if forgetful of everything but the picture, and suddenly, as if obeying an irresistible impulse, she took it down, looked long and fondly at it, then, shaking her curls about her face, as if to hide the act, pressed it to her lips and seemed to weep over it in an uncontrollable paroxysm of tender grief. A sound startled her, and like a guilty thing, she turned to replace the picture; but it dropped from her hand as she uttered a faint cry and hid her face, for Sir John stood before her, with an expression which she could not mistake.

"Jean, why did you do that?" he asked, in an eager, agitated voice.

No answer, as the girl sank lower, like one overwhelmed with shame. Laying his hand on the bent head, and bending his own, he whispered, "Tell me, is the name John Coventry?"

Still no answer, but a stifled sound betrayed that his words had gone home.

"Jean, shall I go back and write the letter, or may I stay and tell you that the old man loves you better than a daughter?"

She did not speak, but a little hand stole out from under the falling hair, as if to keep him. With a broken exclamation he seized it, drew her up into his arms, and laid his gray head on her fair one, too happy for words. For a moment Jean Muir enjoyed her success; then, fearing lest some sudden mishap should destroy it, she hastened to make all secure. Looking up with well-feigned timidity and half-confessed affection, she said softly, "Forgive me that I could not hide this better. I meant to go away and never tell it, but you were so kind it made the parting doubly hard. Why did you ask such dangerous questions? Why did you look, when you should have been writing my dismissal?"

"How could I dream that you loved me, Jean, when you refused the only offer I dared make? Could I be presumptuous enough to fancy you would reject young lovers for an old man like me?" asked Sir John, caressing her.

"You are not old, to me, but everything I love and honor!" interrupted Jean, with a touch of genuine remorse, as this generous, honorable gentleman gave her both heart and home, unconscious of deceit. "It is I who am presumptuous, to dare to love one so far above me. But I did not know how dear you were to me till I felt that I must go. I ought not to accept this happiness. I am not worthy of it; and you will regret your kindness when the world blames you for giving a home to one so poor, and plain, and humble as I."

"Hush, my darling. I care nothing for the idle gossip of the world. If you are happy here, let tongues wag as they will. I shall be too busy enjoying the sunshine of your presence to heed anything that goes on about me. But, Jean, you are sure you love me? It seems incredible that I should win the heart that has been so cold to younger, better men than I."

"Dear Sir John, be sure of this, I love you truly. I will do my best to be a good wife to you, and prove that, in spite of my many faults, I possess the virtue of gratitude."

If he had known the strait she was in, he would have understood the cause of the sudden fervor of her words, the intense thankfulness that shone in her face, the real humility that made her stoop and kiss the generous hand that gave so much. For a few moments she enjoyed and let him enjoy the happy present, undisturbed. But the anxiety which devoured her, the danger which menaced her, soon recalled her, and forced her to wring yet more from the unsuspicious heart she had conquered.

"No need of letters now," said Sir John, as they sat side by side, with the summer moonlight glorifying all the room. "You have found a home for life; may it prove a happy one."

"It is not mine yet, and I have a strange foreboding that it never will be," she answered sadly.

"Why, my child?"

"Because I have an enemy who will try to destroy my peace, to poison your mind against me, and to drive me out from my paradise, to suffer again all I have suffered this last year."

"You mean that mad Sydney of whom you told me?"

"Yes. As soon as he hears of this good fortune to poor little Jean, he will hasten to mar it. He is my fate; I cannot escape him, and wherever he goes my friends desert me; for he has the power and uses it for my destruction. Let me go away and hide before he comes, for, having shared your confidence, it will break my heart to see you distrust and turn from me, instead of loving and protecting."

"My poor child, you are superstitious. Be easy. No one can harm you now, no one would dare attempt it. And as for my deserting you, that will soon be out of my power, if I have my way."

"How, dear Sir John?" asked Jean, with a flutter of intense relief at her heart, for the way seemed smoothing before her.

"I will make you my wife at once, if I may. This will free you from Gerald's love, protect you from Sydney's persecution, give you a safe home, and me the right to cherish and defend with heart and hand. Shall it be so, my child?"

"Yes; but oh, remember that I have no friend but you! Promise me to be faithful to the last—to believe in me, to trust me, protect and love me, in spite of all misfortunes, faults, and follies. I will be true as steel to you, and make your life as happy as it deserves to be. Let us promise these things now, and keep the promises unbroken to the end."

Her solemn air touched Sir John. Too honorable and upright himself to suspect falsehood in others, he saw only the natural impulse of a lovely girl in Jean's words, and, taking the hand she gave him in both of his, he promised all she asked, and kept that promise to the end. She paused an instant, with a pale, absent expression, as if she searched herself, then looked up clearly in the confiding face above her, and promised what she faithfully performed in afteryears.

"When shall it be, little sweetheart? I leave all to you, only let it be soon, else some gay young lover will appear, and take you from me," said Sir John, playfully, anxious to chase away the dark expression which had stolen over Jean's face.

"Can you keep a secret?" asked the girl, smiling up at him, all her charming self again.

"Try me."

"I will. Edward is coming home in three days. I must be gone before he comes. Tell no one of this; he wishes to surprise them. And if you love me, tell nobody of your approaching marriage. Do not betray that you care for me until I am really yours. There will be such a stir, such remonstrances, explanations, and reproaches that I shall be worn out, and run away from you all to escape the trial. If I could have my wish, I would go to some quiet place tomorrow and wait till you come for me. I know so little of such things, I cannot tell how soon we may be married; not for some weeks, I think."

"Tomorrow, if we like. A special license permits people to marry when and where they please. My plan is better than yours. Listen, and tell me if it can be carried out. I will go to town tomorrow, get the license, invite my friend, the Reverend Paul Fairfax, to return with me, and tomorrow evening you come at your usual time, and, in the presence of my discreet old servants, make me the happiest man in England. How does this suit you, my little Lady Coventry?"

The plan which seemed made to meet her ends, the name which was the height of her ambition, and the blessed sense of safety which came to her filled Jean Muir with such intense satisfaction that tears of real feeling stood in her eyes, and the glad assent she gave was the truest word that had passed her lips for months.

"We will go abroad or to Scotland for our honeymoon, till the storm blows over," said Sir John, well knowing that this hasty marriage would surprise or offend all his relations, and feeling as glad as Jean to escape the first excitement.

"To Scotland, please. I long to see my father's home," said Jean, who dreaded to meet Sydney on the continent.

They talked a little longer, arranging all things, Sir John so intent on hurrying the event that Jean had nothing to do but give a ready assent to all his suggestions. One fear alone disturbed her. If Sir John went to town, he might meet Edward, might hear and believe his statements. Then all would be lost. Yet this risk must be incurred, if the marriage was to be speedily and safely accomplished; and to guard against the meeting was Jean's sole care. As they went through the park—for Sir John insisted upon taking her home—she said, clinging to his arm:

"Dear friend, bear one thing in mind, else we shall be much annoyed, and all our plans disarranged. Avoid your nephews; you are so frank your face will betray you. They both love me, are both hottempered, and in the first excitement of the discovery might be violent. You must incur no danger, no disrespect for my sake; so shun them both till we are safe—particularly Edward. He will feel that his brother has wronged him, and that you have succeeded where he failed. This will irritate him, and I fear a stormy scene. Promise to avoid both for a day or two; do not listen to them, do not see them, do not write to or receive letters from them. It is foolish, I know; but you are all I have, and I am haunted by a strange foreboding that I am to lose you." Touched and flattered by her tender solicitude, Sir John promised everything, even while he laughed at her fears. Love blinded the good gentleman to the peculiarity of the request; the novelty, romance, and secrecy of the affair rather bewildered though it charmed him; and the knowledge that he had outrivaled three young and ardent lovers gratified his vanity more than he would confess. Parting from the girl at the garden gate, he turned homeward, feeling like a boy again, and loitered back, humming a love lay, quite forgetful of evening damps, gout, and the five-and-fifty years which lay so lightly on his shoulders since Jean's arms had rested there. She hurried toward the house, anxious to escape Coventry; but he was waiting for her, and she was forced to meet him.

"How could you linger so long, and keep me in suspense?" he said reproachfully, as he took her hand and tried to catch a glimpse of her face in the shadow of her hat brim. "Come and rest in the grotto. I have so much to say, to hear and enjoy."

"Not now; I am too tired. Let me go in and sleep. Tomorrow we will talk. It is damp and chilly, and my head aches with all this worry." Jean spoke wearily, yet with a touch of petulance, and Cov-

226 THE FEMINIST ALCOTT

entry, fancying that she was piqued at his not coming for her, hastened to explain with eager tenderness.

"My poor little Jean, you do need rest. We wear you out, among us, and you never complain. I should have come to bring you home, but Lucia detained me, and when I got away I saw my uncle had forestalled me. I shall be jealous of the old gentleman, if he is so devoted. Jean, tell me one thing before we part; I am free as air, now, and have a right to speak. Do you love me? Am I the happy man who has won your heart? I dare to think so, to believe that this telltale face of yours has betrayed you, and to hope that I have gained what poor Ned and wild Sydney have lost."

"Before I answer, tell me of your interview with Lucia. I have a right to know," said Jean.

Coventry hesitated, for pity and remorse were busy at his heart when he recalled poor Lucia's grief. Jean was bent on hearing the humiliation of her rival. As the young man paused, she frowned, then lifted up her face wreathed in softest smiles, and laying her hand on his arm, she said, with most effective emphasis, half shy, half fond, upon his name, "Please tell me, Gerald!"

He could not resist the look, the touch, the tone, and taking the little hand in his, he said rapidly, as if the task was distasteful to him, "I told her that I did not, could not love her; that I had submitted to my mother's wish, and, for a time, had felt tacitly bound to her, though no words had passed between us. But now I demanded my liberty, regretting that the separation was not mutually desired."

"And she—what did she say? How did she bear it?" asked Jean, feeling in her own woman's heart how deeply Lucia's must have been wounded by that avowal.

"Poor girl! It was hard to bear, but her pride sustained her to the end. She owned that no pledge tied me, fully relinquished any claim my past behavior had seemed to have given her, and prayed that I might find another woman to love me as truly, tenderly as she had done. Jean, I felt like a villain; and yet I never plighted my word to her, never really loved her, and had a perfect right to leave her, if I would."

"Did she speak of me?"

"Yes."

"What did she say?"

"Must I tell you?"

"Yes, tell me everything. I know she hates me and I forgive her, knowing that I should hate any woman whom *you* loved."

"Are you jealous, dear?"

"Of you, Gerald?" And the fine eyes glanced up at him, full of a brilliancy that looked like the light of love.

"You make a slave of me already. How do you do it? I never obeyed a woman before. Jean, I think you are a witch. Scotland is the home of weird, uncanny creatures, who take lovely shapes for the bedevilment of poor weak souls. Are you one of those fair deceivers?"

"You are complimentary," laughed the girl. "I *am* a witch, and one day my disguise will drop away and you will see me as I am, old, ugly, bad and lost. Beware of me in time. I've warned you. Now love me at your peril."

Coventry had paused as he spoke, and eyed her with an unquiet look, conscious of some fascination which conquered yet brought no happiness. A feverish yet pleasurable excitement possessed him; a reckless mood, making him eager to obliterate the past by any rash act, any new experience which his passion brought. Jean regarded him with a wistful, almost woeful face, for one short moment; then a strange smile broke over it, as she spoke in a tone of malicious mockery, under which lurked the bitterness of a sad truth. Coventry looked half bewildered, and his eye went from the girl's mysterious face to a dimly lighted window, behind whose curtains poor Lucia hid her aching heart, praying for him the tender prayers that loving women give to those whose sins are all forgiven for love's sake. His heart smote him, and a momentary feeling of repulsion came over him, as he looked at Jean. She saw it, felt angry, yet conscious of a sense of relief; for now that her own safety was so nearly secured, she felt no wish to do mischief, but rather a desire to undo what was already done, and be at peace with all the world. To recall him to his allegiance, she sighed and walked on, saying gently yet coldly, "Will you tell me what I ask before I answer your question, Mr. Coventry?"

"What Lucia said of you? Well, it was this. 'Beware of Miss Muir.

We instinctively distrusted her when we had no cause. I believe in instincts, and mine have never changed, for she has not tried to delude me. Her art is wonderful; I feel yet cannot explain or detect it, except in the working of events which her hand seems to guide. She has brought sorrow and dissension into this hitherto happy family. We are all changed, and this girl has done it. Me she can harm no further; you she will ruin, if she can. Beware of her in time, or you will bitterly repent your blind infatuation!' "

"And what answer did you make?" asked Jean, as the last words came reluctantly from Coventry's lips.

"I told her that I loved you in spite of myself, and would make you my wife in the face of all opposition. Now, Jean, your answer."

"Give me three days to think of it. Good night." And gliding from him, she vanished into the house, leaving him to roam about half the night, tormented with remorse, suspense, and the old distrust which would return when Jean was not there to banish it by her art.

CHAPTER VIII. SUSPENSE

All the next day, Jean was in a state of the most intense anxiety, as every hour brought the crisis nearer, and every hour might bring defeat, for the subtlest human skill is often thwarted by some unforeseen accident. She longed to assure herself that Sir John was gone, but no servants came or went that day, and she could devise no pretext for sending to glean intelligence. She dared not go herself, lest the unusual act should excite suspicion, for she never went till evening. Even had she determined to venture, there was no time, for Mrs. Coventry was in one of her nervous states, and no one but Miss Muir could amuse her; Lucia was ill, and Miss Muir must give orders; Bella had a studious fit, and Jean must help her. Coventry lingered about the house for several hours, but Jean dared not send him, lest some hint of the truth might reach him. He had ridden away to his new duties when Jean did not appear, and the day dragged on wearisomely. Night came at last, and as Jean dressed for the late dinner, she hardly knew herself when she stood before her mirror, excitement lent such color and brilliancy to her countenance. Remembering the wedding which was to take place that evening, she put on a simple white dress and added a cluster of white roses in bosom and hair. She often wore flowers, but in spite of her desire to look and seem as usual, Bella's first words as she entered the drawing room were "Why, Jean, how like a bride you look; a veil and gloves would make you quite complete!"

"You forget one other trifle, Bell," said Gerald, with eyes that brightened as they rested on Miss Muir.

"What is that?" asked his sister.

"A bridegroom."

Bella looked to see how Jean received this, but she seemed quite composed as she smiled one of her sudden smiles, and merely said, "That trifle will doubtless be found when the time comes. Is Miss Beaufort too ill for dinner?"

"She begs to be excused, and said you would be willing to take her place, she thought."

As innocent Bella delivered this message, Jean glanced at Coventry, who evaded her eye and looked ill at ease.

A little remorse will do him good, and prepare him for repentance after the grand *coup,* she said to herself, and was particularly gay at dinnertime, though Coventry looked often at Lucia's empty seat, as if he missed her. As soon as they left the table, Miss Muir sent Bella to her mother; and, knowing that Coventry would not linger long at his wine, she hurried away to the Hall. A servant was lounging at the door, and of him she asked, in a tone which was eager in spite of all efforts to be calm, "Is Sir John at home?"

"No, miss, he's just gone to town."

"Just gone! When do you mean?" cried Jean, forgetting the relief she felt in hearing of his absence in surprise at his late departure.

"He went half an hour ago, in the last train, miss."

"I thought he was going early this morning; he told me he should be back this evening."

"I believe he did mean to go, but was delayed by company. The steward came up on business, and a load of gentlemen called, so Sir John could not get off till night, when he wasn't fit to go, being worn out, and far from well."

"Do you think he will be ill? Did he look so?" And as Jean spoke, a thrill of fear passed over her, lest death should rob her of her prize.

"Well, you know, miss, hurry of any kind is bad for elderly gentlemen inclined to apoplexy. Sir John was in a worry all day, and not like himself. I wanted him to take his man, but he wouldn't; and drove off looking flushed and excited like. I'm anxious about him, for I know something is amiss to hurry him off in this way."

"When will he be back, Ralph?"

"Tomorrow noon, if possible; at night certainly, he bid me tell anyone that called."

"Did he leave no note or message for Miss Coventry, or someone of the family?"

"No, miss, nothing."

"Thank you." And Jean walked back to spend a restless night and rise to meet renewed suspense.

The morning seemed endless, but noon came at last, and under the pretense of seeking coolness in the grotto, Jean stole away to a slope whence the gate to the Hall park was visible. For two long hours she watched, and no one came. She was just turning away when a horseman dashed through the gate and came galloping toward the Hall. Heedless of everything but the uncontrollable longing to gain some tidings, she ran to meet him, feeling assured that he brought ill news. It was a young man from the station, and as he caught sight of her, he drew bridle, looking agitated and undecided.

"Has anything happened?" she cried breathlessly.

"A dreadful accident on the railroad, just the other side of Croydon. News telegraphed half an hour ago," answered the man, wiping his hot face.

"The noon train? Was Sir John in it? Quick, tell me all!"

"It was that train, miss, but whether Sir John was in it or not, we don't know; for the guard is killed, and everything is in such confusion that nothing can be certain. They are at work getting out the dead and wounded. We heard that Sir John was expected, and I came up to tell Mr. Coventry, thinking he would wish to go down.

A train leaves in fifteen minutes; where shall I find him? I was told he was at the Hall."

"Ride on, ride on! And find him if he is there. I'll run home and look for him. Lose no time. Ride! Ride!" And turning, Jean sped back like a deer, while the man tore up the avenue to rouse the Hall.

Coventry was there, and went off at once, leaving both Hall and house in dismay. Fearing to betray the horrible anxiety that possessed her, Jean shut herself up in her room and suffered untold agonies as the day wore on and no news came. At dark a sudden cry rang through the house, and Jean rushed down to learn the cause. Bella was standing in the hall, holding a letter, while a group of excited servants hovered near her.

"What is it?" demanded Miss Muir, pale and steady, though her heart died within her as she recognized Gerald's handwriting. Bella gave her the note, and hushed her sobbing to hear again the heavy tidings that had come.

Dear Bella:

Uncle is safe; he did not go in the noon train. But several persons are sure that Ned was there. No trace of him as yet, but many bodies are in the river, under the ruins of the bridge, and I am doing my best to find the poor lad, if he is there. I have sent to all his haunts in town, and as he has not been seen, I hope it is a false report and he is safe with his regiment. Keep this from my mother till we are sure. I write you, because Lucia is ill. Miss Muir will comfort and sustain you. Hope for the best, dear.

Yours, G. C.

Those who watched Miss Muir as she read these words wondered at the strange expressions which passed over her face, for the joy which appeared there as Sir John's safety was made known did not change to grief or horror at poor Edward's possible fate. The smile died on her lips, but her voice did not falter, and in her downcast eyes shone an inexplicable look of something like triumph. No wonder, for if this was true, the danger which menaced her was averted for a time, and the marriage might be consummated without such desperate haste. This sad and sudden event seemed to her the mysterious fulfilment of a secret wish; and though startled she was not daunted but inspirited, for fate seemed to favor her designs. She did comfort Bella, control the excited household, and keep the rumors from Mrs. Coventry all that dreadful night.

At dawn Gerald came home exhausted, and bringing no tiding of the missing man. He had telegraphed to the headquarters of the regiment and received a reply, stating that Edward had left for London the previous day, meaning to go home before returning. The fact of his having been at the London station was also established, but whether he left by the train or not was still uncertain. The ruins were still being searched, and the body might yet appear.

"Is Sir John coming at noon?" asked Jean, as the three sat together in the rosy hush of dawn, trying to hope against hope.

"No, he had been ill, I learned from young Gower, who is just from town, and so had not completed his business. I sent him word to wait till night, for the bridge won't be passable till then. Now I must try and rest an hour; I've worked all night and have no strength left. Call me the instant any messenger arrives."

With that Coventry went to his room, Bella followed to wait on him, and Jean roamed through house and grounds, unable to rest. The morning was far spent when the messenger arrived. Jean went to receive his tidings, with the wicked hope still lurking at her heart.

"Is he found?" she asked calmly, as the man hesitated to speak.

"Yes, ma'am."

"You are sure?"

"I am certain, ma'am, though some won't say till Mr. Coventry comes to look."

"Is he alive?" And Jean's white lips trembled as she put the question.

"Oh no, ma'am, that warn't possible, under all them stones and water. The poor young gentleman is so wet, and crushed, and torn, no one would know him, except for the uniform, and the white hand with the ring on it."

Jean sat down, very pale, and the man described the finding of the poor shattered body. As he finished, Coventry appeared, and with one look of mingled remorse, shame, and sorrow, the elder brother went away, to find and bring the younger home. Jean crept into the garden like a guilty thing, trying to hide the satisfaction which struggled with a woman's natural pity, for so sad an end for this brave young life.

"Why waste tears or feign sorrow when I must be glad?" she muttered, as she paced to and fro along the terrace. "The poor boy is out of pain, and I am out of danger."

She got no further, for, turning as she spoke, she stood face to face with Edward! Bearing no mark of peril on dress or person, but stalwart and strong as ever, he stood there looking at her, with contempt and compassion struggling in his face. As if turned to stone, she remained motionless, with dilated eyes, arrested breath, and paling cheek. He did not speak but watched her silently till she put out a trembling hand, as if to assure herself by touch that it was really he. Then he drew back, and as if the act convinced as fully as words, she said slowly, "They told me you were dead."

"And you were glad to believe it. No, it was my comrade, young Courtney, who unconsciously deceived you all, and lost his life, as I should have done, if I had not gone to Ascot after seeing him off yesterday."

"To Ascot?" echoed Jean, shrinking back, for Edward's eye was on her, and his voice was stern and cold.

"Yes; you know the place. I went there to make inquiries concerning you and was well satisfied. Why are you still here?"

"The three days are not over yet. I hold you to your promise. Before night I shall be gone; till then you will be silent, if you have honor enough to keep your word."

"I have." Edward took out his watch and, as he put it back, said with cool precision, "It is now two, the train leaves for London at halfpast six; a carriage will wait for you at the side door. Allow me to advise you to go then, for the instant dinner is over I shall speak." And with a bow he went into the house, leaving Jean nearly suffocated with a throng of contending emotions.

For a few minutes she seemed paralyzed; but the native energy of the woman forbade utter despair, till the last hope was gone. Frail as that now was, she still clung to it tenaciously, resolving to win the game in defiance of everything. Springing up, she went to her room, packed her few valuables, dressed herself with care, and then sat down to wait. She heard a joyful stir below, saw Coventry come hurrying back, and from a garrulous maid learned that the body was that of young Courtney. The uniform being the same as Edward's and the ring, a gift from him, had caused the men to believe the disfigured corpse to be that of the younger Coventry. No one but the maid came near her; once Bella's voice called her, but some one checked the girl, and the call was not repeated. At five an envelope was brought her, directed in Edward's hand, and containing a check which more than paid a year's salary. No word accompanied the gift, yet the generosity of it touched her, for Jean Muir had the relics of a once honest nature, and despite her falsehood could still admire nobleness and respect virtue. A tear of genuine shame dropped on the paper, and real gratitude filled her heart, as she thought that even if all else failed, she was not thrust out penniless into the world, which had no pity for poverty.

As the clock struck six, she heard a carriage drive around and went down to meet it. A servant put on her trunk, gave the order, "To the station, James," and she drove away without meeting anyone, speaking to anyone, or apparently being seen by anyone. A sense of utter weariness came over her, and she longed to lie down and forget. But the last chance still remained, and till that failed, she would not give up. Dismissing the carriage, she seated herself to watch for the quarter-past-six train from London, for in that Sir John would come if he came at all that night. She was haunted by the fear that Edward had met and told him. The first glimpse of Sir John's frank face would betray the truth. If he knew all, there was no hope, and she would go her way alone. If he knew nothing, there was yet time for the marriage; and once his wife, she knew she was safe, because for the honor of his name he would screen and protect her.

Up rushed the train, out stepped Sir John, and Jean's heart died within her. Grave, and pale, and worn he looked, and leaned heavily on the arm of a portly gentleman in black. The Reverend Mr. Fairfax, why has he come, if the secret is out? thought Jean, slowly advancing to meet them and fearing to read her fate in Sir John's face. He saw her, dropped his friend's arm, and hurried forward with the ardor of a young man, exclaiming, as he seized her hand with a beaming face, a glad voice, "My little girl! Did you think I would never come?"

She could not answer, the reaction was too strong, but she clung to him, regardless of time or place, and felt that her last hope had not failed. Mr. Fairfax proved himself equal to the occasion. Asking no questions, he hurried Sir John and Jean into a carriage and stepped in after them with a bland apology. Jean was soon herself again, and, having told her fears at his delay, listened eagerly while he related the various mishaps which had detained him.

"Have you seen Edward?" was her first question.

"Not yet, but I know he has come, and have heard of his narrow escape. I should have been in that train, if I had not been delayed by the indisposition which I then cursed, but now bless. Are you ready, Jean? Do you repent your choice, my child?"

"No, no! I am ready, I am only too happy to become your wife, dear, generous Sir John," cried Jean, with a glad alacrity, which touched the old man to the heart, and charmed the Reverend Mr. Fairfax, who concealed the romance of a boy under his clerical suit.

They reached the Hall. Sir John gave orders to admit no one and after a hasty dinner sent for his old housekeeper and his steward, told them of his purpose, and desired them to witness his marriage. Obedience had been the law of their lives, and Master could do nothing wrong in their eyes, so they played their parts willingly, for Jean was a favorite at the Hall. Pale as her gown, but calm and steady, she stood beside Sir John, uttering her vows in a clear tone and taking upon herself the vows of a wife with more than a bride's usual docility. When the ring was fairly on, a smile broke over her face. When Sir John kissed and called her his "little wife," she shed a tear or two of sincere happiness; and when Mr. Fairfax addressed her as "my lady," she laughed her musical laugh, and glanced up at a picture of Gerald with eyes full of exultation. As the servants left the room, a message was brought from Mrs. Coventry, begging Sir John to come to her at once.

"You will not go and leave me so soon?" pleaded Jean, well knowing why he was sent for.

"My darling, I must." And in spite of its tenderness, Sir John's manner was too decided to be withstood.

"Then I shall go with you," cried Jean, resolving that no earthly power should part them.

CHAPTER IX. LADY COVENTRY

When the first excitement of Edward's return had subsided, and before they could question him as to the cause of this unexpected visit, he told them that after dinner their curiosity should be gratified, and meantime he begged them to leave Miss Muir alone, for she had received bad news and must not be disturbed. The family with difficulty restrained their tongues and waited impatiently. Gerald confessed his love for Jean and asked his brother's pardon for betraying his trust. He had expected an outbreak, but Edward only looked at him with pitying eyes, and said sadly, "You too! I have no reproaches to make, for I know what you will suffer when the truth is known."

"What do you mean?" demanded Coventry.

"You will soon know, my poor Gerald, and we will comfort one another."

Nothing more could be drawn from Edward till dinner was over, the servants gone, and all the family alone together. Then pale and grave, but very self-possessed, for trouble had made a man of him, he produced a packet of letters, and said, addressing himself to his brother, "Jean Muir has deceived us all. I know her story; let me tell it before I read her letters."

"Stop! I'll not listen to any false tales against her. The poor girl has enemies who belie her!" cried Gerald, starting up.

"For the honor of the family, you must listen, and learn what fools she has made of us. I can prove what I say, and convince you that she has the art of a devil. Sit still ten minutes, then go, if you will."

Edward spoke with authority, and his brother obeyed him with a foreboding heart.

"I met Sydney, and he begged me to beware of her. Nay, listen, Gerald! I know she has told her story, and that you believe it; but her own letters convict her. She tried to charm Sydney as she did us, and nearly succeeded in inducing him to marry her. Rash and wild as he is, he is still a gentleman, and when an incautious word of hers roused his suspicions, he refused to make her his wife. A stormy scene ensued, and, hoping to intimidate him, she feigned to stab herself as if in despair. She did wound herself, but failed to gain her point and insisted upon going to a hospital to die. Lady Sydney, good, simple soul, believed the girl's version of the story, thought her son was in the wrong, and when he was gone, tried to atone for his fault by finding Jean Muir another home. She thought Gerald was soon to marry Lucia, and that I was away, so sent her here as a safe and comfortable retreat."

"But, Ned, are you sure of all this? Is Sydney to be believed?" began Coventry, still incredulous.

"To convince you, I'll read Jean's letters before I say more. They were written to an accomplice and were purchased by Sydney. There was a compact between the two women, that each should keep the other informed of all adventures, plots and plans, and share whatever good fortune fell to the lot of either. Thus Jean wrote freely, as you shall judge. The letters concern us alone. The first was written a few days after she came.

> *"Dear Hortense:*
>
> *"Another failure. Sydney was more wily than I thought. All was going well, when one day my old fault beset me, I took too much wine, and I carelessly owned that I had been an actress. He was shocked, and retreated. I got up a scene, and gave myself a safe little wound, to frighten him. The brute was not frightened, but coolly left me to my fate. I'd have died to spite him, if I dared, but as I didn't, I lived to torment him. As yet, I have had no chance, but I will not forget him. His mother is a poor, weak creature, whom I could use as I would, and through her I found an excellent place. A sick mother, silly daughter, and two eligible sons. One is engaged to a handsome iceberg, but that only renders him more interesting in my eyes, rivalry adds so much to the charm of one's conquests. Well, my dear, I went, got up in the meek style, intending to do the pathetic; but before I saw the family, I was so angry I could hardly control myself. Through the indolence of Monsieur the young master, no carriage was sent for me, and I intend he shall atone for that rudeness by-and-by. The younger son, the mother, and the girl received me patron-*

izingly, and I understood the simple souls at once. Monsieur (as I shall call him, as names are unsafe) was unapproachable, and took no pains to conceal his dislike of governesses. The cousin was lovely, but detestable with her pride, her coldness, and her very visible adoration of Monsieur, who let her worship him, like an inanimate idol as he is. I hated them both, of course, and in return for their insolence shall torment her with jealousy, and teach him how to woo a woman by making his heart ache. They are an intensely proud family, but I can humble them all, I think, by captivating the sons, and when they have committed themselves, cast them off, and marry the old uncle, whose title takes my fancy."

"She never wrote that! It is impossible. A woman could not do it," cried Lucia indignantly, while Bella sat bewildered and Mrs. Coventry supported herself with salts and fan. Coventry went to his brother, examined the writing, and returned to his seat, saying, in a tone of suppressed wrath, "She did write it. I posted some of those letters myself. Go on, Ned."

"I made myself useful and agreeable to the amiable ones, and overheard the chat of the lovers. It did not suit me, so I fainted away to stop it, and excite interest in the provoking pair. I thought I had succeeded, but Monsieur suspected me and showed me that he did. I forgot my meek role and gave him a stage look. It had a good effect, and I shall try it again. The man is well worth winning, but I prefer the title, and as the uncle is a hale, handsome gentleman, I can't wait for him to die, though Monsieur is very charming, with his elegant languor, and his heart so fast asleep no woman has had power to wake it yet. I told my story, and they believed it, though I had the audacity to say I was but nineteen, to talk Scotch, and bashfully confess that Sydney wished to marry me. Monsieur knows S. and evidently suspects something. I must watch him and keep the truth from him, if possible.

"I was very miserable that night when I got alone. Something in the atmosphere of this happy home made me wish I was anything but what I am. As I sat there trying to pluck up my spirits, I thought of the days when I was lovely and young, good and gay. My glass showed me an old woman of thirty, for my false locks were off, my paint gone, and my face was without its mask. Bah! how I hate sentiment! I drank your health from your own little flask, and went to bed to dream that I was playing Lady Tartuffe—as I am. Adieu, more soon."

No one spoke as Edward paused, and taking up another letter, he read on:

"My Dear Creature:

"All goes well. Next day I began my task, and having caught a hint of the character of each, tried my power over them. Early in the morning I ran over to see the Hall. Approved of it highly, and took the first step toward becoming its mistress, by piquing the curiosity and flattering the pride of its master. His estate is his idol; I praised it with a few artless compliments to himself, and he was charmed. The cadet of the family adores horses. I risked my neck to pet his beast, and he was charmed. The little girl is romantic about flowers; I made a posy and was sentimental, and she was charmed. The fair icicle loves her departed mamma, I had raptures over an old picture, and she thawed. Monsieur is used to being worshipped. I took no notice of him, and by the natural perversity of human nature, he began to take notice of me. He likes music; I sang, and stopped when he'd listened long enough to want more. He is lazily fond of being amused; I showed him my skill, but refused to exert it in his behalf. In short, I gave him no peace till he began to wake up. In order to get rid of the boy, I fascinated him, and he was sent away. Poor lad, I rather liked him, and if the title had been nearer would have married him.

"Many thanks for the honor." And Edward's lip curled with intense scorn. But Gerald sat like a statue, his teeth set, his eyes fiery, his brows bent, waiting for the end.

"The passionate boy nearly killed his brother, but I turned the affair to good account, and bewitched Monsieur by playing nurse, till Vashti (the icicle) interfered. Then I enacted injured virtue, and kept out of his way, knowing that he would miss me. I mystified him about S. by sending a letter where S. would not get it, and got up all manner of soft scenes to win this proud creature. I get on well and meanwhile privately fascinate Sir J. by being daughterly and devoted. He is a worthy old man, simple as a child, honest as the day, and generous as a prince. I shall be a happy woman if I win him, and you shall share my good fortune; so wish me success.

"This is the third, and contains something which will surprise you," Edward said, as he lifted another paper.

"Hortense:

"I've done what I once planned to do on another occasion. You know my handsome, dissipated father married a lady of rank for his second wife. I never saw Lady H_____d but once, for I was kept out of the way. Finding that this good

Sir J. knew something of her when a girl, and being sure that he did not know of the death of her little daughter, I boldly said I was the child, and told a pitiful tale of my early life. It worked like a charm; he told Monsieur, and both felt the most chivalrous compassion for Lady Howard's daughter, though before they had secretly looked down on me, and my real poverty and my lowliness. That boy pitied me with an honest warmth and never waited to learn my birth. I don't forget that and shall repay it if I can. Wishing to bring Monsieur's affair to a successful crisis, I got up a theatrical evening and was in my element. One little event I must tell you, because I committed an actionable offense and was nearly discovered. I did not go down to supper, knowing that the moth would return to flutter about the candle, and preferring that the fluttering should be done in private, as Vashti's jealousy is getting uncontrollable. Passing through the gentlemen's dressing room, my quick eye caught sight of a letter lying among the costumes. It was no stage affair, and an odd sensation of fear ran through me as I recognized the hand of S. I had feared this, but I believe in chance; and having found the letter, I examined it. You know I can imitate almost any hand. When I read in this paper the whole story of my affair with S., truly told, and also that he had made inquiries into my past life and discovered the truth, I was in a fury. To be so near success and fail was terrible, and I resolved to risk everything. I opened the letter by means of a heated knife blade under the seal, therefore the envelope was perfect; imitating S.'s hand, I penned a few lines in his hasty style, saying he was at Baden, so that if Monsieur answered, the reply would not reach him, for he is in London, it seems. This letter I put into the pocket whence the other must have fallen, and was just congratulating myself on this narrow escape, when Dean, the maid of Vashti, appeared as if watching me. She had evidently seen the letter in my hand, and suspected something. I took no notice of her, but must be careful, for she is on the watch. After this the evening closed with strictly private theatricals, in which Monsieur and myself were the only actors. To make sure that he received my version of the story first, I told him a romantic story of S.'s persecution, and he believed it. This I followed up by a moonlight episode behind a rose hedge, and sent the young gentleman home in a half-dazed condition. What fools men are!"

"She is right!" muttered Coventry, who had flushed scarlet with shame and anger, as his folly became known and Lucia listened in astonished silence.

"Only one more, and my distasteful task will be nearly over," said Edward, unfolding the last of the papers. "This is not a letter, but a copy of one written three nights ago. Dean boldly ransacked Jean

Muir's desk while she was at the Hall, and, fearing to betray the deed by keeping the letter, she made a hasty copy which she gave me today, begging me to save the family from disgrace. This makes the chain complete. Go now, if you will, Gerald. I would gladly spare you the pain of hearing this."

"I will not spare myself; I deserve it. Read on," replied Coventry, guessing what was to follow and nerving himself to hear it. Reluctantly his brother read these lines:

> "*The enemy has surrendered! Give me joy, Hortense; I can be the wife of this proud monsieur, if I will. Think what an honor for the divorced wife of a disreputable actor. I laugh at the farce and enjoy it, for I only wait till the prize I desire is fairly mine, to turn and reject this lover who has proved himself false to brother, mistress, and his own conscience. I resolved to be revenged on both, and I have kept my word. For my sake he cast off the beautiful woman who truly loved him; he forgot his promise to his brother, and put by his pride to beg of me the worn-out heart that is not worth a good man's love. Ah well, I am satisfied, for Vashti has suffered the sharpest pain a proud woman can endure, and will feel another pang when I tell her that I scorn her recreant lover, and give him back to her, to deal with as she will.*"*

Coventry started from his seat with a fierce exclamation, but Lucia bowed her face upon her hands, weeping, as if the pang had been sharper than even Jean foresaw.

"Send for Sir John! I am mortally afraid of this creature. Take her away; do something to her. My poor Bella, what a companion for you! Send for Sir John at once!" cried Mrs. Coventry incoherently, and clasped her daughter in her arms, as if Jean Muir would burst in to annihilate the whole family. Edward alone was calm.

"I have already sent, and while we wait, let me finish this story. It is true that Jean is the daughter of Lady Howard's husband, the pretended clergyman, but really a worthless man who married her for her money. Her own child died, but this girl, having beauty, wit and a bold spirit, took her fate into her own hands, and became an actress. She married an actor, led a reckless life for some years; quarreled with her husband, was divorced, and went to Paris; left the stage, and tried to support herself as governess and companion. You know how she fared with the Sydneys, how she has duped us, and but for this discovery would have duped Sir John. I was in time to prevent this, thank heaven. She is gone; no one knows the truth but Sydney and ourselves; he will be silent, for his own sake; we will be for ours, and leave this dangerous woman to the fate which will surely overtake her."

"Thank you, it has overtaken her, and a very happy one she finds it."

A soft voice uttered the words, and an apparition appeared at the door, which made all start and recoil with amazement—Jean Muir leaning on the arm of Sir John.

"How dare you return?" began Edward, losing the self-control so long preserved. "How dare you insult us by coming back to enjoy the mischief you have done? Uncle, you do not know that woman!"

"Hush, boy, I will not listen to a word, unless you remember where you are," said Sir John, with a commanding gesture.

"Remember your promise: love me, forgive me, protect me, and do not listen to their accusations," whispered Jean, whose quick eye had discovered the letters.

"I will; have no fears, my child," he answered, drawing her nearer as he took his accustomed place before the fire, always lighted when Mrs. Coventry was down.

Gerald, who had been pacing the room excitedly, paused behind Lucia's chair as if to shield her from insult; Bella clung to her mother; and Edward, calming himself by a strong effort, handed his uncle the letters, saying briefly, "Look at those, sir, and let them speak."

"I will look at nothing, hear nothing, believe nothing which can in any way lessen my respect and affection for this young lady. She has prepared me for this. I know the enemy who is unmanly enough to belie and threaten her. I know that you both are unsuccessful lovers, and this explains your unjust, uncourteous treatment now. We all have committed faults and follies. I freely forgive Jean hers, and desire to know nothing of them from your lips. If she has innocently offended, pardon it for my sake, and forget the past."

"But, Uncle, we have proofs that this woman is not what she

seems. Her own letters convict her. Read them, and do not blindly deceive yourself," cried Edward, indignant at his uncle's words.

A low laugh startled them all, and in an instant they saw the cause of it. While Sir John spoke, Jean had taken the letters from the hand which he had put behind him, a favorite gesture of his, and, unobserved, had dropped them on the fire. The mocking laugh, the sudden blaze, showed what had been done. Both young men sprang forward, but it was too late; the proofs were ashes, and Jean Muir's bold, bright eyes defied them, as she said, with a disdainful little gesture, "Hands off, gentlemen! You may degrade yourselves to the work of detectives, but I am not a prisoner yet. Poor Jean Muir you might harm, but Lady Coventry is beyond your reach."

"Lady Coventry!" echoed the dismayed family, in varying tones of incredulity, indignation, and amazement.

"Aye, my dear and honored wife," said Sir John, with a protecting arm about the slender figure at his side; and in the act, the words, there was a tender dignity that touched the listeners with pity and respect for the deceived man. "Receive her as such, and for my sake, forbear all further accusation," he continued steadily. "I know what I have done. I have no fear that I shall repent it. If I am blind, let me remain so till time opens my eyes. We are going away for a little while, and when we return, let the old life return again, unchanged, except that Jean makes sunshine for me as well as for you."

No one spoke, for no one knew what to say. Jean broke the silence, saying coolly, "May I ask how those letters came into your possession?"

"In tracing out your past life, Sydney found your friend Hortense. She was poor, money bribed her, and your letters were given up to him as soon as received. Traitors are always betrayed in the end," replied Edward sternly.

Jean shrugged her shoulders, and shot a glance at Gerald, saying with her significant smile, "Remember that, monsieur, and allow me to hope that in wedding you will be happier than in wooing. Receive my congratulations, Miss Beaufort, and let me beg of you to follow my example, if you would keep your lovers."

Here all the sarcasm passed from her voice, the defiance from her

244 THE FEMINIST ALCOTT

eye, and the one unspoiled attribute which still lingered in this woman's artful nature shone in her face, as she turned toward Edward and Bella at their mother's side.

"You have been kind to me," she said, with grateful warmth. "I thank you for it, and will repay it if I can. To you I will acknowledge that I am not worthy to be this good man's wife, and to you I will solemnly promise to devote my life to his happiness. For his sake forgive me, and let there be peace between us."

There was no reply, but Edward's indignant eyes fell before hers. Bella half put out her hand, and Mrs. Coventry sobbed as if some regret mingled with her resentment. Jean seemed to expect no friendly demonstration, and to understand that they forbore for Sir John's sake, not for hers, and to accept their contempt as her just punishment.

"Come home, love, and forget all this," said her husband, ringing the bell, and eager to be gone. "Lady Coventry's carriage."

And as he gave the order, a smile broke over her face, for the sound assured her that the game was won. Pausing an instant on the threshold before she vanished from their sight, she looked backward, and fixing on Gerald the strange glance he remembered well, she said in her penetrating voice, "Is not the last scene better than the first?"

Taming a Tartar

✦

*D*ear Mademoiselle, I assure you it is an arrangement both profitable and agreeable to one, who, like you, desires change of occupation and scene, as well as support. Madame la Princesse is most affable, generous, and to those who please her, quite child-like in her affection."

"But, madame, am I fit for the place? Does it not need accomplishments and graces which I do not possess? There is a wide difference between being a teacher in a *Pensionnat pour Demoiselles* like this and the companion of a princess."

"Ah, hah, my dear, it is nothing. Let not the fear of rank disturb you; these Russians are but savages, and all their money, splendor, and the polish Paris gives them, do not suffice to change the barbarians. You are the superior in breeding as in intelligence, as you will soon discover; and for accomplishments, yours will bear the test anywhere. I grant you Russians have much talent for them, and acquire with marvelous ease, but taste they have not, nor the skill to use these weapons as we use them."

"The princess is an invalid, you say?"

"Yes; but she suffers little, is delicate and needs care, amusement, yet not excitement. You are to chat with her, to read, sing, strive to fill the place of confidante. She sees little society, and her wing of the hotel is quite removed from that of the prince, who is one of the lions just now."

"Is it of him they tell the strange tales of his princely generosity, his fearful temper, childish caprices, and splendid establishment?"

"In truth, yes; Paris is wild for him, as for some magnificent savage beast. Madame la Comtesse Millefleur declared that she never knew whether he would fall at her feet, or annihilate her, so impetuous were his moods. At one moment showing all the complaisance and elegance of a born Parisian, the next terrifying the beholders by some outburst of savage wrath, some betrayal of the Tartar blood that is in him. Ah! it is incredible how such things amaze one."

"Has the princess the same traits? If so, I fancy the situation of companion is not easy to fill."

"No, no, she is not of the same blood. She is a half-sister; her mother was a Frenchwoman; she was educated in France, and lived here till her marriage with Prince Tcherinski. She detests St. Petersburg, adores Paris, and hopes to keep her brother here till the spring, for the fearful climate of the north is death to her delicate lungs. She is a gay, simple, confiding person; a child still in many things, and since her widowhood entirely under the control of this brother, who loves her tenderly, yet is a tyrant to her as to all who approach him."

I smiled as my loquacious friend gave me these hints of my future master and mistress, but in spite of all drawbacks, I liked the prospect, and what would have deterred another, attracted me. I was alone in the world, fond of experiences and adventures, self-reliant and self-possessed; eager for change, and anxious to rub off the rust of five years' servitude in Madame Bayard's Pensionnat. This new occupation pleased me, and but for a slight fear of proving unequal to it, I should have at once accepted madame's proposition. She knew everyone, and through some friend had heard of the princess's wish to find an English lady as companion and teacher, for a whim had seized her to learn English. Madame knew I intended to leave her, my health and spirits being worn by long and arduous duties, and she kindly interested herself to secure the place for me.

"Go then, dear mademoiselle, make a charming toilet and present yourself to the princess without delay, or you lose your opportunity. I have smoothed the way for you; your own address will do the rest, and in one sense, your fortune is made, if all goes well."

I obeyed madame, and when I was ready, took a critical survey of myself, trying to judge of the effect upon others. The long mirror showed me a slender, well-molded figure, and a pale face—not beautiful, but expressive, for the sharply cut, somewhat haughty features betrayed good blood, spirit and strength. Gray eyes, large and lustrous, under straight, dark brows; a firm mouth and chin, proud nose, wide brow, with waves of chestnut hair parted plainly back into heavy coils behind. Five years in Paris had taught me the art of dress, and a good salary permitted me to indulge my taste. Although simply made, I flattered myself that my promenade costume of silk and sable was *en règle,* as well as becoming, and with a smile at myself in the mirror I went my way, wondering if this new plan was to prove the welcome change so long desired.

As the carriage drove into the court-yard of the prince's hotel in the Champs Élysées, and a gorgeous *laquais* carried up my card, my heart beat a little faster than usual, and when I followed the servant in, I felt as if my old life ended suddenly, and one of strange interest had already begun.

The princess was not ready to receive me yet, and I was shown into a splendid *salon* to wait. My entrance was noiseless, and as I took a seat, my eyes fell on the half-drawn curtains which divided the room from another. Two persons were visible, but as neither saw me in the soft gloom of the apartment, I had an opportunity to look as long and curiously as I pleased. The whole scene was as unlike those usually found in a Parisian *salon* as can well be imagined.

Though three o'clock in the afternoon, it was evidently early morning with the gentleman stretched on the ottoman, reading a novel and smoking a Turkish chibouk—for his costume was that of a Russian seigneur in *déshabillé. A* long Caucasian caftan of the finest white sheepskin, a pair of loose black velvet trowsers, bound round the waist by a rich shawl, and Kasan boots of crimson leather, ornamented with golden embroidery on the instep, covered a pair of feet which seemed disproportionately small compared to the unusually tall, athletic figure of the man; so also did the head with a red silk handkerchief bound over the thick black hair. The costume suited the face; swarthy, black-eyed, scarlet-lipped, heavybrowed and beardless, except a thick mustache; serfs wear beards, but Russian nobles never. A strange face, for even in repose the indescribable difference of race was visible; the contour of the head, molding of the features, hue of hair and skin, even the attitude, all betrayed a trace of the savage strength and spirit of one in whose veins flowed the blood of men reared in tents, and born to lead wild lives in a wild land.

This unexpected glance behind the scenes interested me much, and I took note of everything within my ken. The book which the slender brown hand held was evidently a French novel, but when a lap-dog disturbed the reader, it was ordered off in Russian with a sonorous oath, I suspect, and an impatient gesture. On a guéridon, or side-table, stood a velvet *porte-cigare,* a box of sweetmeats, a bottle of Bordeaux, and a tall glass of cold tea, with a slice of lemon floating in it. A musical instrument, something like a mandolin, lay near the ottoman, a piano stood open, with a sword and helmet on it, and sitting in a corner, noiselessly making cigarettes, was a half-grown boy, a serf I fancied, from his dress and the silent, slavish way in which he watched his master.

The princess kept me waiting long, but I was not impatient, and when I was summoned at last I could not resist a backward glance at the brilliant figure I left behind me. The servant's voice had roused him, and, rising to his elbow, he leaned forward to look, with an expression of mingled curiosity and displeasure in the largest, blackest eyes I ever met.

I found the princess, a pale, pretty little woman of not more than twenty, buried in costly furs, though the temperature of her boudoir seemed tropical to me. Most gracious was my reception, and at once all fear vanished, for she was as simple and wanting in dignity as any of my young pupils.

"Ah, Mademoiselle Varna, you come in good time to spare me from the necessity of accepting a lady whom I like not. She is excellent, but too grave; while you reassure me at once by that smile. Sit near me, and let us arrange the affair before my brother comes. You incline to give me your society, I infer from the good Bayard?"

"If Madame la Princesse accepts my services on trial for a time, I much desire to make the attempt, as my former duties have become irksome, and I have a great curiosity to see St. Petersburg."

"*Mon Dieu!* I trust it will be long before we return to that detestable climate. *Chère* mademoiselle, I entreat you to say nothing of this desire to my brother. He is mad to go back to his wolves, his ice and his barbarous delights; but I cling to Paris, for it is my life. In the spring it is inevitable, and I submit—but not now. If you come to me, I conjure you to aid me in delaying the return, and shall be forever grateful if you help to secure this reprieve for me."

So earnest and beseeching were her looks, her words, and so entirely did she seem to throw herself upon my sympathy and goodwill, that I could not but be touched and won, in spite of my surprise. I assured her that I would do my best, but could not flatter myself that any advice of mine would influence the prince.

"You do not know him; but from what Bayard tells me of your skill in controlling wayward wills and hot tempers, I feel sure that you can influence Alexis. In confidence, I tell you what you will soon learn, if you remain: that though the best and tenderest of brothers, the prince is hard to manage, and one must tread cautiously in approaching him. His will is iron; and a decree once uttered is as irrevocable as the laws of the Medes and Persians. He has always claimed entire liberty for himself, entire obedience from every one about him; and my father's early death leaving him the head of our house, confirmed these tyrannical tendencies. To keep him in Paris is my earnest desire, and in order to do so I must seem indifferent, yet make his life so attractive that he will not command our departure."

"One would fancy life could not but be attractive to the prince in the gayest city of the world," I said, as the princess paused for breath.

"He cares little for the polished pleasures which delight a Parisian, and insists on bringing many of his favorite amusements with him. His caprices amuse the world, and are admired, but they annoy me much. At home he wears his Russian costume, orders the horrible dishes he loves, and makes the apartments unendurable with his samovar, chibouk and barbarous ornaments. Abroad he drives his droschky with the Ischvostchik in full St. Petersburg livery, and wears his uniform on all occasions. I say nothing, but I suffer."

It required a strong effort to repress a smile at the princess's pathetic lamentations and the martyr-like airs she assumed. She was infinitely amusing with her languid or vivacious words and attitudes; her girlish frankness and her feeble health interested me, and I resolved to stay even before she asked my decision.

I sat with her an hour, chatting of many things, and feeling more and more at ease as I read the shallow but amiable nature before me. All arrangements were made, and I was about taking my leave when the prince entered unannounced, and so quickly that I had not time to make my escape.

He had made his toilet since I saw him last, and I found it difficult to recognize the picturesque figure on the ottoman in the person who entered wearing the ordinary costume of a well-dressed gentleman. Even the face seemed changed, for a cold, haughty expression replaced the thoughtful look it had worn in repose. A smile softened it as he greeted his sister, but it vanished as he turned to me, with a slight inclination, when she whispered my name and errand, and while she explained he stood regarding me with a look that angered me. Not that it was insolent, but supremely masterful, as if those proud eyes were accustomed to command whomever they looked upon. It annoyed me, and I betrayed my annoyance by a rebellious glance, which made him lift his brows in surprise as a half smile passed over his lips. When his sister paused, he said, in the purest French, and with a slightly imperious accent:

"Mademoiselle is an Englishwoman?"

"My mother was English, my father of Russian parentage, although born in England."

I knew not by what title to address the questioner, so I simplified the matter by using none at all.

"Ah, you are half a Russian, then, and naturally desire to see your country?"

"Yes, I have long wished it," I began, but a soft cough from the princess reminded me that I must check my wish till it was safe to express it.

"We return soon, and it is well that you go willingly. Mademoiselle sets you a charming example, Nadja; I indulge the hope that you will follow it."

As he spoke the princess shot a quick glance at me, and answered, in a careless tone:

"I seldom disappoint your hopes, Alexis; but mademoiselle agrees with me that St. Petersburg at this season is unendurable."

"Has mademoiselle tried it?" was the quiet reply, as the prince fixed his keen eyes full upon me, as if suspecting a plot.

"Not yet, and I have no desire to do so—the report satisfies me," I answered, moving to go.

The prince shrugged his shoulders, touched his sister's cheek, bowed slightly, and left the room as suddenly as he had entered.

The princess chid me playfully for my *maladresse,* begged to see me on the morrow, and graciously dismissed me. As I waited in the great hall a moment for my carriage to drive round, I witnessed a little scene which made a curious impression on me. In a small anteroom, the door of which was ajar, stood the prince, drawing on his gloves, while the lad whom I had seen above was kneeling before him, fastening a pair of fur-lined overshoes. Something was amiss with one clasp, the prince seemed impatient, and after a sharp word in Russian, angrily lifted his foot with a gesture that sent the lad backward with painful violence. I involuntarily uttered an exclamation, the prince turned quickly, and our eyes met. Mine I know were full of indignation and disgust, for I resented the kick more than the poor lad, who, meekly gathering himself up, finished his task without a word, like one used to such rebukes.

The haughtiest surprise was visible in the face of the prince, but no shame; and as I moved away I heard a low laugh, as if my demonstration amused him.

"Laugh if you will, Monsieur le Prince, but remember all your servants are not serfs," I muttered, irefully, as I entered the carriage.

CHAPTER II

All went smoothly for a week or two, and I not only found my new home agreeable but altogether luxurious, for the princess had taken a fancy to me and desired to secure me by every means in her power, as she confided to Madame Bayard. I had been in a treadmill so long that any change would have been pleasant, but this life was as charming as anything but entire freedom could be. The very caprices of the princess were agreeable, for they varied what otherwise might have been somewhat monotonous, and her perfect simplicity and frankness soon did away with any shyness of mine. As madame said, rank was nothing after all, and in this case princess was but a name, for many an untitled Parisienne led a gayer and more splendid life than Nadja Tcherinski, shut up in her apartments and dependent upon those about her for happiness. Being younger than myself, and one of the clinging, confiding women who must lean on some one, I soon felt that protective fondness which one cannot help feeling for the weak, the sick, and the unhappy. We read English, embroidered, sung, talked, and drove out together, for the princess received little company and seldom joined the revels which went on in the other wing of the hotel.

The prince came daily to visit his sister, and she always exerted herself to make these brief interviews as agreeable as possible. I was pressed into the service, and sung, played, or talked as the princess signified—finding that, like most Russians of good birth, the prince was very accomplished, particularly in languages and music. But in spite of these gifts and the increasing affability of his manners toward myself, I always felt that under all the French polish was hidden the Tartar wildness, and often saw the savage in his eye while his lips were smiling blandly. I did not like him, but my vanity was gratified by the daily assurances of the princess that I possessed and exerted an unconscious influence over him. It was interesting to match him, and soon exciting to try my will against his in covert ways. I did not fear him as his sister did, because over me he had no control, and being of as proud a spirit as himself, I paid him only the respect due to his rank, not as an inferior, but an equal, for my family was good, and he lacked the real princeliness of nature which commands the reverence of the highest. I think he felt this instinctively, and it angered him; but he betrayed nothing of it in words, and was coolly courteous to the incomprehensible *dame-de-compagnie* of his sister.

My apartments were near the princess's, but I never went to her till summoned, as her hours of rising were uncertain. As I sat one day awaiting the call of Claudine, her maid came to me looking pale and terrified.

"Madame la Princesse waits, mademoiselle, and begs you will pardon this long delay."

"What agitates you?" I asked, for the girl glanced nervously over her shoulder as she spoke, and seemed eager, yet afraid to speak.

"Ah, mademoiselle, the prince has been with her, and so afflicted her, it desolates me to behold her. He is quite mad at times, I think, and terrifies us by his violence. Do not breathe to any one this that I say, and comfort madame if it is possible," and with her finger on her lips the girl hurried away.

I found the princess in tears, but the moment I appeared she dropped her handkerchief to exclaim with a gesture of despair: "We are lost! We are lost! Alexis is bent on returning to Russia and taking me to my death. *Chère* Sybil, what is to be done?"

"Refuse to go, and assert at once your freedom; it is a case which warrants such decision," was my revolutionary advice, though I well knew the princess would as soon think of firing the Tuileries as opposing her brother.

"It is impossible, I am dependent on him, he never would forgive such an act, and I should repent it to my last hour. No, my hope is in you, for you have eloquence, you see my feeble state, and you can plead for me as I cannot plead for myself."

"Dear madame, you deceive yourself. I have no eloquence, no power, and it is scarcely for me to come between you and the prince. I will do my best, but it will be in vain, I think."

"No, you do not fear him, he knows that, and it gives you power; you can talk well, can move and convince; I often see this when you read and converse with him, and I know that he would listen. Ah, for my sake make the attempt, and save me from that dreadful place!" cried the princess imploringly.

"Well, madame, tell me what passed, that I may know how to conduct the matter. Is a time for departure fixed?"

"No, thank heaven; if it were I should despair, for he would never revoke his orders. Something has annoyed him; I fancy a certain lady frowns upon him; but be that as it may, he is eager to be gone, and desired me to prepare to leave Paris. I implored, I wept, I reproached, and caressed, but nothing moved him, and he left me with the look which forebodes a storm."

"May I venture to ask why the prince does not return alone, and permit you to join him in the spring?"

"Because when my poor Feodor died he gave me into my brother's care, and Alexis swore to guard me as his life. I am so frail, so helpless, I need a faithful protector, and but for his fearful temper I should desire no better one than my brother. I owe everything to him, and would gladly obey even in this matter but for my health."

"Surely he thinks of that? He will not endanger your life for a selfish wish?"

"He thinks me fanciful, unreasonably fearful, and that I make this an excuse to have my own way. He is never ill, and knows nothing of my suffering, for I do not annoy him with complaints."

"Do you not think, madame, that if we could once convince him of the reality of the danger he would relent?"

"Perhaps; but how convince him? He will listen to no one."

"Permit me to prove that. If you will allow me to leave you for an hour I fancy I can find a way to convince and touch the prince."

The princess embraced me cordially, bade me go at once, and return soon, to satisfy her curiosity. Leaving her to rest and wonder, I went quietly away to the celebrated physician who at intervals visited the princess, and stating the case to him, begged for a written opinion which, coming from him, would, I knew, have weight with the prince. Dr. Segarde at once complied, and strongly urged the necessity of keeping the princess in Paris some months longer. Armed with this, I hastened back, hopeful and gay.

The day was fine, and wishing to keep my errand private, I had not used the carriage placed at my disposal. As I crossed one of the long corridors, on my way to the princess, I was arrested by howls of pain and the sharp crack of a whip, proceeding from an apartment near by. I paused involuntarily, longing yet fearing to enter and defend poor Mouche, for I recognized his voice. As I stood, the door swung open and the great hound sprang out, to cower behind me, with an imploring look in his almost human eyes. The prince followed, whip in hand, evidently in one of the fits of passion which terrified the household. I had seen many demonstrations of wrath, but never anything like that, for he seemed literally beside himself. Pale as death, with eyes full of savage fire, teeth set, and hair bristling like that of an enraged animal, he stood fiercely glaring at me. My heart fluttered for a moment, then was steady, and feeling no fear, I lifted my eyes to his, freely showing the pity I felt for such utter want of self-control.

It irritated him past endurance, and pointing to the dog, he said, in a sharp, low voice, with a gesture of command:

"Go on, mademoiselle, and leave Mouche to his fate."

"But what has the poor beast done to merit such brutal punishment?" I asked, coolly, remaining where I was.

"It is not for you to ask, but to obey," was the half-breathless answer, for a word of opposition increased his fury.

"Pardon; Mouche takes refuge with me; I cannot betray him to his enemy."

The words were still on my lips, when, with a step, the prince reached me, and towering above me like the incarnation of wrath, cried fiercely, as he lifted his hand menacingly:

"If you thwart me it will be at your peril!"

I saw he was on the point of losing all control of himself, and seizing the upraised arm, I looked him in the eye, saying steadily:

"Monsieur le Prince forgets that in France it is dastardly to strike a woman. Do not disgrace yourself by any Russian brutality."

The whip dropped from his hand, his arm fell, and turning suddenly, he dashed into the room behind him. I was about to make good my retreat, when a strange sound made me glance into the room. The prince had flung himself into a chair, and sat there actually choking with the violence of his passion. His face was purple, his lips pale, and his eyes fixed, as he struggled to unclasp the great sable-lined cloak he wore. As he then looked I was afraid he would have a fit, and never stopping for a second thought, I hurried to him, undid the cloak, loosened his collar, and filling a glass from the *carafe* on the sideboard, held it to his lips. He drank mechanically, sat motionless a moment, then drew a long breath, shivered as if recovering from a swoon, and glanced about him till his eye fell on me. It kindled again, and passing his hand over his forehead as if to collect himself, he said abruptly:

"Why are you here?"

"Because you needed help, and there was no one else to give it," I answered, refilling the glass, and offering it again, for his lips seemed dry.

He took it silently, and as he emptied it at a draught his eye glanced from the whip to me, and a scarlet flush rose to his forehead.

"Did I strike you?" he whispered, with a shame-stricken face.

"If you had we should not have been here."

"And why?" he asked, in quick surprise.

"I think I should have killed you, or myself, after such degradation. Unwomanly, perhaps, but I have a man's sense of honor."

It was an odd speech, but it rose to my lips, and I uttered it impulsively, for my spirit was roused by the insult. It served me better than tears or reproaches, for his eye fell after a furtive glance, in which admiration, shame and pride contended, and forcing a smile, he said, as if to hide his discomposure:

"I have insulted you; if you demand satisfaction I will give it, mademoiselle."

"I do," I said, promptly.

He looked curious, but seemed glad of anything which should divert his thoughts from himself, for with a bow and a half smile, he said quickly:

"Will mademoiselle name the reparation I shall make her? Is it to be pistols or swords?"

"It is pardon for poor Mouche."

His black brow lowered, and the thunderbolt veins on his forehead darkened again with the angry blood, not yet restored to quietude. It cost him an effort to say gravely:

"He has offended me, and cannot be pardoned yet; ask anything for yourself, mademoiselle."

I was bent on having my own way, and making him submit as a

penance for his unwomanly menace. Once conquer his will, in no
matter how slight a degree, and I had gained a power possessed by no
other person. I liked the trial, and would not yield one jot of the
advantage I had gained; so I answered, with a smile I had never worn
to him before:

"Monsieur le Prince has given his word to grant me satisfaction;
surely he will not break it, whatever atonement I demand! Ah, pardon
Mouche, and I forget the rest."

I had fine eyes, and knew how to use them; as I spoke I fixed
them on the prince with an expression half-imploring, half-com-
manding, and saw in his face a wish to yield, but pride would not
permit it.

"Mademoiselle, I ordered the dog to follow me; he refused, and
for that I would have punished him. If I relent before the chastisement
is finished I lose my power over him, and the offense will be repeated.
Is it not possible to satisfy you without ruining Mouche?"

"Permit one question before I reply. Did you give yourself the
trouble of discovering the cause of the dog's unusual disobedience
before the whip was used?"

"No; it is enough for me that the brute refused to follow. What
cause could there have been for his rebelling?"

"Call him and it will appear."

The prince ordered in the dog; but in vain; Mouche crouched
in the corridor with a forlorn air, and answered only by a whine. His
master was about to go to him angrily, when, to prevent another
scene, I called, and at once the dog came limping to my feet. Stoop-
ing, I lifted one paw, and showed the prince a deep and swollen
wound, which explained the poor brute's unwillingness to follow his
master on the long daily drive. I was surprised at the way in which
the prince received the rebuke; I expected a laugh, a careless or a
haughty speech, but like a boy he put his arm about the hound, saying
almost tenderly:

"Pardon, pardon, my poor Mouche! Who has hurt thee so cruelly? Forgive the whip; thou shalt never feel it again."

Like a noble brute as he was, Mouche felt the change, understood, forgave, and returned to his allegiance at once, lifting himself

to lick his master's hand and wag his tail in token of affection. It was a pretty little scene, for the prince laid his face on the smooth head of the dog, and half-whispered his regrets, exactly as a generous-hearted lad would have done to the favorite whom he had wronged in anger. I was glad to see it, childish as it was, for it satisfied me that this household tyrant had a heart, and well pleased with the ending of this stormy interview, I stole noiselessly away, carrying the broken whip with me as a trophy of my victory.

To the princess I said nothing of all this, but cheered her with the doctor's note and somewhat rash prophecies of its success. The prince seldom failed to come morning and evening to inquire for his sister, and as the time drew near for the latter visit we both grew anxious. At the desire of the princess I placed myself at the piano, hoping that "music might soothe the savage breast," and artfully prepare the way for the appeal. One of the prince's whims was to have rooms all over the hotel and one never knew in which he might be. That where I had first seen him was near the suite of the princess, and he often stepped quietly in when we least expected him. This habit annoyed his sister, but she never betrayed it, and always welcomed him, no matter how inopportune his visit might be. As I sat playing I saw the curtains that hung before the door softly drawn aside, and expected the prince to enter, but they fell again and no one appeared. I said nothing, but thundered out the Russian national airs with my utmost skill, till the soft scent of flowers and a touch on my arm made me glance down, to see Mouche holding in his mouth a magnificent bouquet, to which was attached a card bearing my name.

I was pleased, yet not quite satisfied, for in this Frenchy little performance I fancied I saw the prince's desire to spare himself any further humiliation. I did not expect it, but I did wish he had asked pardon of me as well as of the dog, and when among the flowers I found a bracelet shaped like a coiled up golden whip with a jeweled handle, I would have none of it, and giving it to Mouche, bid him take it to his master. The docile creature gravely retired, but not before I had discovered that the wounded foot was carefully bound up, that he wore a new silver collar, and had the air of a dog who had been petted to his heart's content.

The princess from her distant couch had observed but not understood the little pantomime, and begged to be enlightened. I told the story, and was amused at the impression it made upon her, for when I paused she clasped her hands, exclaiming, theatrically:

"*Mon Dieu,* that any one should dare face Alexis in one of his furies! And you had no fear? you opposed him? made him spare Mouche and ask pardon? It is incredible!"

"But I could not see the poor beast half killed, and I never dreamed of harm to myself. Of that there could be no danger, for I am a woman, and the prince a gentleman," I said, curious to know how that part of the story would affect the princess.

"Ah, my dear, those who own serfs see in childhood so much cruelty, they lose that horror of it which we feel. Alexis has seen many women beaten when a boy, and though he forbids it now, the thing does not shock him as it should. When in these mad fits he knows not what he does; he killed a man once, a servant, who angered him, struck him dead with a blow. He suffered much remorse, and for a long time was an angel; but the wild blood cannot be controlled, and he is the victim of his passion. It was like him to send the flowers, but it will mortally offend him that you refuse the bracelet. He always consoles me with some bijou after he has made me weep, and I accept it, for it relieves and calms him."

"Does he not express contrition in words?"

"Never! he is too proud for that. No one dares demand such humiliation, and since he was not taught to ask pardon when a child, one cannot expect to teach the lesson now. I fear he will not come to-night; what think you, Sybil?"

"I think he will not come, but what matter? Our plan can be executed at any time. Delay is what we wish, and this affair may cause him to forget the other."

"Ah, if it would, I should bless Mouche almost as fervently as when he saved Alexis from the wolves."

"Does the prince owe his life to the dog?"

"In truth he does, for in one of his bear hunts at home he lost his way, was beset by the ferocious beasts, and but for the gallant dog would never have been saved. He loves him tenderly, and—"

"Breaks whips over the brave creature's back," I added, rudely enough, quite forgetting etiquette in my indignation.

The princess laughed, saying, with a shrug:

"You English are such stern judges."

CHAPTER III

I was intensely curious to see how the prince would behave when we met. Politeness is such a national trait in France, where the poorest workman lifts his cap in passing a lady, to the Emperor, who returns the salute of his shabbiest subject, that one soon learns to expect the little courtesies of daily life so scrupulously and gracefully paid by all classes, and to miss them if they are wanting. When he chose, the prince was a perfect Frenchman in this respect, but at times nothing could be more insolently haughty, or entirely oblivious of common civility. Hitherto I had had no personal experience of this, but had observed it toward others, and very unnecessarily angered myself about it. My turn came now; for when he entered his sister's apartment next day, he affected entire unconsciousness of my presence. Not a look, word, or gesture was vouchsafed me, but, half turning his back, he chatted with the princess in an unusually gay and affectionate manner.

After the first indignant impulse to leave the room had passed, I became cool enough to see and enjoy the ludicrous side of the affair. I could not help wondering if it was done for effect, but for the first time since I came I saw the prince in his uniform. I would not look openly, though I longed to do so, for covert glances, as I busied myself with my embroidery, gave me glimpses of a splendid blending of scarlet, white and gold. It would have been impossible for the prince not to have known that this brilliant costume was excessively becoming, and not to have felt a very natural desire to display his handsome figure to advantage. More than once he crossed the room to look from the window, as if impatient for the droschky, then sat himself down at the piano and played stormily for five minutes, marched back to the princess's sofa and teased Bijou the poodle, ending at length by standing erect on the rug and facing the enemy.

Finding I bore my disgrace with equanimity, he was possessed to play the master, and show his displeasure in words as well as by silence. Turning to his sister, he said, in the tone of one who does not deign to issue commands to inferiors:

"You were enjoying some book as I entered, Nadja; desire Mademoiselle Varna to continue—I go in a moment."

"Ma chère, oblige me by finishing the chapter," said the princess, with a significant glance, and I obeyed.

We were reading George Sand's *Consuelo,* or rather the sequel of that wonderful book, and had reached the scenes in which Frederick the Great torments the prima donna before sending her to prison, because she will not submit to his whims. I liked my task, and read with spirit, hoping the prince would enjoy the lesson as much as I did. By skillfully cutting paragraphs here and there, I managed to get in the most apposite and striking of Consuelo's brave and sensible remarks, as well as the tyrant's unjust and ungenerous commands. The prince stood with his eyes fixed upon me. I felt, rather than saw this, for I never lifted my own, but permitted a smile to appear when Frederick threatened her with his cane. The princess speedily forgot everything but the romance, and when I paused, exclaimed, with a laugh:

"Ah, you enjoy that much, Sybil, for, like Consuelo, you would have defied the Great Fritz himself."

"That I would, in spite of a dozen Spondous. Royalty and rank give no one a right to oppress others. A tyrant—even a crowned one—is the most despicable of creatures," I answered, warmly.

"But you will allow that Porporina was very cold and coy, and altogether provoking, in spite of her genius and virtue," said the princess, avoiding the word "tyrant," as the subjects of the czar have a tendency to do.

"She was right, for the humblest mortals should possess their liberty and preserve it at all costs. Golden chains are often heavier than iron ones: is it not so, Mouche?" I asked of the dog, who lay at my feet, vainly trying to rid himself of the new collar which annoyed him.

A sharp "Here, sir!" made him spring to his master, who ordered him to lie down, and put one foot on him to keep him, as he showed signs of deserting again. The prince looked ireful, his black eyes were kindling, and some imperious speech was trembling on his lips, when Claudine entered with the *mal-apropos* question.

"Does Madame la Princesse desire that I begin to make preparations for the journey?"

"Not yet. Go; I will give orders when it is time," replied the princess, giving me a glance, which said, "We must speak now."

"What journey?" demanded the prince, as Claudine vanished precipitately.

"That for which you commanded me to prepare," returned his sister, with a heavy sigh.

"That is well. You consent, then, without more useless delay?" and the prince's face cleared as he spoke.

"If you still desire it, after reading this, I shall submit, Alexis," and giving him the note, his sister waited, with nervous anxiety, for his decision.

As he read I watched him, and saw real concern, surprise, and regret in his face, but when he looked up, it was to ask:

"When did Dr. Segarde give you this, and wherefore?"

"You shall know all, my brother. Mademoiselle sees my sufferings, pities my unhappiness, and is convinced that it is no whim of mine which makes me dread this return. I implore her to say this to you, to plead for me, because, with all your love, you cannot know my state as she does. To this prayer of mine she listens, but with a modesty as great as her goodness, she fears that you may think her officious, over-bold, or blinded by regard for me.

Therefore she wisely asks for Segarde's opinion, sure that it will touch and influence you. Do not destroy her good opinion, nor disappoint thy Nadja!"

The prince *was* touched, but found it hard to yield, and said, slowly, as he refolded the note, with a glance at me of annoyance not anger:

"So you plot and intrigue against me, ladies! But I have said we shall go, and I never revoke a decree."

"Go!" cried the princess, in a tone of despair.

"Yes, it is inevitable," was the answer, as the prince turned toward the fire, as if to escape importunities and reproaches.

"But when, Alexis—when? Give me still a few weeks of grace!" implored his sister, approaching him in much agitation.

"I give thee till April," replied the prince, in an altered tone.

"But that is spring, the time I pray for! Do you, then, grant my prayer?" exclaimed the princess, pausing in amazement.

"I said we must go, but not *when;* now I fix a time, and give thee yet some weeks of grace. Didst thou think I loved my own pleasure more than thy life, my sister?"

As he turned, with a smile of tender reproach, the princess uttered a cry of joy and threw herself into his arms in a paroxysm of gratitude, delight and affection. I never imagined that the prince could unbend so beautifully and entirely; but as I watched him caress and reassure the frail creature who clung to him, I was surprised to find what a hearty admiration suddenly sprung up within me for "the barbarian," as I often called him to myself. I enjoyed the pretty tableau a moment, and was quietly gliding away, lest I should be *de trop,* when the princess arrested me by exclaiming, as she leaned on her brother's arm, showing a face rosy with satisfaction:

"*Chère* Sybil, come and thank him for this kindness; you know how ardently I desired the boon, and you must help me to express my gratitude."

"In what language shall I thank Monsieur le Prince for prolonging his sister's life? Your tears, madame, are more eloquent than any words of mine," I replied, veiling the reproach under a tone of respectful meekness.

"She is too proud, this English Consuelo; she will not stoop to confess an obligation even to Alexis Demidoff."

He spoke in a half-playful, half-petulant tone, and hesitated over the last words, as if he would have said "a prince." The haughtiness was quite gone, and something in his expression, attitude and tone touched me. The sacrifice had cost him something, and a little commendation would not hurt him, vain and selfish though he might be. I was grateful for the poor princess's sake, and I did not hesitate to show it, saying with my most cordial smile, and doubtless some of the satisfaction I could not but feel visible in my face:

"I am not too proud to thank you sincerely for this favor to Madame la Princesse, nor to ask pardon for anything by which I may have offended you."

A gratified smile rewarded me as he said, with an air of surprise: "And yet, mademoiselle desires much to see St. Petersburg?"

"I do, but I can wait, remembering that it is more blessed to give than to receive."

A low bow was the only reply he made, and with a silent caress to his sister he left the room.

"You have not yet seen the droschky; from the window of the ante-room the courtyard is visible; go, mademoiselle, and get a glimpse of St. Petersburg," said the princess, returning to her sofa, weary with the scene.

I went, and looking down, saw the most picturesque equipage I had ever seen. The elegant, coquettish droschky with a pair of splendid black Ukraine horses, harnessed in the Russian fashion, with a network of purple leather profusely ornamented with silver, stood before the grand entrance, and on the seat sat a handsome young man in full Ischvostchik costume. His caftan of fine cloth was slashed at the sides with embroidery; his hat had a velvet band, a silver buckle, and a bunch of rosy ribbons in it; a white-laced neck-cloth, buckskin gloves, hair and beard in perfect order; a brilliant sash and a crimson silk shirt. As I stood wondering if he was a serf, the prince appeared, wrapped in the long gray capote, lined with scarlet, which all military Russians wear, and the brilliant helmet surmounted by a flowing white plume. As he seated himself among the costly furs he glanced up at his sister's windows, where she sometimes stood to see him. His quick eye recognized me, and to my surprise he waved his hand with a gracious smile as the fiery horses whirled him away.

That smile haunted me curiously all day, and more than once I glanced into the courtyard, hoping to see the picturesque droschky again, for, though one cannot live long in Paris without seeing nearly every costume under the sun, and accustomed as I was to such sights, there was something peculiarly charming to me in the martial figure, the brilliant equipage and the wild black horses, as full of untamed grace and power as if but just brought from the steppes of Tartary.

There was a dinner party in the evening, and, anxious to gratify her brother, the princess went down. Usually I enjoyed these free hours, and was never at a loss for occupation or amusement, but on this evening I could settle to nothing till I resolved to indulge an odd whim which possessed me. Arranging palette and brushes, I was soon absorbed in reproducing on a small canvas a likeness of the droschky and its owner. Hour after hour slipped by as the little picture grew, and horses, vehicle, driver and master took shape and color under my touch. I spent much time on the principal figure, but left the face till the last. All was carefully copied from memory, the white tunic, golden cuirass, massive epaulets, and silver sash; the splendid casque with its plume, the gray cloak, and the scarlet trowsers, half-hidden by the high boots of polished leather. At the boots I paused, trying to remember something.

"Did he wear spurs?" I said, half audibly, as I leaned back to survey my work complacently.

"Decidedly yes, mademoiselle," replied a voice, and there stood the prince with a wicked smile on his lips.

I seldom lose my self-possession, and after an involuntary start, was quite myself, though much annoyed at being discovered. Instead of hiding the picture or sitting dumb with embarrassment, I held it up, saying tranquilly:

"Is it not creditable to so bad an artist? I was in doubt about the spurs, but now I can soon finish."

"The horses are wonderful, and the furs perfect. Ivan is too handsome, and this countenance may be said to lack expression."

He pointed to the blank spot where his own face should have been, and eyed me with most exasperating intelligence. But I concealed my chagrin under an innocent air, and answered simply:

"Yes; I wait to find a portrait of the czar before I finish this addition to my little gallery of kings and queens."

"The czar!" ejaculated the prince, with such an astonished expression that I could not restrain a smile, as I touched up the handsome Ivan's beard.

"I have an admiration for the droschky, and that it may be quite complete, I boldly add the czar. It always pleased me to read how freely and fearlessly he rides among his people, unattended, in the gray cloak and helmet."

The prince gave me an odd look, crossed the room, and returning, laid before me an enameled casket, on the lid of which was a portrait of a stout, light-haired, somewhat ordinary, elderly gentleman, saying in a tone which betrayed some pique and much amusement:

"Mademoiselle need not wait to finish her work: behold the czar!"

I was strongly tempted to laugh, and own the truth, but something in the prince's manner restrained me, and after gravely regarding the portrait a moment, I began to copy it. My hand was not steady nor my eye clear, but I recklessly daubed on till the prince, who had stood watching me, said suddenly in a very mild tone:

"I flatter myself that there was some mistake last evening; either Mouche failed to do his errand, or the design of the trinket displeased you. I have endeavored to suit mademoiselle's taste better, and this time I offer it myself."

A white-gloved hand holding an open jewel-case which contained a glittering ring came before my eyes, and I could not retreat. Being stubborn by nature, and ruffled by what had just passed, as well as bent on having my own way in the matter, I instantly decided to refuse all gifts. Retreating slightly from the offering, I pointed to the flowers on the table near me, and said, with an air of grave decision:

"Monsieur le Prince must permit me to decline. I have already received all that it is possible to accept."

"Nay, examine the trifle, mademoiselle, and relent. Why will you not oblige me and be friends, like Mouche?" he said, earnestly.

That allusion to the dog nettled me, and I replied, coldly turning from the importunate hand.

"It was not the silver collar which consoled poor Mouche for the blows. Like him I can forgive, but I cannot so soon forget."

The dainty case closed with a sharp snap, and flinging it on to a table as he passed, the prince left the room without a word.

I was a little frightened at what I had done for a moment, but soon recovered my courage, resolving that since he had made it a test which should yield, *I* would not be the one to do it, for I had right on my side. Nor would I be appeased till he had made the *amende honorable* to me as to the dog. I laughed at the foolish affair, yet could not entirely banish a feeling of anger at the first violence and at the lordly way in which he tried to atone for the insult.

"Let us wait and see how the sultan carries himself to-morrow," I said; "if he become tyrannical, I am free to go, thank heaven; otherwise it is interesting to watch the handsome savage chafe and fret behind the bars of civilized society."

And gathering up my work, I retired to my room to replace the czar's face with that of the prince.

CHAPTER IV

"Chère amie, you remember I told you that Alexis always gave me some trifle after he had made me weep; behold what a charming gift I find upon my table to-day!" cried the princess, as I joined her next morning.

She held up her slender hand, displaying the ring I had left behind me the night before. I had had but a glimpse of it, but I knew it by the peculiar arrangement of the stones. Before I could say anything the princess ran on, as pleased as a girl with her new bauble:

"I have just discovered the prettiest conceit imaginable. See, the stones spell 'Pardon;' pearl, amethyst, ruby, diamond, opal, and as there is no stone commencing with the last letter, the initial of my name is added in enamel. Is not that divine?"

I examined it, and being a woman, I regretted the loss of the jewels as well as the opportunity of ending the matter, by a kinder reply to this fanciful petition for pardon. While I hesitated to enlighten the princess, for fear of further trouble, the prince entered, and I retreated to my seat at the other end of the room.

"Dear Alexis, I have just discovered your charming souvenir; a thousand thanks," cried his sister, with effusion.

"My souvenir; of what do you speak, Nadja?" he replied, with an air of surprise as he approached.

"Ah, you affect ignorance, but I well know whose hand sends me this, though I find it lying carelessly on my table. Yes, that start is very well done, yet it does not impose upon me. I am charmed with the gift; come, and let me embrace you."

With a very ill grace the "dear Alexis" submitted to the ceremony, and received the thanks of his sister, who expatiated upon the taste and beauty of the ring till he said, impatiently:

"You are very ingenious in your discoveries; I confess I meant it for a charming woman whom I had offended; if you had not accepted it I should have flung it in the fire. Now let it pass, and bid me adieu. I go to pass a week with Bagdonoff."

The princess was, of course, desolated to lose her brother, but resigned herself to the deprivation with calmness, and received his farewell without tears. I thought he meant to ignore me entirely, but to my surprise he approached, and with an expression I had never seen before, said, in a satirical tone:

"Mademoiselle, I leave the princess to your care, with perfect faith in your fidelity. Permit me to hope that you will enjoy my absence," and with a low bow, such as I had seen him give a countess, he departed.

The week lengthened to three before we saw the prince, and I am forced to confess that I did *not* enjoy his absence. So monotonous grew my days that I joyfully welcomed a somewhat romantic little episode in which I was just then called to play a part.

One of my former pupils had a lover. Madame Bayard discovered the awful fact, sent the girl home to her parents, and sternly refused to give the young man her address. He knew me, and in his despair applied to me for help and consolation. But not daring to seek me at the prince's hotel, he sent a note, imploring me to grant him an interview in the Tuileries Garden at a certain hour. I liked Adolph, pitied my amiable ex-pupil, and believing in the sincerity of their love, was glad to aid them.

At the appointed time I met Adolph, and for an hour paced up and down the leafless avenues, listening to his hopes and fears. It was a dull April day, and dusk fell early, but we were so absorbed that neither observed the gathering twilight till an exclamation from my companion made me look up.

"That man is watching us!"

"What man?" I asked, rather startled.

"Ah, he slips away again behind the trees yonder. He has done it twice before as we approached, and when we are past he follows stealthily. Do you see him?"

I glanced into the dusky path which crossed our own, and caught a glimpse of a tall man in a cloak just vanishing.

"You mistake, he does not watch us; why should he? Your own disquiet makes you suspicious, *mon ami*," I said.

"Perhaps so; let him go. Dear mademoiselle, I ask a thousand pardons for detaining you so long. Permit me to call a carriage for you."

I preferred to walk, and refusing Adolph's entreaties to escort me, I went my way along the garden side of the Rue de Rivoli, glad to be free at last. The wind was dying away as the sun set, but as a last freak it blew my veil off and carried it several yards behind me. A gentleman caught and advanced to restore it. As he put it into my hand with a bow, I uttered an exclamation, for it was the prince. He also looked surprised, and greeted me courteously, though with a strong expression of curiosity visible in his face. A cloak hung over his arm, and as my eyes fell upon it, an odd fancy took possession of me, causing me to conceal my pleasure at seeing him, and to assume a cold demeanor, which he observed at once. Vouchsafing no explanation of my late walk, I thanked him for the little service, adjusted my veil, and walked on as if the interview was at an end.

"It is late for mademoiselle to promenade alone; as I am about to return to the hotel, she will permit me to accompany her?"

The prince spoke in his most gracious tone, and walked beside me, casting covert glances at my face as we passed, the lamps now shining all about us. I was angry, and said, with significant emphasis:

"Monsieur le Prince has already sufficiently honored me with his protection. I can dispense with it now."

"Pardon, I do not understand," he began hastily; but I added, pointing to the garment on his arm:

"Pray assume your cloak; it is colder here than in the garden of the Tuileries."

Glancing up as I spoke, I saw him flush and frown, then draw himself up as if to haughtily demand an explanation, but with a sudden impulse, pause, and ask, averting his eyes:

"Why does mademoiselle speak in that accusing tone? Are the gardens forbidden ground to me?"

"Yes; when Monsieur le Prince condescends to play the spy," I boldly replied, adding with a momentary doubt arising in my mind, "Were you not there watching me?"

To my infinite surprise he looked me full in the face, and answered briefly:

"I was."

"Adolph was right then—I also; it is well to know one's enemies," I said, as if to myself, and uttered not another word, but walked rapidly on.

Silent also the prince went beside me, till, as we were about to cross the great square, a carriage whirled round the corner, causing me to step hastily back. An old crone, with a great basket on her head, was in imminent danger of being run over, when the prince sprang forward, caught the bit and forced the spirited horses back till the old creature gathered herself up and reached the pave in safety. Then he returned to me as tranquilly as if nothing had occurred.

"Are you hurt?" I asked, forgetting my anger, as he pulled off and threw away the delicate glove, torn and soiled in the brief struggle.

"Thanks—no; but the old woman?"

"She was not injured, and went on her way, never staying to thank you."

"Why should she?" he asked, quietly.

"One likes to see gratitude. Perhaps she is used to such escapes, and so the act surprised her less than it did me."

"Ah! you wonder that I troubled myself about the poor creature, mademoiselle. I never forget that my mother was a woman, and for her sake I respect all women."

I had never heard that tone in his voice, nor seen that look in his face before, as he spoke those simple words. They touched me more than the act, but some tormenting spirit prompted me to say:

"Even when you threaten one of them with a—"

I got no further, for, with a sudden flash that daunted me, the prince cried imploringly, yet commandingly:

"No—no; do not utter the word—do not recall the shameful scene. Be generous, and forget, though you will not forgive."

"Pardon, it was unkind, I never will offend again."

An awkward pause followed, and we went on without a word, till glancing at me as we passed a brilliant lamp, the prince exclaimed:

"Mademoiselle, you are very pale—you are ill, over-wearied; let me call a carriage."

"By no means; it is nothing. In stepping back to avoid the horses, I hurt my ankle; but we are almost at the hotel, and I can reach it perfectly well."

"And you have walked all this distance without a complaint, when every step was painful? *Ma foi!* mademoiselle is brave," he said, with mingled pity, anxiety and admiration in his fine eyes.

"Women early learn to suffer in silence," I answered, rather grimly, for my foot was in agony, and I was afraid I should give out before I reached the hotel.

The prince hastened on before me, unlocked the side-door by which I usually entered, and helping me in, said earnestly:

"There are many steps to climb; let me assist you, or call some one."

"No, no, I will have no scene; many thanks; I can reach my room quite well alone. *Bon soir,* Monsieur le Prince," and turning from his offered arm, I set my teeth and walked steadily up the first seven stairs. But on reaching the little landing, pain overcame pride, and I sank into a chair with a stifled groan. I had heard the door close, and fancied the prince gone, but he was at my side in an instant.

"Mademoiselle, I shall not leave you till you are safely in your apartment. How can I best serve you?"

I pointed to the bell, saying faintly:

"I cannot walk; let Pierre carry me."

"I am stronger and more fit for such burdens. Pardon, it must be so."

And before I could utter a refusal, he folded the cloak about me, raised me gently in his arms, and went pacing quietly along the corridors, regarding me with an air of much sympathy, though in his eyes lurked a gleam of triumph, as he murmured to himself:

"She has a strong will, this brave mademoiselle of ours, but it must bend at last."

That annoyed me more than my mishap, but being helpless, I answered only with a defiant glance and an irrepressible smile at my little adventure. He looked keenly at me with an eager, yet puzzled air, and said, as he grasped me more firmly:

"Inexplicable creature! Pain can conquer her strength, but her spirit defies me still."

I hardly heard him, for as he laid me on the couch in my own little *salon,* I lost consciousness, and when I recovered myself, I was alone with my maid.

"What has happened?" I asked.

"Dear mademoiselle, I know not; the bell rings, I fly, I find you fainting, and I restore you. It is fatigue, alarm, illness, and you ring before your senses leave you," cried Jacobine, removing my cloak and furs.

A sudden pang in my foot recalled me to myself at once, and bidding the girl apply certain remedies, I was soon comfortable. Not a word was said of the prince; he had evidently vanished before the maid came. I was glad of this, for I had no desire to furnish food for gossip among the servants. Sending Jacobine with a message to the princess, I lay recalling the scene and perplexing myself over several trifles which suddenly assumed great importance in my eyes.

My bonnet and gloves were off when the girl found me. Who had removed them? My hair was damp with eau-de-cologne; who had bathed my head? My injured foot lay on a cushion; who placed it there? Did I dream that a tender voice exclaimed, "My little Sybil, my heart, speak to me"? or did the prince really utter such words?

With burning cheeks, and a half-sweet, half-bitter trouble in my heart, I thought of these things, and asked myself what all this was coming to. A woman often asks herself such questions, but seldom answers them, nor did I, preferring to let time drift me where it would.

The amiable princess came herself to inquire for me. I said nothing of her brother, as it was evident that he had said nothing even to her.

"Alexis has returned, *ma chère;* he was with me when Jacobine told me of your accident; he sends his compliments and regrets. He is in charming spirits, and looking finely."

I murmured my thanks, but felt a little guilty at my want of frankness. Why not tell her the prince met and helped me? While debating the point within myself, the princess was rejoicing that my accident would perhaps still longer delay the dreaded journey.

"Let it be a serious injury, my friend; it will permit you to enjoy life here, but not to travel; so suffer sweetly for my sake, and I will repay you with a thousand thanks," she said, pleadingly.

Laughingly I promised, and having ordered every luxury she could imagine, the princess left me with a joyful heart, while I vainly tried to forget the expression of the prince's face as he said low to himself:

"Her spirit defies me still."

CHAPTER V

For a week I kept my room and left the princess to fabricate what tales she liked. She came to me every day reporting the preparations for departure were begun, but the day still remained unfixed, although April was half over.

"He waits for you, I am sure; he inquires for you daily, and begins to frown at the delay. To appease him, come down to-morrow, languid, lame, and in a charming dishabille. Amuse him as you used to do, and if anything is said of Russia, express your willingness to go, but deplore your inability to bear the journey now."

Very glad to recover my liberty, I obeyed the princess, and entered her room next day leaning on Jacobine, pale, languid, and in my most becoming morning toilet. The princess was reading novels on her sofa by the fire; the prince, in the brilliant costume in which I first saw him, sat in my chair, busy at my embroidery frame. The odd contrast between the man and his employment struck me so ludicrously that a half laugh escaped me. Both looked up; the prince sprang out of his chair as if about to rush forward, but checked himself, and received me with a silent nod. The princess made a great stir over me, and with some difficulty was persuaded to compose herself at last. Having answered her eager and the prince's polite inquiries, I took up my work, saying, with an irresistible smile as I examined the gentleman's progress:

"My flowers have blossomed in my absence, I see. Does M. le Prince possess all accomplishments?"

"Ah, you smile, but I assure you embroidery is one of the amusements of Russian gentlemen, and they often excel us in it. My brother scorned it till he was disabled with a wound, and when all other devices failed, this became his favorite employment."

As the princess spoke the prince stood in his usual attitude on the rug, eying me with a suspicious look, which annoyed me intensely and destroyed my interesting pallor by an uncontrollable blush. I felt terribly guilty with those piercing black eyes fixed on me, and appeared to be absorbed in a fresh bit of work. The princess chattered on till a salver full of notes and cards was brought in, when she forgot everything else in reading and answering these. The prince approached me then, and seating himself near my sofa, said, with somewhat ironical emphasis on the last two words:

"I congratulate mademoiselle on her recovery, and that her bloom is quite untouched by her *severe sufferings*."

"The princess in her amiable sympathy doubtlessly exaggerated my pain, but I certainly *have* suffered, though my roses may belie me."

Why my eyes should fill and my lips tremble was a mystery to me, but they did, as I looked up at him with a reproachful face. I spoke the truth. I *had* suffered, not bodily but mental pain, trying to put away forever a tempting hope which suddenly came to trouble me. Astonishment and concern replaced the cold, suspicious expression of the prince's countenance, and his voice was very kind as he asked, with an evident desire to divert my thoughts from myself:

"For what luxurious being do you embroider these splendid slippers of purple and gold, mademoiselle? Or is that an indiscreet question?"

"For my friend Adolph Vernay."

"They are too large, he is but a boy," began the prince, but stopped abruptly, and bit his lip, with a quick glance at me.

Without lifting my eyes I said, coolly:

"M. le Prince appears to have observed this gentleman with much care, to discover that he has a handsome foot and a youthful face."

"Without doubt I should scrutinize any man with whom I saw mademoiselle walking alone in the twilight. As one of my household, I take the liberty of observing your conduct, and for my sister's sake ask of you to pardon this surveillance."

He spoke gravely, but looked unsatisfied, and feeling in a tormenting mood, I mystified him still more by saying, with a bow of assent:

"If M. le Prince knew all, he would see nothing strange in my promenade, nor in the earnestness of that interview. Believe me, I may seem rash, but I shall never forget what is due to the princess while I remain with her."

He pondered over my words a moment with his eyes on my face, and a frown bending his black brows. Suddenly he spoke, hastily, almost roughly:

"I comprehend what mademoiselle would convey. Monsieur Adolph is a lover, and the princess is about to lose her friend."

"Exactly. M. le Prince has guessed the mystery," and I smiled with downcast eyes.

A gilded ornament on the back of the chair against which the prince leaned snapped under his hand as it closed with a strong grip. He flung it away, and said, rapidly, with a jar in his usually musical voice:

"This gentleman will marry, it seems, and mademoiselle, with

the charming freedom of an English woman, arranges the affair herself."

"Helps to arrange; Adolph has sense and courage; I leave much
to him."

"And when is this interesting event to take place, if one may
ask?"

"Next week, if all goes well."

"I infer the princess knows of this?"

"Oh, yes. I told her at once."

"And she consents?"

"Without doubt; what right would she have to object?"

"Ah, I forgot; in truth, none, nor any other. It is incomprehensible! She is to lose you and yet is not in despair."

"It is but for a time. I join her later if she desires it."

"Never, with that man!" and the prince rose with an impetuous
gesture, which sent my silks flying.

"What man?" I asked, affecting bewilderment.

"This Adolph, whom you are about to marry."

"M. le Prince quite mistakes; I fancied he knew more of the
affair. Permit me to explain."

"Quick, then; what is the mystery? who marries? who goes? who
stays?"

So flushed, anxious and excited did he look, that I was satisfied
with my test, and set about enlightening him with alacrity. Having
told why I met the young man, I added:

"Adolph will demand the hand of Adele from her parents, but if
they refuse it, as I fear they will, being prejudiced against him by
Madame Bayard, he will effect his purpose in another manner.
Though I do not approve of elopements in general, this is a case
where it is pardonable, and I heartily wish him success."

While I spoke the prince's brow had cleared, he drew a long
breath, reseated himself in the chair before me, and when I paused,
said, with one of his sudden smiles and an air of much interest:

"Then you would have this lover boldly carry off his mistress in
spite of all obstacles?"

"Yes. I like courage in love as in war, and respect a man who conquers all obstacles."

"Good, it is well said," and with a low laugh the prince sat regarding me in silence for a moment. Then an expression of relief stole over his face as he said, still smiling:

"And it was of this you spoke so earnestly when you fancied I watched you in the gardens?"

"Fancied! nay, M. le Prince has confessed that it was no fancy."

"How if I had not confessed?"

"I should have believed your word till you betrayed yourself, and then—"

I paused there with an uncontrollable gesture of contempt. He eyed me keenly, saying in that half-imperious, half-persuasive voice of his:

"It is well then that I obeyed my first impulse. To speak truth is one of the instincts which these polished Frenchmen have not yet conquered in the 'barbarian,' as they call me."

"I respected you for that truthful 'yes,' more than for anything you ever said or did," I cried, forgetting myself entirely.

"Then, mademoiselle has a little respect for me?"

He leaned his chin upon the arm that lay along the back of his chair, and looked at me with a sudden softening of voice, eye, and manner.

"Can M. le Prince doubt it?" I said, demurely, little guessing what was to follow.

"Does mademoiselle desire to be respected for the same virtue?" he asked.

"More than for any other."

"Then will she give me a truthful answer to the plain question I desire to ask?"

"I will;" and my heart beat rebelliously as I glanced at the handsome face so near me, and just then so dangerously gentle.

"Has not mademoiselle feigned illness for the past week?"

The question took me completely by surprise, but anxious to stand the test, I glanced at the princess, still busy at her writing-table

278 THE FEMINIST ALCOTT

in the distant alcove, and checking the answer which rose to my lips,
I said, lowering my voice:

"On one condition will I reply."

"Name it, mademoiselle?"

"That nothing be said to Madame la Princesse of this."

"I give you my word."

"Well, then, I answer, yes;" and I fixed my eyes full on his as I
spoke.

His face darkened a shade, but his manner remained unchanged.

"Thanks; now, for the reason of the ruse?"

"To delay a little the journey to Russia."

"Ha, I had not thought of that, imbecile that I am!" he exclaimed with a start.

"What other reason did M. le Prince imagine, if I may question
in my turn?"

His usually proud and steady eyes wavered and fell, and he made
no answer, but seemed to fall into a reverie, from which he woke
presently to ask abruptly:

"What did you mean by saying you were to leave my sister for a
time, and rejoin her later?"

"I must trouble you with the relation of a little affair which will
probably detain me till after the departure, for but a week now remains of April."

"I listen, mademoiselle."

"Good Madame Bayard is unfortunately the victim of a cruel
disease, which menaces her life unless an operation can be successfully
performed. The time for this trial is at hand, and I have promised to
be with her. If she lives I can safely leave her in a few days; if she dies
I must remain till her son can arrive. This sad duty will keep me for a
week or two, and I can rejoin madame at any point she may desire."

"But why make this promise? Madame Bayard has friends—why
impose this unnecessary sacrifice of time, nerve, and sympathy upon
you, mademoiselle?" And the prince knit his brows, as if ill-pleased.

"When I came to Paris long ago a poor, friendless, sorrowful girl,
this good woman took me in, and for five years has been a mother to

me. I am grateful, and would make any sacrifice to serve her in her hour of need."

I spoke with energy; the frown melted to the smile which always ennobled his face, as the prince replied, in a tone of forgetful acquiescence:

"You are right. I say no more. If you are detained I will leave Vacil to escort you to us. He is true as steel, and will guard you well. When must you go to the poor lady?"

"To-morrow; the princess consents to my wish, and I devote myself to my friend till she needs me no longer. May I ask when you leave Paris?" I could not resist asking.

"On the last day of the month," was the brief reply, as the prince rose, and roamed away with a thoughtful face, leaving me to ponder over many things as I wrought my golden pansies, wondering if I should ever dare to offer the purple velvet slippers to the possessor of a handsomer foot than Adolph.

On the following day I went to Madame Bayard; the operation was performed, but failed, and the poor soul died in my arms, blessing me for my love and care. I sent tidings of the event to the princess, and received a kind reply, saying all was ready, and the day irrevocably fixed.

I passed a busy week; saw my best friend laid to her last rest; arranged such of her affairs as I could, and impatiently awaited the arrival of her son. On the second day of May he came, and I was free.

As soon as possible I hastened to the hotel, expecting to find it deserted. To my surprise, however, I saw lights in the *salon* of the princess, and heard sounds of life everywhere as I went wonderingly toward my own apartments. The windows were open, flowers filled the room with spring odors, and everything wore an air of welcome as if some one waited for me. Some one did, for on the balcony, which ran along the whole front, leaned the prince in the mild, new-fallen twilight, singing softly to himself.

"Not gone!" I exclaimed, in unfeigned surprise.

He turned, smiled, flushed, and said, as he vanished:

"I follow mademoiselle's good example in yielding my wishes to the comfort and pleasure of others."

CHAPTER VI

The next day we set out, but the dreaded journey proved delightful, for the weather was fine, and the prince in a charming mood. No allusion was made to the unexpected delay, except by the princess, who privately expressed her wonder at my power, and treated me with redoubled confidence and affection. We loitered by the way, and did not reach St. Petersburg till June.

I had expected changes in my life as well as change of scene, but was unprepared for the position which it soon became evident I was to assume. In Paris I had been the companion, now I was treated as a friend and equal by both the prince and princess. They entirely ignored my post, and remembering only that I was by birth a gentlewoman, by a thousand friendly acts made it impossible for me to refuse the relations which they chose to establish between us. I suspect the princess hinted to her intimates that I was a connection of her own, and my name gave color to the statement. Thus I found myself received with respect and interest by the circle in which I now moved, and truly enjoyed the free, gay life, which seemed doubly charming, after years of drudgery.

With this exception there was less alteration in my surroundings than I had imagined, for the upper classes in Russia speak nothing but French; in dress, amusements, and manners, copy French models so carefully that I should often have fancied myself in Paris, but for the glimpses of barbarism, which observing eyes cannot fail to detect, in spite of the splendor which surrounds them. The hotel of the prince was a dream of luxury; his equipages magnificent; his wealth apparently boundless; his friends among the highest in the land. He appeared to unusual advantage at home, and seemed anxious that I should observe this, exerting himself in many ways to impress me with his power, even while he was most affable and devoted.

I could no longer blind myself to the truth, and tried to meet it honestly. The prince loved me, and made no secret of his preference, though not a word had passed his lips. I had felt this since the night he carried me in his arms, but remembering the difference in rank, had taught myself to see in it only the passing caprice of a master for a servant, and as such, to regard it as an insult. Since we came to St. Petersburg the change in his manner seemed to assure me that he sought me as an equal, and desired to do me honor in the eyes of those about us. This soothed my pride and touched my heart, but, alluring as the thought was to my vanity and my ambition, I did not yield to it, feeling that I should not love, and that such an alliance was not the one for me.

Having come to this conclusion, I resolved to abide by it, and did so the more inflexibly as the temptation to falter grew stronger. My calm, cool manner perplexed and irritated the prince, who seemed to grow more passionate as test after test failed to extort any betrayal of regard from me. The princess, absorbed in her own affairs, seemed apparently blind to her brother's infatuation, till I was forced to enlighten her.

July was nearly over, when the prince announced that he was about to visit one of his estates, some versts from the city, and we were to accompany him. I had discovered that Volnoi was a solitary place, that no guests were expected, and that the prince was supreme master of everything and everybody on the estate. This did not suit me, for Madame Yermaloff, an Englishwoman, who had conceived a friendship for me, had filled my head with stories of Russian barbarity, and the entire helplessness of whomsoever dared to thwart or defy a Russian seigneur, especially when on his own domain. I laughed at her gossip, yet it influenced my decision, for of late the prince had looked ireful, and his black eyes had kept vigilant watch over me. I knew that his patience was exhausted, and feared that a stormy scene was in store for me. To avoid all further annoyance, I boldly stated the case to the princess, and decidedly refused to leave St. Petersburg.

To my surprise, she agreed with me; and I discovered, what I had before suspected, that, much as she liked me as a friend, the princess would have preferred her brother to marry one of his own rank. She delicately hinted this, yet, unwilling to give me up entirely, begged me to remain with Madame Yermaloff till she returned, when some new arrangement might be made. I consented, and feeling unequal to a scene with the prince, left his sister to inform him of my decision, and went quietly to my friend, who gladly received me.

Next morning the following note from the princess somewhat reassured me:

MA CHERE SYBIL—*We leave in an hour. Alexis received the news of your flight in a singular manner. I expected to see him half frantic; but no, he smiled, and said, tranquilly: "She fears and flies me; it is a sign of weakness, for which I thank her." I do not understand him; but when we are quiet at Volnoi, I hope to convince him that you are, as always, wise and prudent. Adieu! I embrace you tenderly.*

N.T.

A curious sense of disappointment and uneasiness took possession of me on reading this note, and, womanlike, I began to long for that which I had denied myself. Madame Yermaloff found me a very dull companion, and began to rally me on my preoccupation. I tried to forget, but could not, and often stole out to walk past the prince's hotel, now closed and silent. A week dragged slowly by, and I had begun to think the prince had indeed forgotten me, when I was convinced that he had not in a somewhat alarming manner. Returning one evening from a lonely walk in the Place Michel, with its green English square, I observed a carriage standing near the Palace Galitzin, and listlessly wondered who was about to travel, for the coachman was in his place and a servant stood holding the door open. As I passed I glanced in, but saw nothing, for in the act sudden darkness fell upon me; a cloak was dexterously thrown over me, enveloping my head and arms, and rendering me helpless. Some one lifted me into the carriage, the door closed, and I was driven rapidly away, in spite of my stifled cries and fruitless struggles. At first I was frantic with anger and fear, and rebelled desperately against the strong hold which restrained me. Not a word was spoken, but I felt sure, after the first alarm, that the prince was near me, and this discovery, though it increased my anger, allayed my fear. Being half-suffocated, I suddenly feigned faintness, and lay motionless, as if spent. A careful hand withdrew the thick folds, and as I opened my eyes they met those of the prince fixed on me, full of mingled solicitude and triumph.

"You! Yes; I might have known no one else would dare perpetrate such an outrage!" I cried, breathlessly, and in a tone of intense scorn, though my heart leaped with joy to see him.

He laughed, while his eyes flashed, as he answered, gayly:

"Mademoiselle forgets that she once said she 'liked courage in love as in war, and respected a man who conquered all obstacles.' I remember this, and, when other means fail dare to brave even her anger to gain my object."

"What is that object?" I demanded, as my eyes fell before the ardent glance fixed on me.

"It is to see you at Volnoi, in spite of your cruel refusal."

"I will not go."

And with a sudden gesture I dashed my hand through the window and cried for help with all my strength. In an instant I was pinioned again, and my cries stifled by the cloak, as the prince said, sternly:

"If mademoiselle resists, it will be the worse for her. Submit, and no harm will befall you. Accept the society of one who adores you, and permit yourself to be conquered by one who never yields— except to you," he added, softly, as he held me closer, and put by the cloak again.

"Let me go—I will be quiet," I panted, feeling that it was indeed idle to resist now, yet resolving that he should suffer for this freak.

"You promise to submit—to smile again, and be your charming self?" he said, in the soft tone that was so hard to deny.

"I promise nothing but to be quiet. Release me instantly!" and I tried to undo the clasp of the hand that held me.

"Not till you forgive me and look kind. Nay, struggle if you will, I like it, for till now you have been the master. See, I pardon all your cruelty, and find you more lovely than ever."

As he spoke he bent and kissed me on forehead, lips and cheek with an ardor which wholly daunted me. I did pardon him, for there was real love in his face, and love robbed the act of rudeness in my eyes, for instead of any show of anger or disdain, I hid my face in my hands, weeping the first tears he had ever seen me shed. It tamed him in a moment, for as I sobbed I heard him imploring me to be calm, promising to sin no more, and assuring me that he meant only to carry me to Volnoi as its mistress, whom he loved and honored above all women. Would I forgive his wild act, and let his obedience in all things else atone for this?

I must forgive it; and if he did not mock me by idle offers of obedience, I desired him to release me entirely and leave me to compose myself, if possible.

He instantly withdrew his arm, and seated himself opposite me, looking half contrite, half exultant, as he arranged the cloak about my feet. I shrunk into the corner and dried my tears, feeling unusually weak and womanish, just when I most desired to be strong and stern. Before I could whet my tongue for some rebuke, the prince uttered an exclamation of alarm, and caught my hand. I looked, and saw that it was bleeding from a wound made by the shattered glass.

"Let it bleed," I said, trying to withdraw it. But he held it fast, binding it up with his own handkerchief in the tenderest manner, saying as he finished, with a passionate pressure:

"Give it to me, Sybil, I want it—this little hand—so resolute, yet soft. Let it be mine, and it shall never know labor or wound again. Why do you frown—what parts us?"

"This," and I pointed to the crest embroidered on the corner of the *mouchoir*.

"Is that all?" he asked, bending forward with a keen glance that seemed to read my heart.

"One other trifle," I replied sharply.

"Name it, my princess, and I will annihilate it, as all other obstacles," he said, with the lordly air that became him.

"It is impossible."

"Nothing is impossible to Alexis Demidoff."

"I do not love you."

"In truth, Sybil?" he cried incredulously.

"In truth," I answered steadily.

He eyed me an instant with a gloomy air, then drew a long breath, and set his teeth, exclaiming:

"You are mortal. I shall *make* you love me."

"How, monsieur?" I coldly asked, while my traitorous heart beat fast.

"I shall humble myself before you, shall obey your commands, shall serve you, protect you, love and honor you ardently, faithfully, while I live. Will not such devotion win you?"

"No."

It was a hard word to utter, but I spoke it, looking him full in the eye and seeing with a pang how pale he grew with real despair.

"Is it because you love already, or that you have no heart?" he said slowly.

"I love already." The words escaped me against my will, for the truth would find vent in spite of me. He took it as I meant he should, for his lips whitened, as he asked hoarsely:

"And this man whom you love, is he alive?"

"Yes."

"He knows of this happiness—he returns your love?"

"He loves me; ask no more; I am ill and weary."

A gloomy silence reigned for several minutes, for the prince seemed buried in a bitter reverie, and I was intent on watching him. An involuntary sigh broke from me as I saw the shadow deepen on the handsome face opposite, and thought that my falsehood had changed the color of a life. He looked up at the sound, saw my white, anxious face, and without a word drew from a pocket of the carriage a flask and silver cup, poured me a draught of wine, and offered it, saying gently:

"Am I cruel in my love, Sybil?"

I made no answer, but drank the wine, and asked as I returned the cup:

"Now that you know the truth, must I go to Volnoi? Be kind, and let me return to Madame Yermaloff."

His face darkened and his eyes grew fierce, as he replied, with an aspect of indomitable resolve:

"It is impossible; I have sworn to make you love me, and at Volnoi I will work the miracle. Do you think this knowledge of the truth will deter me? No; I shall teach you to forget this man, whoever he is, and make you happy in my love. You doubt this. Wait a little and see what a real passion can do."

This lover-like pertinacity was dangerous, for it flattered my woman's nature more than any submission could have done. I dared not listen to it, and preferring to see him angry rather than tender, I said provokingly:

"No man ever forced a woman to love him against her will. You will certainly fail, for no one in her senses would give her heart to *you!*"

"And why? Am I hideous?" he asked, with a haughty smile.

"Far from it."

"Am I a fool, mademoiselle?"

"Quite the reverse."

"Am I base?"

" No."

"Have I degraded my name and rank by any act?"

"Never, till to-night, I believe."

He laughed, yet looked uneasy, and demanded imperiously:

"Then, why will no woman love me?"

"Because you have the will of a tyrant, and the temper of a madman."

If I had struck him in the face it would not have startled him as my blunt words did. He flushed scarlet, drew back and regarded me with a half-bewildered air, for never had such a speech been made to him before. Seeing my success, I followed it up by saying gravely:

"The insult of to-night gives me the right to forget the respect I have hitherto paid you, and for once you shall hear the truth as plain as words can make it. Many fear you for these faults, but no one dares tell you of them, and they mar an otherwise fine nature."

I got no further, for to my surprise, the prince said suddenly, with real dignity, though his voice was less firm than before:

"One dares to tell me of them, and I thank her. Will she add to the obligation by teaching me to cure them?" Then he broke out impetuously: "Sybil, you can help me; you possess courage and power to tame my wild temper, my headstrong will. In heaven's name I ask you to do it, that I may be worthy some good woman's love."

He stretched his hands toward me with a gesture full of force and feeling, and his eloquent eyes pleaded for pity. I felt my resolution melting away, and fortified myself by a chilly speech.

"Monsieur le Prince has said that nothing is impossible to him; if he can conquer all obstacles, it were well to begin with these."

"I have begun. Since I knew you my despotic will has bent more than once to yours, and my mad temper has been curbed by the remembrance that you have seen it. Sybil, if I do conquer myself, can you, will you try to love me?"

So earnestly he looked, so humbly he spoke, it was impossible to resist the charm of this new and manlier mood. I gave him my hand, and said, with the smile that always won him:

"I will respect you sincerely, and be your friend; more I cannot promise."

He kissed my hand with a wistful glance, and sighed as he dropped it, saying in a tone of mingled hope and resignation:

"Thanks; respect and friendship from you are dearer than love and confidence from another woman. I know and deplore the faults fostered by education and indulgence, and I will conquer them. Give me time. I swear it will be done."

"I believe it, and I pray for your success."

He averted his face and sat silent for many minutes, as if struggling with some emotion which he was too proud to show. I watched him, conscious of a redoubled interest in this man, who at one moment ruled me like a despot, and at another confessed his faults like a repentant boy.

CHAPTER VII

In Russia, from the middle of May to the 1st of August, there is no night. It is daylight till eleven, then comes a soft semi-twilight till one, when the sun rises. Through this gathering twilight we drove toward Volnoi. The prince let down the windows, and the summer air blew in refreshingly; the peace of the night soothed my perturbed spirit, and the long silences were fitly broken by some tender word from my companion, who, without approaching nearer, never ceased to regard me with eyes so full of love that, for the first time in my life, I dared not meet them.

It was near midnight when the carriage stopped, and I could discover nothing but a tall white pile in a wilderness of blooming shrubs and trees. Lights shone from many windows, and as the prince led me into a brilliantly lighted *salon,* the princess came smiling to greet me, exclaiming, as she embraced me with affection:

"Welcome, my sister. You see it is in vain to oppose Alexis. We must confess this, and yield gracefully; in truth, I am glad to keep you, *chère amie,* for without you we find life very dull."

"Madame mistakes; I never yield, and am here against my will."

I withdrew myself from her as I spoke, feeling hurt that she had not warned me of her brother's design. They exchanged a few words as I sat apart, trying to look dignified, but dying with sleep. The princess soon came to me, and it was impossible to resist her caressing manner as she begged me to go and rest, leaving all disagreements till the morrow. I submitted, and, with a silent salute to the prince, followed her to an apartment next her own, where I was soon asleep, lulled by the happy thought that I was not forgotten.

The princess was with me early in the morning, and a few moments' conversation proved to me that, so far from her convincing her brother of the folly of his choice, he had entirely won her to his side, and enlisted her sympathies for himself. She pleaded his suit with sisterly skill and eloquence, but I would pledge myself to nothing, feeling a perverse desire to be hardly won, if won at all, and a feminine wish to see my haughty lover thoroughly subdued before I put my happiness into his keeping. I consented to remain for a time, and a servant was sent to Madame Yermaloff with a letter explaining my flight, and telling where to forward a portion of my wardrobe.

Professing herself satisfied for the present, and hopeful for the future, the princess left me to join her brother in the garden, where I saw them talking long and earnestly. It was pleasant to a lonely soul like myself to be so loved and cherished, and when I descended it was impossible to preserve the cold demeanor I had assumed, for all faces greeted me with smiles, all voices welcomed me, and one presence made the strange place seem like home. The prince's behavior was perfect, respectful, devoted and self-controlled; he appeared like a new being, and the whole household seemed to rejoice in the change.

Day after day glided happily away, for Volnoi was a lovely spot, and I saw nothing of the misery hidden in the hearts and homes of the hundred serfs who made the broad domain so beautiful. I seldom saw them, never spoke to them, for I knew no Russ, and in our drives the dull-looking peasantry possessed no interest for me. They never came to the house, and the prince appeared to know nothing of them beyond what his Stavosta, or steward reported. Poor Alexis! he had many hard lessons to learn that year, yet was a better man and master for them all, even the one which nearly cost him his life.

Passing through the hall one day, I came upon a group of servants lingering near the door of the apartment in which the prince gave his orders and transacted business. I observed that the French servants looked alarmed, the Russian ones fierce and threatening, and that Antoine, the valet of the prince, seemed to be eagerly dissuading several of the serfs from entering. As I appeared he exclaimed:

"Hold, he is saved! Mademoiselle will speak for him; she fears nothing, and she pities every one." Then, turning to me, he added, rapidly: "Mademoiselle will pardon us that we implore this favor of her great kindness. Ivan, through some carelessness, has permitted the favorite horse of the prince to injure himself fatally. He has gone in to confess, and we fear for his life, because Monsieur le Prince loved the fine beast well, and will be in a fury at the loss. He killed poor Androvitch for a less offense, and we tremble for Ivan. Will mademoiselle intercede for him? I fear harm to my master if Ivan suffers, for these fellows swear to avenge him."

Without a word I opened the door and entered quietly. Ivan was on his knees, evidently awaiting his doom with dogged submission. A pair of pistols lay on the table, and near it stood the prince, with the dark flush on his face, the terrible fire in his eyes which I had seen before. I saw there was no time to lose, and going to him, looked up into that wrathful countenance, whispering in a warning tone:

"Remember poor Androvitch."

It was like an electric shock; he started, shuddered, and turned pale; covered his face a moment and stood silent, while I saw drops gather on his forehead and his hand clinch itself spasmodically. Suddenly he moved, flung the pistols through the open window, and turning on Ivan, said, with a forceful gesture:

"Go. I pardon you."

The man remained motionless as if bewildered, till I touched him, bidding him thank his master and begone.

"No, it is you I thank, good angel of the house," he muttered, and lifting a fold of my dress to his lips Ivan hurried from the room.

I looked at the prince; he was gravely watching us, but a smile touched his lips as he echoed the man's last words, " 'Good angel of the house'; yes, in truth you are. Ivan is right, he owes me no thanks; and yet it was the hardest thing I ever did to forgive him the loss of my noble Sophron."

"But you did forgive him, and whether he is grateful or not, the victory is yours. A few such victories and the devil is cast out forever."

He seized my hand, exclaiming in a tone of eager delight:

"You believe this? You have faith in me, and rejoice that I conquer this cursed temper, this despotic will?"

"I do; but I still doubt the subjection of the will," I began; he interrupted me by an impetuous—

"Try it; ask anything of me and I will submit."

"Then let me return to St. Petersburg at once, and do not ask to follow."

He had not expected this, it was too much; he hesitated, demanding, anxiously:

"Do you really mean it?"

"Yes."

"You wish to leave me, to banish me now when you are all in all to me?"

"I wish to be free. You have promised to obey; yield your will to mine and let me go."

He turned and walked rapidly through the room, paused a moment at the further end, and coming back, showed me such an altered face that my conscience smote me for the cruel test. He looked at me in silence for an instant, but I showed no sign of relenting, although

I saw what few had ever seen, those proud eyes wet with tears. Bending, he passionately kissed my hands, saying, in a broken voice:

"Go, Sybil. I submit."

"Adieu, my friend; I shall not forget," and without venturing another look l left him.

I had hardly reached my chamber and resolved to end the struggle for both of us, when I saw the prince gallop out of the courtyard like one trying to escape from some unfortunate remembrance or care.

"Return soon to me," I cried; "the last test is over and the victory won."

Alas, how little did I foresee what would happen before that return; how little did he dream of the dangers that encompassed him.

A tap at my door roused me as I sat in the twilight an hour later, and Claudine crept in, so pale and agitated that I started up, fearing some mishap to the princess.

"No, she is well and safe, but oh, mademoiselle, a fearful peril hangs over us all. Hush! I will tell you. I have discovered it, and we must save them."

"Save who? what peril? speak quickly."

"Mademoiselle knows that the people on the estate are poor ignorant brutes who hate the Stavosta, and have no way of reaching the prince except through him. He is a hard man; he oppresses them, taxes them heavily unknown to the prince, and they believe my master to be a tyrant. They have borne much, for when we are away the Stavosta rules here, and they suffer frightfully. I have lived long in Russia, and I hear many things whispered that do not reach the ears of my lady. These poor creatures bear long, but at last they rebel, and some fearful affair occurs, as at Bagatai, where the countess, a cruel woman, was one night seized by her serfs, who burned and tortured her to death."

"Good heavens! Claudine, what is this danger which menaces us?"

"I understand Russ, mademoiselle, have quick eyes and ears, and for some days I perceive that all is not well among the people. Ivan is changed; all look dark and threatening but old Vacil. I watch and listen, and discover that they mean to attack the house and murder the prince."

"Mon Dieu! but when?"

"I knew not till to-day. Ivan came to me and said, 'Mademoiselle Varna has saved my life. I am grateful. I wish to serve her. She came here against her will; she desires to go; the prince is away; I will provide a horse to-night at dusk, and she can join her friend Madame Yermaloff, who is at Baron Narod's, only a verst distant. Say this to mademoiselle, and if she agrees, drop a signal from her window. I shall see and understand.' "

"But why think that the attack is to be to-night?"

"Because Ivan was so anxious to remove you. He urged me to persuade you, for the prince is gone, and the moment is propitious. You will go, mademoiselle?"

"No; I shall not leave the princess."

"But you can save us all by going, for at the baron's you can procure help and return to defend us before these savages arrive. Ivan will believe you safe, and you can thwart their plans before the hour comes. Oh, mademoiselle, I conjure you to do this, for we are watched, and you alone will be permitted to escape."

A moment's thought convinced me that this was the only means of help in our power, and my plans were quickly laid. It was useless to wait for the prince, as his return was uncertain; it was unwise to alarm the princess, as she would betray all; the quick-witted Claudine and myself must do the work, and trust to heaven for success. I dropped a handkerchief from my window; a tall figure emerged from the shrubbery, and vanished, whispering:

"In an hour—at the chapel gate."

At the appointed time I was on the spot, and found Ivan holding the well-trained horse I often rode. It was nearly dark—for August brought night—and it was well for me, as my pale face would have betrayed me.

"Mademoiselle has not fear? If she dares not go alone I will guard her," said Ivan, as he mounted me.

"Thanks. I fear nothing. I have a pistol, and it is not far. Liberty is sweet. I will venture much for it."

"I also," muttered Ivan.

He gave me directions as to my route, and watched me ride away, little suspecting my errand.

How I rode that night! My blood tingles again as I recall the wild gallop along the lonely road, the excitement of the hour, and the resolve to save Alexis or die in the attempt. Fortunately I found a large party at the baron's, and electrified them by appearing in their midst, disheveled, breathless and eager with my tale of danger. What passed I scarcely remember, for all was confusion and alarm. I refused to remain, and soon found myself dashing homeward, followed by a gallant troop of five and twenty gentlemen. More time had been lost than I knew, and my heart sunk as a dull glare shone from the direction of Volnoi as we strained up the last hill.

Reaching the top, we saw that one wing was already on fire, and distinguished a black, heaving mass on the lawn by the flickering torchlight. With a shout of wrath the gentlemen spurred to the rescue, but I reached the chapel gate unseen, and entering, flew to find my friends. Claudine saw me and led me to the great saloon, for the lower part of the house was barricaded. Here I found the princess quite insensible, guarded by a flock of terrified French servants, and Antoine and old Vacil endeavoring to screen the prince, who, with reckless courage, exposed himself to the missiles which came crashing against the windows. A red light filled the room, and from without arose a yell from the infuriated mob more terrible than any wild beast's howl.

As I sprang in, crying, "They are here—the baron and his friends—you are safe!" all turned toward me as if every other hope was lost. A sudden lull without, broken by the clash of arms, verified my words, and with one accord we uttered a cry of gratitude. The prince flung up the window to welcome our deliverers; the red glare of the fire made him distinctly visible, and as he leaned out with a ringing shout, a hoarse voice cried menacingly:

"Remember poor Androvitch."

It was Ivan's voice, and as it echoed my words there was the sharp crack of a pistol, and the prince staggered back, exclaiming faintly:

"I forgive him; it is just."

We caught him in our arms, and as Antoine laid him down he looked at me with a world of love and gratitude in those magnificent eyes of his, whispering as the light died out of them:

"Always our good angel. Adieu, Sybil. I submit."

How the night went after that I neither knew nor cared, for my only thought was how to keep life in my lover till help could come. I learned afterward that the sight of such an unexpected force caused a panic among the serfs, who fled or surrendered at once. The fire was extinguished, the poor princess conveyed to bed, and the conquerors departed, leaving a guard behind. Among the gentlemen there fortunately chanced to be a surgeon, who extracted the ball from the prince's side.

I would yield my place to no one, though the baron implored me to spare myself the anguish of the scene. I remained steadfast, supporting the prince till all was over; then, feeling that my strength was beginning to give way, I whispered to the surgeon, that I might take a little comfort away with me:

"He will live? His wound is not fatal?"

The old man shook his head, and turned away, muttering regretfully:

"There is no hope; say farewell, and let him go in peace, my poor child."

The room grew dark before me, but I had strength to draw the white face close to my own, and whisper tenderly:

"Alexis, I love you, and you alone. I confess my cruelty; oh, pardon me, before you die!"

A look, a smile full of the intensest love and joy, shone in the eyes that silently met mine as consciousness deserted me.

One month from that night I sat in that same saloon a happy woman, for on the couch, a shadow of his former self but alive and out of danger, lay the prince, my husband. The wound was not fatal, and love had worked a marvelous cure. While life and death still fought for him, I yielded to his prayer to become his wife, that he might leave me the protection of his name, the rich gift of his rank and fortune. In my remorse I would have granted anything, and when the danger was passed rejoiced that nothing could part us again.

As I sat beside him my eyes wandered from his tranquil face to the garden where the princess sat singing among the flowers, and then passed to the distant village where the wretched serfs drudged their lives away in ignorance and misery. They were mine now, and the weight of this new possession burdened my soul.

"I cannot bear it; this must be changed."

"It shall."

Unconsciously I had spoken aloud, and the prince had answered without asking to know my thoughts.

"What shall be done, Alexis?" I said, smiling, as I caressed the thin hand that lay in mine.

"Whatever you desire. I do not wait to learn the wish, I promise it shall be granted."

"Rash as ever; have you, then, no will of your own?"

"None; you have broken it."

"Good; hear then my wish. Liberate your serfs; it afflicts me as a free-born Englishwoman to own men and women. Let them serve you if they will, but not through force or fear. Can you grant this, my prince?"

"I do; the Stavosta is already gone, and they know I pardon them. What more, Sybil?"

"Come with me to England, that I may show my countrymen the brave barbarian I have tamed."

My eyes were full of happy tears, but the old tormenting spirit prompted the speech. Alexis frowned, then laughed, and answered, with a glimmer of his former imperious pride:

"I might boast that I also had tamed a fiery spirit, but I am humble, and content myself with the knowledge that the proudest woman ever born has promised to love, honor, and—"

"*Not* obey you," I broke in with a kiss.